A REFLECTION OF HORROR

She saw her image in the glass. As she watched, mesmerized, she saw her face broaden and lengthen into the dreaded reptilian countenance; her own sultry almond-shaped eyes become the color of blood; her own sensuous mouth reshape itself into a wide, lipless grimace full of long, dagger-like teeth from between which shot a slender lolling black tongue.

Shaking her head in a last desperate denial, she opened that hideous mouth, feeling the scream boiling and churning inside her, but instead of sound pouring forth, a vile vomit erupted, blackish bile full of filthy, crawly things—toads and salamanders; huge brown spiders and pink-colored worms; crusty, wriggly-legged beetles and formless, colorless, slithering things. She had become an open geyser connected to the bowels of hell.

A crowd had begun to gather, forming a semicircle at a safe distance from Marija, not seeing what she saw, but seeing merely a disreputable looking female gone mad, screaming continuously at the plate glass window of an old bookstore.

The wailing siren of a police car grew in volume, abruptly cutting off as the car screeched to a halt in front of the building. But even as the uniformed officers leapt out, a gasp went up from the crowd, followed by the shattering music of broken glass.

Marija, in a final desperate act of self-immolation,—or survival—had plunged headfirst through the store window.

PINNACLE'S HORROR SHOW

BLOOD BEAST (17-096, $3.95)
by Don D'Ammassa

No one knew anymore where the gargoyle had come from. It was just an ugly stone creature high up on the walls of the old Sheffield Library. Little Jimmy Nicholson liked to go and stare at the gargoyle. It seemed to look straight at him, as if it knew his most secret desires. And he knew that it would give him everything he'd ever wanted. But first he had to do its bidding, no matter how evil.

LIFEBLOOD (17-110, $3.95)
by Lee Duigon

Millboro, New Jersey was just the kind of place Dr. Winslow Emerson had in mind. A small township of Yuppie couples who spent little time at home. Children shuttled between an overburdened school system and every kind of after-school activity. A town ripe for the kind of evil Dr. Emerson specialized in. For Emerson was no ordinary doctor, and no ordinary mortal. He was a creature of ancient legend of mankind's darkest nightmare. And for the citizens of Millboro, he had arrived where they least expected it: in their own backyards.

DARK ADVENT (17-088, $3.95)
by Brian Hodge

A plague of unknown origin swept through modern civilization almost overnight, destroying good and evil alike. Leaving only a handful of survivors to make their way through an empty landscape, and face the unknown horrors that lay hidden in a savage new world. In a deserted midwestern department store, a few people banded together for survival. Beyond their temporary haven, an evil was stirring. Soon all that would stand between the world and a reign of insanity was this unlikely fortress of humanity, armed with what could be found on a department store shelf and what courage they could muster to battle a monstrous, merciless scourge.

Available wherever paperbacks are sold, or order direct from the Publisher. Send cover price plus 50¢ per copy for mailing and handling to Pinnacle Books, Dept.17-251, 475 Park Avenue South, New York, N.Y. 10016. Residents of New York, New Jersey and Pennsylvania must include sales tax. DO NOT SEND CASH.

BLOODMASTER
MARY L. QUIJANO

PINNACLE BOOKS
WINDSOR PUBLISHING CORP.

PINNACLE BOOKS

are published by

Windsor Publishing Corp.
475 Park Avenue South
New York, NY 10016

First printing: August, 1989

Printed in the United States of America

To Bill McKinney

Thanks for believing in me.
I believe in you, too.

One
Courtship

. . . And they had a king over them, which is the angel of the bottomless pit, whose name in the Hebrew tongue is Abaddon, but in the Greek tongue hath his name Apollyon.

Revelations 9:11

1

The red "No Smoking—Fasten Seat Belts" sign had lit up a few minutes ago, flashing its message sequentially through five different languages per minute. Now the cabin lights flared on as well, while weary flight attendants—still bravely trying to look fresh and attractive after nearly ten hours in the air—began the final chore of gently waking the few rumpled and snoring passengers not yet aware that their transatlantic flight from New York to Rome was nearly at an end.

Soon the jumbo jet began its initial lurch into a stomach-floating descent, the powerful engines backroaring noisily as the nose seemed to lift, the belly to sink. Stiff, swept-back wings tilted to give the bleary-eyed passengers their first glimpse of the magical, sparkling city below, the rolling green countryside beyond, as the plane made its wide, lazy spiral back to earth.

Archbishop Quillans stretched the cramped muscles of his long, sinewy legs one last time before pulling his seat to the required upright position for landing. He was nattily attired in a neat, wrinkle-resistant suit of charcoal gray silk blend over a pale blue Yves St. Laurent shirt and silvery-gray silk tie. The close-cropped military cut of his salt-and-pepper hair was equally neat; even his cool gray eyes above the lightly tanned face had refused to redden like those of his fellow passengers under the barrage of canned air they'd been forced to endure since San Francisco.

He looked more like a successful business executive than some humble successor to the twelve apostles of Jesus.

But he wasn't using his title on this journey.

This journey to Rome, he mused, his eyes distant: to Destiny.

"The Pope is dead, long live the Pope." He felt it deep inside, felt it with a sense of terrible excitement, half-exultation, half-horror. Yet he had no justification for these emotions, no promises given or even alluded to in the terse phone call he'd received yesterday from the Cardinal Secretary of State. Just get himself to the Vatican forthwith.

He glanced out the window, wondering if he could see the Vatican from here, but his was the uptilted side of the airplane, displaying only swift tufts of screaming clouds, a too-blue backdrop of sky.

One cloud was darker than the others, and for just a moment it took on the shape of a face—a ghostly face, vacant eyes, mouth a long oval O that grew and grew in a silent howl of wrath as it chased the plane. He shook his head slightly, passing a well-manicured hand across his eyes.

Suddenly a vivid picture of another dark face appeared in his mind, the ghetto priest . . . what was his name? Muldoon, yes, the San Francisco Archdiocese's token nigger. He saw the face as it looked that day, a week or so ago, when the man had come bursting into his office carrying a tape of some sort, babbling an absurd tale of demonic possession, with a petition for the Rites of Exorcism in his briefcase. Rites of Exorcism, indeed! He'd set the nigger straight on church policy regarding such matters right off, unequivocally. Schizophrenia, not demon possession. Psychiatric intervention, not archaic religious ceremonies with holy water, beads, and arcane litanies. What did he think this was, the

10

dark ages? Damn superstitious . . . Rarely had he felt such instant loathing.

He supposed the reason the man was still on his mind was that last night, even as he waited for his driver to bring the official limousine around to take him to the airport, the phone had rung. The priest again. His thick, soft voice was filled with some kind of shaking emotion, demanding immediate action on the exorcism due to some new crisis.

Demanding! A subordinate, a *black* subordinate at that, ordering *him!* Even now he shook with anger at the memory of this effrontery (and with something else he couldn't recognize, something deep in the pit of his belly).

Now, as the black priest's face faded, another memory rose to take its place: this was the soft, hesitant voice of the woman on the tape Muldoon had left with him on that first visit, the woman the priest claimed was being plagued by demons, telling her own story. Something about that voice — or was it her incredible tale? — had set up an itch at the back of his skull, like something he should know about, or remember, but couldn't.

Even now, in memory, it itched. And because he couldn't scratch it, it irritated.

2

Friday rose uncharacteristically clear and warm for a San Francisco morning in June: brimming with sunshine, hope, a sense of rejuvenation. Marija awoke convinced that the strange dreams and presence that had been haunting her since Memorial Day had by now left her apartment for good, had given up waiting for her to come home and had moved on, perhaps to find some other misfortunate soul to terrorize.

"*Their* problem," she thought mercilessly.

She started to sing in the shower, sang robustly in the car all the way to work, her radio at full blast, her foot pumping the accelerator in time to the heavy beat. She was still humming cheerfully as she entered Brotherton's Sportswear at 6:55 AM.

She even had a warm smile and friendly greeting for Betty Sue, who looked up from behind her desk in open-mouthed surprise at the unusual amity. She was trying to fasten the strap of her high-heeled sandal and breathe all at the same time.

"Oh, hiya," she slurped, straightening up and trying to pull her too-tight, pink knit dress back down over her voluptuous hips, "Feelin' better now?"

12

"No, the doctor said it was terminal, so I thought I'd come back here and spend my final days doing something I really enjoy," MJ deadpanned, continuing past the perplexed receptionist and on into the large inner office where her own desk with its perpetual pile of unfinished paperwork awaited her return.

"God am I glad to see *you!*" Shelly burst out as Marija came into view. "You cannot imagine what kind of garbage the fetid frog" — she indicated Fred Wellesby's office with a jerk of her head — "has been shoveling my way since you've been gone. You *are* all okay now?" she nodded hopefully.

"Sure Shel, I'm fine; but I'm really sorry my absence made extra work for you."

"Oh, only the fun parts. You know, stuff like trying to appease grumpy customers screaming about their overdue orders; or harassing our suppliers about late deliveries, only to find they've put a hold on our shipment because we haven't paid our bills. The good, challenging *meat* of a manufacturing business . . . it puts hair on your chest," she grimaced. Honestly, MJ, I don't know how you put up with it day after day. I'd get sick, too . . . on purpose!"

"Mr. Wellesby shouldn't have dumped that on you!" Marija exclaimed in mild outrage. "It's actually *his* responsibility, but he's gotten so used to shunting it over to me, I guess he figured he could pass it on down the line. I've half a mind to tell him off right now!"

"Listen to the other half," Shelly muttered tersely.

"Huh?"

"Just let it go, hon'," the tall, gaunt, middle-aged woman advised. "Anyway, you know what they say, about you-know-what rolling downhill . . . it's just part of the old ballgame."

"I thought the expression was 'It always floats to the top,'" MJ corrected with a half-grin.

"At Brotherton's, it's *e*verywhere." Shelly laughed, a short, explosive bark.

MJ nodded, tried to smile, but something was bugging her.

"Why?" she demanded suddenly, her incongruous question catching the older woman off guard.

"Why what?"

"Why shouldn't I get on Wellesby about this?"

"For one thing, he's not in yet."

"*Seriously*, Shel," Marija persisted, "what's going on?"

"Ah, it may be nothing . . . but I overheard him on the phone yesterday talking to Mr. B."

"And?"

"He was getting chewed out for something pretty good, by the sound of it; so I kind of tilted my ear toward his office door," she shrugged. "Then I heard him mention your name a couple of times. I couldn't hear *exactly* what was being said, but I got the impression that the fat little toad was trying to shift the blame for whatever it was onto you: you know, you not being here to defend yourself and all."

MJ nodded; that would be just like Wellesby.

"Anyway, that *really* ticked me off," she rumbled hotly, "so I started eavesdropping in earnest, and I heard him say something about putting you on probation once you got back."

"Probation!" The word exploded from her. Then, as the receptionist peered curiously around the doorjamb, she lowered her voice to a fuming whisper. "He gets twice the salary I do, and for what? Picking his nose? He couldn't even do that right without instructions; and he's got the balls to put *me* on probation?"

"MJ, it's a job," Shelly said, putting her hand on the younger women's shoulder. "You either want it or you don't. If you don't, go tell him to take a flying leap at the moon, and more power to you. But if you *do* want it, or even *need* it, you've just got to accept the fact that—"

"Yeah, yeah, I know. 'Shit rolls downhill,' " Marija sighed in exasperation. "Only does there have to be a continuous avalanche of the stuff?"

The news had faded the bloom off her day—completely wilted it—and all morning, as she caught up on her memos and correspondence, refamiliarizing herself with the progress of the various jobs in the shop, MJ vacillated between anger and depression over Wellesby's treachery.

At 11 AM, shortly before the temporary reprieve of lunch—and just as she was beginning to think Shelly might have been mistaken about Wellesby's comments—the intercom on her desk buzzed.

"Ms. Draekins," Fred Wellesby's nasal voice piped imperiously through the small metal box. "Please drop whatever you are doing and come into my office immediately."

The line clicked off before she had a chance to respond. Her stomach knotted, her legs grew weak as they propelled her unwillingly across the room through the heavy door and into the production chief's office. The door wheezed shut behind her, sending a little chill prickling across the back of her hairline.

A scattering of reports were spread across the highly polished, and seldom used, surface of the oversized desk, dwarfing the small, middle-aged man behind it. He was hunched over the reports studiously, bulging in his too-tight Brooks Brothers' suit, twirling his thin mustache, tapping his pencil against the papers importantly. Actually he was doing nothing productive, simply making Marija wait what he felt was an appropriate period of time before acknowledging her presence—as she knew only too well.

"Sit down, Ms. Draekins," he said at last, barely glancing up. It was an order, not an act of hospitality, designed to get her down to a physical level where he could, at his choosing, rise to loom over her threateningly with all sixty-five inches of his squat, Italian–Welsh body. After six years working for the man, she was wise to all his tricks. Despite her quaking knees, Marija remained standing.

"What's up, Mr. Wellesby?" she asked, trying to keep both the fear and the belligerence out of her voice.

"Ms. Draekins! I asked you to be seated; I suggest you comply!" Anger shook his pudgy jowls, bulged his already protuberant eyes. He looked like an ineffectual, wrong-side-of-Europe Hitler. MJ hesitated a minute longer, wanting to defy him. But since he was obviously looking for any excuse to jump on her, she finally, grudgingly, sat — sullen, silent, waiting for him to get on with his prepared speech.

"Our summer line of new floral overalls," he said, once he realized she was just going to sit there glaring at him through narrowed eyes with that stubborn, sulky pout on her face. "Our summer *designer* line, Ms. Draekins," he repeated ominously, "is not selling as well as we'd projected . . . and do you know why?"

Yeah, because they suck. MJ thought, compressing her lips. Aloud she said nothing; she knew she didn't need to. He was obviously going to tell her anyway, and it was ninety-nine-percent certain to be pure BS. She waited.

"Because they were *late* getting to our distributors, Ms. Draekins," he went on, beginning to huff, working his way up to believing what he was about to say. *"That's* why they aren't selling, *Ms.* Draekins; too late to compete. And do you know *why* they were late getting out?" His voice dripped venom.

MJ grimaced, looking toward the ceiling.

"Don't give me that look!" Wellesby shrieked, jumping out of his chair and banging a pudgy fist on the desk so hard his pens jumped in their holder. His face was beet-red and his trembling lips were making the wispy little mustache twitch. "You *know* you dragged your heels on this project from the very start; continued to drag them all the way through production. *That's* why the damn things were late, and *that's* why they haven't sold!"

"Wellesby," Marija answered in a calm and weary voice, "that's a pile of crap and you know it."

The little man sputtered in shock and outrage, waving his soft, professionally manicured hand frantically in the air. But MJ had held this back too long. Not about to be stopped now, she made her voice grow stronger, releasing months of pent-up indignation and resentment at the mini-tyrant.

"The order was less than two weeks overdue, well within our four-week margin, *Mister* Wellesby. If the design had been worth a shit, our regular customers would have bought them up anyway. But frankly, sir, your precious creation stank!"

"Miss Draekins, you'd better watch yourself!" Wellesby interjected shrilly.

"Oh yeah? Well in case you've forgotten, I've still got your order to me *in writing* from the first of March, compelling me to schedule production of this new line of yours without a proper preliminary survey — *contrary* to company policy. Sorry, Wellesby," she taunted. "But if you're trying to shift the blame to me, using this fiasco of your own making as an excuse to get me fired, you'd better think again. Because if you push it, it's gonna be *your* ass on the line, not mine!"

Marija had risen to her feet during this declamation, pointing her finger at the supervisor for emphasis; but now she paused, her anger-contorted features fading to a look of puzzlement. Something had subtly changed in the atmosphere of the office. The air seemed thicker, cloying; she thought she could hear a faint echo of her final words still resounding in the after-silence.

"Oh no!" a small voice in the pit of her stomach cried, running to hide beneath the lower curve of her spine. She could sense what was coming, but there was nothing she could do to prevent it.

There was a certain aura to the room, a feeling that reality had once more been displaced. She sensed the onset of that too-familiar, sound-swallowing silence — not an absence of sound, but a suppression of it under an even louder quiet — filling her ears with its nothingness as it filled the vast reaches of the endless empty universe.

Her heart roared wildly in her chest.

"Mr. Wellesby?" she queried softly, for the man — rather than leaping around in characteristic fury as he had been —

was now reseated behind his desk, looking up at her with an eerie, mocking smile which bent the corners of his lips but left the eyes strangely cold, brittle, dead.

He didn't answer, but for an instant his features seemed to melt and ripple, as if a wave had passed through them. MJ blinked rapidly to clear the haze from her vision: then it happened again.

"No," she squeaked, shaking her head. Pressing her fingertips against her eyes, she willed the visual deformity gone; and when she looked up a minute later everything seemed normal. Then the wavering motion passed through the man again, and this time the phenomenon continued.

Wellesby's face *was* changing. It was melting, remolding! First it turned into a caricature of itself: the chin receding further and further until it disappeared altogether; the wide, thin-lipped mouth stretching and exaggerating to grossness; the bulbous eyes enlarging until they seemed about to pop from his head.

MJ gasped, tried to speak, and then to turn her head away, but she could do neither. Her hand shot up to her mouth, the knuckles pushed into her teeth, and there they stayed, frozen.

The squat little man's nose had grown shorter and shorter, flattening into nothing but two slightly ridged nasal apertures; his pasty complexion took on a greenish hue, deepening finally into an ugly mossy shade, while the chubby body became even more hunched and rounded.

" 'Toad,' huh?" the voice croaked in a hoarse rasp from deep inside the bulging throat. " 'Freddy the Gremlin,' you call me — you and that large-assed, tight-cunted spinster secretary. You thought I didn't *know?*"

"But, but Mr. Wellesby," MJ stammered, "your face —" She reached a tentative hand out toward him, but her terrified overture was cut short.

"Oh, shut up, you ignorant slut," the voice wheezed derisively, now seeming to originate from somewhere behind the oversized frog face which gaped ludicrously out of the three-

18

piece suit. "Don't you know *yet* who this is? Here, let me give you a little hint."

A roar of horrible, spine-curling laughter filled the spaces between the silence as the shape before the woman rapidly reformed itself again. The bulging eyes closed, then reopened slowly to expose two fiery red, almond shaped orbs with vertical black slits for pupils. The fat round head elongated and narrowed into a lizardlike appendage; the lipless reptilian mouth gaped to display gleaming white rows of carnivorous teeth pushing forth from the swollen black gums. From deep in the throat a narrow black ribbon of tongue uncoiled and flicked out an alarming length, nearly touching Marija's face eight feet away, where she stood paralyzed—either by fear or by something outside her holding her in place.

The demon's eyes locked onto hers, fierce and unrelenting in their power. As she was forced to look back into them she felt herself being drawn slowly into their depths, pulled under the control of the entity behind them as a swimmer is pulled under by a deadly riptide.

The scaly, greenish-black skin of the monster's face loomed closer, the crimson windows widening as if to envelop her, while beyond this visage, normal space and dimension were continuing to abdicate their hold on reality.

MJ felt torn between fear and fascination, attraction and repulsion. She wanted to pull her attention away, to run, to hide her face from this hideous creature, but at the same time found herself mysteriously drawn to it with a magnetism of perverse longing.

It was during this vacillation that she first noticed a small blemish within one of the hypnotic red eyes, a black spot near the pupil that appeared to be moving, catching her attention in a sudden, overpowering curiosity—a curiosity that overwhelmed even her own terror. She looked a little closer, a bit closer still, not realizing that while trying to bring the object into focus she was leaving her resistance behind.

As the dragon grew more and more prominent, the reality

of the rest of her surroundings faded away, quietly obliterated by the presence of the beast . . . just as it had during her dream.

The intertwined fabric of time and space was being warped and flattened into a two-dimensional curtain; when it dissipated entirely into a single-dimensioned nothingness, Marija knew she would be beyond recall, dissipated along with it. Nevertheless she continued to probe the mystery of that small spot in the devil's eye: just a second more, she almost had it now . . . vaguely rationalizing that the answer might provide a clue to his vulnerability, to her own ultimate escape.

The spot grew suddenly clearer and larger, discernible now as two tiny, dark silhouettes, like figurines carved from obsidian, then thrown back into the fire of their origins; writhing and moving in thick, sluggish, almost dancelike postures inside the brightly burning eye.

She peered more closely, and the tiny figures became even more well-defined. One was a naked woman, the other some sort of winged beast, the pair separate but seemingly linked, the woman alternately attempting to tear herself away, then flinging herself with destructive abandon back into its grasp.

Suddenly as if Marija had entered the eye of the dragon itself, the figures were large as the characters on a movie screen, larger than life, and at that moment MJ realized with a heart-dropping shock that the female human and the large, dragonlike animal were engaged in sexual intercourse, a violent, grunting, painful act of lust and hatred.

The woman's face turned slowly toward her, grinning in empty-eyed, slavish eroticism. And Marija saw that the face was her own.

She screamed then, driving her fists hard into her offending eyes, hurling herself from the awful truth — while deep in a cowering corner of her mind a tiny, maniacal part of her burst into hysterical, side-splitting glee at the joke.

Slowly, slowly, she forced herself to breathe, then to breathe deeply; hold it, let it out, try to force control on the quivering hysteria, beat it into submission. At last she opened her eyes, hoping it was all gone, all back to normal, a mere hallucination that she had vanquished by force of will to some form of acceptable reality.

But as her vision cleared from the electrical stars pressed into her eyeballs, she saw again the winged beast, now standing directly in front of her, the redness all around them both, and from the recesses of his lower belly there protruded an enormous, sweating, spiral-tipped organ. It was fully engorged, held in the grasp of a scaly green clawed hand, flipping up and down and pulsing at her hungrily. She felt the hysterical laughter begin to rise in her throat again, but when it reached her mouth it turned into sour-tasting bile.

The beast grinned, lapping his black serpent's tongue suggestively out at her. The tongue ensnared the hem of her brushed nylon skirt on its sticky tip, lifting the soft fabric high above her waist to expose the scantily clad pubic area peeking out from behind her lace bikini panties.

The dragon rolled his hips, slowly and lasciviously, then abruptly thrust his pelvis forward, the huge oily penis prodding at her genitals. As the pointed tip touched her there, she felt an intense fiery cold penetrate her, coursing through her vaginal area in an aching shudder.

Then, somewhere within her mind, something snapped. Screams erupted from deep inside her, tearing their way out through her throat in painful, shattering explosions, one after the other. She backed and whirled, blindly shoving her way past some soft, inconsequential forms that had materialized in the room behind her, grabbing the more solid outlines of the doorframe as she propelled herself into the outer office like a metal projectile in a pinball machine, bouncing and careening off the haphazard array of desks as she ran.

The echoes of her continuous screaming—punctuated by shriller shrieks each time she hit, bounced, and caromed forward—ended abruptly as she reached the main entrance. Throwing the outer door open, she stopped short, dazzled by the glare of the noonday sun, then began running again in a crazy, stumbling gait across the parking lot. Some inner sense of propriety had stilled her awful cries the second she'd reached the outside world; but though no sound now escaped her lips, except for a muffled, whimpering noise; the gut-tearing sounds carried on inside her until she became little more than one tremendous, unreleased howl running through the darkest part of the day.

Twenty minutes later, when Joe called, the office was still in a turmoil, buzzing with the angry confusion of a hive whacked by a stick.

When Marija had begun screaming, Shelly was the first to leap from her desk and burst unannounced through the heavy oak doors into Wellesby's office, with Carol and Pat, two clerk-typists, close behind.

But when she'd reached out to help her friend, she was met by a smashing blow to the chest as MJ blindly fought her way past—a blow that hurled the older woman against the door with such force that her head snapped back and received a solid crack on the hard wood, giving her a nasty lump beneath the graying hair and a throbbing headache for her efforts.

"What the hell did you *do* to her, Wellesby?" she'd demanded angrily through her dizziness and pain, making him the target for her own injury as well as whatever had happened to Marija.

The production manager's pretentiousness had dissolved in a cold sweat.

"Nothing, I don't know . . . I did *nothing!*" he insisted, bodily shoving the women out and slamming his office door behind them. He sat back down behind his massive desk, his head in his damp little hands, trying to figure out what had happened.

He remembered chewing out Ms. Draekins for delaying production of his summer lines, remembered her angry retort couched in various obscene expletives, and how furious he'd in turn become with her. But then his memory blurred around the edges, got mushy in the middle.

He'd felt a sudden dizziness . . . had had to sit back down; recalled thinking that he might be having a stroke—"Jesus, not at *my* age"—and then a kind of blankness took over. Next thing he knew, this screwy broad was screaming like a stuck pig, running through his office as if her ass were on fire.

The distraught little man shook his head, rubbed his temples, shook his head again. "Hell, I don't know . . . she's just crazy, that's all." He stood up, ran a hand through his limp, sweaty hair, sat back down. Even *he* was unconvinced by that simplistic a conclusion.

Replaying the scene in his head, once more he saw her angry outburst, felt his growing fury—then the dizziness, followed by a feeling less that he had blacked out than that he was missing something, as if a small segment of time had been permanently removed from his life, something for which he hadn't—would *never* have—any recollection. And much as he dwelt on that blank period, dug at it, picked about in his mind for any stray memories lying around unattended, he could find nothing, not even any evidence to support the purported blackout. Until at last he concluded—quite naturally for someone of his perceptiveness—that he hadn't lost consciousness at all, *couldn't* have. If he had, surely it was not for more than a second or two.

Which meant that any screaming and carrying on Marija had done were strictly the result of her own hysterical temperament. *Had* to be. They certainly weren't *his* fault. He tugged his tie into a more comfortable fit, jutting out his little chin as he did so. He felt he was beginning to get a handle on this thing now, dismissing once and for all the imponderables, setting his mind back to the narrow realities he could accept and deal with.

The bitch had to go.

Enough was enough. As a responsible executive he had no choice but to recommend her immediate termination. He

23

exhaled deeply — not aware till he did so that he'd been holding his breath — and tried to put on an appropriate look of regret. He took a clean white handkerchief from his vest pocket, carefully mopped his brow, fastidiously removed any traces of dirt from his fingertips, and folded the cloth neatly back into a perfect square before replacing it.

"Perhaps," he mused, intertwining his fingers and cracking his knuckles, "an extended sick leave — without pay, of course — would be considered more, shall we say, acceptable; more humane, under the circumstances? Yes," he smiled broadly, picking up the interoffice phone line and punching the four-digit code for Whitney Brotherton's private suite; "an *extended* sick leave ought to be just the ticket."

At the same moment that Fred Wellesby was cheerfully putting the ax to Marija, Joe was on the other line, vainly trying to get hold of her through the hopelessly uncommunicative receptionist.

"Ah'm sorry suh, she's not in," the soft southern drawl repeated.

Joe sighed. "I know, you already said that," he reminded the woman patiently, "but did she say *where* she was going?"

"Not to mah knawledge, suh," the sugary voice drawled.

"Well do you know when she'll be back?" His voice was tightening.

A little of the syrup dried up at his tone. "No, I don't!" Joe caught a slight waiver in the voice, a hint of tension that set a small gnawing worry nipping at his stomach.

"Listen, this is her fiancé . . . is something wrong? We were supposed to meet for lunch. She wouldn't just leave."

"I, I don't know. I'm not sure what I'm supposed to say." The woman's composure was definitely breaking down, her drawl disappearing into a tearful-sounding whine. "You wanna talk to Mr. Wellesby?" she added hopefully.

The growing alarm Joe had been feeling suddenly exploded in a full blown, white-hot flash of terror. He saw Marija's face again as it had been four days ago, wild-eyed and ashen

24

behind the vomitlike globs of oatmeal cookie dough that ran down from the overturned orange mixing bowl she wore like a construction helmet, wielding a heavy cast iron skillet above her head, and screaming about armies of bugs. Bugs that weren't there. About doors and windows that wouldn't open, ghosts and goblins that screamed her name, a stench of sewage that filled the apartment . . . when all he'd heard was her own screams, all he'd smelled was the acrid smoke from the batch of cookies she'd burnt black in the oven.

Now she was at it again! Was she?

"Wait a minute, what the hell's going on down there?" Joe asked.

"Please hold, suh." The receptionist backed up again behind her Georgia drawl. "Ah'll put you through to Mr. Wellesby as soon as his line is free."

The connection clicked dead, cutting off all further protest. In a second the Muzak switched on, its supposedly soothing orchestration— music to drum fingers by—becoming more annoying by the minute.

Too many minutes . . . too much time . . . Time to get scared . . . time to get angry. Damn, Marija, why? Why did this have to happen to you . . . whatever the fuck it is! To *us*. *Me*. Why couldn't you just be a nice normal sexy girl like you were when I met you?

Sure, they'd had their little metaphysical discussions over a glass of chablis or two—how many people in love didn't? It went with the territory—but these were of safe things, airy things, entertaining things: the essential spiritual nature of man, the possibility of reincarnation, soulmates, karma, ghosts . . . things you could discuss all day and night without ever proving a thing.

But it had all gotten a lot less entertaining when her dreams began, dreams which had increasingly taken a bigger, greedier bite out of his own reality. They were *her* dreams— her hallucinations—but over the past ten days they'd been dragging him unwillingly down there with her, down to the

25

blackness of that other reality, until he'd almost begun to believe, to see things too. . . .

Soul mates, yeah. Soul mates in lunacy.

"I'm getting tired of your jokes," he said suddenly to the air, although someone walking past the office door right then might have thought he was speaking to the person on the other line. He slammed down the receiver, grabbed his keys from the desk, and bolted for the door.

Fifteen minutes later he ripped into the Brotherton parking lot in fourth gear, quickly downshifting to a screeching halt in one of the visitor spaces near the entrance.

As he got out, he glanced across the rows of cars and almost immediately spotted MJ's old Datsun parked in its usual space. A great draining sense of relief washed over him, followed by a wave of unwarranted anger at her for there being nothing wrong after all . . . after scaring the piss out of him. He almost got back into his Alfa and drove away, then reason and doubt overcame the impulse. *Something* must have happened to cause the receptionist to act the way she had, even if it wasn't so serious as he'd imagined.

The plump, attractively decorated woman manning the front desk glanced up as he stormed in.

"May I *help* y'all?" she said.

"I want to see Marija, I'm her fiancé," he stated flatly.

"Oh. Well, she's not here, like I told you before."

"Just what kind of game are you playing?" he demanded, roughly grabbing the woman by the shoulder and turning her to face him.

"Ow, leggo. That *hurts!*" She whined, grabbing at his hand.

"I call on the phone and you tell me she's gone," he raged on. "You refuse to say where, let on like something's happened. Then you put me on hold for half a fucking hour waiting for answers. So I leave my own goddam job and drive over here, and what do I see? What do I see?" His jaw was clenched and he was spitting out the words, his teeth an inch from her pale frightened face. "MJ's car! It's right out there in the lot; but

26

you're still trying to tell me she's not here?! What are you trying to pull? Who put you up to this?" In his increasing fury his grip tightened on the receptionist's shoulder until she was squirming, whimpering in pain.

"Please," she cried, tears beginning to form in big pools within her heavily mascaraed lower lashes, "that really hurts!"

Joe released her, shocked by the realization of what he was doing. He was about to apologize when the girl spoke up.

"She really *isn't* here, mister," the bleached blonde said tearfully, rubbing at her shoulder. "She went kind of . . . crazy-like. I don't know what happened; I don't even *want* to know. Wouldja please just go talk to Mr. Wellesby?"

But Joe was already past her, hurrying towards the production chief's office, a sick fear churning through his stomach. His mind stuck like a needle in a cracked groove, replaying the receptionist's words over and over: *"She went kind of . . . crazy-like . . . she went kind of crazy-like . . . she went kind of crazy. . . ."*

Ten minutes later he emerged from Wellesby's private office much subdued. As he passed through the clerical area a hand reached out and softly plucked at his shirt sleeve.

"Joe?" A voice whispered through his blackness. He turned, scowling, to face a middle-aged woman who looked nearly as bad as he felt.

"I'm Shelly, MJ's friend," she introduced herself, still in that soft, throaty whisper that might have sounded seductive had her face not been so grave. "Can I talk to you a minute . . . outside?"

Joe nodded curtly. MJ had spoken of this woman from time to time, always in very favorable terms. As he held open the heavy glass entrance door for the lady, he noticed the receptionist giving the two of them a furtive look before picking up her interoffice line.

"Your friend in there . . ." he warned with a flick of his eyes in that direction.

"Screw her," the secretary said tartly, openly glaring

through the glass at the buxom blonde inside. "Joe," she turned back to him earnestly, an intense expression on her lined face, "I don't know what Wellesby told you happened in there, but I just want to say that . . . well, that it *had* to be a lie if you walked out of there without punching him. I've never seen anyone so completely terrified as MJ when she came tearing out of that office, and I'm telling you"—the words were spewing out, building on their own momentum—"that it is *not* like Marija. I've known that lady for over six years now, worked with her eight hours a day, five days a week, and she's as cool as they come. Oh, she gets mad, yeah, don't we all from time to time? But never anything like this. My advice to you is get a lawyer, press charges. That asshole had to do *something*, something really terrible, to make her react that way!"

"Yeah, maybe . . . " Joe said, putting a hand on Shelly's bony shoulder and keeping his private doubts private, "but the first thing I've got to do is find her, get *her* side of the story. Have you any idea where she went, why she didn't take her car?"

"Sure. She went out in such a rush she left her purse on her desk; her keys are probably still in it. I saw her fumbling at her car door and ran inside to fetch it for her, but when I got back she was gone."

"You don't know which way she was heading, do you?"

"No, but maybe one of the other girls noticed. Wait here while I get her purse for you and I'll see what I can find out."

Two minutes later Shelly was back with the purse and the information that MJ was last seen running north on Potrero toward Franklin Square. "Um, could you . . . " she faltered, pressing a torn slip of paper with a phone number into his hand, "could you keep me posted? I'm—I'm very fond of her." She wiped a stray tear from the corner of her eye, hurrying away embarrassed.

After a few blocks Marija's headlong flight had slowed to a stumbling shuffle, her body bent with the pain of her ragged breathing, her hand pressed to her side to ease a muscle spasm. The terror that had spurred her was slowing somewhat, but reality failed to return in its place. Instead she was bewildered, disoriented—not knowing where she was or what she was doing there, not even *who* she was, knowing only that she had to keep going, to escape, find a safe haven somewhere.

When she reached the intersection of Seventeenth and Potrero, she turned left, following her instincts unerringly, toward a home she couldn't remember in a neighborhood nearly three miles away.

As she walked slowly west along Seventeenth, the industrial complexes of the Potrero district gave way to the Hispanic barrios of the Mission. Small mom-and-pop markets, dusty pawnshops, dark-fronted bars, secondhand clothing stores, slumlord realties, dirty, graffiti-scarred laundromats, TV repair shops. The culturally deficient enterprises that bespoke a poverty-ridden clientele lined either side of the broad thoroughfare, their windows protected by wrought-iron bars against their own local compadres.

Fragrant, peppery odors floated out from numerous Mexican eateries along the route, making Marija aware of the gnawing emptiness in her stomach. But her mind was incapable of making the necessary connection between the aromas and her hunger, the medium of exchange needed to bring them together. All she could do was move reluctantly on.

Ahead, a group of cholos—teenage Mexican street toughs—were leaning their lanky, perfumed forms against the corner of an old brick building, careful not to get their hip-length, starched white T-shirts dirty. She saw one of the youths—a tall, mustachioed chicano with greased-back hair held in place by a ladies' hairnet, and swarthy, acne-pocked skin—jab an elbow into the ribs of one of his buddies. Next thing she knew, her way was blocked by a semicircle of the five leering adolescents.

Their mouths were moving, but the words made no sense: MJ didn't even recognize it as language. She stared dumbly from one to the other, wanting only to get by, wondering why they were preventing her from doing so.

"Hey, huera. Whassa matter?" "Hey, mamacita!" They were moving forward now. "You slummin' today, baby doll?" "Looking good!"

"Chupala mi vergas, puta!" one of them shouted, causing the others to laugh in a way that frightened her. A brown arm shot out, mean fingers grabbing her nipple through the thin fabric of her blouse, giving it a vicious tweak.

As the five closed in, pressing toward her, their sultry brown eyes blinked languorously beneath long, thick lashes. When they reopened each was a glowing red.

A silent shriek coursed down her spine; her teeth clamped onto her lower lip, drawing a bright speck of blood. She looked helplessly from one to the other. Before her wide, staring eyes the cholos' tanned skins were growing darker, their leering smiles widening into lipless, gaping mouths. Then, from the recesses of those open pits, elongated, slender black tongues snaked out at the horrified woman, touching her cheeks, her neck and lips, with their slimy wetness.

Marija's sudden keening shattered the afternoon air. The teenagers backed off quickly, displaying shifty-eyed surprise, suppressed fear. They began defensively muttering their disdain for "crazy white bitches" coming into their turf and "makeeng traboul". Then they rapidly dispersed down the boulevard before anyone could finger them for whatever the crazy *gringa* thought she was yelling about.

As soon as they took off, Marija turned in the other direction, her terror back, full blown, running blindly around the corner and up the quiet street beyond. Halfway up the block, attracted by the sound of her pounding feet on the sunlit, cracked concrete, an old yellow cur came charging out, hackles raised and barking wildly.

As she paused in midstride, the animal's face began to

30

change into a semblance of the same demonic effigy, crimson eyes laughing with evil humor, barks becoming a nasty, mocking cachinnation.

"*Nooo*. Oh come on, please, not again," she whimpered, taking a step backward from the awful sight. Her heel slipped off the edge of the curb and, losing her balance, arms pinwheeling, she tumbled ass-first into the filth of the gutter, whiplashing her head in a solid crack against the asphalt. Streaks of light shot through her brain, her ears rang with the blow. Dazed, she rose slowly to her elbows, looking about cautiously. The dog had by now retreated, scurrying out of sight before the hobbling rush of an elderly couple who'd passed by to witness the accident — to them nothing more than a woman frightened by an ordinary mongrel.

As they hurried to her side, Marija looked up with a weak smile of gratitude, struggling to rise. But the wrinkled, age-spotted hands that grabbed her arms turned into scaly green claws. Rather than lifting her to safety, they carelessly flung her backward nearly into the traffic.

"Oh my God!" she cried feverishly, scrabbling away from them, her eyes wild with panic. "Get away, get away from me! Leave me alone!"

The old man hesitated, uncertain how far Christian duty required him to go. His wife had already retreated to her little aluminum cart of groceries, clucking and shaking her head. *He* saw a young woman groveling in the gutter, her features contorted with some indecipherable anguish, her hair and clothing a filthy mess. He shook his head and returned to his wife, leading her away, his expression a mixture of sadness and contempt for the drug-crazed creature they'd tried to help.

A while after they'd departed, MJ clambered slowly to her feet, dusting herself off with exaggerated care. Her dress was torn and soiled, her panty hose shredded, her elbows skinned. The heel on one shoe had broken off, giving her an awkward limp as she hobbled up the street.

The midday sun burned down in a shadowless glare, but its warmth didn't touch Marija. She walked in her own shadow — cold, alone, a displaced person dumped harshly into a hostile foreign land full of secret enemies. Her head was low, her shoulders hunched about her neck, her eyes following the shuffling limp of her feet. What few other pedestrians she encountered gave her a wide berth, staring after her and mumbling deprecating comments to one another as she passed.

A few blocks farther on, she noticed a small, beautiful, blond-haired child playing in his front yard. As she approached he ran up to the white picket fence and called out to her in a sweet innocent voice.

"Lady — hey lady! Look at thith," he lisped.

She turned her head slowly, numbly, somehow knowing . . . resignedly she looked anyway. The four-year-old had unzipped his blue jeans and was dangling a horribly outsized, sewage-green penis from between the slats in the fence, waving it at her with his chubby pink fist. Now that he had her attention, he began urinating on her feet, giggling wickedly, red eyes glowing with a malignant and knowing humor.

Marija gasped, doubling over as if she'd been hit in the stomach. Tears welled up and streamed down her face while she looked stupidly at her wet feet. She kicked off the sodden, ruined sandals, working loose the heel strap of one with the sole of the other, her head bent in complete degradation. When she finally looked up again, the boy had disappeared.

Muffling her sobs, biting the knuckles of her clenched fist until the salty-sweet, metallic taste of her own blood made her gag, she blindly stumbled on. Forty feet above her the afternoon traffic roared along the central skyway, the drivers part of an indifferent world of speed and power in their own time and space, no longer men of flesh and blood but mere extensions of the steel-and-chrome machines they controlled.

A red Alfa Romeo flashed by on the arcing ribbon of concrete overhead, but it was on the opposite side of the freeway, traveling north, as she was. Marija never saw it. Nor did the frowning, mustachioed man behind the wheel see the small, desolate figure below, though it was she he was searching for, her home he was headed toward in hopes she might be there.

Disoriented, she moved through the sights and sounds of the city like a sleepwalker, a derelict in a drunken stupor, little of what she saw getting through, none of it making any sense.

But as she passed the corner of Mission and Duboce Streets, Marija's attention was suddenly drawn toward the display window of a small, dusty bookstore. She stopped, though she had no desire to. Her feet simply refused to move. With what little scrap of will she had left, she tried to resist the powerful urge to turn her head toward it, knowing deep inside she must not, *must not*. Yet slowly, inexorably, as if under the control of an unseen hand, her head was being moved, twisted against the top of her spine until she was face to face with the reflective surface of the glass. Within it she saw her own disarrayed image staring back.

Then, as she watched, mesmerized, she saw her *own* face lengthen and broaden into the dreaded reptilian countenance, her own sultry almond-shaped eyes become the color of blood, her own sensuous mouth reshape itself into a wide, lipless grimace full of long, daggerlike teeth from between which shot a slender, lolling black tongue.

Shaking her head in a last desperate denial, MJ opened that hideous mouth, feeling the scream boiling and churning inside her, seeking escape. But instead of sound pouring out in an ear-splitting release of agony, a vile vomit burst forth, blackish bile full of filthy, crawly things: toads and salamanders, huge brown spiders and pink worms, crusty, wrigglylegged beetles, and formless, colorless, slithering things. An unbelievable volume upgorged from the beast that was Marija, more than any human form could possibly contain, spewing out her mouth as if she'd become an open geyser connected to the bowels of hell.

A crowd had begun to gather, forming a semicircle at safe

distance from the woman — seeing merely a disreputable-looking female gone mad, screaming continuously at the plate glass window of an old bookstore.

"What is happening to me, what is happening to me, what is happening to me, what am I becoming . . . *what have I become?!*

The wailing siren of a police car grew louder, abruptly cutting off as the black-and-white coasted to a halt in front of the building. But even as the uniformed officers leapt with businesslike urgency from their unit, a gasp went up from the crowd, followed by the shattering of breaking glass.

Marija, in a final desperate act of self-immolation or survival, had plunged headfirst through the store window.

The doctor in the emergency ward was overly reassuring, the way doctors are when they're not really sure what to do. He was also inordinately loud.

"Yes, yes. She's in satisfactory condition," he bellowed in response to Joe's quiet inquiry, causing heads to turn curiously. "No real danger Mr. . . . Marten, is it?"

The doctor beamed, proud of his ability to remember names.

"We thought we'd better keep her here a day or two for observation — psychiatric evaluation and all that, you understand. Does she carry any insurance that you know of?" the medic boomed on, oblivious to the other man's discomfort.

"I have no idea," Joe replied coldly, ignoring the doctor's disparaging look.

"I see." The doctor scribbled a notation on his clipboard. "Well, we've notified the patient's mother; she's on her way over now. Perhaps *she* can be of more help."

Joe wanted to sock him. Instead he muttered another question.

"What's that?" The doctor stopped midstride, impatient to get back to his rounds. "Her injuries? No, as I said, nothing serious. A few superficial lacerations on her hands and fore-arms, and one that required a couple of stitches on her fore-head . . . but not to worry, it's way up here." He indicated a point just below his prematurely receding hairline. "The scar won't even show."

"Fine. I was really worried about that," Joe retorted sarcastically.

"Oh, by the way, do you know if she's ever suffered any prior mental disorders?"

Joe shook his head, his hands curling and uncurling inside his pockets, his neck hot and red. Either this asshole was a total jerk, or he was deliberately broadcasting their private calamity for his own amusement.

"*On* anything?" the resident probed further, his lips twitching with an ill-suppressed urge to smirk.

"I beg your pardon?"

"*You* know, has she been taking any drugs, prescription or otherwise?" Then, noting that Joe cast a worried glance around the crowded waiting room, he laid a hand on Joe's shoulder. "Hey, this is strictly confidential, doctor–patient stuff, you know?"

Joe took a deep breath, trying to control the anger . . . the son-of-a-bitch was actually enjoying embarrassing him.

"*No, doctor*," he said. "She's totally opposed to drugs of any sort . . . 'prescription or otherwise.'"

"Okay!" the grinning physician gave in, holding his hands palms outward, making it obvious he didn't believe the denial for a minute. "We have to cover all bases. And about my first question, any knowledge of prior mental illness?"

Joe hesitated. "I said 'no,'" he answered at last, but the lack of conviction was evident in his voice and the doctor picked up on it at once.

"Something you're not saying?" he inquired, at last lowering his voice confidentially.

Joe looked around. Though the emergency room was filled with people too deep in their own miseries to pay much attention to someone else's, he still felt as if a hundred ears had just perked up to listen in.

"She's been . . . under a bit of a strain lately," he faltered. "Been seeing a priest about it."

"His name?" The doctor drew his pen from the clipboard.

"Muldoon . . . Michael Muldoon. Listen, when can I see her?"

"We've got her under sedation right now . . . would you happen to have this priest's address or phone number?"

Joe fished a business card out of his wallet. "What kind of sedation?" he asked nervously as he handed over the card.

"Oh, just a little something to help her sleep . . . Seconal, I believe," the resident replied as he jotted down the information.

"Seconal! Isn't that a barbiturate?"

"Not to worry," the doctor said again. "We use it all the time in cases like this. It's perfectly safe."

"Yeah, well," Joe ran his hand through his hair distractedly. "Could I stay with her tonight, anyway? I'd like to be there in case she wakes up."

"Sorry, but we can't allow visitors here beyond regular hours, particularly in the psych wing . . . regulations, you know." He put his arm around the worried man's shoulders in a fatherly fashion, though he was no older than Joe, and began steering him toward the ward. "If you like, you can see her now for a while, though I'm sure she'll be sleeping. She's on the third floor, just ask at the desk for her room number." He glanced at his watch. "You've got about forty-five minutes until visiting hours are over."

He was sitting by the bedside, holding one of Marija's bandaged hands while she slept, when Mike burst into the room about thirty minutes later.

"What happened, how is she?" he whispered.

"I don't know exactly," Joe said as he rose to shake the

priest's hand. "She apparently freaked out at work today, though no one there seems to know why; she ran screaming from the factory in hysterics." He began pacing back and forth at the foot of MJ's bed, his voice low as he related what little he knew of the incident. When he was done he sighed deeply, shoving his fists into his pockets, looking up at the priest as if from a vast distance, his eyes not too proud to beg for help.

"Have you talked to Marija about what happened?" Mike asked, subdued.

Joe shook his head. "By the time I got here they'd knocked her out so they could sew up the lacerations. I guess she was still . . . agitated," he grimaced. "Doc says they gave her Seconal, says she'll be out all night."

"What? Seconal! But Joe, don't you realize what that could do, how helpless the drug will make her to resist if . . . that is, if this was caused by . . ."

He was remembering the way he'd met Marija.

A pounding on the rectory door in the middle of the night; voices, the old-world brass of his aging housekeeper Mrs. McGilvroy shooing the intruder away; the soft, breathless terror in the voice outside the door that had compelled him to intervene. Wide hazel eyes, huge with fright in the dimly lit parlor, peeking over the edge of a steaming cup of tea while the frightened girl told her story.

She'd been fooling around with the idea of astral projection, experimenting, when in the midst of what seemed to be an out-of-body experience she'd suddenly been confronted by the shadowy form of a huge, dragonlike monster which beckoned from behind the fading screen of reality. He called her by name, she said, told her secret things. His eyes opened wider as he talked — huge, almond-shaped, glowing red — holding her, caressing her, drawing her slowly in.

Almost too late she'd realized what was happening (although in retelling it she said she could not remember exactly what that was, just that it had frightened her so badly she'd begun to scream deep inside, to fight to pull away). When at last she'd finally managed to pop her eyes open — back in her bed and bathed in sweat — she'd heard in the corners of her empty room a faint echo of distant thunder — or laughter.

Later she'd tried to dismiss the whole experience, she told him, write it off as a very bad nightmare. Until tonight, when the same red eyes had blinked to life inside her blackened TV screen, the same insidious voice had hissed her name: "Marija . . . you can't escape me, Marija."

Mike felt again the slow sickness that seemed to crawl around his stomach like a bellyful of wet slugs, remembered not wanting to hear any more of this, aware of the cold, pasty slickness of his forehead. Yet he was too polite, too aware of his office, to tell her to shut up.

She'd broken down at this point in her story, broken into racking sobs that were almost convulsions. Agony. It was this that had sent her fleeing blindly through the night streets in her pajamas and overcoat, and into his life.

He'd gone through the motions then, comforting, consoling, promising to help. Finally he'd driven her home. But when he'd returned to his own bed he'd just lain there, unable to sleep. At last he'd turned on the light, picked up his Bible from the nightstand, and watched with a trembling amazement while the pages riffled as if turned by an unseen hand, falling open to a place near the end. It was the Book of Revelations, Chapter Twelve.

Even now he could see the gilt and the black words leaping into his mind.

And he'd read:

And there appeared another wonder in heaven, and behold a great red dragon . . . And the great dragon was cast out, that old serpent, called the Devil, and Satan. . . . And the dragon was wroth with the woman, and went to make war with the remnant of her seed. . . .

The beginning of Armageddon.

At that moment he'd sensed a piece of a very old, but as yet unknown, puzzle click into place somewhere in the universe.

So much had happened in the five days since that first meeting! He looked over now at Joe, knowing that he too was remembering their hushed discussions, their disputed strategies, as the incidents had increased in frequency and intensity.

"I know she shouldn't be drugged," the younger man was saying. "Damn it, you think I don't *know?* But what can I do? They won't even let me stay with her tonight—some goddam regulations—and if I told them why I think I must . . ."

"Well, maybe they'll let *me* stay," and in answer to Joe's quizzical look, he fingered the stiff clerical collar. "I'm a priest. They wouldn't throw a priest out, would they?"

"Yeah, maybe . . ."

"All right, then. I'll go scout up the doctor and get his okay, then I'd better call the parish and let Mrs. M know where I'll be." He was already heading for the door. "You'll still be here when I get back?"

"Where else?" Joe waved wearily, sitting down by the bed. He couldn't help resenting the way Mike always seemed to take charge, the fact that the priest had the right to stay with his fiancée when *he* couldn't. . . .

Just then Marija's mother hurried into the room wringing her hands. "Oh Joe, Joe! What *are* we to *do?*" she cried, bursting into melodramatic tears as she flung herself into his arms. He gave her shoulder a couple of awkward pats, then extracted himself as politely as possible.

She peered over at her daughter's bandaged and unconscious form. "How is she, Joe? I mean *really?* I just couldn't *believe* it when the doctor called me and said she was in the *psychiatric* ward!" The older women's voice was beginning to undulate in pitch, "*Nothing* like this has *ever* happened on *my* side of the family before," she continued, tears beginning to well up again in her eyes.

"Here here, sit down," Joe said, pulling out a chair, careful not to let his impatience show.

Marija had explained her mother to him, but no one had ever explained Marija to her mother.

Mrs. Draekins — Dolores — remembered all too well their discussions during Marija's youth. Their debates had ranged over all manner of things from moral values to ESP to UFOs. She couldn't remember when they'd stopped having those little talks, when MJ had finally given up trying to convince her mother of the existence — or even of the *possibility* — of this or that or the other thing that no one in his right mind would ever want to believe in. But she did remember the relief she'd felt when she finally realized there were no more such discussions on the agenda.

Over the past few years Dolores had thought her daughter had finally grown out of such weird ideas, leveled off, grown up. Now she realized that Marija had only stopped talking to her about it all. The result was that she'd landed in the psycho ward for all the world to see.

Joe took hold of her arm.

"She apparently had a little upset at work — she's been under a lot of pressure there lately, Mrs. Draekins," he explained, looking directly into the woman's eyes. "She, ah, left work, took a little walk to cool off, and along the way somehow lost her footing — she was crying, from what I understand — and tumbled into the display window of a small bookstore. It was simply an accident," he reassured her, taking her hands comfortingly. "But you know how psychiatrists are. If you aren't reacting to life exactly the way they think you should, they immediately want to evaluate your state of mind and throw a fancy label on it." He forced a small chuckle. "I suppose that's how they make the kind of bucks it takes to live in Atherton, don't you think?"

"Oh." The woman sounded almost disappointed. "Well, do you think I should spend the night with her?" She'd already tucked her handkerchief back into her purse and edged forward in her chair as if to rise.

"Not at all," he replied, helping her to her feet — as eager to have her out of there as she was to leave. "I don't believe regulations permit overnight visitors in the hospital, even if you wanted to stay, Mrs. Draekins . . . but not to worry," he subconsciously mimicked the attending doctor's pet phrase. "I've arranged for a close personal friend who happens to be a priest to sit with her tonight."

"A priest! Oh my," she exclaimed, sensing a new drama.

"A close personal friend," Joe reemphasized. "They'll let a priest skirt hospital regulations."

"I see," she said, not really seeing at all. "Well, then, I guess I might as well get along home. . . ."

"Yes, that's a good idea," Joe agreed, walking her to the door.

"You *will* let her know I came by."

"Of course, Mrs. Draekins, of course. I'll be in touch." He quickly closed the door behind her, feeling immediate relief.

A few minutes later, when the priest reappeared, Joe took his leave as well — too drained and depressed to make more than a perfunctory attempt at conversation before saying good night. After a double shot of Wild Turkey to quell the worry, he flopped fully clothed on his waterbed, listening to the miniwaves lap beneath his ears as they rocked him into the temporary respite of sleep.

3

Saturday, June 10th

Joe leapt from his bed at the first jarring ring, sensing even before he was fully awake that the phone call must be about Marija.

The bedside clock read out the time in an endless succession of changing red digits: at the moment it was moving through 2:56:14.

He grabbed the phone in the middle of its third ring.

"Joe, this is Mike. Can you get down here right away?"

"What's happened?" Joe asked, sitting stonelike on the edge of the bed, steeled for the bad news.

"She's had another episode — the doctors think it was some kind of mild seizure, but it's *him*, Joe; I know it is! I pulled her out of this one, talked her out, but now the doctor wants to increase her medication and I don't have the authority to stop him. I have a plan, but it requires your help. . . ." The desperation in the priest's usually controlled voice shocked Joe out of his apathy.

"I'll be there in ten minutes," he said and hung up.

When he arrived on the third floor, the psychiatric unit, he strode purposefully past the nurses' station without so much as a glance at the young woman sitting behind the desk, her attention immersed in a Harlequin romance.

He'd almost reached the double doors which closed off the psych wing, the thick, double-paned windows reinforced by chicken wire, when her voice caught up with him, well ahead of her gum-soled shoes.

"Sir! Hey, wait a minute, sir . . . you can't go in there!"

A burly uniformed guard materialized in front of him from out of nowhere, the lights gleaming cooly off the snout of his dull gray .38 automatic.

Joe turned from him, keeping one eye on the weapon, directing his entreaty to the pretty, dark-haired nurse, warily poised in the shadowless glare of the fluorescent lighting." Please Miss, Miss . . . Feinstein," he read off the plastic name tag. "I've got to see my fiancée. I just got a call from the priest who's here with her; it's a . . . a life-and-death matter."

"Oh! You must be Mr. Marten. It's okay, Sam," she said to the guard. "Dr. Richardson gave special permission for this man to pass."

Reluctantly the guard replaced his pistol, then withdrew a set of keys from a chain attached to his belt. He opened the double doors and moved aside, the hint of a smile curling his lips.

"Room 357," the nurse announced, "about halfway down the hall. Sam'll have to accompany you as far as the door. I believe the doctor's still in with her."

Marija was now sitting up in bed, her eyes enormous beneath the gauzy white bandage covering her forehead, her face a sickly gray.

The three other occupants of the room turned at the sound of the door.

Mike's bulky frame was positioned protectively between MJ and the two hospital personnel — the young resident Joe had met earlier, and an old, salty-looking RN who hovered near the foot of the bed. The nurse was holding a stainless steel tray containing vials of medication and a pair of paper-packaged syringes. She shifted her ample weight from one foot to the other, impatient to get on with it. The doctor busied himself consulting the patient's chart and checking his watch, an annoyed expression on his face.

Marija was staring at Joe through a gradually clearing fog. "Joe!" she exclaimed weakly as recognition came. She held out her arms to him.

He held her tightly, surprised to find tears coursing down his cheeks.

After a moment he felt a gentle tug at his arm. It was Mike. "I need to talk to you for a minute, outside," he said in a low voice. "We'll be right back, sweetie," he assured Marija, giving her arm an affectionate squeeze.

Joe winced at the man's familiarity with MJ. He bent to kiss her. "Be right back," he repeated, following the priest into the hall.

"So, what now, Father?" he asked, once they were out of earshot. The door to the hospital room had been purposely left ajar, affording them an unobstructed view of the injured woman—and the medics.

"As things stand, they won't allow Marija to decide for herself if she should be put on drug therapy or not . . . they've deemed her incompetent to act on her own behalf." Mike's voice was edged in irony. "After she and I refused to allow such treatment, they called her mother of all people for permission to proceed. The old lady is on her way over now, gleefully ready to sign the consent forms, it appears."

"But where do I fit in? Don't I have any say in this?"

"I asked them that. Not as her fiancé, you don't, but as her *husband* you would have the right to stop them. *You'd* be her 'next of kin.'"

"Fine, only I'm not her husband, not yet; how—"

"That's what I wanted to talk to you about. I could marry the two of you here tonight . . . that is, if you're really serious about wanting this marriage with her. If you're not," he warned, "please have the courage to say so right now. In the Catholic Church, marriage is a sacrament. I don't perform sacraments lightly, no matter what the circumstances."

"Of course I'm serious," Joe said. "It's just that . . . I don't see how we can possibly get married *tonight*; we haven't had the blood tests, the three-day wait. Why, we don't even have a license!"

"The tests and three-day wait can be waived under California law in certain instances," explained the pastor. "You *have*, in essence, been cohabitating as man and wife for at least thirty days?"

"In essence," Joe agreed.

"As for the license, I took the liberty of asking Mrs. McGilvroy to bring over a blank one from my supply at the church . . . just in case," he offered a weak smile. "She should be here any minute. So . . . ?"

Joe looked at the other man, his doubtful expression slowly giving way to an ever-widening grin.

"Well, I'll be damned," he laughed at last; "I've been checkmated. I'm really going to get married!"

A few minutes later the duty nurse delivered a manila envelope addressed to the Rev. Michael Muldoon, containing the blank marriage certificate. She then remained, at the priest's request and with the physician's reluctant approval, to witness the brief religious ceremony that followed.

The ceremony was complete—the final "Amen" still hanging in the air—when, without warning, Mike began to laugh—a deep, rolling laugh that quickly infected Joe and Marija (though they had even less idea than he what was so funny.) Even the young nurse began to laugh. As the four of them collapsed in helpless glee, tears streaming down their cheeks, the doctor and the dour-faced nurse, trying in vain to quiet the raucous group, exchanged looks that said they'd like to ECT the whole lot.

When at last the laughter had run itself out, the doctor drew Joe aside. "May I assume you wish to take your new bride home with you tonight?"

"If I *can*, of course," Joe answered in surprise.

"In that case, I have a few forms for you to sign before we

can release her into your custody . . . a legal waiver and so forth." The resident's eyes were red-rimmed with exhaustion by this time, his earlier buoyancy reduced to a plodding roteness as he neared the end of his shift. It would be far easier, he'd decided, to do the paperwork on a release-against-medical-advice than try to explain to the chief of psychiatry tomorrow why the woman was still occupying a much-needed bed while refusing all medication and treatment.

By the time Joe returned from the front desk, Marija had already been helped into her clothes by the older nurse and was waiting in a wheelchair with Mike close by her side. The nurse insisted on doing the pushing herself. "Regulations," she explained tersely, still bristling with barely controlled outrage at having been thwarted from putting the woman under.

"Your mother's downstairs," Joe warned in MJ's ear as he bent to kiss her cheek while they waited for the elevator.

"Mmmmm," Marija smiled drowsily, leaning her head against his side, still affected by the earlier dose of Seconal. The memory of her recent ordeal was safely tucked away for now under a cover of protective forgetfulness; it faded like a nightmare does once the prison of sleep has been escaped.

"Want me to get rid of her?" Joe suggested.

"Mmm-hmm," she nodded. She could hardly keep her eyes open in the thick, honeyed glow of well-being that the drugs, coupled with a mystically unreal notion that she had just gotten married, infused in her.

Joe sent Mike on ahead to dispatch Mrs. Draekins on whatever pretext he could muster while he, Marija, and the nurse waited for the next elevator down.

Once Marija was settled into the deep bucket seat of Joe's sportscar, and the iron-haired RN had retreated, Joe and Mike stood alone in the cool mist of early morning, trying to decide what to do next.

"This is ridiculous," Joe said, "Here it is, my wedding

46

night," he glanced up at the lightening sky — "morning," he corrected himself, "and all I can think of is the fact that I've got to go to work in three hours."

"On a Saturday?" Mike interrupted.

"I took off early yesterday, left a job half done," Joe sighed. "If it's not completed by Monday morning, it's my sweet ass."

"Well, frankly," Mike looked down through the windshield at Marija, already fast asleep with her head lolled comfortable to one side, her lips slightly parted, "it doesn't look like Marija's got her mind on much of a honeymoon at the moment anyway."

Joe glanced through the window, smiled fondly. "Sleep's what she needs most right now."

"I've got an idea," the priest offered. "Why don't you bring her on over to the rectory? Mrs. McGilvroy can keep an eye on her while you're at work . . . I've got a pretty busy day ahead myself," he reflected, thinking of the half-written sermon lying on his desk, the long hours he'd be spending in the confessional later today. "You can come back as soon as you're finished and decide what you want to do then."

Mrs. McGilvroy met them at the door. Her nightly costume of robe and curlers had been traded for a calf-length, blue print housedress. A bulky homeknit sweater covered her shoulders and a red kerchief was tied babushka-style over the yellowish-gray mass of uncombed frizz that framed her round, wrinkled apple face. With her practical low-heeled shoes and woolen stockings, she was the personification of an old world peasant: staid, sturdy, unflappable, with an iron-bound code of ethics that could never be compromised in the least . . . unless she chose to.

"I've made up the bed in your room for her, Father," the woman said brusquely, turning to lead the way as Mike and Joe, the latter carrying the still-sleeping Marija in his arms, followed obediently.

"Mind you," Mrs. M argued to the air as she limped arthritically down the hall, "I *did* have some serious reservations as to the propriety of putting a pretty young woman to bed in a priest's own quarters. But then I said to myself, 'Who's to know, as long as none of us tell 'em?' " She paused a moment to give each in turn a look that could best be described as tacitly threatening.

Opening the door to the monsignor's sparsely furnished bedroom and stepping aside to let the others pass before her, she prattled on. "More important, I told myself, is to keep this poor soul safe from further harm — and what place could be more sanctified than a Father's own bedroom? Naturally the entire rectory has been blessed, but I'll wager the very bed a man of the cloth puts his cares to rest in each night must be doubly so, wouldn't you think? In any case, it's not the same as if she were a single lady, is it, now? I mean to say, she *is* a respectable married woman, blessed by the sacrament this very night." She bestowed the slightest hint of an approving smile on Joe. She turned down the bedsheets and took a step back to allow Joe to lay his new wife gently on the mattress. MJ stirred slightly in her sleep, but did not wake up.

"It's fine, Mrs. McGilvroy," the priest said warmly, giving her shoulder an affectionate squeeze. "Thank you very much for thinking of it."

"Go on, now," the woman squirmed and blushed. "You two just scoot on out of here and go about your business. I'll keep careful watch over the little lady, don't you worry. Nothing's going to bother her as long as I'm here. Oh, there's a fresh pot of coffee on the warmer, Father. You just help yourselves."

"How did she know?" Joe asked suspiciously as soon as they were seated in the comfortable kitchen. "I didn't see you stop to call her on our way back from the hospital."

Mike finished pouring the coffee and set the old blue enamel pot back on the burner before answering. "How did she know what? You mean that Marija would be staying here today?" He chuckled, giving Joe a direct look over the rim of his steaming mug, a glint of amusement in his brown eyes. "No, I didn't plan this beforehand," he answered, "though I did brief Mrs. M on what's been happening to MJ when I called her to bring the marriage certificate to the hospital . . . I felt I owed some explanation for dragging her out of bed in the middle of the night," he apologized. "No breach of confidence intended."

"No, that's all right . . . but then how *did* she know we'd bring MJ over here?"

"Mrs. McGilvroy, for all her old world conservatism, is an extremely sensitive person," the priest said, smiling. "Which is just another way of saying she's got a bit of the magic in her, I think. Purely white magic, to be sure—but she does blow my mind from time to time. Frankly," he admitted, "I feel very good about leaving Ms. Draekins—pardon me, Mrs. Marten—in her care today. I'm afraid I'm going to be tied up most of the day in the confessional. With you also working, it's a great relief to know there's someone like her to take charge. I promise I'll look in on them from time to time, just to be sure everything is going well, but I don't think you have anything to worry about. Do you want me to give you a call after each check so you can rest easier, too?"

Joe exhaled, rubbing his temples. "I guess not," he answered after a bit. "I'll probably be out on a service call most of the day, and I've no idea how you could reach me, in any case. If I get too worried, I suppose I could always give Mrs. McGilvroy a ring myself."

"Sure, that'd be fine," Mike nodded, draining the contents of his cup and pushing away from the table. "So, my friend, just relax and finish your coffee—have a second, if you like, it's right there—but as for me, if you'll excuse my rudeness, I'm afraid I've got to get cleaned up and changed into the proper vestments. The confessional opens at 6 AM and there's always a line of impatient sinners waiting for quick absolution so they can get out to the links ahead of the crowds." He grinned as he spoke, but it failed to disguise the bitter edge to his voice. Joe darted him a quick, appraising look, but aside from a barely perceptible shrug, Mike pretended not to notice.

Thirty minutes later, when he went around the front of the old brick church to unlock the large double doors at the main entrance, there was already a short, informal queue formed. The priest flipped on the low-intensity illumination for the chapel from the master control box near the doorway, then proceeded ahead of the parishioners, genuflecting at the center aisle before continuing with unhurried deliberation through the nave to the chancel to light the altar candles. He managed to ignore the impatient coughs and shuffles of his restless flock while performing these rituals. When he finally entered the dark cubicle of the confessional, it was 6:16 AM.

Over the next five hours the pastor listened halfheartedly to the endless series of trivial, boring revelations from the stream of sinners who came to clear their consciences that day.

When at last the morning session ended shortly after eleven, the distracted priest all but leapt from the tiny booth, his hasty exit nearly bowling over his last parishioner, who looked back over her shoulder at him, embarrassed, cringing beneath her print silk scarf to hide her identity as she hurried to the altar.

He left through a side door in the vestry, rushing across to the rectory, a knot of anxiety tightening his stomach muscles. But when he entered the house he saw Marija and Mrs. McGilvroy sitting amiably at the kitchen table over cups of strong English tea, his usual lunch laid out on the table beside them. Though he really hadn't much appetite, he ate what he could so as not to offend the housekeeper.

Finally he pushed the plate away and got to his feet. "Thank you, Mrs. M—delicious, as usual," he said gallantly. "Now if you'll excuse me and Mrs. Marten . . . I'd like to have a little talk with you in my office," he said, reaching down to take Marija's hand and draw her to her feet. She followed placidly enough, though still abnormally quiet as he'd noticed during his brief lunch, a barely perceptible resistance in her steps. She sat meekly where he indicated as he closed his office door behind them, one hand playing aimlessly with her hair while the other picked at imaginary lint on her woolen skirt.

He hated to ask the question they both knew was coming, but if he was to help her he had to know.

"What happened yesterday, Marija?"

Her mouth opened and closed several times as if to reply. Then the tears began, choking off any further attempts. All she could do was cry, shake her head, cry some more, her great green eyes lonely and lost.

"Was it the dragon again, Marija?"

She nodded and the flow of tears increased alarmingly— rivers of tears, more than he would have thought possible.

"In the office . . . your boss?" He was going on instinct.

She nodded again, her face twisting in agony at the awful memory. Her mouth opened to speak, but only a low gurgling moan escaped.

"And later, in front of that store . . . the bookstore?" He persisted. "Was it he who made you fall into the glass?"

Once more the start of a nod, a hesitation, then quickly she shook her head to the negative. The tears were drying up now, her body's store of them drained and depleted, yet her body continued to shake and tremble in silent, convulsive sobs.

"Then what *did* happen there, Marija? Please, I *must* know." He resisted the urge to come around the side of the desk that separated them, take her in his arms, hold her until the pain and fear went away. He knew that his strength, not his sympathy, was what she needed now, and to give that strength, distance must be maintained.

"The reflection . . . " she faltered at last in a low, quavering voice barely audible to his straining ears. "In the glass. Me, the demon . . . it was me, the demon was *me!*" Her whisper

51

had the overtones of a scream, all the more terrifying in its quiet, dead certainty.

Mike got around the desk just in time to catch her collapsing form as it slid from the chair to the floor. She had fainted. He hoisted the unconscious woman easily into his arms, holding her with the gentle strength of a father carrying a sleeping child, bellowing for Mrs. McGilvroy as he headed for the bedroom. The elderly housekeeper was right on his heels, clucking like an anxious mother hen as he laid MJ on the bed.

The housekeeper immediately took over, pushing him firmly out of the way while she ministered to the girl, pinching and prodding at her cheeks, arms, and shoulders to bring her around. As soon as Mike saw Marija begin to stir, saw her cradled in the soothing arms of Mrs. M while she sobbed and hiccuped like a little girl, he strode back to his office, slamming the door behind him.

The priest was shaking with fury, determined to break through the bureaucratic bullshit of the church hierarchy and get that woman the help— the *exorcism*—she needed now. Yet even as he picked up the phone he hesitated, remembering the slap in the face he'd received five days earlier when he'd taken Marija's case before the archbishop the first time, the cold look of hatred in Quillans' eyes when he'd handed him the petition for the rites.

"This, Your Excellency," he'd said, "contains a taped account of a young woman's recent experiences with what seems to be a powerful demon. There are lesser evil spirits involved as well, possibly under his control. I am of the opinion that it is a genuine case of diabolical obsession."

"I see," the archbishop had said after an interminable moment of deadly scrutiny, his fingers forming a thoughtful V as the tips touched his pursed lips. "And has she sought psychiatric help?"

Mike had shaken his head.

"Have you recommended that she do so?"

"I, uh, I know that as a rule we are supposed to advise those professing such . . . symptoms to go first to a mental health service for diagnosis and treatment. But in this situation I believe such a course could be potentially devastating. Their likely course of treatment would be electroshock or drug therapy, which might dull her mind and spirit to the extent that she would become at the complete mercy of these evil forces."

"Are you suggesting," the official had demanded, "that a doctor who's spent ten or twelve years learning about mental disorders — and who knows how many more in practical application — is more likely to misdiagnose a case of mental illness than you are?"

"No," Mike had replied, resisting the urge to back up in his chair. "What I'm saying is that a psychiatrist would never recognize a case of genuine *possession*, because there's no room for such options in his texts or his philosophy."

"Well, Father Muldoon, since you have presumed to bypass all regular channels to come here with this information today," he indicated Mike's materials with a dismissive wave of his hand, "you might as well leave it. I'll look it over when I find the time."

With that, Archbishop Quillans had extended his ring hand to be kissed. Father Michael Muldoon, rising obediently to perform the ritual, had been summarily dismissed.

Muldoon now looked at the phone in his hand, then down the hall where the woman still cried quietly in his housekeeper's ample arms. He began to dial.

The cultured voice on the other end of the line was hard and cold as tempered steel.

"You seem to have a great deal of influence with my personal secretary, Father Muldoon." The words were clipped, the sharp-edged tongue just short of sarcastic, "I do hope, for both your sakes, that this call is as important as you purport.

53

I am extremely busy."

"Then I must apologize for disturbing Your Excellency," Mike said without real sincerity. "But I do believe the matter must not wait another minute. It's the possession of the young woman I spoke to you about Wednesday — I'm afraid true diabolic possession is now occurring . . . you *must* approve an exorcism at once if we are to save this lady's eternal soul!"

A long disquieting silence greeted Mike's entreaty. Finally the archbishop spoke, his tone a study in controlled outrage.

"Do you presume to *order* this office, *Father* Muldoon?"

"No, sir, no, Your Excellency. Forgive my unfortunate choice of words," he faltered, backpedaling, his clean line of purpose now confused and wavering. "I merely wished to urge, to *implore* your office to act with merciful haste in light of what has just happened to this unfortunate young woman."

"Which is?" came the icy voice.

"She was, it seems, confronted by a physical manifestation of Satan in broad daylight . . . while she was at work yesterday. I don't have the complete picture yet." His words were beginning to rush out. "Of course she's still distraught; but it appears she fled in terror after the encounter and began running through the city streets. Then she saw her reflection in a shop window, saw her own face turn into that of the devil — as if she had now become him. She hurled herself through the glass in an apparent attempt to thwart the incipient possession."

"And what professional care has she been given? Have you sought psychiatric consultation for her — either before or after this incident — as I advised?"

"Yes . . . in a sense. That is, she was taken to a hospital and kept there for psychiatric observation and treatment last night. But the drugs they were giving her were making her more susceptible to this . . . possession. I personally observed it. They were going to give her even more drugs, until I stepped in and got her released early this morning."

"You *what!*" the voice bellowed, all semblance of control shattered. The deadly silence resumed, broken only by rapid, harsh breathing that slowly diminished. After a while the voice resumed, its icy calm restored.

"Father Muldoon, it might interest you to know that I have been reviewing your personnel records since I last spoke with you. It appears you have often displayed something of a preoccupation—a personal fetish, I might suggest—with the subject of demon possession and exorcism. It appears you were placed on probation while in the seminary for this very matter, presuming to know better than your superiors how such things should be dealt with—were you not?"

"Well, Archbishop, I . . . "

"Yes or no, Muldoon."

"Yes." A heavy sigh.

"Well, then, you may consider yourself on probation again." It was like a book slamming closed. "And if your parish is of any importance to you, I would advise you to tread very carefully on this and any other religious matters from here on out. Do you understand?"

"You pissbrain!" Mike thought angrily, slamming his fist against the desk in frustration. Well, he wouldn't just let this drop. "I understand, Your Excellency," he said aloud, his voice now as cold as the archbishop's. "But what about the woman, what about her welfare?"

"Put your information on the proper lines, sir, and it will be dealt with properly, in due time." Quillans had changed now to a formal, end-of-conversation tone. "If you will excuse me now, I have much to do before my flight to Rome tonight."

"Rome?" Mike exclaimed, shocked - a jumble of worried questions assaulting his mind. "Why? For how long? What about the petition while you're gone? What about *Marija?*"

"Where have you been, Father Muldoon, aside from chasing imaginary dragons, that is?" the archbishop said. "It's been all over the news. The Holy Father was stricken last

55

night with a cerebral hemorrhage; his condition is now extremely critical. Comatose, I understand. But just before he lapsed into unconsciousness he specifically ordered that I be flown to his side." The prideful Quillans gloated. "I depart for the Vatican at seven tonight, and it is of course uncertain how long I will remain. Bishop Dumore will be handling the normal business of the diocese in my absence, but other matters will just have to wait till I return."

What he meant by "other matters" was all too clear.

Stunned, Mike mumbled his condolences and hung up, his mind in turmoil.

Chapter 4

When Joe finished his work that afternoon, he got in his Alfa and headed for the rectory, but never got there.

He wasn't ready.

"I love you, Marija, I love you, I do," he muttered aloud as he passed Fell Street without turning. "But my God, I don't know what I've gotten myself into here! I don't understand what's happening to you and I don't know what to do to get you out of it!"

He drove on through the city streets like an automaton, his reflexes gearshifting, steering, turning, while his mind boiled darkly. The man felt tormented, and unreasonably angry with Marija for causing him such anguish.

Joe wished he could simply write off the previous day's experience as some sort of psychotic episode. That would simplify things. Yet he couldn't, any more than he could the event that had started this nightmare two weeks ago — or any of the increasingly horrifying happenings that had plagued their lives since.

On one side he felt pulled by the rational, real, physical world he'd always stood by like a loyal friend. On the other, he was teased and tormented by that weird, intangible world lying just below the surface, a world better ignored.

As he downshifted now at a traffic light, he found himself staring at the lit orb in the top of the stanchion, like a little red glowing ball. A memory came floating in on that ball. The light was comforting, somehow. It hung beside his bed in the old wooden farmhouse where he'd grown up. Yes, he remembered now; it was a red ball balanced on the nose of a small gray plastic seal plugged into the outlet beside his bed. A night light, the one he'd had for a little while after Harold had left.

Harold!

Suddenly Joe realized he hadn't always been so firmly entrenched in the world of hard-core realism. There was, after all, his "invisible friend" Harold, with whom he'd talked and played for hours on end when he was too little to know better.

Harold had left for good the day his daddy delivered seven-year-old Joey a solid, open-hand roundhouse to the right cheek, telling him never to mention "that imaginary fag friend of yours again."

He winced now, almost feeling the pain, the lingering bruise, and then the pain inside the pain.

No, Dad, he didn't want the guys down at the factory teasing you about having a pansy for a son. Sure, Dad, he knew there was no such thing as an invisible person. No, he'd never talk to or about Harold again. No, there was no Harold.

But there was still his fear of darkness, a fear which mounted to almost uncontrollable panic after the banishment of Harold, who had served to keep the nighttime boogeymen under control. When his father discovered that Joey's sympathetic mother had been allowing a night light on in his room, he'd wrenched it from the wall socket and smashed it to bits beneath his heavy work boots.

"Ya wanna turn him into a goddam sissy, Ethel? Is that what you want? You'd like that, wouldn't you, make him into a little mama's boy!" His father was bellowing, his rage reaching its peak, and when his mother had started to protest, understanding the degree of her son's night terror, his father had slapped her so hard she'd fallen back on the floor, bleeding

58

from the nose and mouth.

So the light had stayed off, the door closed, and the ominous darkness had mounted like impending doom each night, filling the wide-eyed hours of gloom until weariness would finally overcome the boy, despite his certainty that to sleep was to succumb.

"Now, Son," his father had explained later with phony geniality, his bearish arm around the small boy's quivering shoulders, "you know that what you can't see can't hurt you, right? If you can't see it, smell it, touch it, or give it a good goose, it just ain't there . . . and don't you forget it, Boy, hear?"

Joey had just nodded, too afraid to open his mouth, the vision of his mother — plopped down there on the floor, legs askew, sobbing — still too vivid in his mind.

Once his mother had tried to sneak a new night light into his room after his father had gone to bed, but the boy had just kissed her and shaken his head. "No, Mom. It's okay. I'm doing fine." *Nothing* was worth seeing her hurt again. But it was months, years even, before he got a good night's sleep.

In the end, his father's philosophy had won out, made him comfortable with the dark, the dark side. Because, you see, there *was* no dark side. Because, you see, "If you can't see it, smell it, or give it a good goose, it just ain't there."

Right, Dad.

"Only what do you do with *this* shit, Joey, m'boy?" he asked himself aloud, pounding the heel of his hand against the rim of the steering wheel in a steady rhythm. "How do you goose this old crappola, huh? How do you hold onto Marija and still hold onto reality, huh? You wanna dump the crazy bitch, or what, *huh?*"

He felt like crying, so empty was the thought. Suddenly he *was* crying, so hard that he had to pull over to the curb.

He couldn't lose her.

Right now he didn't care what it took to get a handle on this thing — faith and all the hokum that went with it were just fine, so long as they worked. And he didn't want to understand, not any of it. He just wanted it out of their lives, *all* this shit out of their lives, God, the devil, whoever and whatever. Just go away and leave us alone, okay?

"I'll do anything, okay?"

Joe had been driving as if on automatic pilot the past half hour, not knowing where he was going, nor particularly interested. Now, as he looked up to get his bearings, he discovered that he'd parked down in the marina district. Directly across the street was an oversized Victorian mansion, its surrounding grounds an unkempt profusion of hedges and gardens gone wild, its exterior freshly painted, black on black. Startled, he jerked his foot, stalling the engine.

He restarted the car and circled the block so that he could come back around in front, pulling up to read the neatly printed wooden signboard attached to the high wrought iron fence that surrounded the three-story mansion: "Church of Satanic Principles — Alton B. Hawley, Founder and High Priest."

His breath came out in a slow whoosh, an inadvertent shudder at the capriciousness of Fate. This was one of the cults at the top of his list, one of the metaphysical groups he'd found in the phone book one day when Marija's situation began to worsen. He'd intended to check them out as possible alternatives to this exorcism thing, but hadn't yet gotten around to it.

He moved his shoulders uneasily, as if to dislodge the invisible hand he felt pushing him along. Of course it could have been mere coincidence that he ended up here. Or, better yet, since it had been his hand that had originally written this place down on his list, perhaps he had subconsciously steered the car to this exact destination. That must be it.

He continued to stare at the contrived, sinister-looking house, the engine of his Alfa still humming. It was movement that finally made up his mind — the slightest flick at the side of the heavy black drapes that covered the tall bay windows fronting the house. He'd obviously been spotted by someone. Now he must either go up to the door or scratch the place off his list. No way could he drive off and come back later.

"Okay, I'll go in," he said aloud, turning off the ignition, flexing his legs under the low steering column as he opened the car door.

He walked up to the gate, trying to be nonchalant, but his heart thudded loudly. His hand slipped the first time he tried the latch, and he had to clench it into a hard fist to stop its shaking before trying again.

There was an errant hope at the back of his mind that the gate would be locked, but it slid open easily under his touch, the well-oiled noiselessness of its movement somehow more eerie than the creak he expected.

The blackness of the massive entryway was relieved only by a single spot of color, a greenish metal gargoyle-head doorknocker with bright red eyes made of glass. A little smile twitched the corners of Joe's mouth. The place was just a bit too Hollywood.

The door was opened on his second tentative rap by a tall, slender girl of about nineteen. His mouth opened involuntarily, the carefully rehearsed line stuck somewhere around his Adam's apple, forgotten.

She was breathtakingly beautiful, with a waist-length mane of reddish-gold hair flowing down her back and over the front of her purple robe, along the creamy white curves of her firm young breasts.

The deep V-neck of the silky gown was laced from waist to cleavage with a velvet ribbon, and he felt an almost uncontrollable urge to reach out and loosen it.

His eyes lifted to her face. An amused, subtly seductive smile played about her lips, her lavender eyes twinkling mischievously as she slid a slender hand across her chest, toying with the ribbon.

"Yes?" she enquired in a low voice.

"I . . . ahem." He cleared his throat noisily, annoyed with himself for his nervous habit. "I wish to see Mr. Hawley."

"I'm sorry, that's quite impossible," the girl said, shaking her head. Thick, silken tresses moved in gentle waves about her face. She continued to look at him, emanating sensuality; but when he failed to respond she frowned and moved as if to close the door.

"Wait, please — it's very important," he pleaded.

"Well?" the young woman prodded impatiently, tiring of the game.

"My fiancé . . . that is, my wife," he corrected lamely, feeling a little guilty now about the way he had been staring at her, "has been having some . . . unusual experiences. She seems to think demons are after her." He held up his hands as if to say, "You know how it goes."

The woman looked at him for a moment without speaking, a quizzical expression on her face. Then she opened the door just wide enough to allow him entrance.

He was in a long, broad hallway from which a steep bannistered stairway rose gracefully on the left, an open doorway invited to the right. The interior of the house, just like the exterior, was painted entirely black. A thick blood-red carpet graced the floor and stairs.

The only illumination came from an old brass chandelier directly overhead and three or four wall sconces along the stairwell, their dim bulbs casting a pale reddish glow in weird shadows.

The girl led him into the front parlor and indicated a plush purple velvet chair.

"Wait here. I'll go get my mother."

There was something so mundane, so intrinsically human in that last statement — especially in the context of this cabalistic atmosphere — that he nearly laughed aloud.

The parlor was another Disneylike effort at Halloween — black walls, black drapes, red lights and carpet, a human skeleton in a glass case, a stuffed, doglike creature neatly labeled "Albanian Werewolf" beside the fireplace. There was a surgical cabinet containing, among other magical appurtenances, several small gray packets marked "graveyard dust," while a matched set of genuine human skulls grinned happily down from the mantlepiece, absurd-looking fat wax candles protruding from their crania.

Joe was watching the doorway for the red-haired girl's return when he felt a sudden chill on the back of his neck. He turned to see a woman float soundlessly into the room from an unseen door behind him. At first, in the dim light, he thought it was the daughter returning alone.

"What happened, where is your mother?" he started to ask; but before the words were formed, the woman stepped into the light, smiling coldly.

"I *am* the mother," she said, "Diana, high priestess of the Devil's temple." She extended her hand. It was soft, smooth, exquisitely well cared for. Her face, but for a sprinkling of giveaway age lines at the corners of the large gray eyes, was also flawless. Had he not known she had a grown daughter, he would have guessed her age at no more than thirty. The river of thick blond hair was identical to her daughter's—though perhaps a trace paler, a touch longer. The gown, of similar cut and design to the younger woman's, was black, and the breasts and thighs outlined beneath the sleek, clinging fabric were a little fuller.

Suddenly he wanted her so much that he ached.

She smiled in acknowledgment of his desire, as if it were expected, then got on with business. Sitting carefully on the edge of the black Victorian sofa across from him, she leaned forward confidentially, her soft, hot hand placed gently on his knee, her snow-white breasts heaving against the ribbon lacing.

"Now," she said in a low, conspiratorial whisper, "why don't you tell me what's on your mind?"

Fucking, he thought. He swallowed hard.

"I'd hoped to speak to Mr. Hawley personally," Joe faltered.

"Well, first you must speak to me," the woman said, a chill stealing into her voice. "I'll decide if what you have to say is worthy of the Black Pope's consideration. And frankly, I'm a

63

bit short on time," she declared, the warning implicit in her tone as she flounced back against the cushions and waved her arm imperiously for him to proceed.

Pointedly staring at his feet, Joe related in a rushed monotone an abbreviated version of what had been happening to Marija since the first incident in the old hotel up the coast.

"Why come to us?" Diana asked when he was finished. "Why not just let her have her little Catholic exorcism and be done with it?"

"Because I think it's a pile of crap!" Joe burst out, surprising her with his vehemence. "And even it could do some good, I don't think the church is about to approve it, nor does Monsignor Muldoon, *really* . . . all he wants is to . . . I don't know." Joe stopped himself from voicing the unfair accusation, rubbing his forehead. "It's just that I don't want to see Marija going off the deep end like this while the Catholic hierarchy puts her on hold, playing their weird-ass bureaucratic games, you know?"

"But why us?" She smiled in a pleased way. "What do you think Satan worshipers are going to do to help?"

"I'm not sure." He shook his head. "I just thought if anyone knew how to deal with the devil, it'd be you."

"Deal?" A plucked and painted eyebrow rose a fraction. "You want to make a *deal* with the devil?"

"No! Yes . . . I don't know," Joe stammered, confused. "I didn't mean deal in *that* way, exactly. I just want all this bullshit to stop; I want things back to normal. I want to get on with our life. No religions, no ghosts, no devils . . . just us, you understand? The way it was before."

"All right." The woman rose decisively. Joe stumbling clumsily to his feet. "Tomorrow, three PM. Bring the woman with you."

"But . . ."

"Bring the woman. Nothing can be done without her consent. No woman, no audience."

As the door closed heavily behind him, Joe, blinking in the

painfully bright sunlight, could only wonder how he was going to convince Marija to come here with him tomorrow.

"So—what do you think?" the big, bearded man said between mouthfuls of spaghetti, the bright yellow light of a modern chrome chandelier reflecting dully off his gleaming bald head as he bent over the blue-and-white Wedgwood plate.

"Mmm, I don't know. He seems to have money . . . drives a late-model Alfa Romeo."

"Well, that's a start," the bald man smiled jovially, pinching his wife's well-formed bottom through the tight jeans hard enough to make her jump, sending the dishes rattling dangerously in her hands. "What else?"

"His wife has some sort of hang-up about demons—she's started seeing a priest about it," the blond woman answered as she rinsed the china before putting it into the dishwasher. "Anyway, Joe—that's the guy's name—he's jealous of the priest, hates religion, and just wants everything to get back to normal. I think he'll pay to get it. I think he'll pay plenty," she winked, looking up.

"Is he a wimp?" Hawley asked, pushing back from the table with a satisfied burp.

"Noo," Diana smiled slyly.

He raised a heavy black brow at her, his brown eyes surprisingly warm in a face that looked chiseled from granite.

"I sensed something rather remarkable in him," she mused. "He *could* be quite powerful, I think, but he's afraid to be anything but tiresomely 'normal.' "

"Attractive?"

"Mmm-hmm." She smiled mysteriously.

"And his . . . libido?"

"Oh, definitely present—only he fights it so, poor man."

Alton B. Hawley threw back his large head and roared with laughter. "So," he said after a moment, "what does he expect *me* to do about his problem?"

"Something, anything . . . I don't think he's got a specific plan in mind," she answered as she cleared the rest of the dishes from the table. "As I said, he just wants things 'normal' again between him and his old lady. He's apparently ready to try anything. And with his obvious sexual hang-ups, plus his money—shit, we could milk him for quite some time."

"My dear, you have convinced me." The Satanist smiled, rising. "Tomorrow then, at 3 PM, I shall greet your latest find in full diabolic regalia. But for now, if you'll excuse me, I think I'll retire to the tube to see if I can't conjure up enough black magic to make the Giants win at least one game this season against those outrageous Pirates."

Joe failed to return to her that afternoon, and as afternoon ticked slowly toward evening, Marija's fears mounted by the minute.

What if he never came back? He'd married her, sure . . . but that was just because he had to, just because he was too nice a guy to let her sit in that hospital and be destroyed.

She tried anger for a while—"Yeah, *nice* guy . . . whatever happened to 'for better or worse'?"—storming around the small barren bedroom like a caged lion. That lasted about five minutes.

Then she'd begun to cry—hard, burning tears that dropped to puddle on the polished wood floor between her feet where she sat on the little bed. The tears relieved nothing, and still he did not return.

After a time she'd stopped, feeling worse than ever. Her head was heavy, her eyes swollen. A throbbing headache had begun in her temples, then moved to form a tightening band around her skull, causing her stomach to churn uneasily. Weak and dizzy, she'd propelled herself into the bathroom and vomited. It was like a release of the bitter yellow bile of her emotions.

66

Dampening a clean white washcloth under the tap in the basin, she'd wiped her face, relishing the cool relief it temporarily brought. She wet it again, then folded it into a neat rectangle and pressed it to her forehead across her tired eyes.

Stumbling to the bed, Marija had laid herself carefully back onto the pillow. After a time she lifted her legs up onto the mattress one at a time, her body stretched out on the bed in a tense equilibrium between passivity and pain. Finally, blessedly, she slept.

It was 9 PM before Joe had finally gotten enough liquid courage down him at a corner bar to return to the rectory.

The priest himself answered the door, looking rough and woodsy in his Pendleton plaid shirt and Levis. "Mrs. M and Marija are both sleeping," he whispered as he opened the door wider for Joe to enter. "Come on into my study, where we can talk."

"Scotch?" Muldoon offered, taking down a small water glass from the shelf behind his desk, wiping out the dust with his shirttail.

"Fine," Joe nodded, noting the half-empty glass already on the pastor's desk with mild surprise.

Mike caught his look and nodded, topping off his own drink. "It's been that kind of day," he said, then raised his glass in a toast. "Here's to a better tomorrow."

They drank in silence, savoring the taste of the liquor, the sensation of liquid fire that coursed down their throats, sending its bolts of warmth radiating outward through the veins to soothe and numb and take the edge off their pain.

Joe noticed, without seeming to look at it, the made-up cot in the corner, feeling strangely relieved.

"So," he said casually, raising his eyes to Mike's. "What's the progress on getting that exorcism approved?"

"It's bad, Joe," the priest admitted morosely, sitting back in his creaky wooden chair, pressing the heel of both hands against his forehead as if he'd just remembered a headache. "The archbishop's gone off to Rome and the auxiliary bishop left in charge during his absence wouldn't pee without written permission. There's no way I can get an exorcism approved until Quillans' return."

"So how far does that set things back?"

"I don't know, I really don't. The Pope, it seems, is dying, and he's summoned the archbishop to his side—why or for how long, no one seems to have any idea."

"Then why didn't you push for his okay on this thing before he left?" Joe demanded, his voice rising in exasperation.

"I did," Mike answered quietly, looking up. "All I got for my trouble was a royal chewing out. That, and now I'm on 'official probation.' "

Mike refilled his guest's glass and his own, then both men sat there, looking at nothing, sipping their drinks.

"Well, you did all you could," Joe said at last.

Mike nodded.

"Looks like it's time to try something else."

"Like what?" the priest asked, looking hard at Joe. "An exorcism is what's indicated. It's the only thing I know of that could handle a . . . a situation like Marija's. We'll just have to keep her here where it's safe, protect her, until the approval comes through. That's all we can do."

"Maybe not quite all," Joe replied elliptically, a little wave of satisfaction passing through him. Convincing Marija to go to the black church with him tomorrow would not be the insurmountable problem it had first seemed, now that the priest and his religion had obviously failed.

5

Sunday, June 11th

By the time MJ awoke the next morning, Mike had already left to serve early Mass, but Mrs. McGilvroy was up — MJ could hear her bustling about the small apartment beyond the bedroom. After a few minutes the older woman peeked in the doorway, caught Marija's eye, held up an index finger — "Wait a minute" — and disappeared. She was back quickly, a folded and sealed note in her hand. She handed it to the younger woman.

"From the Father," she explained, backing politely away as MJ tore the letter open. "He said to be sure you got it first thing."

"Mrs. Marten," the note began with a genial formality, *"Your husband dropped by to see you last night after you were asleep. He asked me not to wake you, but said to tell you that he would come by again this morning.*

"I also wanted you to know that I will be offering the first Mass this morning on your behalf — in prayer that you and your new marriage may overcome these present adversities to flourish and prosper. Best regards, the Reverend M. Muldoon."

Marija felt a momentary surge of elation as she reread the note. Joe *had* come back to see her!

Then, as the morning wore on with no sign of the man,

even that small elation withered, and hope gradually turned to an ugly dread that what Joe had come back to tell her last night—what he was coming again this morning to say once he got up his nerve—was that it was all too much, he couldn't take anymore . . . that it was over.

It was past eleven before MJ heard the unmistakable throaty growl of Joe's car as it pulled into the rectory drive-way. Her heart leapt with joy and fear, her hands trembling so badly that she had to set down her mug of coffee to keep the hot liquid from slopping onto the table. She lit a ciga-rette, inhaled deeply, fumbled a mirrored compact out of the purse on her lap to check her makeup. She fluffed her hair, pulled her bangs back over her forehead, wet her lips, and by the time Joe walked through the door she was willing to do almost anything to keep him.

After a brief, superficial round of the required amenities—mostly for Mrs. McGilvroy's benefit—the two of them, at Joe's suggestion, went for a drive.

They rode in silence, each casting an occasional worried glance at the other. At last Joe pulled into a dirt parking area on the bluff overlooking the Cliff House restaurant, sheltered from prying eyes and the insistent Pacific wind by a small grove of bent and tortured Monterey pines. Turning to the somber, dark-haired woman beside him, he began immedi-ately his rehearsed speech.

"Marija, there's something very important I have to talk to you about."

She felt her heart stop momentarily and gripped the side of the seat cushion waiting for the blow, steeling herself.

"The reason I brought you out here to talk," he went on, "is because I feel, as your husband, that I have a right to insist that you try other avenues of approach besides Catholicsm for this . . . problem you've been having."

Marija had already started to cry; big, soft quiet tears of relief. "Husband," he'd said! She'd hardly heard a word past that.

Misinterpreting her reaction, Joe quickly went on to convince her. "Now come on, babe," he said, turning her to him. "You promised me a while back that you'd check out other methods of dealing with this thing, and since exorcism's just about a dead issue anyway . . ."

"Dead issue?" she paled. "What do you mean?"

"Mike hasn't told you?"

"No—told me what? What's happened?"

"It seems the archbishop flew off to Rome for an indefinite stay at the summons of the Pope without approving your petition. Nothing can be done about the exorcism until the man gets back . . . if then."

"But . . . but what about me? What am I supposed to do in the meantime?"

"That's what I wanted to talk to you about. There's this place I want to take you, today," Joe answered. "I think maybe we can get some answers there."

"What place?" she queried, taking his hand.

"Listen, hon," he said, slipping an arm around her shoulder to draw her close. "I want you to keep an open mind about this."

"Mmm-hmm," she acknowledged, laying her cheek against his chest.

"It's just that right now the Catholic exorcism plan is not panning out—it could take weeks, possibly months, for an approval to come down. I don't want to wait that long to, well, to get back to normal. Do you?"

"No, of course I don't," she mumbled into the scratchy softness of his lambswool sweater.

"And until we find something that works, I guess you'll have to keep staying at the rectory . . . it's okay, I understand," he assured her as she jerked her head up to deny it. "If that's where you feel safest, that's where you'll stay—but I can't very well make love to you there, can't hold you in the night. I really miss that, you know." He smiled, tweaking her nose.

"Me too," she sighed, snuggling back against him. "What place, Joe?"

"It's over in the marina area, one of the places on my list — you remember the list I made? The occult groups we were going to check out?"

"Yes, I remember," she smiled. "Which one?"

"The Church of Satanic Principles."

"The *what?* Oh, Christ, Joe — not that!" she exclaimed, jerking back from his embrace. "Has everything I've been going through slipped by you?"

"No, Marija, I don't think so."

"Sorry . . . I didn't mean it to come out quite that way. It's just . . ." She sighed deeply, fidgeted, knowing there was no way ever to convey the depth of her horror to him, no way he could comprehend the full reality of what had happened to her, no matter how many times she tried to explain it. She tended to reject it herself, to deny or at least downgrade it. If she didn't, she wouldn't be able to function at all. Yet the enormity of what was happening to her hovered just below the surface, like a caged beast waiting to break free at the first opportunity and devour her entirely.

"I'm afraid, Joe," she said finally, looking to him to grasp the rest.

"Because it's supposedly the Church of Satan, the enemy stronghold?" he suggested. She gave a tiny nod.

"I understand, believe me," he said, pulling her close again, "only it's not like that, MJ — really it's not. The place is more Disneyland than anything else. I stopped by there yesterday," he admitted. "It's not for real, I'm sure of it."

"Then why go at all?" she asked over the lump of fear in her throat, trying to sound calm. "I mean, if it'll make you happy, and you're sure it can't hurt . . . I suppose I could go. But why bother? If they're just a bunch of phonies, how can they possibly help?"

"Maybe they can't," he acknowledged, pulling his arm back from around her shoulder to turn the ignition, knowing he'd

72

won. "I just happened across the place by accident yesterday, but now I'm kind of curious to meet this crackpot Hawley, see if he has anything useful to say. It *is* possible," he shrugged, shifting into reverse and backing cautiously out of the lot. "He's reputed to be something of an expert on the subject, an 'extremely articulate and well-read student of the occult,' according to the books I read. Majored in demonology at Weirdo Tech," he winked. "So even if he is basically a carny con man, as far as his own powers go, he still might be able to steer us onto something that will help. Now," he concluded, flashing a winning smile in her direction, "how about some lunch?"

6

Archbishop Robert Quillans seethed beneath his well-tailored business suit. The fact that this clandestine journey had required him shedding the robes and title of his office had — and this he'd *not* foreseen — also shed him of the prestige and privileges of that office, the respect.

He'd been standing in this line of foot-shifting, alternately grumbling and wisecracking tourists — as if he were one of them — for more than an hour, waiting to pass through customs. He hated their closeness, the smell of their breath, the little touches as their bodies inadvertently brushed against his; their stupidity, their cowlike patience, their doglike impatience . . . God, wouldn't this line ever come to an end?

It was nearly 9:45 that Sunday evening before he was finally allowed to depart the customs offices for the main airline terminal. As he walked through the revolving doors into the cooler, mosaic-tiled expanse of the waiting area, a short, plump, middle-aged and offensively greasy-looking Italian in a sweat-stained tan suit hurried up to meet him. The man was surreptitiously holding a small dog-eared photograph in his left hand. He slipped it into his pocket as he reached to shake the archbishop's hand.

"I see they made sure you'd find me." Quillans smiled with a curt nod at the poorly hidden snapshot of himself, setting down his luggage to give the man's proffered hand a reluctant squeeze.

"Oh!" The chubby Italian blushed, pumping the visitor's hand in both of his own with great enthusiasm. "Yes sir, yes Your Excellency . . . although if you so easily spotted my little ruse, then I am afraid I am not so clever as I thought." His accent was not so pronounced as the American visitor had expected.

Quillans noted that the emissary was beginning to perspire again voluminously—his body odor as well as his breath permeated by an unshakable essence of garlic. He turned away with a distasteful expression curling his upper lip and gently pulled his hand free of the functionary's wet clasp, wiping it carefully with a white linen handkerchief before taking up his briefcase once more.

"Shall we proceed?" he inquired icily, moving toward the exit, pointedly leaving the larger suitcases behind for his assigned chauffeur to carry.

None of this condescension was lost on the Vatican's representative. The fact that names had not even been exchanged in greeting was an omission of courtesy and custom which made the little Italian fairly itch with discomfiture. But he had been instructed by the Papal Secretary to exercise utmost discretion in dealing with the archbishop, and in all matters to follow the American's lead. So, if His Excellency wished to be rude, then rude it would be.

He shrugged, then picked up the heavy suitcases easily beneath his stubby arms and dutifully fell in behind the older, taller man.

Outside, a warm, humid blast of night air—filled with the fragrances of sweet wine, pungent spices, a whiff of sea air, and a solid dose of diesel fumes—wrapped itself around the obdurate visitor, flapping the bottom of his neat gray suit. Suddenly his sensibilities were shattered by a shrill, piercing whistle. Annoyed, he turned with a scowl to see his escort—two fingers inserted to either side of his pursed lips—wildly hailing a cab out of the whirring maelstrom of traffic in the broad avenue that encircled the international airport at Fumicino.

With studied obsequiousness, the former nuncio to Spain—himself an archbishop only recently recalled to the Vatican for this special assignment—opened the rear door of the taxi for his eminent foreign guest, saying in a barely audible voice which Quillans mistook for abject humility, "The official limousine is parked where it will draw no undue attention. We'll be transferring to it shortly. I must apologize to Your Excellency for any inconvenience caused by our precautions."

The archbishop from San Francisco acknowledged and dismissed the other man's apology with a preemptive wave of his hand, closing the door behind him and relegating what he presumed to be an inferior to the front seat beside the cabbie.

Even later, once they were safely ensconced in the privacy of the sleek black limousine, the steely gray man occupying the lavish rear seat maintained his aura of silent aloofness, breaking it only once to ask if there had been any change in the Pope's condition.

"I'm afraid not," the Italian archbishop announced sadly. "He remains comatose. It's a very grave situation."

"I see," said Quillans, settling back into the deep, soft cushions of the rear seat. His voice had conveyed just the right note of concern, but had the other man not been so preoccupied with surviving the chaos of Rome's evening traffic, he might have glanced into the rearview mirror in time to see the incongruous little smile that momentarily touched the American's lips at this news.

And he might have wondered just for a second what sort of man the archbishop from San Francisco really was.

7

"They're here!" Leta squealed excitedly, letting the heavy drapes fall back over the window.

She lifted the hem of her long, flowing dress above her bare feet and proceeded to take the steps two at a time, bursting into her mother's private office on the second floor without knocking. "They've just pulled up outside, Mom!" she exclaimed.

Diana looked up from the accounts ledger with a slight frown of displeasure. "You want to try that again?" she suggested tersely.

The younger woman sighed deeply, dropping her shoulders, and walked out of the small, plush room, closing the door carefully behind her. She then turned and knocked twice, waited a second, and gave it one more rap.

"Come in." Diana's voice floated out, strong and musical despite the physical barrier between them.

Leta reentered, quietly this time, and waited for her mother to raise her languid, heavily made-up gray-blue eyes from her work.

"Yes?"

"The couple we've been expecting has arrived, Priestess,"

the red-haired beauty said, with only the vaguest trace of petulance in her voice.

Just then they both heard the clacking of the gargoyle knocker on the front door downstairs.

"All right; show them into the parlor, then go and inform Alton." The tone was brisk and strident now, all business. "On your way back, retrieve them and escort them up here so I can collect their"—she smiled—"donation."

The brooding exterior of the black Victorian mansion had been malignant enough in the hazy afternoon sunlight, but even that was not sufficient to prepare MJ for what she saw inside.

Although the glass-fronted cabinet full of "graveyard dust" was laughable, she didn't feel much like laughing at the other paraphernalia of Mr. Hawley's trade—in particular a braided leather nine-thonged whip and a gleaming razor-sharp halberd, hung in ominous decoration on the wall.

The human skeleton in its glass-domed case and the two skulls on the mantlepiece, illuminated as they were by well-placed ultraviolet spotlights, seemed to glow with an inner light of their own, while the red, flame-shaped light bulbs in the chandelier cast eerie shadows on the deep red carpet, the coal-black walls, and everything in between.

And if, as Joe had observed, the atmosphere was essentially theatrical in nature, MJ still had to wonder what kind of people would go to such lengths to contrive this sort of ambience.

Before she had time to worry the question further, however, Leta reappeared in the doorway like a noiseless apparition, looking as solemn and mystic as her role demanded. "Follow me," she ordered, moving immediately away again so that they were forced to jump up in a hurry to catch her.

They found her hovering at the foot of the stairs; as soon as she saw their heads poke out from the parlor she turned wordlessly and began to move up the stairs, so gracefully—with virtually no movement of her head or shoulders—that she gave the appearance of floating.

Leta heard the woman behind her give out a slight gasp, and a self-satisfied smile crept across her face for an instant before it retreated beneath the carefully cultivated layer of mysterious remoteness. If she knew how many times I've been up and down these blasted stairs perfecting that walk she wouldn't be so amazed, the girl thought.

If the parlor had been designed to chill the blood, the office of the high priestess was surely meant to heat it back up again.

The wet-looking black walls promised the secret pleasures of a moonless night, while the amber glow from two fat, beeswax candles—lit but a moment before to replace the more functional but far less seductive light of the fluorescent tubes hidden behind ceiling valances—softly ignited the beautiful blonde's ivory skin until it seemed to be lit from within.

MJ was finding it difficult to keep from staring at the woman's voluminous bosom—the breasts straining against the thin fabric, bulging behind satin lacings. The taut nipples threatened to pop out from either side of the widely cut, deep V at every heaving breath as Diana invited them to be seated.

Stealing a quick sideways glance at Joe, MJ found his eyes riveted as if hypnotized, his mouth hanging stupidly open. A surge of jealous anger colored MJ's face. She had a strong urge to kick him in the shin.

As if reading the dark-haired woman's mind, Diana slowly stretched her long arms back above her head, like a cat waking from a nap, so that the edge of one hard pink nipple did indeed peek out mischievously for a moment.

Joe kept his hands carefully in his lap to hide the erection that was starting to make a noticeable bulge in his jeans. He forced his eyes elsewhere.

Almost immediately his gaze was caught by a large oil painting on the wall above Diana's head. It depicted a huge white swan mounted in sexual posture upon a crouching, full-figured nude. The woman's face wore an odd expression of ecstasy mixed with terror; the swan's long neck was fully extended, head tilted up, black beak gaping open, as if it were crowing its triumph to all the world.

Joe's organ twitched and strained against his tightly cut Levis and he squirmed uncomfortably. It took him a while to realize MJ was speaking, her voice impatient as she repeated his name.

"I'm sorry," he blushed; "what were you saying?"

"They require a donation before we go any further," Marija said, looking at him stonily.

"Oh, oh sure," Joe turned to Diana. "How much?"

"The standard donation for an initial consultation with the Black Pope is thirty-five dollars . . . apiece," the high priestess replied, giving a dismissive little shrug.

"Jacoby and Myers would have been half the price," Joe kidded the woman as he fished the money from his wallet.

As if on cue, Leta reappeared at the door almost the moment the money changed hands.

"Leta, will you please escort Mr. Marten and his . . . bride back down to the parlor, then find out when the high priest will be ready to receive them?"

Following Marija and the younger woman back down the narrow staircase, Joe was glad to note that his erection was subsiding almost as quickly as it had appeared: somehow handing over cash had always had a distinctly debilitating effect on that part of his anatomy.

They'd anticipated being brought before the august presence of Alton Hawley within a minute or two, but as if by design they were kept waiting somewhere closer to twenty in the dark, chilly display room—long enough for the heavy walls to close in on them, the dankness to settle deep into their clothes and skin, the skeleton and werewolf to seem almost to move. Marija in particular was beginning to feel as if she'd been trapped inside an ancient tomb replete with former occupants and other artifacts of horror. Gradually their idle nervous chatter and attempts at humor fell prey to longer and longer silences.

At last Leta reappeared in the doorway, a candle held in both hands just beneath her chin, illuminating the planes of her face ghoulishly.

"Please follow me," she said, her voice soft and not unkind. She always felt a little sorry for new clients at this phase of the initiation. One woman, a hypertensive claustrophobic, it turned out, had come totally unglued during the twenty-minute confinement in the "scare room." They'd had to call paramedics after all attempts to snap her out of her hysterics had failed. Once she'd recovered, she was foolish enough to initiate a lawsuit against the church but, Leta smiled to remember, the old biddy had suddenly dropped all charges when her hair began to fall out. When her teeth started loosening in her gums, she changed her name and moved to another state.

Most people coming here get just about what they deserve anyway, she told herself, pausing before the massive door to her father's study just long enough to ensure that the already nervous couple received full impact from the eerily illuminated brass replica of Pan's horned, satyric visage leering down at them from above the doorway. Then she rapped on the carved mahogany door.

"Enter," boomed a strong masculine voice, hollowly amplified by hidden speakers in the upper corners of the narrow hall.

Leta pulled open the door, standing to one side so that Joe and Marija could pass before her. Then she closed it with an intentional bang, making the initiates jump in spite of themselves.

This room, though also black, was better illuminated than any of the others in the house. By comparison it might have been almost cheery, were it not for the weird diabolic symbols covering the walls — and the awesome presence of the man

81

behind the desk.

Alton B. Hawley was an impressive figure, over six feet tall, a muscular two hundred and forty pounds. His sharp-featured face sported a neatly trimmed and distinctly evil-looking beard; his clean-shaven skull, encased in a black leather helmet with small ivory horns, was bent studiously over a sheaf of official-looking documents on his desk.

"Be seated," he ordered after a moment, eyes still on the papers before him.

Just when the pair was about to get itchy, he raised his head, his small dark eyes glittering as if with some beguiling inner secret. "Now," he boomed, catching Joe off guard. "What did you wish to see me about?"

Joe turned. His blue eyes locked into Hawley's black ones. A force not unlike electricity shot instantly between the two men, binding them, riveting them to each other. Joe felt a strange, floating sensation come over him, and with it a sense of his own innate power, something he had never before known he had.

The self-proclaimed priest of Satan jerked back involuntarily, his narrow eyes beginning to widen, first with surprise, then wider still with something akin to fear.

The huge man, usually a master of control, wrenched his gaze away from the pull of the blue eyes, turning his attention to the woman. But in her, too, was something disturbing, something either too close to that power he'd been seeking and pretending all these years — the ultimate evil — or else so far at the opposite end of the spectrum that she formed a reflection of his own aspirations, mocking the unbreachable gap in the otherwise closed circle of infinity.

"I . . . I cannot help you. Please leave, both of you. Leave at once," he commanded in a cracked voice.

"But you *must* help us," Joe spoke with quiet reason. "You've taken our fee."

"I'll return your damned fee!" shouted the satanist, turning to face the back wall, his burly arms crossed against his chest.

"I don't want the money. I want your help. You've made a deal. If you can't help us, you must give us someone who can."

"Oh, very well, very well," said Hawley, turning back to his desk. Sweat was beginning to bead up on his forehead beneath the heavy helmet. He longed to tear it off, but wouldn't lower himself to that degree in front of these . . . people. Shuffling busily through the papers and artifacts in his top drawer, he finally extracted a wrinkled, coffee-stained business card. His broad nostrils flared as he remembered with disgust the fat, sniveling little woman who had come to him last fall seeking training in harmless tricks that she could use in her tea room consultations. She'd been accompanied by a tall, austere-looking woman — a local medium of some repute — who was apparently her friend. After he'd successfully reduced the first to tears with his harangue on her hypocrisy and she'd fled the room, the second woman had lingered a moment longer to hand him her card.

"If you ever run into a client in need of *real* help," she'd smiled, then turned and quickly left to catch up with her blubbering companion.

It was this card that he now handed to Joe, still avoiding the man's eyes, withdrawing his hand before their flesh could touch.

"This is a renowned medium," he said as Joe turned the card over, inspecting it. "Perhaps she can be of assistance." He pressed a white button on his desk and a bell was heard ringing in the outer hall. Within seconds Leta appeared.

"Please escort our guests out," Hawley said wearily, looking only at his daughter. "Have Diana refund their donation before they go."

"That won't be necessary . . . " Joe began, but the big man cut him off with an upraised palm.

"Take it and go," he ordered hoarsely. "Then I owe you nothing. And don't come back."

They sat outside the black manse, Marija waiting for Joe to start the car, or the conversation. He seemed to be off somewhere, staring at the house they had just left with a somber, unblinking gaze.

Finally she broke the silence. "*What*, Joe . . . what is it?"

"I don't know," he answered, his voice slow, measured. "I felt, I *feel* strange. Something happened in there, but I'm not sure what it was."

He turned to her now, looked directly in her eyes, and she felt a small shock. "Did you feel . . . anything, anything odd, when we were talking to Hawley?"

She caught her breath, looked away. "Kind of," she murmured. "He seemed scared," she added after a moment.

"Yeah, but more than that." Joe glanced up at the house again. "It was like — recognition, like he knew me. And then all of a sudden I felt like *I* knew me too, but I don't know why."

Marija met this in silence. Whatever she'd felt, she didn't want to know about it. There'd been way too much of this kind of knowing lately.

"Can we go now, Joe?" She asked quietly.

After a few minutes of driving, however, it became apparent that Joe was not heading back toward the rectory.

"I thought we'd stop by and see the medium for a minute," he responded to her questioning look.

Marija started to protest, not up to any more heavy encounters that day, but then she didn't want any heavy encounters with Joe over the issue, either. She looked out the window instead.

"Tired?" Joe inquired with a glance in her direction.

"Mmm, a little."

"Don't worry, we won't be there long. I'd just like to check on this dame while we're still out and about, see if she opens up any new possibilities." He smiled, and she noticed a certain glint in his eyes that hadn't been there before, a new undercurrent of strength.

"Shouldn't we call first, Joe?"

"We're almost there; if she's out, we'll just come back another time."

About a half block past Clement Street he slowed and began scouting the houses and curbs for their street addresses, finally pulling up in front of an older, Mediterranean-style stucco—a clone of every other house on the street, differing only in their individual shades of peeling pastel. This one was a faded rose hue.

"Wait here a minute," he ordered, jumping energetically from the car. "I'll be right back."

She watched him in mild fascination—the spring to his step, the confidence in his bearing as he strode up the cement walk towards the front of the house. What had happened in there between him and Hawley to cause such a visible difference in his character?

As she looked on from the car, the front door opened a few inches, still held from within by a heavy brass safety chain; and a tall dark-haired woman, her features mostly hidden in the shadows, appeared behind it. He pulled out the business card from his pocket and handed it to her, talking with animated gestures. He waved a hand in the direction of the car, partially turning toward Marija, who resisted the impulse to cringe beneath the window as the woman poked her head through the crack in the door to peer at her appraisingly. Finally she gave a brief nod, and Joe ran back to the passenger side of the car.

"Come on," he said, opening the door and grasping MJ lightly beneath the elbow to help her out.

"What'd you tell her?" Whispered MJ as she clambered awkwardly from the low slung vehicle.

"Not much; just that Hawley had recommended her and we wanted to talk for a few minutes."

MJ shrugged and followed him docilely up the cracked cement pathway, stepping carefully over the tufts of grass and dandelions that filled its broken gaps. As they arrived on the front stoop the door swung open and a husky voice from the shadows bade them enter.

The medium *looked* ordinary enough: She was a tall, gaunt, somewhat masculine woman clad in old blue jeans and a faded cotton shirt. Her thick black waist-length hair, streaked with silver about the temples, was drawn back into a low pony tail tied with a narrow blue satin ribbon.

"I've just made a fresh pot of coffee; will you join me?" She offered, showing them into her comfortable living room.

"I'd love some," Marija smiled gratefully. Joe nodded his assent.

"Just sit anywhere," the woman invited. "Nothing's precious. I'll be back in a jif."

The man and woman lowered themselves onto the slightly frayed floral print sofa, then sank back with a whoosh of relief, instantly comfortable and at ease. The late afternoon sun slipped through the half-open slats of the venetian blinds, shimmering golden shafts of light that warmed their faces, raised their hopes.

"Oh dear," exclaimed their hostess as she returned with a tray. "That sun is right in your eyes! Would you like me to close the blinds?"

"No!" Marija nearly shouted, then laughed as she apologized. "I'm sorry, it's just so nice to be in some light again."

"After Hawley's tomb?" the spiritualist grimaced. "I know what you mean."

She served them coffee and thin slices of fruitcake laden with creamy butter, and for a few minutes they nibbled and sipped and discussed nothing more threatening than the weather and baseball.

It was Marija who finally broached the subject of their visit, not so much from any desire to talk about it, but more from concern that they were beginning to take up too much of this pleasant woman's time.

"I'm not sure what Joe told you about my problem," she

86

began.

"Nothing, really," the medium smiled, looking directly at her.

"I, I'm not sure what a medium can do for me," MJ said with a nervous laugh, "but we seem to be running out of alternatives." She looked over at Joe, her eyes asking for help, and together they proceeded to tell the occultist all the things that had happened to Marija over the past few weeks.

As they talked, the handsome woman's face began to harden, her expression less open and friendly than it had been earlier. The bright turquoise eyes faded to a distant, cloudy gray. Her lips thinned into an uncompromising line.

Sensing they were losing the medium's attention, Marija began to talk faster, adding more and more details in an attempt to convince the woman, though why or of what, she couldn't have said. At last she gave up, sensing each word was only making the rift between them deeper. She leaned back against the cushions, hands folded primly in her lap, waiting for sentence.

Joe had wisely stopped talking some time before.

"I'm afraid I can be of no use to you," the spiritualist stated flatly when she saw they were done.

"But why?" Marija protested.

"A séance under these circumstances — assuming even part of what you've told me is true — could be extremely dangerous. You have *no idea* what you're asking," she admonished, shaking her head almost angrily. "Even contact with relatively benign spirits is an extreme drain on me psychically as well as physically, and it always contains an element of risk. But to attempt to contact spiritual entities of the magnitude of evil power you've described could be deadly. I wouldn't even consider it," she shook her head again firmly, her face grim.

"Then what are we to do, how are we to communicate with these things so they will *leave me alone?*" MJ cried.

"My advice is that you forget it — do *not* pursue this matter

87

any further at all!"

"You don't seem to understand: It is *they* who are pursuing *me!*" the younger woman cried. "I just want them to stop!"

"Marija," Joe's voice broke in, calm and commanding. "Why don't you go on back to the car. I'll be out in a minute."

"But . . ."

"It's all right, go on. I just want a word with Ms. Salvida . . . it won't take long," he said reassuringly, his hand on her shoulder, guiding her to the door.

In less than five minutes the front door reopened and MJ noticed Joe slipping something into his pocket as he stepped into the twilight. He was grinning again as he came down the walk.

"What was that?" she pounced as he climbed into the driver's seat.

"The name of another medium she thinks might be willing to help," Joe said.

"But she was so adamant, so against it!" Marija exclaimed in genuine amazement. "How did you ever . . . ?"

"Trade secret," he chuckled, preening his long curly mustache smugly. "You willing to give it one more shot?"

"Yeah, what else is there . . . ?" she admitted reluctantly. "But not tonight, okay?"

Madame Salvida watched the pair from her window, fiddling with her pendant worriedly. She'd have to give Mildred a call, let her know about these two. Her friend was a total fraud—a "Tea Room Hypocrite," Hawley'd called her—but at least she was aware of her own psychic limitations . . . *and* she could put on a pretty good show. Maybe that would be enough to satisfy these two. Who knew, it might even help, as the man had just suggested. If the woman could be convinced that she had communicated with and banished the dark forces that tormented her, her fear might also disappear—and with *it* gone, the evil spirits might have less power over her, might even tire of the game and leave the girl alone completely.

She sighed, turning away from the window as the red sports car pulled out and drove off down the street. But as she reached for the phone, the other side of the equation — the one she'd been avoiding — reached up to slap her face: *"Then again, a phony séance might only serve to anger the demons further. And if it does . . ."*

About the same time that Joe and MJ were entering a small cafe for a quick meal before returning to the rectory, Mike was pushing his plate of Irish stew away untouched. Well, nearly untouched — he *had* mixed it about, poking at it distractedly with his fork for a while before giving up.

"Sorry, Mrs. M.," he apologized at last, getting up from the table. "I just don't seem to have much appetite tonight."

He'd waited until nearly eight to dine, hoping Marija would be back to join him, before finally giving in to Mrs. McGilvroy's nagging about the potatoes getting soggy and the carrots overcooked.

Now it was after eight-thirty, and still no Marija.

The priest retreated moodily to his study, taking with him a clean water glass which he promptly filled with bourbon, the Scotch having been finished the night before.

"What am I gonna do?" he sighed, rubbing his fingers back through his hair. "What — am — I — going — to — do?"

Regardless of his earlier assurances to Joe, he knew deep in his heart that Marija's exorcism was never going to be approved. And he knew he had to tell her — tell them both — without any more procrastination.

"But I'm still going to help her, with or without official sanction," he said aloud, slamming his palms down flat against the desktop. "One way or another. Because I have to. Because . . . she was *sent* to me!"

As the truth of this hit him, he also knew that more was involved, though he was not yet ready to determine quite what. Like the bud of a rose or the first line of a sonnet, what had happened so far was merely a promise of what was to come.

It was nearly ten before Joe and Marija arrived back at the rectory.

Marija entered first, looking a little sheepish, uncertain of her welcome. Mike took care of that in short order, hugging her warmly while heartily shaking Joe's hand, as one would greet treasured guests.

"How about a nightcap?" He suggested hospitably, leading them towards the study. "It's not quite as comfortable as the living room," he noted apologetically as they settled onto the hard little chairs and he poured their drinks, "but it is a bit more private."

As it turned out, Marija and Joe took the news about the exorcism better than expected, although he did notice funny looks passing between the two as he spoke.

When he got to the end of his speech, the part about Marija being *sent* to him for help, there were tears sparkling in the woman's eyes, and even Joe was smiling.

But a little later, when they decided to confide in him where they'd been that day, he found his own smile faltering.

"I can understand your eagerness to get something done on this," he said, "and I know I haven't been much help so far."

"Oh, but you have . . ." Marija began to protest.

"It's not your fault, you gave it your best shot," Joe added. "And we do appreciate it, but . . ."

"But I haven't come through with the goods," Mike finished for him, smiling to lighten the words. "I know. Listen, I can't tell you *not* to try other things, but I'd just like to ask you one favor, take me along next time, okay? Maybe, well . . . if something goes awry, I'd like to be there. I don't know how 'divine' I am, but I think I might be able to call on some friends upstairs in a tight situation. I know a couple of good prayers I could throw in," he grinned disarmingly.

Later that night, after Joe had left and Marija was tucked safely into bed, Mike came to one more decision. If the church would not provide an exorcism for the woman soon, *he* would, *one way or another*.

He knew there must be literature on those arcane rites available somewhere besides the Catholic Church — he'd read enough on the subject during his seminary days to discover that the Catholics had only adopted the rites from earlier occult practices, not invented them.

Of course, the church hierarchy considered exorcism a sanctified ritual *only* when confined to a practice within their religion. Outside this official sanction it became heresy, a sacrilege of the first magnitude. If he were to go ahead without their okay, they might terminate his position not only as a priest but as a practicing Catholic as well. *Excommunication.*

"So?" He dismissed the concern with forced indifference, turning out the lights and climbing onto his uncomfortable cot. "They're leaving me few options. I've at least got to be prepared to go ahead with it, for Marija's sake. I just hope I never have to make that final choice."

8

If Archbishop Luigi Magliano was less than thrilled with his current assignment for the Vatican, he'd at least accepted it with as much grace as anyone could hope to muster under the circumstances — willing himself, as always, to remain the ever-humble servant, even when his fiery Italian temper itched to rebel. Like last night.

"I wonder what makes our eminent visitor from San Francisco so sure of his own importance that he can justify rudeness to a fellow servant of God?" he wondered aloud as he recalled with renewed displeasure the American's snobbish manner of the previous night.

Cautiously the portly Italian emissary slid the nose of the sleek black limousine out into the midmorning traffic that whirred past the northern corner of Vatican City, noting out of the corner of his eye the crowds of dowdy housewives and tired old men, ragged indigents and camera-laden tourists, and particularly the hoards of media people already beginning to gather in ever-increasing droves in the Piazza di San Pietro.

"Like a flock of vultures," he thought, "waiting for word of Il Papa's death. And what will they do when it is announced, burst into tears and lamentations? No. They will run for the bank of public telephones in a mad race to scoop each other. That will be the only thing on their minds."

Shaking his large head sadly, he withdrew a well-worn strand of carved rosary beads from the pocket of his jacket and began mumbling the rote prayers.

Archbishop Magliano's sudden recall three days earlier from the comfortable and prestigious position of Nuncio to Madrid had come as an unexpected shock. Though he'd been told it had to do with the Holy Father's illness, he could not help but feel a certain disappointment at the abrupt curtailment of all his plans and projects, his loss of stature, there in Madrid.

Of course he'd accepted the orders without question, willing always to do whatever was asked, go wherever he was needed—even, he supposed, if it meant playing lackey to a pompous fool like Archbishop Quillans. He began stroking the beads more passionately as he felt the anger blossom in him again, praying faster against this disturbing, persistent fault in himself.

While one hand continued to work its way through the succession of beads, the other guided the big car expertly through Rome's morning traffic. Soon he was heading west, out of the city proper and toward the suburban town of Fumicino, toward the international airport just inland from the sunwashed, golden beaches of the Tyrrhenian Sea.

There had been no need for him to carry an identifying snapshot of today's arrival: Patriarch Synarus of Alexandria, head of the Eastern Sees, was a frequent visitor to the Vatican, well known not just to the Roman Curia but to the Italian media as well, since the ancient schism between the two main bodies of Catholicism had been resolved the previous year. That tall, imposing figure with his hawklike nose, piercing black eyes, and full gray beard would have been recognized anywhere. Trying to conceal his identity would only have aroused undue suspicion from the newspeople.

So today, at least, Luigi was spared the elaborate and discomfiting precautions of the night before. "No," he smiled, beginning to whistle the opening bars of a popular operetta, his cheerfulness returning under the bright blue skies and rolling green fields of his beloved countryside, "today, if I must play chauffeur, at least I may do so with a certain degree of respectability and grace."

Magliano was by no means a dull-witted man. On the contrary, the keen, probing mind beneath his placid countenance was the source of his sorest trial as a priest: his continuing difficulty in accepting the rules and decrees of the church hierarchy without question or criticism. He found himself forever wanting to dig, to examine, to understand — rather than simply to accept their mandates on faith, as products of divine guidance as a good Catholic should.

But the depth of his love and devotion to God and to Christ, acquired as a street child growing up under the shadow of the Vatican, which had become a physical symbol of that God to him, more than matched this inherent intellectual flaw.

He had worked as hard as any man could to overcome his upsetting human frailty. If he hadn't succeeded entirely, he had at least learned to suppress it well, learned to outwardly accept all his orders and assignments with such unquestioning faith, such convincing enthusiasm, that he had rapidly earned a somewhat gilded reputation for obedience and fervor. It was this as much as anything which had elevated him from a simple parish priest to archbishop and official representative of the Pope in Spain by the relatively young age of 45.

Today, however, the old battle raged within again: events of the past few days had been so curious, the reasons behind them so oblique, that the unasked whys burned in his mind like a fever.

Why had the archbishop from San Francisco been called to Rome so hurriedly, without so much as a single aide, and under such a blanket of secrecy? Why was the powerful Eastern Patriarch sent for with equal haste, and again no entourage? Why had he himself been recalled from Madrid with no replacement, no time to set affairs in order, told to speak to no one about his assignment, and then told so little about it himself that he couldn't have sunk any ships if he'd wanted to?

Early this morning as he was leaving the Cardinal Secretary's office suite, he'd chanced to look down through the glass wall of the second story hallway into the small, enclosed piazza of the main entry just as two of the cardinal bishops from the suburban sees were arriving. In addition to their usual briefcases of church business, both carried large overnight bags as well. Curious indeed!

"Stop it!" he ordered himself, as he pulled deftly into the reserved parking zone before the airline terminal, "Whatever you need to know you will be told—no more, no less. Where is your faith?"

In the short time it took him to lock the car, argue with a parking attendant and a taxi driver about his right to use the space, and cover the forty feet to the entrance in his short, swinging gait, he was already perspiring profusely. He entered the cool sanctuary of the air-conditioned building gratefully, mopping his brow with a large white handkerchief.

According to the electronic airline schedule on the lobby wall, the flight from Cairo would be only 45 minutes late— not too bad for an Egyptian airline. A few minutes after the plane's arrival was finally announced, the Patriarch—dressed in the flowing robes of his office—was hustled through customs with the minimum of apologetic, cursory inspection.

Magliano came forward to introduce himself, but though Cardinal Synarus had met him on only one previous occasion, the impressive religious leader seemed to recognize the Italian archbishop immediately, even in street clothes, and dropping his luggage, he hurried toward the smaller man with outstretched arms, a warm friendly smile creasing his austere face.

They embraced, kissing each other on either cheek in the European fashion. It was such a contrast to the cool snub he'd received the night before that tears of gratitude sprang momentarily to Luigi's eyes. He stepped back and bowed his forehead to the cardinal's ring with humble admiration and respect. "Your Eminence," he said hoarsely.

Suddenly the two men were separated by a silvery sphere at the end of a slender black rod, rudely thrust between their faces by a small white hand, the long tapered fingers tipped in bright red enamel.

They turned as one to the heavily made-up face of an otherwise pretty young woman who flashed a smile at them as she switched on her hand-held cassette recorder.

"Cardinal Synarus?" she began, with a slight hesitation. Magliano was about to take advantage of her uncertainty when the Patriarch smiled, answering ingenuously, "Yes, my child?"

"DiGuccione from *Il Messaggero*," she identified herself, clumsily flashing her press card with one hand while attempting to juggle the tape recorder and microphone with the other. "I was given a tip," she stopped and blushed at her artless choice of terms, promptly correcting herself, *"information*, that you were en route to the Vatican. Does this concern the death of the Pope?"

Shock registered on the bearded Patriarch's face. His skin paled beneath the swarthy tan. "Death?" he repeated numbly, his voice a rough whisper. "You mean he is . . . gone?"

"Oh! Oh, *no*, Your Eminence . . ." she stammered. "At least, not that I'm aware of." She was blushing furiously, had almost dropped the recorder. Under all that makeup she now looked like a foolish little girl. "I'm so very sorry for my, my poor choice of words," she apologized, near tears.

Magliano noticed the small gold crucifix peeking out from behind the open collar of her blouse, the tailored wool suit that, like his, was too hot for the season, and he found himself in sympathy for her despite his aversion to pushy reporters. Obviously she was new to this game.

"I only meant to say, are you here because his death seems imminent?" She was straining bravely to regain some semblance of professional composure.

"In the face of eternity, death is imminent for us all," the eastern holy man stated, seeming to enjoy being enigmatic. "As for the Pontiff, the time of his death, like ours, is in the hands of God."

"I'm afraid we have no further comment at this time," interposed the former diplomat to Spain, gently taking charge as he picked up the suitcases and began to move the cardinal away.

"And who are *you?*" she asked pertly, giving a sly once-over to his rumpled, ill-fitting suit, his unimpressive stature. She shoved the obnoxious mike under Magliano's oversized mustache.

"Why, this is Archbishop Magliano, Nuncio to Spain," Cardinal Synarus answered with innocent pride in his fellow servant.

He *should* have been briefed, Magliano thought in exasperation, turning his head so that Synarus wouldn't see him roll his eyes. Aloud he simply repeated, "No further comment," hurrying the patriarch away before the reporter could regain her composure.

On the drive back into the city, the unassuming head of the Eastern Churches chose to forgo the comforts of the expansive rear section — "You can't *see* anything from back there" — and joined Magliano in comradely discomfort in the front, chatting animatedly the whole way home.

From their conversation it appeared he was as much in mystery about the strange and urgent summons that had brought him to the Holy See as was the little Italian, who could provide few answers to the visitor's multitude of questions.

Magliano perceived, beneath the intelligence, wit, and curiosity of the cardinal bishop, a pervasive, childlike simplicity, a naivete that was foremost in his character. In that sense he was the Italian's polar opposite, with all the unstrained qualities of grace Luigi found so lacking in himself. He had the feeling the cardinal could have received any answer to his questions, no matter how shocking or unorthodox, and come through with his faith unshaken.

For this reason Magliano wished he were able to confide in Synarus about the American archbishop, his disturbing qualities. The patriarch would undoubtedly have said something upbeat and reassuring, making Luigi more comfortable about the man. But he kept his mouth shut, his doubts hidden. He had sworn to the Papal Secretary complete silence on the subject of Quillans' visit, and until that most holy man, second in command to the Pope, relieved him of this promise, he had to bear the burden of his uncertainty alone. For reasons he could not name, the very thought of the man filled him with foreboding.

While Archbishop Magliano and Cardinal Synarus were en route, Archbishop Robert F. Quillans was pacing the small, richly furnished apartment in which he'd been sequestered within the Vatican Palace.

Instructions had arrived in a sealed envelope on his breakfast tray that morning requesting that he remain in his quarters until his personal steward returned from the airport with further data. The memo was on letterhead engraved in gold leaf: "From the Office of the Secretary of State, Vatican City," and had been signed by Cardinal Bishop Mendice himself. Quillans guessed that made the request official.

He was annoyed by the restrictions, but not really perturbed. Things were moving along as they were supposed to, the game being played out on cue. Still there *was* this native restlessness, this impatient nature to hold in check — a nature which railed against the enforced realities of time and place and protocol which had to be observed. He ached for the power soon to be his, hating every delay. But it wasn't wise to mess with the plan.

So he paced the little room to release some of the nervous energy snarling within his unquiet soul, determined to let events take their predetermined course if it killed him.

It was after 1 PM when a light rap at the door broke the enveloping silence. Quillans had been staring out his third-story window at the crowds gathered in the great circular plaza below, wondering how these throngs of the faithful would react to the momentous changes destined to take place shortly. The knocking jolted him back from his speculations before he'd followed them to conclusion.

"Enter," he called out. The door opened to reveal his portly chauffeur from the night before.

"Your Excellency," the Italian said with a little bow, "you are well, I trust?"

"Well as could be expected," Quillans said curtly. "You are, I presume, my long-awaited 'personal steward'?" The quotation marks hung in the air.

The man's aptitude for discourtesy is truly amazing, thought Luigi. "Yes, I am your 'personal steward,' archbishop, as part of a *temporary* assignment at the Holy See."

"And what, may I ask, is your usual function?"

"I'm afraid I'm not at liberty to say," the Italian answered cooly, wishing he could, so that the other man would be appropriately embarrassed. Instead he asked politely, "Have you had lunch?"

"They brought me something a while ago. I hadn't much appetite for it."

We'll see how you feel about that when you discover that dinner isn't served around here until after eight, the nuncio thought with a certain satisfaction. Aloud he said, "In that case, I am instructed to take you at once for a personal audience with the Papal Secretary . . . if you are ready?" He extended a hand

99

toward the door.

As they walked together down the long, ornately decorated hall, the silence between them grew burdensome to Magliano. He began speaking, but kept his voice low and confidential, lest someone overhear.

"As I'm sure you are aware, Excellency," he said, "your true identity is, for the present, a fact known only to myself and the Secretary. My instructions are to serve as your personal escort wherever you might wish to venture within the Vatican grounds. His Eminence has asked me to convey his apologies for any discomfort or inconvenience this may cause you."

They were descending a curved, inner stairwell now, their footsteps echoing in the narrow vaulted chamber. The legate lowered his voice even further.

"If I am compelled to introduce you, it will be as Robert Blake, a reporter for the *American Catholic Journal*." Magliano looked over his shoulder into the cool, impassive face of the San Franciscan, who waved a hand dismissively.

Luigi's mood blackened. Turning away, he led the man the rest of their short journey without another word.

They moved through a twisting maze of hallways on the second floor, finally stopping before a nondescript door at the rear of the palace apartment complex. His knock was answered within seconds by a small, slender man with a silvery fluff of hair ringing his bald pate.

"Your Eminence," the Italian archbishop said, bending his forehead to the sapphire ring. "I have delivered your guest."

The transformation in the other archbishop's demeanor, now that he was in the august presence of the Cardinal Secretary of State, was as complete as it was — to Magliano — contrived.

Quillans was the essence of charm, humbly respectful, exuding warmth and kindliness and perfect manners until Luigi wanted to spit. But a moment later he was delivered satisfaction.

"Archbishop Quillans, may I introduce to you the man

who has most graciously agreed to act as your personal steward during your stay here," said the diminutive head of state. "The Most Reverend Archbishop Luigi Magliano, just recalled from his position as Nuncio to Spain to help us in this delicate matter."

Color flooded the American's face. "I had no idea," he murmured, taking the proffered hand.

"Obviously," the other man muttered through his smile, nodding graciously.

"As you know from the telex I sent you, Archbishop Quillans," the Secretary went on, innocent of the tension between the two men, "you are here at the personal behest of Pope Marcus. It was his specific instruction that your visit be conducted in absolute secrecy."

He seated himself gingerly on an uncomfortable wooden chair, wrapping his robes carefully across his lap and indicating that the archbishops sit. "The Holy Father requested that certain members of the Sacred College be likewise sequestered in the palace: these have arrived this morning and will remain until . . ." at this point he threw his hands up in the air with typical Italian exaggeration. "I'm really not certain what his Holiness has in mind for us all from this point. I shall have to let you make your own judgment after dinner tonight. I intend to play a recording of the Pontiff's last message, the one that has brought you all under this roof, in hopes that we — with some help from the heavenly Father — may be able to reach an inspired conclusion. In the meantime, we wait, I'm afraid," he smiled gently.

A hand raised shoulder-high requesting permission to speak, and at the cardinal bishop's nod, the American asked with stilted courtesy, "Was Archbishop Mangini here . . ."

"Magliano," corrected the Italian politely.

"Pardon me . . . *Magliano*," Robert Quillans amended with feigned contrition. Then turning back to the Secretary of State, he continued: "Was my esteemed colleague here also specifically requested by the Pontiff?"

If the gentle little cardinal had noticed the undercurrent between the two archbishops, he gave no sign. "No, it was my own decision to recall Archbishop Magliano to help me in this task," the Secretary admitted. "I needed someone with the necessary experience and dedication to act as courier and emissary for the six cardinal bishops of Rome, so that vital church business in their suburban sees might continue in their absence. We also needed a man of utmost discretion and diplomacy to carry out our little ruse at the airport, as well as serve the needs of our guests once they'd arrived. I could think of no man to fit the task so well." He turned to beam at Magliano.

"I see," said the San Franciscan thoughtfully, rubbing his jaw.

"As I mentioned, we shall be having a private supper this evening in my apartment suite," the papal statesman concluded, edging out of his chair. Then, noting the questioning glance of the taller man, he laughed—a light little chuckle. "No, not *here*; this is merely a spare bedroom I borrowed for this meeting, in keeping with our temporary need for security."

It occurred to Magliano that the cardinal was actually enjoying all this cloak-and-dagger stuff despite his profuse apologies to the contrary.

"Your Eminence?" It was Quillans again. "Is it necessary for me to remain in my quarters, now that I have been briefed?"

"Oh, not at all, not at all," Cardinal Mendice assured him. "Archbishop Magliano is at your service the rest of the day. He can give you a first-class guided tour of our city, if you like. He has, I presume, briefed you on your assumed identity?"

"Yes, Your Eminence."

"Excellent," smiled the secretary, rising from the chair and extending his hand for the customary reverence. "Do enjoy your tour, archbishop . . . it *is* your first visit here, is it not?"

The archbishop nodded. "Then there is much to see; don't let me keep you any longer."

Cardinal Bishop Mendice's suite was more like a small gothic manor than an apartment. It was set apart from the main rooms of the palace, and though slightly newer than the main building, reflected the same aura of opulence that had flourished during the sixteenth and seventeenth centuries when the palace and basilica were constructed. Mosaic tiles adorned the floors and arches, heavy baroque-gilt tapestries hung from the panelled walls, richly colored oriental carpets covered most of the open floor space, and immense brass and crystal chandeliers hung from the ceilings. These filled the rooms with a softly patterned light, like pale sun through leaves. It was through this light that the nine somber guests of the papal secretary now moved, in slow procession from the dining chamber to the living area.

Archbishop Quillans, the only stranger in the group, had been introduced to the others during the quiet supper, but his presence in that ennobled group had not been explained to the seven old ecclesiastics in their red-ucchetti — except for an enigmatic assurance by their host that the forthcoming tape would clarify the reasons for His Excellency's attendance there.

Now the head of the San Francisco archdiocese carefully, surreptitiously studied the six Italian cardinal bishops from the suburban sees of Rome, while all were awaiting the reappearance of the Secretary of State with the much-anticipated tape.

An aide quietly moved about the room, serving crystal snifters of brandy to the elderly cardinals, who stood beside their chairs in a semicircle around the unlit fireplace, ignoring the discomfort of old muscles and arthritic bones in respect for the senior cardinal bishop whose return was imminent.

103

All but one of these top church officials were above 65, and three appeared to be close to the end of their active careers in the college, nearing the 80-year mark — after which they would no longer be allowed to vote on church matters.

Quillans studied these eldest three first, deciding quickly that they were so nearly identical in physical appearance and mannerisms — age, belief, and shared rituals being the great levelers — that to study one was to know them all. They were undoubtedly intelligent men, once quite dynamic, but now there was a certain fuzziness of intellect. An old man's weariness had settled in about each one, a tendency to avoid looking at anything too closely, to avoid controversy, confrontation, and conflict. They would not be dangerous, not at all, he concluded, mentally dismissing them and turning his attention to the next member of the council.

The Patriarch of Alexandria, as head of the Reunified Eastern Churches, could carry a great deal of weight and deserved particular study. Quillans had already devoted most of his time during dinner to feeling out this man's character, and his final resolution was much the same as Archbishop Magliano had intuited during the drive back from the airport that morning. Cardinal Synarus, though vital in mind and spirit, was trusting to a fault in the Doctrine of Divine Guidance. He would offer no objection to anything the Pope decreed, even if it were orders to blow up the Vatican and torch all the pilgrims in St. Peter's Square.

He cast a final glance toward the corner where Synarus and Magliano stood chatting and caught a thoughtful look from the latter. Casually he averted his gaze, pretending to admire the tapestries that covered the cool stone walls, clenching his fists in secret ire.

Magliano was too shrewd, too much of a rebel for all his seeming deference. Quillans read him well: he could be very dangerous indeed . . . were it not for the fact that as an archbishop he would be powerless to influence the decisions of the Sacred College of Cardinals. He would not be allowed into the secret consistory nor the special elective conclave, thus he could do no real harm. Let him worry and suspect to his heart's content, Quillans smiled, accepting a brandy from the aide with a little nod; he's helpless to stop me.

That left the three remaining cardinal bishops to consider: Cardinal Bertini. Bishop of Frascati and Camerlingo of the Holy Roman Church; Cardinal Mertinello of Porto and Santa Rufina, the Sub-Dean; and Cardinal Falliano of Ostia, all-important Dean of the College of Cardinals.

But before the American had a chance to pursue his evaluation of the trio, the Papal Secretary reentered the room with the precious tape. The murmur of conversation ceased instantly, all heads turning to follow the man across the room.

"Please be seated," the cardinal invited, indicating the arc of chairs arranged before the knee-high hearth. He seated himself primly on the raised stone structure in front of them, tucking his long red cassock beneath him.

For a prolonged moment he fiddled in silence with the portable cassette player — testing, playing it fast forward, testing again, reversing slightly until he had the tape cued to his satisfaction. His bright blue eyes looked up, twinkling mischievously at the breathless anticipation in the faces surrounding him.

"I see we are all *quite* ready," he said. "If you will bear with me one moment longer, I believe a brief explanation as to how I came to make this recording is in order."

Quillans leaned forward, his expression perhaps a shade more intense than that of the others in the room.

"As you know," Cardinal Mendice continued, "Pope Marcus was stricken with a massive cerebral hemorrhage shortly after dinner Friday night. He had dined alone that evening, and complained of feeling unwell, and when he collapsed his personal servant immediately summoned me.

"His Holiness had lapsed into a stupor by the time I got to him, so I sent the steward to summon his personal physician. While I awaited the doctor's arrival, the Holy Father came back to himself momentarily — he appeared to be struggling against unconsciousness — and beseeched me to fetch his cassette recorder, the one he keeps in the drawer of his bedside table to record inspirations that come to him in dreams.

"I removed the tape recorder and inserted a new blank cartridge. When he saw that this was done he raised himself painfully to his elbows — an effort the attending physician was later to say was nothing short of miraculous, considering the extent of brain damage His Holiness had suffered — and began to speak in a surprisingly strong voice."

The little cardinal stopped for a moment, a slight frown knitting his normally placid brow. "His voice took on a strange quality. You will notice it, I'm sure. I mention it only to assure you that it is not a fault of the equipment; the reproduction is accurate. His voice is exactly as I heard it that night."

He sighed heavily for no apparent reason, giving his ear-lobe a distracted tug.

"As for the rest of it — the reason the Pope is being cared for in the palace infirmary instead of the Hospital-General; the reason you have all been called away from your normal realms of duty in the dead of night, as it were, and shut away here for an indeterminate period; the effect of these recent events on the future of the entire Roman Catholic Religion — these you may discern for yourselves from the Pope's own words. I am merely the messenger for His Holiness, carrying out his last orders, which are found faithfully recorded herein."

With that last dramatic verbal flourish, he pushed the PLAY button and the voice of Pope Marcus filled the room.

"This is Pope Marcus the Third, Bishop of Rome, Vicar of Jesus Christ, Servant of the Servants of God." The dying pontiff's words had begun as a weak, halting rasp, but rapidly increased in strength and volume until they were loud enough to be heard easily by everyone. Yet the voice was strangely lacking in resonance, as flat and one-dimensional as the thin magnetic tape on which it had been recorded.

"Present with me now, as my witness and faithful servant, in whom I hereby entrust the responsibility for carrying out the divine orders which I am about to deliver, is Cardinal Mendice, the Secretary of State of our Statto della Città del Vaticano."

At this point there was a burst of static, as if the recorder mike had been dropped or jarred in a clumsy transfer of hands, and the secretary's voice came on a moment later, identifying himself awkwardly as if uncertain of what he was supposed to say. Quillans chanced a quick look at the man, whose ears were pink with embarrassment. Then the Pope's haunting voice returned.

"I have been drawn into the body of God for these past few minutes, and in this brief time has been revealed to me His great plan for us all. I am with Him now, and He with me. It is only through Him that I am made able now to speak with you . . . it is actually Him speaking with you, through me."

The words were uttered with extreme care, the hollow voice speaking slowly and clearly, as if to ensure there would be no misinterpretation of his arcane message. A significant pause concluded the statement, the death rattle of his breathing—which had been heard between the precisely measured words—now the only sound in the room. The secretary took this moment to stop the tape and inquire if anyone would like to hear that last section again.

The cardinals looked at one another, then one by one shook their heads to the negative. Mendice nodded and restarted the tape without comment.

"First, to my able physician Doctor Frederico, these instructions: I am *not* to be removed from the Vatican palace no matter how grave my condition. Further, I am to be given no drugs or medications of the nature that impair or alter the functioning of the central nervous system—only antibiotics for secondary infections, should the need arise. However, as it is God's desire that this mortal body be kept alive until its purpose has been fulfilled, you are strongly enjoined to use all the other so-called miracles of modern medicine to that end, including life-support machines, if necessary.

"Next, to my Secretary of State, Cardinal Mendice: my first mandate is that you ensure that the rest of what I am about to say is kept in strictest confidence, to be revealed to none save those whom I specifically name herein, until such time as I give permission to release the context of this tape to the rest of the Sacred College and thence to the world."

The tape was halted again, and the little statesman stood to face the other men in the room, his ruddy face creased in worry.

"Eminent brothers in God, at this point I must stop and consult you on a matter to which I have given a good deal of reflection the past few days. Let me say first that the Pontiff was so adamant on this last point that he had me lock the door to his chambers and admit no one, not even the physician, until he was finished speaking. Near the end of the tape, you will hear a pounding noise in the background . . . Doctor Frederico demanding entry," he smiled.

"Now, all of you here tonight save one has been ordained by the Holy Father to be present for the further playing of this tape. Whether or not that one not so designated should be allowed to stay for the remainder of the message, I now leave to you to decide."

Several of the cardinals glanced at Archbishop Quillans, the stranger in their midst, with well-mannered distrust.

"The person not specifically deemed eligible to hear the Pope's message is our beloved Nuncio to Spain." The Secretary nodded with a look of apologetic regret at the portly Italian churchman, "Archbishop Luigi Magliano."

Expressions of surprise registered on the faces of the seven cardinal bishops as they turned toward the archbishop, who wriggled uncomfortably in his chair, his cheeks glowing redly. A flicker of amusement passed over Quillans' face and was instantly gone, like the shadow of a racing cloud across a sunburnt hillock.

"The problem with which I was faced initially was that in order to carry out the Holy Father's directives in this sensitive matter, it was vital that I call in an outside assistant." The Papal Secretary hesitated for a minute, as if considering, then turned to the Italian nuncio. "Archbishop Magliano, please forgive my rudeness, but perhaps it would be better were you to wait in the study. There are some points made in the later portion of the tape which the others will need to be made aware of before they can make a learned decision on this problem."

The cardinal rang a small silver bell, and almost immediately his aide appeared from the kitchen, wiping his hands on an apron at his waist. "Please escort His Excellency to my study and see to his comfort, if you will, Deacon Armandi. I will ring you again when he is to be summoned."

As soon as the pair were safely out of earshot, the diminutive cardinal, fidgeting nervously with his sapphire ring, continued.

"The Pope, as you will soon hear for yourselves, left explicit instructions regarding the secrecy with which the members of this group were to be brought and maintained here, stressing the necessity for each of you to be sequestered within a few minutes of his Holiness's bedside."

Several men in the audience nodded—they had already learned this much in their initial private meetings with the secretary.

"I was therefore faced with the exquisite dilemma of how to carry out these mandates of secrecy. Obviously *I* could not personally meet the guests who arrived by air without being recognized by our inquisitive and ever-watchful media nor without drawing attention to these arrivals. There was also the problem of maintaining a semblance of normalcy in the suburban sees, not letting the vital church business lapse— again to avoid undue attention and publicity about the conspicuous absence of the cardinal bishops who run them.

Someone knowledgeable, trustworthy, and discreet was needed to personally courier the more vital dispatches between your auxiliaries and yourselves. There are several matters of important business in progress at the moment which cannot be postponed for any length of time.

"Thus my gordian knot," he sighed, raising his palms upward. "To be sure, I have already abridged the Holy Father's directives by bringing Archbishop Magliano into this, but I assure you I could not have carried out the initial phases of the Pontiff's design without His Excellency's assistance. Also, we *do* still need a courier to the Sees, and I feel we'd be much safer utilizing the archbishop for this than to attempt our business through uninformed and possible indiscreet couriers."

"Up to this time I have told the archbishop only as much as I have told the rest of you," he explained, rubbing his hands together nervously; "that you were brought here *in camera* at the specific request of Pope Marcus. His first instructions were only to ensure that Archbishop Quillans' arrival be achieved incognito, and that Patriarch Synarus be similarly met and escorted to the palace with a minimum of attention from the press — both of which tasks he carried out admirably."

He rubbed his eyes wearily, perhaps a bit guiltily. "I may have gone further than I should have, but it soon seemed necessary to inform him of the presence and circumstances of the rest of you here as well — he had observed your arrivals in any case — in order to alert him to the fact that he might be required to act as courier while you are in residence."

"Your Eminence?" It was the youngest of the cardinal bishops, fifty-eight-year-old Paolo Bertini, Camerlingo of the College of Cardinals.

"Yes, Cardinal Bertini?"

"Is it really necessary for Archbishop Magliano to know the remainder of what is on that tape in order to carry out the functions to which you've already assigned him?"

110

The old statesman hesitated a moment before replying, "No, I guess it really isn't. I felt that, having taken him into my confidence this far, it would be only . . . *considerate* to include him in on the rest of it as well." He lifted his shoulders almost to his ears with an apologetic grimace. "I see now, thanks to your question, that this would be ill advised. Any further breach of the Holy Father's command to secrecy would be unwarranted. I am grateful to you for pointing this out, Cardinal."

The Bishop of Frascati settled back on the dark leather couch with a satisfied expression, his dark eyes darting to the other, older cardinals, whose heads nodded in approval. They looked like lizards basking in the sun, Quillans thought; their sluggish old blood drained from the centers of thought to their overfull stomachs.

But he made a mental note to keep a particular eye on Bertini; thus far he was the only one present who had evinced enough of an independent and functioning mind to question the upcoming plans.

"Well, then," smiled the cardinal secretary, "if we are all in accord?"

They nodded in unison again. Mendice rang for his steward and instructed the young man to take a fresh brandy to the waiting nuncio, "then keep Archbishop Magliano company until our private business here has been concluded."

At the request of the eldest cardinal, white-haired and palsied Carlo Capione of the Sabina See, the secretary reset the tape to its very beginning and replayed the first sections to refresh their memories.

Again the strangeness of the tonal quality struck them all: as hollow and distant as a voice at the bottom of a well, flat as a mirror. This time the Secretary allowed the tape to continue straight through to the end without interruption. The Papal orders, given in that weirdly echoing voice, were direct and to the point: Archbishop Robert F. Quillans of the San Francisco archdiocese was to be brought at once to the Vatican and kept close at hand, in strictest secrecy, for a "special purpose" to be revealed in the near future. (The precise manner of such revelation was not elucidated.) The Patriarch of Alexandria was likewise to be summoned, as were the six other top ranking officials of the Roman Catholic Church.

Basically there was nothing new here other than hearing the directives given in the Pope's own voice, and the sense of redundancy had dulled the listeners' attention so that they almost missed the significance of his final statement. All but Quillans, who heard every word with a thrill of satisfaction.

"Pardon me, Cardinal Mendice." It was the strident baritone of the youthful Camerlingo once again. "Could you please replay that last section, from when the Holy Father adjures us not to heed the doctor's dire prognosis?"

"Yes, certainly . . . I was going to suggest it myself," he agreed, bending to fuss with the buttons again until he had the tape partly rewound. As he pressed the PLAY button, all the men leaned forward in concentration.

"You may be told by the physicians attending my body that I am near death, that recovery is hopeless, that I will never again regain consciousness. They may even say that I am medically dead, that my brain registers no sign of activity. I implore you to have faith, for I will remain and return to you *regardless* of what they say. I am not this body, I am not this brain — though I am *of* the body and brain, to the extent that I need them as tools to communicate in a physical medium . . . It is an unfortunate failing of men that they will only truly accept a message that arrives via one of the body's five sense organs."

The Pope's voice was thinning now, weakening; the rasp of his labored breathing between the words was becoming louder, more pronounced. Obviously struggling, he went on.

"If it comes to the point where it is necessary to keep this body alive by machines, then you must have them brought in. I need this body to bring you God's word in a manner which leaves no doubt as to its meaning, intent, and source —

112

a manner which can be physically recorded, just as this has been. Only in this way will even the most skeptical disbelievers know the Word of God does exist. It is in expectation and anticipation of this holy Word, to be given in my second awakening, that the leaders of our church must be sequestered here, both as witnesses and as devoted generals who will then carry out its decrees without question or hesitation."

The tape ended abruptly, a brief rumble of amplified rustling as the microphone was set down, the recorder shut off— and then just the soft, whirring noise of empty tape running through the reel.

Cardinal Mendice shut the player off and rose from the hearth, his hands clasped before him.

"As you are aware, the Holy Father's condition has gradually deteriorated since this message was recorded," he said, his voice and expression solemn. "As he himself predicted, the doctors have issued reports that he is gravely ill, that he will die without regaining consciousness. Their tests indicate massive brain damage from the pressure of the cerebral hemorrhage. Just this evening I was told by Doctor Frederico that the electroencephalogram was flat, that without the heart–lung machine Pope Marcus has been attached to since Saturday, he would surely succumb within a few hours." He paused, looking from face to face.

"Just how accurate *is* this device?"

Quillans looked up to see who was speaking; it was Cardinal Falliano this time, a man of nearly seventy, moderately tall with a full, handsome mane of white hair above his tanned and deeply lined face. But despite his still-vital appearance, a slight haze had begun to dull the blue of his eyes, and Quillans sensed that he, too, was starting to go.

"What I mean to ask," the Dean of the Sacred College continued; "is can we be absolutely sure, based on this limited and potentially fallible mechanical instrument, that no life, no hope, exists?" His voice quavered, whether with age or emotion Quillans was uncertain.

"A good point, Cardinal Falliano," acknowledged the secretary, "and one which we might do well to pursue from a theological viewpoint at a later date. Luckily we are spared from having to make such a consideration at present. Were it not for this," he patted the tape player on his lap almost fondly, "we should have a most difficult and far-reaching decision to make over what determines life or death—one that would not only affect the Holy Father but would ultimately set a precedent for the entire membership of the Church in such matters. As things stand, however, it is a moot point. The Pontiff's directives are clear cut and indisputable: we simply do *not* disconnect the machinery—not until or unless he himself advises otherwise. Meanwhile, we wait for his next message."

"But while we wait, our church is without a leader, the papal line is broken," protested Camerlingo Bertini with some concern. "How long can we go on like this?"

"As long as we must, Cardinal Bertini." The rebuke was mild but definite. "As long as we must."

Chapter 9

Joe was both mystified and pleased by the transformation that had taken place in him since he'd met with the satanist Alton Hawley three days earlier.

He could remember somewhat similar, if muddier, sensations of euphoria in the past — usually the release stage of alcohol or marijuana. But those feelings had always dissipated overnight, leaving him wooden and depressed the following morning. This time, however, he'd felt even more invigorated on Monday morning than he had the evening before.

Everything he'd done that day at work, and the succeeding two days as well, had gone perfectly, with no particular effort on his part. And the more that things went right, the better he'd felt.

Now, Wednesday evening, he was on his way over to the rectory, humming cheerfully to the radio as he contemplated the night's upcoming event. He was filled with sublime confidence that it would go as well as everything else had lately, that the seance would prove to be the final ultimate resolution of Marija's ongoing problem.

Monday night Joe, Marija and Mike had gone to visit

the medium recommended by Ms. Salvida—one Madame Le Beuc.

This self-proclaimed necromancer occupied the bottom flat of a huge, disreputable old Victorian on Sutter Street, on the fringes of a slum. She'd invited them in only as far as the first streetside room that evening, but Joe had observed several other doors leading off the long, gloomy entry hall.

The front parlor–office into which the medium had led them looked out through an oversized bay window onto the garbage, broken wine bottles, and dog droppings that decorated the wide cement sidewalk outside. It was separated from the next room by a pair of broad, sliding wooden doors—partially opened enough to reveal a large high-ceilinged chamber with an oval table planted squarely in its center. This, Joe deduced, was probably the infamous seance room.

Madame Le Beuc, a.k.a. Mildred Spencer, according to an unpaid gas bill left on her desk, was as overdone as her pseudonym. Fat, blowsy, with puffy little eyes—their watery blueness almost lost entirely under the heavy layers of wrinkled silver eyeshadow and inch-long false eyelashes— she polished off her occultist image in a silver turban and red silk chinese robe embroidered front and back with a large dragon done in metallic threads.

Her lips, painted bright red in a thirties-style cupid's bow, parted to reveal a set of cheap, yellowing dentures when she smiled. Her handshake was clammy.

She'd gabbled and expounded in mysterious, whispery rhetoric—as if the spirits themselves might overhear— about the art and magic of necromancy. She talked of being blessed with a "control"—a spirit named Feena who acted as go-between for her and the nether world, possessed of extraordinary courage and ability. She also spoke modestly of her own gifts as a spiritualist.

But when she got around to the fees, she was all capi-

116

talistic grit.

Obviously she'd been briefed by Ms. Salvida about the intensity of their situation, their desperation to resolve it. "My services will cost you two hundred dollars," she'd stated flatly, sitting down behind her antique rosewood desk and fumbling to don a pair of thick, rhinestone-framed glasses, "plus one hundred apiece for my assistants."

Joe had just as grittily bartered her down—to $150, with a single assistant at $75, assuring her they would provide the second party to make up the minimum of six required for a seance. Mike and Marija had glanced over at him obliquely, wondering who he had in mind. But he'd only smiled.

"Payable in advance," the middle-aged woman had insisted, holding out her chubby palm.

"I'd rather pay you Wednesday night, just before we begin," Joe maintained while she resolutely shook her head and continued to hold out her hand, wiggling her fingers.

They'd finally agreed on $50 as a "good faith" deposit, the balance due Wednesday before the seance got under way.

Marija and the bearded priest politely remained out of the transaction, but as soon as they were back in the car the two turned on Joe with a barrage of questions, doubts, and misgivings about the wisdom of going through with the seance at all.

"I can't believe she's for real, Joe," MJ had complained, Mike basically echoing her sentiments in his own choice phraseology.

"What's the harm, then?" Joe fended off their objections good-naturedly. "If she helps, great; if not, it should at least be entertaining." He winked at them both, but there was an extra message in his eyes for Mike, hinting of more to say once the two men were alone.

Over tumblers of Scotch in Muldoon's private study,

117

after MJ had retired for the night, Joe revealed what was really on his mind.

"Sure the old broad's as phony as a three-dollar bill," he agreed readily. "But she might provide just the sort of placebo Marija needs to get back in control."

Mike's eyebrow lifted a notch as he sank down into an old easy chair and waited for Joe to continue.

"Look," Joe continued earnestly, "this obsession with demons has MJ coming and going—she's afraid to leave the rectory, afraid to sleep. She's lost her job. She can't go on like this much longer."

"Agreed," the priest nodded, waiting for the point to be made.

"It seems to me it's as much through her fear as anything else that this—whatever it is—has such power over her. It eats away at her, grabs hold of her mind. It is *because* she's become so terrified of it, so weakened and immobilized by that terror, that she can no longer hold the source of that fear in check." Joe's eyes, sparkling with a fiery intensity, now wavered slightly as he added, "This would be true whether her experiences are the result of *actual* contact with the spirit world, or purely psychological disturbances . . . wouldn't you agree?"

Mike had taken a long swallow of his drink, letting the amber liquid burn down his throat before he answered. "Yes, I would . . . and I see what you're getting at with regard to the seance. If the medium can put on a good enough show, convince Marija that she has actually communicated with her evil spirits and rendered them harmless, perhaps her fear will dissipate enough that she will be strong against them again. Of course, we're going to have to build the woman's authenticity up a bit in MJ's eyes. At the moment she seems pretty disillusioned with the whole idea. Maybe we could tell her we've checked out the medium, that she has a pretty high reputation as a spiritualist, despite her tendency to overdo the trappings. If MJ buys it, it just might work."

Thoughtfully he stroked his beard, considering the plan. There was something about the logic that vaguely disturbed him.

When Joe had suggested Mrs. McGilvroy as the sixth member of their seance, Mike had smiled, then grinned broadly, then thrown back his big shaggy head and roared with laughter.

"Perfect," he'd gasped, wiping his eyes. "She'll be totally scandalized . . . and love it! Especially when I give her the 'placebo' bit to salve her pangs of conscience." He paused for a minute, letting his laughter subside before asking more seriously, "Do you think one of us ought to talk to Madame Le Beuc . . . ?" But saying the name broke him up again, the last syllable snorting out through his nose as he doubled over in a delicious fit of giggling. "Le Buick . . . '52 model—built like a Sherman tank with chrome skirts."

It was infectious. Joe smirked, then chortled, then gave in to helpless laughter, tears in his eyes. It took several tries before Mike was finally able to complete his question.

"Do you suppose," he said finally, taking deep, slow breaths to calm himself, "that we should talk to . . . this medium about what we're trying to accomplish? Brief her so she doesn't blow it?"

They'd batted around the idea for a while, at last deciding against it. Even if the woman was a phony, she'd never admit it to them.

And she *might* take offense at the suggestion, refusing to do the seance at all. Besides, Ms. Salvida had probably already clued her in.

So they'd left it alone, hoping for the best, figuring the odds were with them that, as an astute businesswoman, "Madame Le Buick" would have sense enough to set things up so that her client would triumph.

119

Now it was Wednesday, and within a few hours they'd know if the gamble had paid off. As Joe pulled into the rectory driveway and cut the engine, he saw Marija waiting for him in the lighted doorway, looking beautiful. He leapt from the car and ran to her arms, hugging her tightly and swinging her around like a schoolgirl.

"Ready for the big night?" he asked, nibbling at her ear.

"I guess," she smiled playfully, "but I can think of something *else* I'd rather be doing."

"Maybe after tonight," he grinned, pushing her back so he could gaze into those wide, hazel eyes reassuringly, noticing the deep pain beneath their cheerful surface. "Maybe everything will be okay again after tonight."

Mike came to the door just then, dressed in his minister's shirt and black jacket. Seeing Joe's appraising look he smiled, fingering the white tab inserted in his cleric collar. "I was tempted to go in my hippie lumberjack disguise, but since this is something bordering on the black arts, I'd feel guilty if I didn't go in proclaiming loud and clear whose side I'm on."

"Gotcha," Joe smiled back, grabbing the man's shoulder. "Now, are you going to invite me in, or what?"

The little wooden clock in the sitting room chimed six times as they walked through the entry hall. They had three hours to go, three hours to fill with nervous small talk, nursing slow drinks, enduring long introspective silences, until the nine o'clock appointment would begin. It seemed forever.

Chapter 10

His sleep was light, his dream intensely sexual, as usual . . . so near the surface of his mind he wasn't even sure he was dreaming until the stout finger poking at his shoulder and the rough whisper calling in his ear dissolved the erotic pictures and pulled him reluctantly back to consciousness.

He opened his eyes slowly against the unwelcome glare of the bare overhead light. The ruddy face of Archbishop Magliano — glistening with perspiration even now in the predawn chill — hovered anxiously over him.

"Archbishop Quillans, *please!*" the voice urged, rising in anxiety. "It is Il Papa; he has awakened. He has summoned *you!* You must come at once to the infirmary!"

The American grunted in acknowledgment and slid his feet over the edge of the narrow bed, holding the blanket modestly across his lap. "If you will allow me a moment to dress in privacy," he suggested, his tone icy.

"I'll wait outside, Excellency," the Italian acquiesced, stung again by the man's rudeness and snobbery. It was not until he was out in the hall that it struck him as odd that the San Franciscan was not in the least excited over

121

the news. Magliano might have been simply announcing breakfast, for all the surprise it engendered. But before he had a chance to pursue this line of thinking further, the door opened and the steely-eyed American walked out into the dark, chilly hallway.

They proceeded in mutually stony silence, Magliano in the lead, taking the ornate, gilded elevator to the first floor, then echoing across the deserted tiled lobby, through a maze of dim hallways, and into the brightly lit corridor outside the suite of offices that constituted the Vatican infirmary.

Magliano opened one of the twin glass-paned doors for his confrere and followed him inside, closing it quietly.

Although normally the palace infirmary served as both outpatient clinic and temporary emergency hospital for the palace staff, ever since the Pope was stricken it had been reserved for his care alone. The few current inpatients and those members of the curia needing emergency care had been routed to Roman hospitals outside the city walls for treatment, leaving the little clinic oddly quiet and empty.

Quillans now preceded Magliano, striding forward as if he knew instinctively where he was headed. They passed through another pair of swinging doors beyond the empty waiting room which led into an examination area where two nursing nuns knelt in a darkened corner murmuring in prayer. From there they proceeded down a broad hall off which were a series of stencil-numbered doors.

As the archbishops hurried forward, one of these opened and two white-jacketed medics emerged, talking in low, excited whispers. Immediately behind them came the short, trim figure of the papal secretary, whose worried expression lifted somewhat as he spotted the American headed his way.

"Praise be," he exclaimed in a hushed voice, "you have arrived in time! The rest are already inside." He began to urge the man through the door, turning his head to convey his regret to the Italian nuncio that he could not be invited to join them as well. "In good conscience, I must adhere to the Pontiff's wishes in this matter, little father," he sighed with an affectionate look at Magliano.

"I understand, Your Eminence," the portly man smiled graciously.

The door closed, leaving him and the two doctors to stare in silent consternation at each other, then at the impassive glass face of the door behind which a miracle of sorts was taking place.

Pope Marcus the Third lay in stately repose, the upper third of his gaunt frame propped up by white linen-covered pillows. His face was gray with the pallor of death; his hair limp, thin, gray also; his long, skeletal yellow fingers splayed against the white sheets.

His eyes shot open as Quillans entered the room, eyes incongruously dark and alive against the deathliness of his body. The thin fingers twitched, beckoning his audience forward.

"Turn on the recorder," the voice hissed from behind nearly unmoving lips. The sound of it was a shock, even to the archbishop from San Francisco. A hollow, sibilant whisper, it seemed to come from somewhere deep within the man. And the breath was so exceedingly foul—a pit of death and decay—that Quillans had to force himself not to recoil from it.

"God speaks through my lips," the Pope pronounced, rasping into the microphone on his chest as the tape recorder whirred. "Let no man doubt this is so. If there are still those who cannot accept this news on faith, then I offer them medical proof as well—the signed and sworn statements of my attending physicians that my awakening, my speaking to you now in this moribund condition, is a physical impossibility. Thus it follows that it *must* be God's will, *His* words spoken *through* me that you hear."

The room filled with the terrible mephitis of the dying Pontiff, with the awesome words, the awful sound of his voice. The six cardinals of the suburban sees leaned forward intently, as if not to miss a single word, yet they kept their heads bent, their eyes averted from the sight of the cadaverous prolocutor. The Patriarch of Alexandria wept openly while the cardinal secretary busied himself with the recorder, trying to hide his complex emotions.

Quillans alone observed the tiniest trace of a smile trying to work its way around a steely resolve which kept his lips tightly compressed, a slight twitch at the corner of his mouth which the others would have taken to be a nervous tic, its only manifestation.

"What I tell you next is God's decree and must be obeyed as such, even though you may find it highly unusual." He paused momentarily, the amplified sound of his strangled breathing penetrating the silence just as his stench penetrated the air.

"You have among you at this moment a very special man, chosen of God for a very special mission."

There was another slight pause in the rasping whisper, long enough for the cardinals in the room to exchange looks.

"The first duty of this secret consistory is to confirm my nomination of that man—Archbishop Robert F. Quillans—to the holy station of cardinal." A brilliant, laser-thin flash of recognition shot between his eyes and those of the tall, composed archbishop at these words, but it went unnoticed amidst the flurry of small gasps and murmurs escaping the other men's lips.

"It shall be done, Your Holiness," the Secretary of State assured him, bending near but not inhaling.

"Good. You shall prepare the biglietto at the conclusion of this meeting," Pope Marcus ordered. "The public ceremony may be waived in this instance, but the presentation of his ring and holy vestments of office must be made in a private ceremony first thing tomorrow, attended only by those cardinals present here tonight; Dean Falliano will do the honors in my stead."

The very room seemed to be darkening while the Pontiff spoke, his words collecting like shadows in the corners of the ward, the stench emanating from him like a slow brown mist discoloring the air.

"Is everything I have ordered thus far understood?" he rumbled.

"Understood, your Holiness," Cardinal Mendice assured him nervously.

"Excellent. Because I have a further revelation from God to impart now." The gray sunken cheeks quivered in an attempt to smile; the black, black eyes shone and sparked. "I have been in the company of God for several days now, and He has revealed to me more of His plans for the future of our church, and the continuing role I am to play in creating that future. He has now ordained that I remain alive *indefinitely* even though I be technically dead, so that from time to time He may again speak directly to the world through these frail lips. When He is not using me in this manner, I will be returned to the deathful coma in which you've found me these past five days." He waited, letting his words sink in.

"The problem you, the administrators of the worldwide church, are faced with as a result of this lingering death-state in your elected Pope, is how to manage over an extended period of time without a functional head of state," the Pontiff stated, voicing their concern.

"Thus the second major task that I hereby assign you in this consistory is to transcribe, as a Motu Proprio, our decree that an auxiliary Pope be elected at once to carry out all the Papal functions, both spiritual and temporal, in my absence.

"One of the most important duties of the auxiliary Pope will be to ensure that any future mandates of God which come through me are carried out surely, promptly, and exactly; without either wasteful deliberation or destructive alteration of their precise import."

The cardinals were murmuring again among themselves, and Cardinal Mendice turned toward them with a fiery warning glance. Their chatter immediately ceased.

The withered old man on the bed continued, his voice both deeply resonant and as flat and lifeless as something originating from an electronic synthesizer. It was unlike anything the learned cardinals at his bedside had ever heard . . . yet there was a woman half a world away who might have recognized it.

"A stipulation of my Motu Proprio is that the election of this auxiliary Pope shall be accomplished by limited delegation rather than through general conclave; the only members are to be the nine of you here tonight. The customary fifteen-day wait after the death of a Pope is, of course, waived, as there is no death involved. And the election must be held within the next three days."

Several of the old, white-haired heads had begun nodding in solemn agreement — or possibly numb amazement — and two more of the cardinal bishops had joined the eastern patriarch, tears flowing freely down their cheeks. The others looked variously stricken, enraptured, or confused. Robert Quillans continued to suppress his smile.

"*Finally,*" the voice echoed out of the depths, catching each member's attention anew with its intensity, "is the matter of whom God has selected for this task, to act in my place as your Pontiff while I remain in this limbo, the humble vessel of God."

Although his head was perfectly still, the Pope's sharp eyes darted from face to face, enjoying the anticipation building in each.

"Usually you, the members of the Sacred College, are left to choose a new Pope on your own initiative, with faith that God's hand is working through you. This time the Father wishes no possibility that His will might be misinterpreted through the fallibilities of human judgment. Therefore let me state clearly that the person *He* has selected, your *only* choice for auxiliary Pontiff, is the new cardinal-designate, Robert F. Quillans, former archbishop to San Francisco."

Audible gasps could be heard around the room. A ring of faces turned as one to Quillans, who stood at the foot of the bed attempting to mask his inner excitement with a solemn expression of piety.

"I tire now, and have said all that I must," the Holy Father said, his voice drawing away. "Before I return to my place with the Father, may I have the word of each one present here tonight that the orders I have commended to you will be carried out precisely as given?"

Mumbled words of assent filled the space around the bed: What else could they say? It *was* God's will.

"Secretary Mendice," the voice came now from far, far away, "as each step in my decree is completed, you may release the news, first to the Roman Catholic hierarchy, then to the media. But *transcripts* of my message only," the voice was disappearing in a whispery hiss. "Release no tapes of my voice to anyone: Lock them in the archives vault. *Never* play the tapes, not the tapes. . . ."

Pope Marcus the Third had gone; the machines that ran his body whirred on. The miracle was over, but something else had begun.

Chapter 11

They'd gathered in the front parlor, a nervous little clot of men and women trying to look self-assured, masking with limited success their own uncertainties, their feelings of awkward foolishness in being party to the upcoming gambit by filling the silences with idle chatter.

Madame Le Beuc had insisted on serving tea to her guests before the seance commenced. It was her traditional "ice breaker," she'd proclaimed, essential to the success of the proceedings. "It will help bring us all closer together, make us feel more comfortable with one another and with our surroundings, bringing our auras into spiritual harmony."

Of course the ample portions of brandy she'd added to their cups of herbal brew might have something to do with the outlook for success, Joe sniggered to Mike—his eyes watering slightly from the heavy alcoholic fumes that were rising from his china mug. If they drank more than one cup of this stuff they'd be so polluted she could make them believe anything.

During tea they'd been introduced to the sixth member of their party—a tall, middle-aged black man with a touch

128

of gray at his temples, a grizzle of gray whiskers on his cheeks and chin, a mocking, tired, supercilious glint in his red-rimmed eyes.

The professor, as the medium called him, was a mediocre philosopher given to rambling erudition and, from the way he was putting away the brandy-laced tea (after the first cup omitting the tea altogether), an unconcernedly committed alcoholic.

He was also, Muldoon suspected in a whispered aside to Joe, a sometime bedroom companion of their hostess, from the close way they snarled at one another.

The preliminaries finally over, they'd been ceremoniously ushered into the dimly lit middle room by the spurious medium—tonight dressed to the hilt in her interpretation of Lady Merlin: a long, flowing black gown decorated in swirling patterns of glittery silver sequins, her silver turban embellished with a huge red paste jewel. Her makeup was, if possible, even more overdone than before, and she seemed a trifle tipsy as she directed them to their places.

The room was nearly as tall as it was wide, the twelve-foot ceiling painted the same deep midnight blue as the walls and floor, but speckled with luminescent silver paint in a half-baked replication of the northern skies.

Dominating the center of the fifteen-foot room was a large oval table, draped to the floor in a cheap black satin throw, a wrinkly hand-sewn seam down its midsection. An odd selection of old wavery mirrors hung in haphazard arrangement about the four walls—their only purpose, Joe guessed, to be used in some optical illusions the medium had in store.

Madame Le Beuc sat at the head of the table, Joe and Mike on either side of her. Marija was placed next to Joe, Mrs. McGilvroy opposite her beside the priest, and the dour black man filled the space between the two ladies at the far end of the table from the medium.

"Before we begin," the spiritualist said, looking around the table with narrowed eyes, "there are a few basic rules you must adhere to without fail. To disobey these would be to court . . . disaster!" The woman was most emphatic in her pronouncement.

Joe cast a worried glance at MJ; he'd spent the last two days trying to play up Le Beuc's credibility, wanting MJ to believe in it so that the psychodrama of the seance would create the desired effect. Now he was beginning to wish he'd briefed the medium after all. An extra fifty or so would have quelled any affront to her professional dignity and ensured her cooperation, he was sure. If she continued to overplay her role this way, Joe feared MJ would see right through her antics and all the hoped-for results would be lost. MJ caught his look and smiled.

"First," the turbaned spiritualist went on, her voice irritatingly high-pitched and nasal, "absolute silence is to be maintained at all times—no chitchat, no comments, remarks, or questions that might break the line of communication with the spirit world.

"The next rule is that no one is to get up from this table for any reason from the moment the lights are dimmed to the conclusion of the seance. Even during ordinary circumstances the spirits evoked through necromancy may be unpredictable, and they can sometimes prove hostile or threatening. In your case," she sent her narrow, pig-eyed gaze in Marija's direction, "the spirits we wish to contact are already known to be antagonistic, at least to you personally. To break the safety of our circle would be to leave yourself totally vulnerable to their power. Beyond this field, once the seance has begun, there will remain only a timeless void, a black abyss full of unknown perils and terrible forces. This table, our joining around it, is the only hold you or any of us will have on this plane of reality. Do not forsake it!"

Mike grabbed Mrs. McGilvroy's hand and gave it a reassuring squeeze; she squeezed back as if to comfort him, as if the big, burly priest were a frightened boy. The medium, seeing she was creating the desired effect, continued with even more fervor.

"You must realize that in our joining hands we become as one being, one mind. What one of us does affects everyone present. Thus if even one of you breaks the circle, you throw all our combined power into the hands of our adversaries, put us all at their mercy. Therefore I must reemphasize this: *never*, for any reason, break the circle of hands. Do you all understand these rules?"

Each person murmured a self-conscious affirmation — except Leroy, the black professor, who took the opportunity to sneak a quick belt of Southern Comfort from the pint bottle tucked into his pocket. This the medium chose to ignore.

"Fine, fine," Madame Le Beuc smiled, exposing her yellowing dentures. "Now then, those are the hard and fast rules. There are, in addition, some suggestions that, though they cannot be enforced, would greatly enhance the success of our necromantic experience here tonight if you would at least *attempt* to carry them out in good faith."

Joe stirred restlessly in his chair, trying to squirm away a persistent itch in a portion of his anatomy best scratched in private. The medium shot him a hard look and continued.

"I would ask you to let yourself flow with the forces that surround us. Do not fight them, do not try to rationalize them away. Try for just one night to put away your self-protective attitudes of cynicism and disbelief; set your

131

spiritual nature free to rise to higher planes of awareness."
She was waving a pink-nailed hand in a swirling motion
above her head. *"Believe,* if you can, ladies and gentlemen:
Believe!!"

With that final dramatic admonition the lights suddenly
went out, leaving only a blue, hazy glow directed at the
table from a hidden spotlight behind the woman's head,
casting the medium in an eerie aura and reflecting in
shadowy patches across the faces of the five other people.

"Join hands in the never-ending circle of eternal life,"
the medium droned. "Join hands and join spirits . . . the
seance has begun!"

Mildred Spencer Le Beuc fluttered her eyelids and let
her head flop forward, ignoring the sharp twinge of pain
the movement sent through her arthritic vertebrae. She
allowed herself a fleeting smile while her face was thus
tucked down out of view. Never having had a real spiritual experience in her life, she nevertheless possessed a
wily flair for the dramatics needed to con the gullible
neurotics who sought her services. She also had an obses-
sive and vivid imagination, fed by the never-dying hope
that she might this time succeed in achieving real contact
with the spirit world. This helped the credibility of her act
considerably. But the majority of credit for her successes
would have to go to the special talents of her technical
assistant, the professor, aka Leroy Turner.

He had been a special effects technician with Universal
Studios until thirteen years ago, when his descent into
alcohol had made his hands too shaky, his performance
too unreliable for even the union to intercede in his behalf
any longer. From Hollywood he'd slowly odd-jobbed his
way north through the hot, dry cities of the sprawling San
Joaquin Valley—Bakersfield, Fresno, Merced, Stockton,
and finally San Francisco—earning just enough to feed his

thirst for oblivion, moving on when the bills piled too high for him to talk his way out of them. He'd been on the verge of moving on again when Mildred Spencer first met him nine years ago. He'd been sent by her reluctant slumlord to piece together some faulty wiring in her flat and had been there ever since. She was a slightly slimmer and firmer thirty-nine then, he a rather withered forty-four with a suffering liver and little hope.

The first thing the woman did was to sober him up. Then she took him to her bed and—with a patience born of desperate loneliness—brought him to the point where he could perform the act he'd given up as lost forever years before. After that it had been no problem to enlist his expertise in creating an elaborate system of electronically controlled magic in the middle room, the eerie effects she dreamed up for her recently acquired avocation as a spiritual medium. With his help she soon had, literally at her fingertips, all those strange and frightening phenomena she imagined *should* happen in a seance but, for all her efforts, had never deigned to occur naturally.

She gave him a room in her home, a cut of the take, and a renewed sense of his manhood. What did it matter that in the succeeding nine years he'd slowly slipped back into the embrace of his former potent mistress, that their sexual encounters had subsequently become less and less frequent over the years? As long as he could still perform at her seances, his lack of performance in the bedroom bothered her very little; it bothered him not at all.

Now the medium moaned loudly, throwing her head back in a strained arch. She clutched hard at the hands of the two men flanking her, rolling her eyes up into her head and mumbling incoherently. It was the professor's signal to press the lever beneath the throw rug at his feet that would begin the first special effect. He pushed on cue

133

with the toe of his worn cowboy boot, but nothing happened. He tapped at the switch again with increased force, seeing the tension of disapproval in the corners of his consort's mouth.

"Oh spirits of the netherworld, hinderers of Hades aura, lost souls of the Earth," she intoned loudly, buying time, "arise and make thy presence known."

The professor pushed the lever again, hard, but the prerecorded moans and synthesized wailing, the refrigerated air blown in on clouds of dry ice fumes through invisible vents in the dark walls, the eerie glowing amorphous shapes created out of cleverly concealed black lights revolving behind stencil-cut "ghosts"—all refused to materialize.

Suddenly there was a deep, low rumbling from somewhere in the bowels of the earth. The floor jumped and the table began to jitter and sway, jolting about on its stiff, thick legs like a drunken sailor. The shuddering of the room increased to a violent tempo, the rumble intensified to a roar. Mirrors were flung from the walls. In the furthest black depths of the room a heavy light fixture crashed to the floor, exploding in a burst of bluish white incandescence.

"My God, it's an earthquake!" Marija exclaimed, leaping up.

"Sit down!" the black man hissed, his large hand tightening on hers, pulling her back into the chair. "Don't break the chain!"

What incredible timing, thought the medium, suppressing her own alarm with the opportunistic craft of a P. T. Barnum. "We hear you, oh spirits of darkness!" she cried out in a quavering tone. "We thank you for answering our call."

A tremendous ear-shattering thunder, like that of a jet

engine at full throttle, filled the air at her words: two black-painted windows to the left clung tenaciously to their rotting frames for a quivering, bulging moment before blowing out in a shattering crash to the concrete side yard beyond. More hidden lights within the seance parlor burst in electrical flashes, illuminating briefly the frightened faces at the table in a strobelike, kaleidoscopic view of horror.

Madame Le Beuc felt the beads of perspiration spring to her skin, pooling into little rivulets on her forehead and beneath her arms, running greasily down her neck and sides. Her sweat was beginning to stink—the smell of fear—at the long-awaited success she now wished had never come.

Joe glanced anxiously at Mike, barely visible across the dark gap that separated them: he too looked concerned. If this was just a show, it was a damned good one.

Marija's eyes looked huge in the shadowy light, her set features grim. She was clinging to Joe's hand with a grip so intense it was painful. Mrs. McGilvroy had her eyes closed, her mouth moving in silent prayer. The professor was staring down in the direction of his coat pocket where the hidden flask of whiskey lay out of reach; he too was perspiring heavily.

Abruptly the roaring cacophony of sound and motion ceased, replaced with an ominous hollow of silence. Slowly this soundless vacuum was filled by a low, almost inaudible moaning . . . sensed first as nothing more than a tremor vibrating the receptors of the inner ear, until the vibrations raised in pitch enough to be discerned by the brain as noise. It was the type of sound that crawled along the spine on its way to the heart.

The moaning gradually increased in key and volume, filling the room with its unbearable anguish. The six mor-

135

tals around the table began to twist their heads back and forth as if seeking escape, but the shrieking persisted, individuating slowly into a dozen different voices. With the voices came a sudden penetrating chill, as from out of the dark a swirling, pulsating phosphorescent cloud began to materialize, then another and another. In seconds the room was filled with trembling, amorphous forms in softly luminescent violet, green, and blue. Moaning, shrieking, sighing, they shot over and through the circle of humans in a spinning dance, a sucking vortex.

No one seemed able to move, to scream, even to shiver. They all sat transfixed, helplessly immobilized by the completeness of their terror.

Faces began to form now within the intangible mists — weird, distorted cadaverous etchings with darkly gaping mouths and black eye sockets sculpted into the vaporous heads. Their encircling motion died out gradually, along with their hideous screams, as the countenances of the tormented spirits lost their skeletal quality, forming into holographic images of their former identities: men and women and children, all pointing accusing fingers toward the circle.

Their mouths opened, they began to speak, but the words were garbled and unintelligible, their voices a hollow, wretched, faraway sound.

Slowly it began to dawn on MJ that they were all saying the same thing, the same word, chanting it over and over. And with a gut-wrenching shock she recognized what it was. A name. *Her name.*

"Noooo!" She wailed, half-rising, her hands still in the grip of the others. "It's like the last time, Joe, just like the time in the kitchen. I told you. I *told* you! Now the bugs will come!"

She heard it now as she had then: a faint, skittering,

scurrying noise in the walls, in the ceiling above her head; an infinitesimal scratching magnified by the multitude of its sources, like the faint thunder of a distant army marching off to war, the beat of thousands upon thousands of tiny chitinous boots tromping out their wrath on a lath-and-plaster battlefield.

She saw it again now as she had then, as if still locked into that night of horror, saw a small bronze bullet dropping from the topmost cupboard shelf in her kitchen, its six tiny legs scrabbling uselessly for a foothold in the air as it free-fell to the counter below. The scurrying sound increased. Another cockroach dived after the first, then another and another. Faster and faster they came, now in twos, then threes, sixes, twenties. The scratch of their clawed appendages had grown to a subdued roar behind the walls of the old Victorian flat.

"Oh my God!" Marija'd screamed as a solid boiling wave of wriggling, shiny brown insects began to spill over the edge of the topmost cupboard. Some poured like a fountain through the air, spraying off the counter shelf and onto the floor below; others wrapped their paths around the edge to run in defiance of gravity along the bottom of the shelf and down the wall. But whatever path they chose, they all appeared to be programmed toward the same point of convergence—they were all running straight at her!

In a moment there were cockroaches everywhere, pouring from all four sides of the room by the hundreds, the thousands, from every conceivable crack and crevice. The ceiling was covered in a moving tide of plump, shiny insects which grew thicker even as she watched, bodies crawling over and clinging to other bodies until in some places the layer was several inches deep.

Then they began falling in a sporadic living rain, landing on her hair, her face, her lips; down between her breasts, running down her neck and arms and shoulders while those already on the floor began crawling in a thick stocking up her legs with an unbearably repulsive prickling.

At some point Marija became aware of a loud, continuous, high-pitched screaming. It took a minute for her to realize that the awful noise was coming from her.

The others around the table saw no bugs—that was Marija's private nightmare—but the rest was real enough to them: the ghostly shapes and voices, the frigid air, the terror. And something else, something slithering through their entrails as MJ's cockroaches had slithered up her legs, something evil, an enormously strong and vile presence that now filled the room and penetrated their innermost beings. It took Marija's hysterical screams to slap them awake.

"Break the circle!" a voice screamed out of the darkness. It was Mildred Spencer—Madame Le Beuc had fled— "Break the fucking circle!"

Mike and Joe both felt the furious yank of her hands against their grip and tried to release her, but their fingers refused to obey the commands of their brains.

The erstwhile medium struggled even more frantically, twisting her fat body one way and the other, to no avail. "Let me go, damn you . . . break the fucking circle!" she cried again hysterically, tears of fright streaming down her face.

The others began struggling now as well, trying to free themselves from one another. A group panic set in when they discovered they couldn't. Their hands were frozen into place like the unmovable rigor of the dead, the unrelenting grip of the linesman who's inadvertently taken hold of a high-voltage wire.

138

All at once their flailings ceased, cut short by an invisible power. Their bodies turned rigid, shaking all over, teeth chattering between clenched jaws as a surge of incredible energy coursed through their unbroken chain. Like stiff rag dolls in the teeth of some huge invisible dog, they were shaken into submission, played with before the jugular was severed in one last heartless slash.

When at last they were released, they fell limply back into their chairs, humbled and unresistant, spent and conquered.

In the center of the table the space inscribed by the circle of their joined hands now began to glow and pulsate with a strange energy field. The black abyss Madame Le Beuc had postulated in her opening dramatics had suddenly grown into a giddying reality for the six: they felt as if they were floating together, suspended in space and time, surrounded by an unknown emptiness, a vast nothing devoid of all light and life, created out of endless cold and unfathomable distances. Their only hold on the physical world lay in the contact of hands around the table, their attention riveted on the newly created reality which occupied the space between them as if it were a life preserver on this dark and sucking sea.

The luminous field had slowly congealed, forming a darkly gleaming, violet-hued orb some twenty inches in diameter, hovering in their midst just above the reflective surface of the black satin plane. Within its depths small shapes began to materialize, rapidly becoming three-dimensional, holographic images—six tiny white marble figures caught in frozen poses of life. Slowly the figures began to take on color and life, and a gasp emerged from the onlookers: *the tiny living statuettes were of them, themselves miniaturized, trapped inside the transparent ball!*

A heaviness pressed in on Marija, Joe, and the others

139

around the table, taking their breath away, making them unable to speak or move. At the same instant their tiny alter egos within the sphere burst fully to life, beating frantically against the invisible walls of their prison, mouths open in soundless screams of terror and protest.

Their fruitless thrashing stopped as abruptly as it had begun, almost as if the little clones were being turned on and off by a switch. Manipulated like marionettes, their hands dropped slackly to their sides, heads flopped forward on tiny necks. Five of the lilliputian figures began to recede, growing tinier and tinier within the transparent ball, gradually fading from view completely. At last only one subject remained, alone and exposed: it was the medium, Madame Le Beuc.

A background began to fill in by degrees around her; a sunny parlor that looked vaguely familiar to two of the guests. Soon another female figure manifested within the blue haze: tall, big-boned and handsome; MJ recognized Ms. Salvida.

Without warning the scene changed; the two middle-aged women were now in another room, a bedroom, and both were totally naked. The dark-haired woman's hands were on Mildred's plump, droopy breasts, caressing them gently, teasing the swollen nipples into a tense erectness.

Her wide, unpainted mouth bent to kiss first one, then the other, lifting the pendulous bosom to her lips. Mildred Spencer, sitting at the table, emitted a strangled choking sound and tried to close her eyes, while her tiny alter ego in the globe continued wriggling happily under the other woman's touch, pushing her thick hips forward to meet her lover's pubic bulge, clasping her hands around the firm, slim buttocks and pulling them crushingly close. The two moved together for a time, standing there in each other's arms, swaying sensuously to music heard only

140

by themselves. Then they kissed, gently at first, but soon harder, more demanding, holding each other tightly.

Without breaking the embrace they sidled closer to the bed, and, as one, folded down upon it, Salvida on top. Tender hands reached for the partner's private sensitive areas, softly, carefully stimulating and caressing. Thighs wrapped around thighs, wetness found wetness and rubbed against it, moved into it — writhing and pushing and touching, clutching in heated embrace, in final shuddering release.

The orb went black. All eyes were pulled against their will to face the medium: she looked back at them unseeing, her face deathly white beneath the black splotches of running mascara, the glaring pink rouge on her cheeks. One of her false eyelashes hung ludicrously from her upper lid. Her painted mouth opened and closed noiselessly.

The inky depths outside their circle darkened suddenly. Danger crept up six rigid spines, fear edged away sympathy. Hands clutched tighter to one another, each member torn between wanting to flee the awful revelations of this self-created world before them, and deadly terror at what might lie beyond the safety of their chain.

Now their heads jerked back to the maleficent orb, which had glowed once more to life. Within its gloomy arena another figure slowly materialized.

This time it was the professor, but a much younger, stronger, more virile man than the withered alcoholic who shared their table tonight. His step was light, jaunty almost, in the early afternoon air. He carried a small bouquet of daisies in his left hand, the soft Southern California winter sunlight glinting off the yellow band that encircled one of the powerful, dark-skinned fingers.

The tall, handsome man could have passed for a college athlete instead of a thirty-nine-year-old as he skipped up the flagstone walk to his comfortable ranch-style house in North Hollywood. His uncanny light green eyes sparkled as he carefully opened the door, tiptoeing over the threshold, the flowers behind his back.

Inside the interior was dim; the man's smile faded as he struck a listening posture, the flowers quietly discarded on the small oval entry table just inside the door. He took a careful step or two forward, pausing, listening again.

The swarthy face hardened, turned cold and blacker still. The powerfully built body moved forward with the stealth of a stalking tiger, around a corner, down a narrow hall.

The silence was broken by a sobbing, grunting noise at the far end of the seance table — the old Negro suffering for what he knew was to come, for his inability to get to the flask of liquid amnesia that had been his escape from these memories for the past 15 years.

Back in the globe a bedroom door was being flung open, the man and woman within caught in the classic pose — shock, guilt and fear on the woman's face as she scurried to pull the sheets over her naked body. The man, a white man even paler in his fright, was grabbing for his discarded trousers and his shoes.

Leroy Turner's rage was directed toward his wife alone: the intruder, the usurper, had become invisible, insignificant. He skittered all but unnoticed past the cuckolded husband, heading for the open door, his pants and shoes clutched protectively over his suddenly flaccid penis.

The black man closed the door behind him, a quietly calculated movement as deadly as that of an aroused cobra.

The woman had begun to whimper; her mouth was moving, an attempt to placate, to explain, to cajole with a quivering smile, begging his forgiveness, his mercy.

Leroy Turner moved forward, jaw set, eyes brittle. A huge hand drew back and swung with the force of a piston, flat and hard against the woman's delicate cheek, spinning her head around, lifting her half out of the bed. The other hand snapped out lightning fast, striking her on the opposite side of her face before she completed her fall, slamming her back in the other direction. Again and again he hit her. The blood from her split mouth and ruptured eardrums covering his palms served only to increase his rage.

Her screams ceased after the fifth or sixth blow: after half a dozen or so more he stopped, only because she was obviously no longer feeling the pain.

Leroy strode into the bathroom, yanking her orange rubber douche bag from its hook in the shower. He filled it at the sink, carrying it back into the bedroom, the bulbous black plastic end piece held high enough to keep the cold water from spraying out onto the carpet. Standing over his wife's sprawled, unconscious form, he smiled and lowered the hose, drenching her face and upper torso until she sputtered, groaned, and returned to a semiconscious state.

Grinning broadly now—a feral grimace—he pulled the sheets roughly from her body and stood looking down at her nakedness: the full beautiful breasts that had been his pillow these past two years, the flat young belly, the coffee-colored thighs. And the matted pubic hair, wet with some other man's need, wet with her own filthy desires. The smile faded.

"You bitch, you fucking traitorous bitch," he hissed, lifting his arm to strike her again. But he checked his swing, looking at the empty douche bag in his hand, an evil glint coming into his eyes.

Striding back to the bathroom—all coherent reason

gone, only hate and revenge filling his mind with sweet poison—he began rummaging through the medicine chest and cupboards, then through the cans and bottles of housecleaning products beneath the vanity cabinet. He pulled out a white plastic bottle of chlorine bleach, gazed at it somberly for a moment, then poured its contents into the orange rubber bag. He moved mechanically back into the bedroom where his wife was still moaning and weeping loudly on the bed, her legs splayed helplessly. He jerked the heavy thighs farther apart, the bag of caustic liquid held high, and with a vicious motion jammed the black end piece deep inside her.

As her screams began he pushed one of her lover's dirty socks into her mouth, leaned his elbow into her chest to hold her down, and continued to let the burning chemical flow into her until the bag was empty.

Later he rinsed the blistered skin with a clear water douche—not out of compassion but to protect himself—then violently and repeatedly raped her, his tormented face a gape-mouthed mixture of lust and hate and unbearable pain.

This picture gradually faded, then one final scene appeared within the holographic ball: the professor sitting on the hearth of his cold dark fireplace, old-looking, beaten, the bottle of Jim Beam in his hand nearly empty. His head did not turn at all as his battered wife limped slowly down the hall with a large suitcase dragging behind, thumping on its little plastic wheels past the wilted daisies in their green paper wrapper on the entry table. The woman turned at the door to give one last despairing look at the man, the house, then walked out into the predawn depths of blackness.

The sphere darkened, obliterating the last vistiges of that image. Five heads were again turned unwillingly to

144

stare at the remains of the man at the foot of their table, but before their horror could be moved to pity, an insane tittering swept through the void around them, growing and fading in an undulating curve, mocking their compassion, reminding them of the unknown powers that surrounded and controlled them. Then it slipped back into the abyss.

Almost immediately the next miniaturized figure began to appear within the globe. It was Mrs. McGilvroy.

"Now what could this dear old woman possibly be concealing?" the priest thought with a sense of anguish, trying to give her hand a comforting squeeze. Too quickly he had his answer.

She lay curled in bed in her little room in the rectory, moaning quietly and writhing inside her prim cotton gown, her sins hidden under the faded yellow coverlet that sheltered her from their view.

Cruelly the covers suddenly vaporized, the gown disappeared, exposing her plump, wrinkled body for all to see. A loud sobbing was heard at the side of the table, the sound of a heart breaking, as the globe went on to display her secret in telescopic close-up: the gnarled, arthritic fingers stroking the genital area, the middle one thrust deep into her opening, rubbing slowly in and out. Her fat, flabby thighs squeezed against the hand, buttocks moving rhythmically, pushing against the hardness of her palm. The old woman's eyes were tightly closed, her lips slightly parted, her breath growing harsh and rasping. And now another picture came to the forefront, partially overlaying the first larger background scene. It was the picture in her mind, the sexual fantasy she was playing out to bring herself to climax.

"No, no! Oh please, God, not that!" the real Mrs. McGilvroy cried out, trying to wrench free from the cir-

145

cle, to stop this somehow. To run. But her head reeled suddenly to one side as a loud slapping sound punctuated the air; red weals immediately appeared on her pale, wrinkled cheek. Her head was jerked cruelly around to face the globe, held there stiffly in an invisible grasp, while her wide-opened eyes drained a continuous flow of helpless tears onto the black satin tablecloth.

Within the spherical stage a second miniature of herself had appeared — but of course, in her fantasy, a younger, firmer, more voluptuous self — lying in the pristine sanctity of her bedroom. Suddenly the door was flung open and the young priest stood before her in his thin cotton pajamas. As she watched, his fly parted under the pressure of his bulging penis; it poked out at her — huge, erect, engorged. He moved sensuously toward her, a glint of lust in his eye, and she pulled the covers up higher around her neck, her eyes wide in alarm.

With a swift, sure gesture he yanked the blanket away. Two strong brown hands took hold of either side of her gown, tearing the fabric from her naked, trembling flesh. She lay there powerless to fight the strength of his passion, while his soft mouth covered her neck with kisses, his beard scratching her breasts, the sharp white teeth biting at her flesh until her back arched involuntarily up to meet him.

And then he was in her, plunging again and again — deep, demanding, ardent. The larger background figure of the lonely woman in her bed squirmed and pumped faster and faster in time to her fantasy's rhythm until both ended in shaking, shuddering completion.

Once more the remaining five felt their eyes being forced toward the member of their group who'd been defamed, but this time, with a small bleat of fury, one refused. Marija, with a sudden, surprising force of will,

146

wrenched her eyes from the housekeeper's unbearable humiliation. Her defiance instantly met with a tremendous roar of rage from their unseen malefactor. A bolt of white fire hurtled around the table, encircling them; a terrible gnawing pain shot up their spines and into their foreheads, exploding behind their eyes in a white-hot burst, a crazing agony. The chastisement lasted only a few seconds, all that was needed. The fire receded and disappeared into the blackness, silence resumed her reign, the hideous little theater regained their attention, dominated their wills—and no one chose to protest further.

The priest's ruination was next, unfolding relentlessly in three-dimensioned detail. The incident of his deepest shame was his part in the death of the young woman he had seduced thirteen years earlier. Mike's dismissal of the faulty brakes in his car was a discarded picture in the back of his mind as he wheedled his beautiful Cathy to go out for cigarettes; Cathy a few minutes later found herself in slow-motion terror, pumping frantically at the unresponsive brake pedal; the ghostly truck lights loomed up through the coastal fog; the slender arms were thrown protectively over her eyes, bulging in horror; and then there came the splintering impact, shards of glass imploding lazily inward, puncturing her face and hands, blood spewing out thick and sluggish from the gaping wounds. The steering wheel folded upwards as it crushed into her chest, its metal column proceeding on like a jagged pile driver to puncture the abdominal wall, the full, sensitive lips opening to release her final scream, disgorging instead a belching sound of blood and death.

"Damn you!" the choked whisper screamed from the tormented priest at the satin-draped table. "God damn you to eternal hell for this!"

With callous indifference the drama proceeded to a se-

147

ries of cameos at the graveside service: Cathy's mother collapsing in grief beside the precisely hewn rectangle of emptiness in the wet, dark earth that waited to receive her daughter's body; a haunting image of the tiny closed coffin containing the unborn male fetus, lying in silent accusation within the larger satin lined box beside its mother. Then the dirt, falling in slow heavy shovelful into the hole — *thump . . . thump . . . thump.*

The final scene was at the graveyard later that night: the man alone in the darkness, hunkered down beside the fresh, soft dirt of her grave, the glowing ember from his cigarette reflecting the deadness in his eyes. He flicked the butt away in a fiery arc, suddenly falling in a paroxysm of anguish to his knees, beginning to claw at the damp soil, aching to hold his love close one last time.

A shooting star passed overhead, like God flicking away His cigarette, in seeming mockery of Mike's pain.

"Fuck you!" he cried out in his agony, the middle finger of his right hand gesticulating wildly at the sky. He collapsed back onto the ground, clutching the cold earth in his arms, burying his face in its musty, unyielding dankness, wanting his forbidden woman. Slowly his hips began moving against the mound, pushing gently back and forth. His hand found his fly and pulled the zipper down, reaching into the opening to yank against the hardening flesh within. His motions became faster, more feverish, almost abusive. Then he rose up on his arms, shaking violently for a second before rolling over on his back, his shame and disgrace at last complete. Then, at last, the tears came.

Back in the seance room Mike's entire body was heaving with the same racking sobs — as much at having his degradation, his sacrilege, exposed so vividly before this company of friends and strangers as from the pain of reliving the episode.

But the unfeeling blue orb merely blinked out — already bored with the destruction of the priest and anxious to proceed with its next subject, who immediately began to appear in its cool depths.

It was Marija's turn this time. She gasped, knowing instinctively what was coming. The demon barker of this lurid sideshow had read her deepest thoughts and found the one thing she most dreaded having exposed, and that was exactly what began now to develop within the mini-world before them.

It was a picture of rampant, uncontrollable gluttony — a feeding frenzy, almost — the slender, attractive, well-groomed female executive almost unrecognizable in a huge, dowdy housecoat, secreted away in the kitchen of her campy Victorian flat, compulsively gorging on unbelievable quantities of virtually anything edible she could get her hands on.

The follow-up scene was even more damning: MJ locking herself in her spotless, white-tiled bathroom, running the bathwater to drown out the sound, then sticking a well-manicured finger down her throat and vomiting all the undigested food back up again, heaving out huge, lumpy volumes of the partially chewed and barely digested feast with a horrid retching noise, spattering it on the sides of the bowl, the toilet rim — splashback from the smelly, slimy mess landing on her face, her arms, her lustrous dark brown hair.

Once her stomach was empty she began to wipe away all the evidence with a practiced, businesslike air — scrubbing the toilet and surrounding floor with a strong-smelling disinfectant. Then she stripped off the soiled robe, turned up the shower hot and steamy, and scrubbed herself from head to toe until all traces of food residue and

149

odor had been vanquished, her secret safe.

The center stage dimmed for a minute—just long enough to allow a tiny surge of wishful thinking to push back the blade of despair from Marija's heart—then it gleamed wickedly and went on to show three, four, five more similar incidents in rapid succession, enough to obliterate all pretense that the first had been an isolated occurrence, making it abundantly clear that the woman went on such food rampages regularly, knowingly, even ritually.

Marija hung her head in shame, sickened with herself. She'd never before realized how awful she looked with her face contorted over the porcelain bowl, vomit spewing from her gaping mouth, running down her chin and hand. Even the expression of glazy-eyed avariciousness as she stuffed her face was disgusting—and the knowledge that the others had seen her this way, knew the truth, saw what a horrible greedy pig she really was and to what perverse lengths she would go to maintain her figure—this was unbearable. She could never face them again, never . . . especially not Joe, or Mike either. God, the expressions of horror and revulsion that must be on their faces!

But though she fought to resist, her head was lifted back up, her eyes forced to meet the others around the table. Surprisingly she saw only compassion in those faces—that and love. She flushed and crumbled under the burden of their understanding.

The next instant the room went completely black; a fierce rumbling shook the air about them, rattling the table, the chairs. Out of the inky depths above Marija's head two large, almond-shaped eyes blinked open, their fiery scarlet irises slashed vertically with evil slits, their gaze as cold and dead as a shark's. A wide, lipless mouth opened beneath the eyes, emitting a fetid rush of heat at the company, a dark wind smelling of some warm, over-ripe pocket of decay, a wind that blew their hair around, burnt their faces, parched their lips, gagged them. *Dragon breath.*

Marija was the only one who couldn't see what was behind her, but then she didn't need to: she already knew the touch of the beast.

Her mouth opened to release a scream: as it did, she could feel her features begin to change. Her nose felt thicker, wrinkly; her cheeks grew heavy, pushing up against her eyes, making her squint. Her ears tickled and didn't feel right, misplaced somehow, too high on her head, and her neck thickened, became weighty against the back of her skull. She tried to jerk her hands away from the others to feel her face, but they remained locked into the unyielding grip of the two men on either side of her.

Now the looks of horrified revulsion she'd been expecting to see on her companions' faces did appear, looks of open-mouthed fear and disgust unanimous among the five around the oval table. And suddenly she didn't need to feel her features to know what she'd been transformed into.

She opened her mouth once more to scream, but the noise she emitted was a terrified, high-pitched animal squeal. At the sound the red-eyed demon exploded with enormous amusement, a deep, rolling laughter that taunted and tormented the woman even further, its glee-fulness infecting and corrupting the others as well until they too began to snicker, then chortle, then erupt in helpless uncontrollable laughter at the bewildered swine face now bulging stupidly above Marija's silk blouse.

After a few minutes even the woman herself could not resist the infectiousness of their amusement; but the noises she made came out as more squeals, grunts, and snorts,

151

setting the rest off even more.

Finally, the insane laughter was abruptly cut off. The beast blinked once and Marija's normal features were restored; it blinked again and disappeared like the cheshire cat, his attention turned wholly to the imminent destruction of his last untarnished guest.

Joe's image rapidly took shape in the mystic spheroid — a Joe barely recognizable to those present in the gangly body of a pimply-faced adolescent, walking through the starry quiet of a country night. His footsteps echoed hollowly on the deserted sidewalk of the small community near his rural home. Joe's jaw was set, but his young eyes were uncertain as he reluctantly searched the darkened side streets for his father's pickup truck, sent by his eternally ailing mother to find and fetch her errant husband home.

A neon sign above the deserted truck stop flashed on and off, beckoning him forward. *Maynard's Diner — Good Food — 24 Hrs* it repeated over and over in bright red letters. He entered quietly, looking around: there was no one to be seen, although a jukebox blared loudly. A couple of half-full coffee cups sat on one of the small formica tables in a darkened corner, their contents still steaming.

He was about to leave when he heard a strange noise from the back of the restaurant. As he tiptoed through the swinging doors into the waitress station, a soft moan could be heard coming from one of the dry storage rooms at the rear of the building.

Pushing open the door, he stopped as if struck, his face drained of all color. His father, still on his hands and knees, turned to stare up at the boy, exposing in that moment the soft pink vulva glistening between a pair of full white thighs that belonged to the woman who had

152

been straddling him. Her short waitress skirt was hiked up over her ample hips, her panty hose dangling in a lumpy mass from one white-shod foot. She'd relaxed back onto the large sacks of flour when she saw the teenager, grinning lazily as she ruminated on a big wad of Juicy Fruit gum.

"What are you doing here?" his father hissed furiously. "Get out!"

Joe began backing away, but the woman's voice had already risen in protest, stopping him. "Wait a minute, honey . . . Bret, listen, if he leaves now he might . . ." and she whispered something in his father's ear. The older man listened thoughtfully, his hard anger softening slightly to be replaced by a slow, crafty smile.

"C'mere, son," he said. It was spoken gently, but it was a solid order, and Joe'd already had too much cuffing from this man during his young life to even consider disobeying.

"How old are you now, son—fourteen, fifteen?" the man asked, rising to put an arm around the teenager's bony shoulder.

"F-fifteen, sir," answered the desperately embarrassed boy, his eyes riveted to the blatantly exposed pubic area of the woman, who'd reclined again on the flour sacks, casually spreading her legs.

"Ever had a woman, son?" the older man inquired lightly. Joe couldn't answer.

" 'Bout time you became a man, dontcha think? Let's see if you've got the equipment." He reached his big, callused hand down and gave Joe's crotch a hard squeeze, feeling the already potent erection there.

"Hey, Maggie," his father sniggered, "the kid's got a hard-on for you."

"Oh yeah?" She smiled lasciviously, chewing on her

gum. "Let's see it."

"Take your pants off, boy," the burly man ordered genially. Joe froze, his erection softening.

"I said, drop 'em," the father snarled, yanking down the Levis from his slim hips.

"Not much of one," pouted the bleach-blonde, looking at his drooping organ, "but ol' Maggie can fix that up. Come here, honey." She swagged an index finger at him.

His father's hand was on his back, pushing. The blushing youngster stumbled forward, tripping over the pants around his ankles and sprawling clumsily across the hard, damp concrete floor. When he raised his head, he found himself face to face with the secret folds of flesh that covered the woman's sacred portal, his nose almost touching her skin.

The woman and his father broke up at this, collapsing in raucous guffaws while Joe's ears burned hot and red. He tried to get to his feet, but a soft pair of hands grabbed the sides of his head and a husky voice said low in his ear, "You're not going anywhere, are you, honey?" He looked up to see Maggie's face bent over him, her eyes glowing with an inner fire. "Lick it for me, won't you, baby?" she said softly, a pleading lilt in her voice.

"Huh?" the adolescent responded stupidly, shocked and confused.

"Lick it, baby, just lick it a little," she breathed, shoving his face into the soft, hot sweetness. His tongue reached out, tentatively at first, then more certainly as she moaned and pushed against him. He explored and tasted her, moving his tongue along the surface, probing her depths, his lips massaging and caressing the flesh. Suddenly she grabbed his hair even harder, pressing his head fully into her, moving her hips wildly against his mouth.

"There, there, there," she cried, "Oh God, oh!" She

154

shrieked, gave one last drawn-out cry, and fell back against the flour sacks, breathing in deep, shuddering sighs.

"You been givin' him lessons, Bret?" she teased between gasps, opening one eye. But Joe's father was lost in a lust of his own, his hand on his organ, his eyes unfocused, jerking furiously.

"Look, baby," she said, turning the boy's head with her soft palms, "let's watch your daddy gettin' off."

Joe did watch, alternately fascinated and repelled, unable to turn his gaze away, feeling the tension growing even more demanding in his already tortured loins.

When the older man had at last climaxed in a grunting, doubled-over spasm of release, the woman turned her attention back to Joe, whose own not yet fully developed penis was protruding from beneath him, swollen and distended. She smiled, bending forward to tease it gently with her tongue, and he felt an almost unbearable pressure building in his scrotum, coursing up the underside of his groin. Her full pink lips closed over the tip, moving it in and out of her mouth only once, and he exploded from every cell in his body.

As the roaring of blood in his ears slowly subsided, he heard another roar replacing it, the roar of laughter from his father as Maggie spat and wiped her mouth on the back of her hand.

"Quick little rabbit, ain't he?" she said, and dissolved in a fit of jeering giggles.

"Get out of here, little rabbit," his father said, slapping Joe's bare behind. "And keep your mouth shut, hear? You're as guilty as I am now, and don't you forget it!"

"And don't guilt just feel *good*, though?" Maggie taunted bawdily. Their laughter joined the confusion of pain and pleasure still churning through the boy.

155

As his tiny figure receded in the gloom, the globe once more darkened, this time remaining that way for nearly fifteen minutes—long enough for the embarrassed, restive participants in this night of horrors to begin to relax ever so slightly, a thin edge of hope beginning to lighten the dark horizon of their seemingly endless ordeal. Perhaps it was all over. Maybe this thing would free them, let them pick up the pieces of their shattered egos and limp away with their ruined lives.

But the evil presence controlling them noiselessly slithered through the surrounding abyss, his red eyes glowing in icy malice.

Now.

The orb ignited into new life with shocking suddenness, six tiny figures re-emerging in its center to play out the too-human secrets of their mortal counterparts, still trapped in their chairs around the table, unable to escape or prevent the oncoming show.

This time, like a thing gone wild with evil, the globe began portraying every sordid hidden act each one had ever committed, even their fantasies. It was a collage of man's weaknesses, his depravities, his hungers, guilts, and shame. Even those incidents they might have considered normal looked perverted and repulsive when put on gross display for all to view.

Most of the scenarios were sexual in nature, and gradually, under the continuous barrage of obscenities and stimulation, the six found themselves changing in their reaction to the incidents. First there had been revulsion and a desire to look away; this was replaced by a growing curiosity, and finally a perversely compelling attraction, a desire to take in every detail of the acts played out before them.

Against their will they began as well to experience a

tingling in their own sexual organs, an increasing hunger that took hold of them physically even as their minds protested and their moralities cried out against it.

They were being used, manipulated, defamed by flesh that was no longer in their control. They knew this, yet their miniaturized alter-egos provided the visual stimuli, their flesh responded, writhing and moaning. Their palms sweated against each other's grip, trying to break free, aching to ease their individual overwhelming needs. Thighs rubbed and pressed and squirmed, only stimulating the genital areas further in their efforts to obtain some sort of relief.

The more they gave in to these feelings the stronger and more uncontrollable the urges became, and the weaker grew their inner protestations of innate decency. They were becoming what the globe portrayed them to be, succumbing to it, embracing it.

The beast hidden behind his shield of darkness smiled in satisfaction. Soon he could release them, soon they would be ready — so lost in desire that their first act would be one of mindless mass copulation, like a den of snakes at the height of mating fever. After that, they would be his completely.

Then, unexpectedly, a voice screamed.

"Nemeroth! Ahriman! Lucifer! I . . I command you, be gone! *Go!* In the name of Ei, in the name of Baal, I command you to *go!*" The voice, Madame Le Beuc's, had begun as an hysterical but fervent scream of supplication to the powers of darkness for aid, brought up from some inner resource of resistance she didn't know she had. But it ended in an agonized shriek of pain and fear as her head, caught in a viselike grip by a pair of furious unseen hands, began to twist to the left. Farther and farther — obscenely, scarily far — it turned on its eroded cervical ver-

157

tebrae until, with a loud snap, it had turned completely around, facing backward on the neck away from the horrified gaze of the helpless onlookers.

Her body had begun to glow, surrounded in a reddish aura while the head continued to turn slowly through the rest of the cycle. As her face came back into view, the rest of the company gasped: Mildred's eyes were bulging sightlessly from their sockets, her blackened tongue protruding grotesquely from her red-painted cupid's-bow lips. Blood-tinged saliva dripped from the slack-hanging mouth and began to spray the satin tablecloth as the head continued to turn, to pick up speed, to spin. The flabby neck stretched taut as it twisted, like a washrag being wrung as Mildred Spencer's auburn-tressed cranium proceeded faster and faster through five, six, seven more revolutions. On the eighth the forces of torque and pressure exceeded the resiliency of the flesh and the head flew off like a sodden shot put. The wall behind materialized out of the void in time to meet it, the sound as it smacked against the solid surface a sickening crunch. Blood from the severed carotid artery spewed onto the table in great gushing pulses, poured from the jugular vein in dark red splotches on the wall and floor where the head had come to rest.

A fierce laugh rolled up from the depths of hell, joined by an insane tittering from the degraded souls of limbo who skittered nervously through the timeless mists beyond all finite places.

All at once a new voice—deep and commanding, yet at the same time feminine in an unearthly way—arose like a foreign entity in Marija's throat, and poured like thunder from her pale, quivering lips.

"Iblis!"

The laughter stopped, movement ceased. Within the central spheroid a shadowy, froglike face appeared, its

158

eyes glowering with a fiery crimson light.

"Iblis, persecutor of mankind, begone from this room!"

At the Vatican two medical professionals scurried for the large ward room where their famous patient lay: a monitoring device had begun to wail loudly, signaling a sudden, dangerous rise in the blood pressure of the frail holy man beneath the white sheets. Vials of medication and paper packages of sterile syringes were ripped open, the withered flesh punctured, veins filled with fluid medication to bring the bodily functions under control.

The frog-like creature withdrew further inside the globe at Marija's command, metamorphosing into a familiar dragon shape. His serpentine tail flailed angrily across the inner sky and a myriad of stars were created in its wake: he whipped the point of his tapered tail around in a show of defiance and anger, and the stars were drawn behind the movement in a luminescent stream, a dozen or so of them hurtling out of the orb to fall like burning splinters on the faces and hands of the onlookers.

"Iblis, I bind you in eternal hell!!" the woman shouted forcefully.

In a richly furnished apartment within the Vatican, a tall gray man of military bearing grabbed the sides of his temples in sudden agony. Queasy waves of hot and cold fear passed through him, then were gone. Momentarily shaken, he got up from the stiff little chair where he'd been reading and peered into the vanity mirror, pulling down his lower lids, inspecting his tongue. Finding nothing amiss, he shrugged, shook his head, and went back to his book.

Within the globe the dragon's tail whipped back and forth in total rage, drawing the stars into a funnel, a glowing maelstrom of highly charged energy particles.

"I, Lilith, command it!"

With a final burst of vengeance and hate the tail of the beast slued across the microcosmic violet sky, flinging the condensed tornadolike cluster of miniature stars into a laser stream of pure, intense power which shot out through the invisible walls of the disintegrating sphere, aimed for the heart of the young dark-haired woman. But her hand, suddenly freed from the grip of the men beside her, raised up, palm extended in protection.

The deadly beam arced in its path, veering away from the opposing force of her intent and into the forehead of the black man on her right. It hung there in the air, buzzing and sparking while the professor's body jumped and twitched as if impaled on a golden spike. Smoke began to curl upward from the singed, smoldering hole that had opened up between his eyes. As the beam went out in one final dazzling pulse of energy, Leroy Turner's body retched in a violent convulsion and collapsed to the floor with a heavy thud.

At that moment the paralyzing spell was lifted. What lights still remained intact flickered and came on. Those who occupied the inky depths of the abyss had returned to their own dimension.

The gambit had been made, but to whose advantage?

Chapter 12

Thursday, June 15th
Rome

At the precise moment the seance guests had been seating themselves around the satin-draped table in Madame Le Beuc's rundown house, more than seven thousand miles away Luigi Magliano had been slipping quietly out of his temporary quarters in the Vatican palace and into the chill, golden light of a Roman summer morning.

When the secret consistory had barred him from their middle-of-the-night conclave with the ailing Pontiff three hours earlier, he'd hung around the infirmary waiting for news. But once the tired and taciturn group of cardinals finally emerged, they would reveal nothing of what had occurred within other than to inform the physicians who had shared his silent vigil that the Pope had lapsed back into his coma and needed their attention.

Returning to his cold, barren room, the portly archbishop tossed and turned fretfully for the next two hours, his mind a turmoil of questions he couldn't quite phrase, before rolling out of the hard, narrow bed in defeat. He showered, shaved the thick stubble from his cheeks and chin, carefully groomed and twisted his large, droopy mustache, and dressed casually in a navy cardigan and slacks, then headed for the solace of a hearty breakfast beyond the city walls.

At that hour few people were about within the palace itself, but beyond its walls Luigi discovered a surprising number of visitors already milling about in the cool, quiet gardens and broad, sunlit avenues surrounding the Basilica. These early birds were mostly silent, standing alone or in little clusters around the grounds.

Perhaps news of the Pope's astonishing, if momentary, recovery had already reached the public somehow; or maybe it was nothing more than the daily growing concern of the faithful over the Holy Father's gradually worsening condition that brought them out at this hour in such numbers.

As he skirted the perimeter of the great circular plaza of St. Peter, walking beneath the huge, columned roof of the gallery that flanked the square, he noticed a flurry of newspeople and television cameras arriving through the central thoroughfare, emanating the nervous intensity that invariably sparked their actions when they knew something was up.

The archbishop quickened his pace, skittering through the arched portals of the colonnade and out onto a side street before he could be spotted and cornered for an interview, heading for a small neighborhood cafe where he often took meals when in Rome.

As he passed a corner newsstand, he saw the reason for the excitement: the early morning edition of *Il Messaggero* blasted a red banner headline in three-inch letters: *MIRACLE AT VATICAN*. Below, in smaller black letters, it added: *Il Papa awakens from death sleep*.

The nuncio handed a two-hundred-lire note to the sleepy-looking newsboy and folded the thin paper under his arm. Characteristically, even though avidly curious to find out what it had to say, he did not open it again until he was seated at a solitary table in a nearby empty cafe, his first cup of coffee at his elbow.

The article, he quickly discovered, was short on fact and long on speculation. "Reliable sources" within the Vatican had apparently contacted the news office shortly before press time to inform them of the Pope's sudden, inexplicable return to consciousness from what had apparently been a state of irreversible brain death. It mentioned a "secret emergency meeting" held in the Pontiff's hospital room, attended by a half dozen or so "top Church officials" immediately following the mysterious revivification.

The paper went on to speculate as to the causes for the Pope's spontaneous recovery, and the possible import of the meeting, but it was obvious reporters had had little to go on, were not even aware—at least at the time they went to press—that the Holy Father had subsequently lapsed back into the deep coma, no better off than before.

Just at that moment his breakfast arrived—three eggs swimming in butter, surrounded by four fat Italian sausages—and he set the paper and its concerns aside momentarily while he attacked his food.

He reread the article carefully, sipping his third cup of black coffee as he scanned the write-up for hidden information. It contained enough medical data to lead Magliano to believe the "reliable source" had been one of the attending physicians, though whether the doctor had called the newspaper directly or merely confided to a wife or associate who'd then leaked it to the press was uncertain.

On his return, the archbishop checked in at the papal secretary's suite of offices and was immediately ushered into the cardinal's private chamber.

"I've been looking for you, archbishop!" The cardinal nodded at the folded paper in Magliano's hand. "Apparently you've seen it. I'll need you to handle the press personally today, and probably for the next couple of days as well. I'll be tied up."

He handed the startled nuncio a typewritten sheet. "This is the basic text of a briefing you are scheduled to give the media today at ten AM. That gives you precisely," he paused, checking the gold Swiss watch on a chain beneath his vestments, "one hour and thirty-six minutes to prepare yourself. I'd like you to read through this now so you can ask any questions that occur to you, offer any suggestions for editing or rewording that you'd feel more comfortable with. When we have it complete, I'll give it to Deacon Frascati to retype . . . he'll also run off a number of copies for you to hand out at the briefing."

Archbishop Magliano looked down at the messy typewritten page in his hands and began to read. In a moment his skin paled and he felt a cold, sickness wash over him. His knees gave way and he sat heavily in a nearby chair, continuing to read intently. *Quillans a cardinal!* The idea struck him as so terribly wrong that he found it hard to concentrate on the rest of the release.

Its text, written in terse, unemotional journalistic prose, gave a chronological account of the previous night's momentous events in subdued understatement. It began with the "spontaneous revival" of the Pope at precisely 2:46 AM, followed by the subsequent summons to his bedside of the secretary of state, the six cardinal bishops of Rome, the patriarch of the Eastern Orthodox churches, and the archbishop of San Francisco—mentioning as an aside that these nine notables had been sequestered in the Vatican palace close at hand for the past few days at the Pontiff's request.

The brief went on to state that there followed a secret consistory lasting approximately 35 minutes during which Pope Marcus appointed the American archbishop Robert F. Quillans a titular cardinal of Rome. This was the point where Magliano's attention stuck. He read and reread the account.

The Holy Father, the press release continued, then gave his cardinals certain instructions regarding the administration of the Church and his own medical maintenance during the remainder of his illness before finally relapsing into a coma.

It concluded by stating that a complete transcript of the Pope's message during this incredible meeting was being prepared from the tape recording made at bedside. This message—which contained "news of immense importance to the Christian world"—would be made public in a few days, in accordance with His Holiness's specific directives.

Magliano looked up at Cardinal Mandice. "I suppose there's no point in my asking for an elucidation of this last point?" he enquired.

"I'm afraid not." The secretary smiled sympathetically.

"Well, then," the archbishop replied, "I'm sure the newspeople will have a lot of medical questions on this; may I have Doctor Frederico present to field those for me?"

"Certainly, good idea!" agreed the cardinal, relaxing somewhat, now that the burden of public relations was being removed from his overwhelming schedule of responsibilities.

"Now, this part, about the members of last night's secret consistory having been sequestered here at the Pope's request—the reporters will surely ask how and when such an order could have been given, considering the gravity of His Holiness's condition almost from the onset. . . ."

"Yes, yes, of course," said the cardinal. "Here, let me see that." He took the paper from Magliano, studied it for a moment, then scribbled something on the page and handed it back. His annotation consisted of a couple of succinct phrases explaining how the Pontiff had made this request from his bed just before slipping into unconsciousness five days earlier.

The Italian archbishop glanced through it. "That'll do,"

he nodded, looking up before adding hesitantly, "There's one other point here, though." He looked back down at the paper to hide his emotions, trying hard to keep his voice neutral. "Regarding the appointment of Archbishop Quillans to cardinal; isn't that a trifle . . . irregular?"

"In what way, archbishop?" There was a strained edge to the normally soft and patient voice.

"I'm not sure. Having him present at his own nomination, for one thing, rather than notified later through a formal biglietto," the larger man suggested, feeling a thin film of perspiration begin to form on his brow. "They'll surely have some questions about that . . . at least the more learned will. I just want to be prepared to answer them properly." He tugged at his mustache with an apologetic grimace. "Also, they'll most likely ask where and when the formal public ceremony of investiture will be held, things of that nature."

"Yes." The white-haired statesman cleared his throat, begging time. "Well, you may tell them that the date of the public ceremony has not yet been set." Magliano was making notes in the margin. "As for the other irregularity you mentioned, just say it was done this way at the Holy Father's behest, owing to unusual circumstances, and constitutes no more than a minor alteration of protocol necessitated by the gravity of the situation." He finished the statement with a satisfied air, pleased with the way it sounded.

As the thick, ornately carved door closed behind him, the archbishop gave one more cursory look at the rough draft in his hands and then, on an impulse quite foreign to his usual conservative nature, inserted the adjective "controversial" before the words "Archbishop Quillans" in the text, then quickly handed the paper to the secretary's assistant before he could talk himself out of it.

While Deacon Frascati was busy preparing the final copies of the press release, Magliano scuttled to his room to change into something more appropriate in which to greet the media.

He strode into the banquet hall at 9:55. It was bustling with men and women, cameras, lights, sound equipment, and filled with a buzz of excitement: soft murmurs, loud chatter, a woman's voice raised in laughter, the whirr of a camera, the squawk of the PA system being tested, the high-pitched skreel of feedback from the mike. And the pounding of his heart.

A half-hour later the meeting was over. The media representatives had been only mildly obnoxious, accepting the information he'd imparted with a minimum of respectful nitpicking, laughing at his droll jokes. The Italian archbishop was enjoying the euphoria of relief as he made his way back through a rear exit, heading for the office he'd been assigned for public relations functions, when a woman's voice, vaguely familiar, hailed him from a darkened corridor.

"Archbishop Magliano?" It was almost a whisper. He turned as the woman stepped out of the shadows. He immediate recognized the young reporter who'd accosted him and Patriarch Synarus at the airport a few days earlier.

"Ah, Signorina DiGuccione, if memory serves," he greeted her with a stately bow.

"Why yes, Your Excellency," she stammered. "How kind of you to remember."

She'd toned down her makeup considerably, he noted with fatherly approval, wondering if someone had taken her aside and given her a few pointers. She was also more polite, almost deferential, in her attitude toward him now. The overall effect was to make her seem even younger, almost childlike in appearance.

"How may I serve you?" he asked graciously.

"I — well, a couple of questions occurred to me in there," she indicated the briefing room, "but I wasn't sure if it

167

would be proper to bring them up . . . at least not formally, in front of all the others, you know. It's more a matter of personal curiosity . . . or maybe ignorance," she explained. "Besides, I wanted to assure you that I'd keep your answers off the record, if you wish."

He smiled despite himself; she certainly was a timid creature. How could she ever hope to compete with that wolf pack in the other room? Anyway, what could be so problematic about a private interview? Curiosity got the better of him and he invited her to follow him to his office.

Once they were safely behind closed doors he turned to her. "You may ask your questions, signorina," he said, showing her to a chair, "but your tape recorder must remain off. I also reserve the right to refuse comment, or to insist that any answers I do give be kept in strictest confidence. Agreed?"

She nodded. "Well," she began, sitting primly on the edge of the stiff wooden chair, "it's about the new cardinal-designate, Robert Quillans."

"Ah," the archbishop faltered slightly, feeling a nervous tension begin to prickle his scalp at the very mention of the man.

"You used the word . . ." she shuffled through her notes, wanting to get it correct, " 'controversial' to describe him. May I ask in what way he is controversial?"

"Perhaps it was a poor choice of word," Magliano hedged, truly uncomfortable now. He should have known better than to include that dig at Quillans; it had created a hole into which he himself was now in danger of falling. His neck had turned hot beneath his clerical collar . . . he hoped it didn't show.

"Couldn't you give me at least a clue as to where I could begin to look for background data," she wheedled coyly, blinking up at him, "some idea which of his activities or views might be considered . . . questionable?"

"He is—*was*—in charge of the first and thus far only Roman Catholic archdiocese to purposely employ an avowed homosexual as a parish priest," Magliano blurted. "He's also been quite vocal, if not outright militant, in his liberalized views on abortion, birth control, and divorce!"

The words had come spilling out with more vehemence than he'd intended, indeed, more than he'd realized he felt. But his outburst seemed only to amuse the girl, who was madly scribbling on her notepad. He took a deep breath, getting hold of his emotions. "I do not wish to be quoted on this, Signorina DiGuccione—neither directly nor indirectly. I am merely pointing you toward the avenues for further exploration as you requested. Is that understood?"

"Perfectly, Your Excellency. You don't much like him though, do you?"

"Let's just say that I'm of the old school," Magliano smiled faintly. "Now then, if there's nothing else . . ." This conversation was making him decidedly edgy; he rose from his chair to end it.

"No, not really," the brown-eyed woman sighed, getting up, "but would you correct me on one more thing, if I'm wrong?"

The middle-aged Italian shrugged noncommittally as he came around the desk, determined to escort the reporter out as rapidly as grace would allow.

"Doesn't Pope Marcus the Third *also* ascribe to these modernized views?" she persisted, moving forward under the gentle but persistent pressure of Luigi's hand against her back. "As a matter of fact, isn't he the one who authorized the new policy allowing homosexuals into the ministry?"

"Yes," the archbishop acknowledged tersely, reaching for the doorknob. It didn't help that she was sticking her nose into areas that were, for him, deeply sensitive.

"One last question, Your Excellency," she begged, holding her palm against the doorjamb in quiet resistance. "It's been rumored that many of the more conservative clergy secretly opposed this new liberal stance by the church. Some even feel that the Sacred College might have erred in their last Papal selection. How do *you* feel about that?"

"I'm sorry, no further comment," Magliano answered coldly, suppressing a sudden urge to shake the impertinent young reporter. He opened the door wide and, abandoning all pretext of diplomacy, virtually shoved her through it.

His last image of the woman, imposed on his mind like a photograph, was her ostensibly innocent face betrayed by a cool spark of knowingness in the big, soft eyes, a hint of sardonic smugness playing about the sensitive lips. He shut the door with a hard, angry snap.

"How dare she!" he fumed, pacing around the empty office. "What does she know of our faith and its tests? How can a layperson ever presume to understand the conflict between a profound desire to support our chosen Pope as the divinely ordained head of the Christian world, and the equally passionate need to defend the basic moral tenets of our religion which *he* seems, even from his deathbed, to threaten with extinction?"

He walked over to one of the tall leaded-glass doors that opened onto a small private garden and banged it gently with the heels of his hands, leaning his forehead against the coolness for a few minutes. He looked up at the ceiling beseechingly. "We're just the watchmen, Lord, not the architect. How can we know which is the right solution?"

Then he leaned his arms heavily against the glass door and, much to his own astonishment, began to cry.

Unbeknownst to Magliano, deep within the vaulted caverns of the Sistine Chapel a secret conclave—its sole purpose a sham ritual of election for the pre-selected "Auxiliary Pope"—was just getting under way. And there was at least one other Catholic official who shared his gnawing concerns.

Cardinal Bertini, the energetic fifty-six-year-old Bishop of Frascati, had prayed fervently for divine guidance during the Mass of the Holy Ghost which preceded their procession to the conclave. But now that the moment was at hand, he felt his inner doubts still eating away at his resolve.

As Camerlingo it had fallen upon him to oversee this special election, directing all preparations and managing its proceedings. It was also customary for the person holding his office to make a brief introductory speech before the first secret ballot was cast, and Bertini had spent the early morning hours following Pope Marcus's resurrection and subsequent relapse trying to compose a suitable message, one which proclaimed with awe and reverence the importance of the roles they were about to play in this ongoing miracle.

But as the light of day erased the metaphysical realities of the night, the dumbstruck wonder he'd felt immediately following the miraculous consistory had slowly dissipated until he was left with not just uncertainty, but a growing, unnamed alarm, one which had intensified during the brief investiture ceremony this morning at which Robert Quillans was presented with his cardinal's robe and ring.

He simply did not like the man.

Now he stood at the dais before the eight other cardinals—tiny figures in the majestic nave—and tried to force the words of invocation from between his stiff, dry lips, the writing blurring in and out of focus as the paper shook in his hands. Myriads of painted angels and saints looked down from all sides, Michelangelo's children, waiting in silent judgment on his decision.

"Fellow servants of God," he began, "we are drawn to-gether here today under most unusual circumstances, to vote on an act which has no precedent in the history of our church." He sighed, gave a slight shake of his head, and crumbled the prepared text in his clenched fist. "So much for that," Bertini decided.

Looking up earnestly at his small, elite audience, he spoke now from his heart. "Bear that in mind while you are casting your vote today, I beseech you. Remember that the Holy Roman Church is far more than any one man, any one decree . . . no matter how great, how necessary or expedient that man or decree might seem. Our religion was established on the word of God as com-municated directly to His apostles through His only-be-gotten son Jesus Christ. It was founded on sacred laws—moral laws—which must be upheld and enforced despite the pressures of corrupt societies and temporal needs, if we are ever to find a place with Him in heaven."

His eloquent voice had begun to waver, taking on a pleading note; his eyes shifted nervously from one to an-other of the faces below, faces whose expressions ranged from the confused expectancy of those still waiting for him to give benediction to their task, to the horrified disappro-bation of those who realized he was not about to.

"We must balance in our minds and souls these tenets which make up the bedrock of our religion against the unusual undertaking we have been assigned to complete today."

Quillans shifted uncomfortably in his seat: what the hell was Bertini up to? The election should have been a mere formality. Now this man was attempting to cast doubt in the minds of the conclavists. The Papal designate sent out a random mental intention, a thought seeking another mind willing to voice it as its own. He must stop this diatribe before it caused any real damage.

"What are you getting at, Cardinal Bertini?" It was the

sharp authoritarian voice of Cardinal Falliano, Dean of the Sacred College. "Are you suggesting we disregard the true word of God so that you can remain within the comfortable confines of your old, outdated dogmata? Can you still deny the infallibility of the Pope, question the Doctrine of Divine Assistance, after last night's miracle? For it *surely* was no less than that!"

The tall, white-haired Bishop of Ostia had risen to his feet as he spoke, leaning forward in a challenging manner, his voice raw with emotion. "Times change, Cardinal Bertini, and our religion must express that change, must adapt to the present needs of the people, if we are to remain a viable force in the world."

He turned his attention to the scandalized faces of the other cardinal bishops. Invoking his ultimate authority as Dean of the College of Cardinals, he called for an immediate vote. "Please remove yourselves to the balloting areas at once," he ordered. "The question before us is whether or not to respect the sacred directive we received last night"—he cast a withering look in the camerlingo's direction—"to elect Cardinal Robert F. Quillans Auxiliary Pope of the Holy Roman Catholic Church. A two-thirds majority, as for any Papal election, is all that is needed to carry the motion."

The cardinals rose obediently to their feet, stunned by the extraordinary outbursts, and began moving toward their individual canopied thrones situated around the walls of the enormous chapel.

The close-cropped, steely-gray head of the American delegate bowed in apparent devotions within his booth, but a smile of tremulous excitement betrayed the set of his lips. A sharp eye stole secret glances from a part in the filmy curtains to ensure he would not be the first to emerge and cast his ballot.

When two had gone before him, he folded his own lengthwise and moved slowly to the altar. He knelt, observing the ritual prayer, before placing his vote in the gold chalice residing on a table in front of the chancel.

It was more than a half-hour later when the last of the conclavists finally emerged from his canopied throne to complete the first round of voting.

The secretary of state came ceremoniously forward, knelt, and prayed for what seemed an endless time before finally removing the scrutinies from the large gold cup. He counted the ballots once, then carefully a second time while Quillans seethed beneath his cool demeanor, wanting to shriek in exasperation. At last the diminutive statesman moved to the center of the aisle and raised the chalice in his hands, facing them. "The vote is five ayes, four nays," he announced without emotion. "We have no decision in this ballot."

Quillans' gray eyes darkened, narrowed; he scanned the group angrily, trying to pick out the dissenters. Bertini, with his smug expression, was one, that was certain. Equally sure was the fact that Dean Falliano was not. Of the six remaining cardinals, three had voted against his confirmation into office. He *must* find out who they were before the next vote was cast.

He studied their faces without appearing to: a quick glance photographed the details of each countenance. Then, closing his eyes, he brought the picture back for an intuitive judgment on what the expression conveyed. Cardinal Capione, the eldest of those present, appeared upset and bewildered; Cardinal Salini, bald and palsied, was open-mouthed in disbelief. Scratch these two, he decided.

The other elderly cardinal, Malagio of Belletri, was harder to read. Even after a second look, Quillans couldn't be sure whose side the old man favored, or if he was even fully aware of what they were voting on. He could have cast a negative ballot simply out of habit — or in senile confusion. By the time Quillans gave up trying to figure him out, it was too late to interpret the rest of the faces; their initial reactions to the disclosure had already receded beneath the practiced decorum of their holy office.

With only one more "aye" needed to secure his victory, the San Franciscan sought to find an area of wavering confusion among the remaining three cardinals in question, one that he might turn to his advantage.

Almost at once the tall, scholarly patriarch of Alexandria rose to his feet, signaling a desire to address the group. Quillans slipped a long, well-manicured hand across his own upper jaw, concealing the involuntary display of pride that bent and parted his thin lips over the even, white teeth. It was getting easier all the time to control the wills of these high holy men . . . and he realized with some amusement how weak and uncertain in their faith they really were. He had no such doubts as to his own powers, nor of the existence and strength of the One who gave them to him.

The papal secretary gave a formal nod of recognition to the speaker, who then turned his attention to the Bishop of Frascati. "May I enquire of our esteemed Cardinal Camerlingo," he asked in a thickly accented but exceedingly gentle voice, "as to the exact nature of his reservations about carrying out the Motu Proprio we were given by Pope Marcus last night? Before you answer, Cardinal Bertini," he added, holding up his long, slender palm in a staying motion, "I wish to state that I personally do not find anything very threatening to the foundations of our Church in electing an Auxiliary Pope while the true Pope is too disabled to carry out the functions of his holy office. There have been a number of major changes in the administrative and electoral procedures surrounding the Papacy since its inception—some far more drastic and controversial, I think, than this current proposal—but the office itself has survived and continued to perform its duties in an unbroken line since St. Peter." He was wagging his head solemnly, his left hand stroking his beard, a wise expression in his black eyes. "Is it, perhaps, not the election of an Auxiliary Pope per se, so much as the personalities involved, that troubles your heart?"

"An astute and very . . . *candid* observation, Patriarch," Bertini admitted with a stiff bow, irritated and defensive now. "It is, in fact, this particular candidate's outspoken, almost maverick, stand on certain key issues that concerns me most.

"Specifically?" prompted Synarus, his face betraying no bias toward one view or another.

"Homosexuality, for one," Bertini retorted bluntly. "Cardinal-designate Quillans is known as the originator of the proposal to reverse the Church's moral position on this blatantly unnatural, hedonistic, and unsanctified act. And once it *was* officially reversed, he immediately gave over a parish in his diocese to an avowedly homosexual priest, who promptly filled the services with an unabashedly homosexual congregation!" His voice had risen in anger as he spoke, his last statement nearly a shout. Now he fell back in uncomfortable silence.

A murmur ran through the small gathering. Bertini felt the weight of disapproval at his obtrusive attack on one of their own. Whether he was right or wrong did not matter—it was unseemly and unforgivable to have brought it up in this manner, right in front of the man in question, who offered no defense other than his humble, downcast expression.

The camerlingo suddenly felt quite alone, estranged from his fellows, and in that isolation less sure of his own stand. Quillans, quick to sense his advantage, sent another thought flying into a weaker mind to be expressed.

"I think in all fairness we should allow Cardinal Quillans to defend his views." It was the mellow, reasonable voice of Secretary Mendice.

"Thank you, Your Eminence," the American said, rising

smoothly and with quiet authority. He looked from one man to the next, making eye contact, his expression warm, forbearing; he wanted them to feel good about him.

He was an artful, confident, convincing speaker. He was quickly able to move the cardinal bishops to compassion for the homosexuals in question, painting a picture of poor souls trapped in bodies that betrayed their innate striving to be good.

"Jesus came to free the sinners, not the saints," he proclaimed in a resonant voice, nodding his head to draw his audience into nodding with him. "He can save these sinners only if we first open our doors to them." His eyes sought theirs again, finding the desired agreement—and even a certain degree of shame for their previously uncharitable attitude.

He had them now; he knew it. Time for the coup de grace.

"As for the priest in question," he nodded toward Bertini with a conciliatory look, "to continue to refer to him as a homosexual would be to deny the power of the Holy Spirit in his life. It is true that at one point in his youth he found himself pulled toward the agonies of homosexual preference. But with the great compassion and understanding of his own parish priest, whom he had served as an altar boy, he was turned from his self-destructive path and taken into the hands of God. Then, forsaking all sexual activities, natural or unnatural, he entered the priesthood, hoping to save others like him through his ministry. How, I ask you, can one be called a homosexual who has taken the vows of celibacy as part of his Holy Orders?"

Once again he looked into the face of each cardinal bishop, his expression kindly, conveying tolerance, forgiveness for their lack of trust, their wavering faith. And he saw their eyes respond, the last shreds of doubt disappear.

The conclave recessed for a brief lunch, then they returned to the primary nave of the Sistine Chapel and their separate thrones for a period of silent prayer.

The second vote, taken at 3 PM, was unanimous. The former archbishop of San Francisco had, in less than twenty-four hours, risen first to cardinal and now to the active head of the Roman Catholic Church, the most powerful, most influential, and richest religious body in the world.

Chapter 13

Thursday, June 15th
San Francisco

After the investigating officer's final admonition not to leave the Bay area, Mike, Joe, and Marija were escorted by a wedge of patrolmen through a barrage of popping flashbulbs, jabbing microphones, and shouted questions to an unmarked car behind the precinct headquarters.

"Where to?" the driver asked impersonally once the doors were locked against the demanding crowd of reporters.

A television camera pushed up against the rear window. Marija cringed and turned her head into Joe's chest. Mike studiously ignored it, giving the driver directions to the rectory. "I don't think they'll bother us there," he said to no one in particular.

The events of the last ten hours had left the three totally spent, drained of all energy, wrung dry of emotion. The only thing any of them wanted now was a safe haven in which to rest, to talk it out—a period of respite to regroup their weary minds and spirits.

The seance's horribly lethal climax seven hours earlier had left the trio dazed. For an indeterminate period of time they'd simply sat in place staring out at the nightmarish reality around them, seeing nothing.

It was Joe who'd pulled out of it first, his eyes slowly bringing into focus the inert form of Mrs. McGilvroy slumped over the table across from him, her slack lips drooling a wet stain on the satin cloth beneath her cheek.

"Mike!" he'd yelped, bringing the bearded priest around. Muldoon had given an anguished cry, bent over his stricken housekeeper, and fumbled for her wrist, checking her pulse.

Marija had begun to struggle her way to reality at that moment, just far enough to begin a keening wail of hysteria. As the noise increased, Joe'd slapped her hard and her screams had dissolved into quiet, wrenching sobs. He'd turned his attention back to Mike, letting her cry it out.

"She's alive!" Mike whispered hopefully, lifting his head.

"I'll go call an ambulance. And the police." As Joe scrambled up, anxious to be out of there, his gaze fell on the bodies of the other two members of their group, contorted and motionless on opposite ends of the room. At the head of the table the decapitated corpse of Madame Le Beuc was still draining blood from the severed arteries and veins of the twisted neck. Joe gagged and leapt backward, the heel of his shoe catching the rung of his chair and sending him sprawling. As he lifted up on his elbows, he found himself face to face with the bulging eyes and protruding tongue of the dead medium's missing head, which had rolled to the corner of the room

The strangled cry trying to force its way from his constricted throat sounded more animal than human. He scrabbled backward in horror, grabbing the wall for support, tearing his gaze forcefully away from the lurid fascination of death. He edged around the far wall, pressing close as he slipped quickly past the other corpse, still smoldering from the burnt round hole in the center of his forehead, a third eye between the pair staring sightlessly out from their bloodshot rims.

The first officials to arrive on the scene were two uniformed patrolmen who'd been cruising the adjacent block when the call came through. The in-charge was a street-tough black cop who'd flashed his badge importantly as he bullied through the door, then scanned the dimly lit room with the bright, wide beam of his flashlight. As the spot focused on the headless medium, his partner, a young, blond, baby-faced rookie, took one look and promptly threw up all over the floor.

"Get the fuck outta here with that shit," the black cop said in disgust, chewing hard on the cigarette clenched between his teeth, "and call for back up, *if you think you can manage it.*"

He quickly moved the beam off the grotesque form, shining it slowly across the floor until it illuminated the other body spread-eagled backward at the opposite end of the room. "Shee-it, another one!" he exclaimed, coming around the table for a closer look.

"Holy God, it's the professor—you fucks have killed the professor!"

His gun, a magnum, was drawn before the words were fully out of his mouth. At his direction Joe helped the still sobbing MJ to her feet and joined Mike in assuming the position against the west wall. The officer rapidly frisked each man in turn.

He was beginning a more thorough search of the woman when the paramedics arrived. The ambulance crew had already removed Mrs. M before the first wave of rumple-suited detectives and crime lab boys arrived, their portable spotlights igniting the room in a merciless glare.

During the body search Marija had stopped her blubbering and lapsed into an apathetic, docile state, but when the dazzling lights exposed the blood pooled in ugly brownish-red blotches — not just on the walls, table, and floor, but all over their faces and clothing as well — her voice erupted from her throat in an endless shattering scream.

"Shut that fuckin' broad up!" the detective in charge growled to a younger assistant, shifting a stale cigar in his mouth. Just then a series of flashbulbs went off like firecrackers: it was the *Chronicle*'s crime report unit, who'd followed the detectives over from police headquarters, smelling a story.

"Keep outta my way, Rooney," the chief warned, signaling for the two uniformed patrolmen to escort the reporter out. MJ had now stopped her terrible screaming and was crying wretchedly onto the blue polyester jacket of the assistant investigator, who patted her on the shoulder helplessly, looking embarrassed.

The older detective turned to Mike, looking him up and down suspiciously as he lit the well-chewed cigar between his teeth. "You really a minister?"

"Yes, sir."

"One of them flaky cults?"

"I beg your pardon?"

"Are you with one of the 'new religions' that seem to be sprouting like fungus all over our fair city, or are you what I might call 'legit,' " he explained, rewording his question with carefully bridled sarcasm.

"I'm a Roman Catholic priest," Mike answered indignantly, "pastor of St. Jude's parish, over on Fell." He proffered a hand which the other man pointedly ignored, instead continuing to look at him with skepticism.

"You have anyone who can verify that?" he asked from

182

behind a cloud of thick, brownish smoke.

"Certainly, call the parish; my housekeeper will . . . oh," he stopped, remembering.

"What?"

"She was here tonight, with us. They took her to the hospital just before you arrived."

"Fine, just fuckin' fine. Okay, Father, assuming for the moment you *are* one—do you mind telling me just what the hell went on here tonight?"

"A seance," the priest replied. "It was being conducted for the psychological benefit of the young woman. Something went wrong."

"I'll say!" the other man snorted humorlessly, looking around at the carnage. "So who did this? You guys get mad when the old broad and her shill wouldn't refund your money or somethin'?"

"No, no," Mike shook his head. Tears were beginning to well up in his eyes, wanting release from the turmoil of emotion which he'd been holding so tightly to him.

"It was the devil!" Marija cried out, startling them all. "It was straight-out-of-hell fucking Satan that did it! And it's my fault he did, all my fault," she wailed, tears flowing down her face. Joe caught her in his arms, holding her protectively. The younger detective looked relieved to be rid of her.

"You gotta be shittin' me!" the fat-jowled investigator exclaimed in disbelief, looking from one then to the other. Joe shook his head, stroking MJ's hair against his chest. "She's right," he whispered. Mike nodded in agreement.

"Take 'em downtown," the older man sighed. "Get their statements, check out their ID's, any wants, records, the works. I'll finish up here and be down by the time you're done."

The formal interviews at headquarters were private, polite affairs, after which their signed and sworn statements

183

were taken apart word by word: belittled, poked at, questioned and requestioned for hours—the three interrogators assigned to the case taking turns trying to break down the stories of the separated witnesses throughout the long night.

Mike was finally allowed a brief respite to phone the hospital at 4:30 AM, when he learned to his relief that Mrs. McGilvroy had suffered only a mild stroke. Her condition was listed as serious but stable. He'd begged to be allowed to see Joe and Marija to share the good news, but no such freedom was permitted. Obviously they were all being kept apart in compliance with some standard of investigative tech, but this was carrying it too far, he decided, slipping into a sullen funk. He refused to answer any more of their inane questions.

Marija had already given up trying to convince her inquisitors of her truthfulness. She laid her head on the dirty, cigarette-scarred table and mumbled "I already told you that" through a steady drizzle of forlorn, exhausted tears each time she was asked another of the same old questions.

Joe, on the other hand, had resorted to sarcastic irony—changing his answers absurdly whenever he was asked something he'd fully responded to at least ten times.

It was after 6 AM when the trio was finally brought together in the senior detective's office, which stank of sweat, stale coffee, old cigar smoke, and frustration.

"The preliminary reports are back from Forensics and Pathology," he said, picking up a sheaf of typewritten notes held together with an oversized paper clip. He sighed, moving his narrow, reddened eyes from face to face with the air of a man who has found a bag of burning dog shit on his front porch—wishing he could kick it, but not wanting the stink on his shoes.

"I find what I read in here hard to believe," he admit-

184

ted, lighting a cigar and slowly, carefully blowing the exhalation from his first good draw in their direction. Marija choked obligingly, her fist against her mouth.

"The medical examiner states that the male victim was initially suspected to have been killed by a gunshot wound, said projectile thought to have entered through the prefrontal area of the brain approximately one inch above the ethmoid . . . the bridge of his nose," he explained, looking up from beneath his heavy scowling brows. "However, on closer inspection, the pathologist could find no signs of posterior egress by the offending particle, nor did subsequent X-rays reveal the bullet to be lodged anywhere within the cranial, thoracic, or even lumbar cavities." He looked up, a wry smirk on his face. "Gunshot wound with no bullet . . . very cute.

"A craniotomy was then performed and an initial pathological survey of the damage to the brain tissue itself. The cortex was found to be virtually disintegrated, with a heavy layer of black residue lining the dura mater next to the skull; chemical analysis of this ash has not yet been completed. Additionally, the normal composition of the white matter beneath the cortex was deteriorated into a pulplike consistency, with deep lesions reaching into the brain stem."

"In short, at this point we have no weapon, no known device capable of causing the kind of trauma responsible for the death of the male victim. As for the second victim, the female," he sighed again, looking like he'd bitten a worm, "the pathologist reports that it would have taken the combined strength of at least two, possibly three well-muscled male adults to have exerted the degree of torque through brute force needed to cause the type of physical damage observed on the remains." Once again his beady eyes peered out wrathfully from beneath the bushy brows, pinning them like moths. "Mysteriously, no marks of any sort—from either fingers or a foreign device—were found on the woman's head, neck, or body. Cause of death is tentatively listed as 'decapitation by persons or objects unknown.' "

Despite the purposely gruesome way the detective was presenting his facts, Joe felt his tension beginning to ease as the coroner's report was read. Mike did too, nodding almost eagerly as if to say, "See, that proves we're telling the truth!"

But Detective Grogan, catching the look, jumped to his feet, slamming his beefy palm against the surface of the desk with a solid thwack that made everyone in the room jump. He leaned his face to within an inch of the priest's and opened up.

"If you think for one second that this means I buy any of the cockamamie bullshit you people have been trying to shovel down my throat for the past five hours, you are out of your ever-lovin' minds!" he screamed.

Satisfied, he backed off, slumped against his gray metal desk, and continued in a dangerously soft voice.

"As far as I'm concerned, you pussies are *it*. All we've got to do is figure out how you did it, and believe me, we will." He pointed his cigar at them threateningly. "Legally we can't hold you, not yet. But don't even *think* about leaving town. I'll be in touch soon . . . bet on it. Sergeant Brown!" he bellowed through the stenciled glass door. "Is the police escort ready?"

"Yes sir," the man replied, poking his head around the door.

"Then get 'em the fuck outta my sight," he ordered, turning away in disgust, his head surrounded by a cloud of cigar smoke, his bleary eyes staring off into space.

The driver let them out in front of the white picket fence that enclosed the sideyard of the church and sped away.

Inside, the little house felt strangely cold and empty. No Mrs. McGilvroy. A lump came into Mike's throat. Marija excused herself almost immediately, desperate to shower and change out of her smelly, blood-spattered clothing. Joe and Mike flopped disconsolately across the two over-stuffed chairs in the parlor, a bottle of Scotch on the table between them. The men were too drained physically and emotionally to bother about social amenities or small talk, and the important things were still too emotionally charged to voice.

After a while MJ came back into the room dressed in a fresh pair of jeans and a pale blue shirt, her damp hair turbaned in a fluffy white towel. She looked somewhat revived, her eyes not quite so glazed-looking as they had been.

"Drink?" Joe offered, holding up Mike's bottle.

"I think I'd rather have coffee," she answered slowly, her voice tired and distant. "But don't get up. I'll make it myself."

While she was in the kitchen, Joe went to take a quick shower himself. When he returned in a borrowed pair of Mike's oversized denims, he found her tucked up in a corner of the sofa, sipping the hot brew moodily.

Silence hung like a heavy curtain across the room, separating each from the others.

"Well . . . how do you feel?" Joe asked finally, throwing the question randomly into the air for whoever chose to pick it up.

"Fine, MJ lied automatically. "Rotten" Mike complained simultaneously. They both laughed, a strained chortle. Joe smiled. Silence resumed.

Then, after a few minutes, Marija spoke up. "Actually, I don't feel as bad as I *think* I should under the circumstances. I'm kind of . . . ambivalent. I can't get over what we went through, the horrible deaths of those poor people." Her shoulders and upper body shook involuntarily as the pictures came into her mind. She took a deep breath. "At the same time, I also feel unaccountably peaceful, like I'm really quiet deep down inside."

Mike tipped his head quizzically, interested, but not quite sure of her meaning.

She lit a cigarette, inhaled deeply, letting the smoke out in a long, lazy curl above her head before continuing. She watched the smoke as she talked. Joe poured another drink; Mike stroked his beard reflectively.

"At first, after all those awful things that happened in the glowing ball . . . I mean *mine*," she clarified with a quick apologetic glance at the two men, "I felt so degraded, so sick at myself, I didn't think I could ever face anyone again. And then that last scene, those grisly murders, the police interrogations . . ." She took another deep drag off the cigarette, watching the ember glow redder, blowing the smoke considerately up over her shoulder. She shrugged eloquently. "But now that it's over, I feel — I don't know, clean, somehow. It's hard to explain." She tilted her head, chancing a brief glance at the priest. "Like someone took one of those little suction tubes — the kind dentists use to suck up your spit? — and poked around into all the dark, dirty little corners of my mind, pulling out all the old secrets, the garbage and guilt I'd tucked away over the years — just sucked it all up and got rid of it, you know?"

Joe had been only half listening, but suddenly he tensed with an odd excitement. She had just put into words his own experience, clarified his own feelings. He too sensed a cleanness, a quiet new freedom at the core of his being.

He looked over at Mike, saw a small movement of the lips beneath the heavy mustache growing into a wide grin as the priest also grasped the full reality of what the woman was saying.

188

"You know what I just realized?" the priest blurted out, drawing a sharp curious look from the woman. "This clean feeling we share . . . this is what a confessional is meant to accomplish, when it's done honestly and fully. All those years and I never really understood," he shook his head. "I just never knew."

Marija tried to smile, but ended up yawning instead.

"I think we could all use some sleep," the priest observed with a warm look at the bleary-eyed pair on the sofa. "Joe, why don't you and Marija use my bed. I'll just lie down out here on the couch."

Too tired to protest, the couple quickly accepted his offer and within moments of collapsing onto the small bed were fast asleep.

Mike crept into the room a few minutes later to get some fresh clothes, then took a long, cool shower, scrubbing himself vigorously.

Once dressed, he lay down on the couch, a hundred questions darting like flies through his mind, each too fast, too erratic to grab hold of, yet too annoying to ignore.

"Maybe," he finally decided, rising to pour another half-tumbler of warm Scotch, "it is not that a person's sins separate him from God directly, but that they separate him from himself, lowering his sense of self-worth so that he can no longer recognize or acknowledge his inherent oneness as part of the Creator as well as the creation.

The drink remained untouched in his hand. He paced, rubbing the glass against his forehead, thinking about the confessional, the power it was capable of. By erasing these self-constructed barriers it could actually rejoin men to God and to all mankind in a spiritual brotherhood not even dreamed of . . . *if* it were used correctly.

Now that he fully understood its purpose, he resolved to make it the focal point of his pastoral duties. He would expand the confessional hours to at least four or five a day to allow ample time for each penitent to achieve true absolution. He'd push the need for confession in every sermon, every counseling session. He'd make it work.

Then he realized with a sinking feeling that he would probably never get the chance, not once the news of his involvement in the tragic seance reached his superiors.

As he lay back on the tattered sofa cushions, a solitary tear was shed, but he found he was too tired to cry. He briefly considered the irony: the demon's ploy to corrupt and control them had backfired, spiritually freeing them from their sins and making them stronger than ever, closer than ever. Yet in a perverse way it had also succeeded, for in his final act of vengeance he had brought a public notoriety into their lives that ruined any chance they might have of putting that new awareness to good use.

Sleep was creeping in on Mike now. The last thought as he drifted off was that it might have all been worth it anyway: Marija had, in the seance, won her battle with Satan. She herself had exorcised him from their midst. God willing, the nightmare for her, at least, was finally over.

Chapter 14

Soon after the conclave had unanimously approved Robert F. Quillans' appointment as Auxiliary Pope, the eight cardinals retired to their quarters for some much needed rest. At 7:30 that evening each was awakened by a personal envoy of the Papal secretary, and after a period of private prayer and meditation all of them met again for dinner in the quarters of Cardinal Bishop Mendice.

In adherence to strict rules of etiquette, the meal itself was a quiet affair, broken only by polite conversation and requests to pass the butter; but once it was concluded the elderly statesmen quickly passed to the secretary's comfortable sitting room to take up the urgent business at hand.

"Esteemed cardinals," he began formally, "we have elected a new Pope—albeit a surrogate Pontiff, as long as Marcus still lives—who has accepted his assignation and all the burdens, duties, and responsibilities such assignation implies."

He looked around the room at the eight senior members of the Roman Catholic Church, most of whom were nodding expectantly. Bertini still wore a look of mild reserve.

"The task that lies before us now is to notify and receive the pledge of obedience from all the members of the College of Cardinals that we represented today in our limited conclave. This must be done before we can make the formal public announcement of this special Papal election to the rest of the world."

He paused here, putting his palms up, mild consternation on his pleasant, pink-cheeked face. "I confess to you," he said; "that I am uncertain how to proceed under such unusual circumstances: I wish to open the floor to any suggestions you might have."

"Cardinal Secretary!" Quillans spoke up at once, rising from the thronelike chair, "I believe the first order of business should be the announcement of my chosen Papal name."

"Oh, yes — certainly," Mendice nodded, surprised.

"I have given this careful thought and prayer, and have decided that the name I will be called henceforth is 'Sixtus the Sixth.' "

A slight murmur of surprise and approval ran through the group. "Viva Il Papa!" one of the eldest burst out in quavery enthusiasm.

"Thank you," acknowledged the new Pope Sixtus with a little smile, remaining standing and thus tacitly in control of the meeting. "Now, as to the manner in which we conduct the remaining required formalities of my election, I would offer the following plan. First, if it has not yet been done, have complete verbatim transcripts made of the two taped messages from Pope Marcus's bedside consistories. Next, write a detailed chronology of the sequence of events which developed out of those meetings — how the messages came to be received and recorded, what was done to carry out the Pope's subsequent directives, and so on. This, I suppose, would fall to you,

Secretary Mendice," he added with a deprecatory glance at the little cardinal hovering beside him, "as you were primarily responsible for recording and administering the Pontiff's last requests."

"Yes, that is so," Mendice agreed, bowing respectfully.

"If the missive is written in this manner," the Pope-elect continued, "with the Holy Father's directives in his own words forming the main body of the narrative, we need merely add at the conclusion that we, having carried out our part faithfully, now require the formal pledge of obedience from each remaining cardinal to complete the Motu Proprio. This should leave no room for argument, no need for further clarification. The cardinals will instantly recognize that my election is truly God's will and not open to question or debate."

"And how should this missive be delivered, Your Holiness?" asked Cardinal Falliano. "Should the cardinals be invited to Rome for the reading of it, or should the message be delivered individually to each member by special courier?"

"Good heavens!" Pope Sixtus laughed, rolling his eyes, "this is the twentieth century, Dean Falliano! We shall send the messages by telex to each cardinal throughout the world just as soon as the text is prepared, instructing them to pledge their obedience in the same manner. Depending on how long it takes the Papal Secretary to prepare the original dispatch, we should be ready by sometime tomorrow morning to let the rest of the outside world in on our good news."

He smiled broadly at the group of men, commanding their smiles in return.

Sixtus continued to control the meeting, now directing the secretary of state on the preparation of the press release—to be identical in form and content to the missive sent the cardinals, except that it would, of course, omit the request for a pledge of obedience. Instead, he instructed Cardinal Mendice, the release should proclaim that the new Auxiliary Pope had received "immediate, enthusiastic, and unanimous acceptance by all members of the Sacred College," and that "congratulatory telexes and pledges of obedience were pouring in from all corners of the globe, et cetera, et cetera."

"Tell them the coronation will take place this Sunday in Saint Peter's," he concluded, "with the traditional blessing from the balcony to be given directly after high mass."

Inadvertent gasps escaped several of the cardinals at this last reversal of form, this unheard-of haste in the ceremonial proceedings.

"It is absolutely necessary, I assure you," Sixtus answered their unspoken disapproval smoothly. "Remember, please, that we were instructed by Pope Marcus to *complete* this election within three days." He looked meaningfully into the eyes of each in turn until all were with him once again, caught up in his aura of power.

"Set up the press conference for tomorrow morning, would you? Say, eleven AM?" He'd turned back to the secretary, who was scribbling furiously on a little notepad. "Oh, and Cardinal Mendice . . ." he waited for the round cherubic face to raise and meet his eyes.

"Yes, Your Holiness?"

"Conduct this one yourself, would you please? I don't want Archbishop Magliano handling any more of my press."

Within two hours the telex machines in the Vatican communications office were sending the messages abroad. Once the 149 cardinals had been dispatched, the secretary of state, by his own inspiration, directed the wireless operators to notify all the archdioceses throughout the world so that they might share in and pass on the joyous news of this miracle to the bishops and priests beneath them, before it reached any by way of the media.

Pope-elect Sixtus the Sixth had followed the classic format of most politicians on election night—retiring early for a short nap, then returning to the telex room just as the first wave of congratulatory acknowledgments and pledges began replacing the temporary silence in the airwaves, pouring in in an urgent, mechanical clatter.

Shortly before 3 AM, one of the telex operators—eyes red-rimmed from visual concentration and lack of sleep—handed a teleprint directly to Sixtus. "This one is from your old archdiocese, Holiness. It contains something of a personal message for you."

"They're *all* personal for me," the new Pope growled, taking the paper torn from the machine. He lowered the rimless reading glasses from their perch above his forehead and began to scan the dispatch, skimming disinterestedly over the expected congratulations and utterances of respect and support. Halfway down the page his gray eyes stopped, a heavy scowl lowering his dark eyebrows, tightening his thin, tense lips. He read the remainder of the message slowly, thoughtfully—and by the time he'd reached the bottom of the page an ironic smile had replaced the frown.

"Deacon, please send a reply at once to Bishop Dumoré, requesting he telex me a complete transcript of the newspaper article he mentioned here. Tell him I await his immediate reply . . . and hold this line open for him."

Less than twenty minutes later the return message chattered in. Pope Sixtus read it in silence, then sat down at a small desk and hastily scribbled out a reply.

"What time would it be in San Francisco right now?" he asked the telex operator.

"Six-thirty PM, Your Holiness."

"Still Thursday there, is it?"

"Yes, Your Holiness."

Without acknowledgment, the Pope returned to his awkward, left-handed scrawl. Minutes later he handed the paper to the waiting deacon. "After you send this off, you may reopen the telex to receive the rest of my confirmations," he ordered, turning briskly away.

Chapter 15

An insistent banging had wormed its way into Mike's dream, becoming an old weather-beaten shutter slamming against the window frame of an ancient New England--style house. Suddenly, as if to explain this phenomenon, his mind concocted a violent, fearsome North Atlantic storm bellowing about the building, hurling the shutter in its rhythmic plunge and retreat against the wooden sashes. A wild rain pelted the glass panes, retreated, pelted again. The whole house shuddered, threatening to give way under the unrelenting onslaught, the shutters continuing to bang insistently.

"Let me in, Muldoon," the voice came now into his wakingness; followed by three more solid raps before it repeated, "Let—me—in!"

"Okay, okay—coming," he called out, rising groggily from the couch in the dim twilight of the room. He glanced at his wristwatch, struggling to focus. The digitals read 7:25. He felt disoriented, not sure if it was still Thursday or had become Friday while he slept. So much

197

had happened in the last twenty-four hours that time had lost all the usual reference points. He pushed the button on his watch for the date; 6.15. Still Thursday, he sighed, tugging open the door.

Two dark-suited figures stood in the dusky gloom, hats partially shielding their faces. For a moment he thought they might be a new team of detectives back for more blood, or possibly a matched set of reporters that had managed a preemptive strike through the insignificant little barrier of his white picket fence.

"May we come in, Muldoon?" the forwardmost said icily, and in that moment, as he recognized the voice, the bottom dropped out of Mike's stomach.

"Certainly, Bishop Dumoré." He found his voice somewhere and coaxed it unwillingly from his throat in a weak bleat. "Come in."

He stepped aside. As the second man passed before him, removing his hat, the priest recognized with a sad sort of surprise his carrot-topped ally from the archbishop's office, Father Murphy.

The two preceded him officiously into his sitting room, the priest following docilely behind, turning on an overhead light as he entered. Not trusting his voice, he waited for them to initiate the inevitable.

"I have a message to read to you," the bishop began without social preamble, looking askance at the half-empty Scotch bottle on the nearby table, the dirty glasses. "I believe you'll find it self-explanatory."

He remained standing, flanked by the boyish deacon, whose chubby face attempted to look stern while the bluish-gray eyes confessed confusion and unhappiness. Bishop Dumoré, on the other hand, was thoroughly enjoying the execution of his duty. His lips and tongue lolled especially lovingly over the words "heresy," "sacrilege," and "excommunication" as he read the xerox sheet held in his soft well-manicured hands.

"Do you have any last words to say on your own behalf?" he sneered once the message had been delivered, the sentence pronounced.

Mike felt weird. There was a huge pressure of tears right behind his eyeballs, threatening to slip through at any moment. At the same time, he felt like laughing, yet he knew once he started it would rapidly get out of control. Questions whirled dizzyingly through his head: how could the Pope have found out about him so soon? Why had he made such an extreme and rapid adjudication of. Mike's guilt, without so much as a hearing to bring forth all the facts? The question he did manage to phrase was seemingly irrelevant: "Who is Pope Sixtus the Sixth?"

"Actually, that's none of your business *now*," replied the bishop stingingly, "although you might check tomorrow's news, if you really want to know."

"May I keep this?" Muldoon asked, holding out his hand for the telex. "As a souvenir," he added with a quirky half-smile.

Dumoré tossed it at him with disdain. "It's a copy anyway," he said, turning on his heel. "I'll be back at midnight to ensure you are gone." The door slammed behind the two, Father Murphy unconsciously mimicking the haughty step of the older man as they went down the walk and out the gate.

Mike stood there leaning his head against the door. He walked wearily back into the sitting room, falling into one of the chairs, and reread the ultimatum. His throat felt thick and painful. His eyes hurt and his nose was starting to run, as if the blocked tears were seeking an alternative outlet.

Marija stood quietly in the darkened hallway, as she'd

199

stood for the past ten minutes—afraid to move, almost afraid to breathe least the discovery of her presence in the rectory by the two visiting church officials make matters even worse for poor Mike.

Now she was torn between wanting to respect the man's private grief and wanting to run to his side, comfort him, do something to help. Indecision won out; she stole back into the bedroom to awaken Joe and ask his advice.

When they came back into the room they found Mike Muldoon weeping openly into his arms like a small boy. Wisely they let him cry it out. Later they helped him pack.

While Joe and Marija finished cramming the last of the monsignor's few personal belongings into every conceivable nook and cranny of their two small foreign cars, Mike excused himself and went off into the large empty church for a last private word with his God.

A dim illumination from the lamps at the corners of the altar shone upward onto the life-size wooden figure of Christ, who gazed benignly from his perpetual agony on the cross at the agony of the priest standing below him. As he knelt, Mike felt a warmth flow over him, a tide of compassion, understanding, strength. He found no accusing finger of God here. Instead, he felt love. He looked up, tears flooding his eyes, and in his wavering vision it seemed as if the carven replica smiled back at him.

After a while he rose to leave; then without conscious forethought, he reached beneath the altar cloth into the hidden receptacle and withdrew a small silver pyx of consecrated host and a glass vial of holy water that had been stored there for morning mass. Looking around almost furtively, he tucked these items into his jacket pocket, then started across the chancel. On his second step his foot kicked against something heavy: it was the tall, ornate silver censer. He bent to reach inside, grabbed a cake of incense, and stuffed it into his other pocket. Quickly now he left the nave by a side entrance, automatically genuflecting and making the sign of the cross on his way out.

The bishop and Deacon Murphy were just arriving as he emerged and locked the chapel door behind him.

"Here are the keys," he said, dangling them at arms' length. "Everything's out that is mine."

"I hope you appreciate the trouble you've caused us," the bishop charged peevishly. "I shall have to conduct your services here personally, on top of *all* my other work." He raised his brows in exasperation.

Mike looked at him a long silent moment, then turned and walked to his car without a word.

Chapter 16

The musty, weakly illuminated theological bookstore, filled with row upon row of floor-to-ceiling bookshelves through which shafts of dust-laden sunbeams fell, took up the entire second floor of a three-story building on the corner of Geary and Mason.

Above the bookstore was a dance studio — heavy feet thumping clumsily in time to a tinny piano's insistent beat, shaking a continuous rain of plaster dust down upon the books, the floor, the aging proprietor, and his sole customer.

"Wednesday, that's the worst," claimed the man, a sour grimace aimed through the ceiling at his hidden adversaries. "We close at noon now on Wednesday. That's the day for beginner tap and acrobatics classes." The nervous little pot-bellied man behind the counter smiled grimly, scratching his hairless scalp. His bulgy eyes, wire-rimmed glasses, and pursed lips made him look like a caricature of a desk clerk of any haunted hotel from a horror flick.

Mike had to smile despite his unease. He still had no

idea what he was doing here.

He'd spent the previous night on the sofa at Joe's apartment, but this morning, while they were still sleeping, had left early to take a long walk, hoping to clear his mind and get things sorted out. When he saw the small, carefully printed sign — "New Age Theological Bookstore, Complete Selection of Literature on the Occult, Theosophy, and Religious Lore" — he couldn't resist the impulse to go in. Just as he hadn't been able to resist the impulse to pocket the holy water, and incense the night before, even as he reassured himself there was no real need for such things anymore, now that MJ had vanquished her demons.

Aloud he said, "What do you have on the rites of exorcism?

A half-hour later he emerged from the steep dark wooden stairwell, squinting into the glare of daylight, a brown-wrapped parcel under his arm. Inside it were two books: the first, a red leather edition entitled *White Magic, Rites and Rituals*, was an anthology of hokum used by various cults purportedly to overcome the influence of evil spirits and spells and to cast out demons. The rubrics ranged from those of modern day Macumba to the ancient exorcism rites of Babylonia. The price was nearly fifty dollars.

He and the old bookseller had also turned up a thin, worn, black-jacketed manual, *Rituale Romanum*, the official Roman Catholic rites of exorcism, though the bespectacled little man seemed as surprised to discover it, lodged at the back of one of his display racks, as Mike was pleased. Taking advantage of the man's temporary confusion, Mike had purchased it for a mere ten dollars. Now he could hardly wait to poke his head inside the fragile forbidden covers.

He was anxious to find some place where he could read

the manuals in private with no distractions. That wouldn't really be possible in Joe's bachelor apartment, he realized. If Marija saw him reading about exorcism at this point, she might think he was worried that the satanic powers which had terrorized her could return . . . not that that was the case. He wasn't really worried. It was just a compulsion to finally possess that knowledge which had been withheld from him for so long and at such cost.

The library, he finally decided . . . that would be the best place. He nearly sprinted the eight blocks to the huge gray granite structure.

Taking the broad stone steps two at a time, he slowed his pace as he entered the cool, quiet reading room. Picking the nearest unoccupied table, he unwrapped the package and withdrew the red volume first, saving the Catholic text as if it were dessert.

As he picked it up, its pages fell open to the glossary. "Demon," he read. "From Daemon, Greek; originally 'genius spirit,' thought to be a spirit that interacted between the gods and men."

The next paragraph really raised Mike's eyebrows. "In the early tenets of monotheistic Judaism, demons were considered to be agents of God, manipulated by *Him* to test or punish His people."

Would it make a difference how you'd conduct an exorcism—or *if* you would, he pondered, pulling at his beard, if you knew the evil spirit possessing someone was controlled by God rather than Satan?

Quickly he scanned the glossary, looking for a reference on Satan. To his surprise he discovered that the concept of a *supreme* evil entity, locked in a power struggle with God over control of the earth, had originated in the doctrine of Christianity alone. No other religion—not even Judaism, out of whose loins Christianity had sprung—ever held such a concept. All had their lesser demons, of course, their evil spirits and tempters, but none claimed the existence of the antithetical adversary of God that Satan was considered to be.

What if Satan *was* just a relatively recent invention of God, a tool, a great "genius spirit" used to carry out His ultimate tests of men's faith and moral strength before the final reckoning? Mike wondered. It made sense, in a way. *If* God is the Creator of the Universe — omnipotent, omnipresent, omniform, omniscient — that means He knows, has power over, and *is* all that he has created. Including Satan. If you believe the first, you *have* to believe the second!

Resolutely Mike turned his attention back into the red volume, determined to get through it. It occurred to him as he was nearing the end of the book that although the side trappings and artifacts varied from cult to cult, the basic ritual for exorcism followed the same essential principles throughout: discover the name of the particular *deity* the demon in question most fears so that his name may be invoked to bind and banish the offending spirit, *and discover the name of the demon himself* in order to address him directly during the exorcism.

Mike skimmed over the glossary list of deities that might be invoked during the rites, then over the names and identities of the many greater and lesser demons that have been known to terrorize man over the ages. Suddenly his eyes stopped and widened, his breath caught in his throat, and his heart began to thud sickeningly in his chest.

"Lilith," he whispered aloud, tracing along the lines with his finger, "considered the most malevolent demon of ancient Judaism. In Jewish folklore she was Adam's first wife, spurned and cast off by him in favor of Eve. In a jealous rage she vowed to destroy all the children of man."

His mind whirled and shuddered. *Lilith*. That was the

205

name Marija had used to exorcise the devil from the seance! He remembered the oddness of MJ's voice at the time—as if it were not really she but someone else speaking through her.

Lilith! Had Lilith herself dispelled the evil monster from their midst? If that were true, could she actually be as terrible as legend had it?

If only he could remember the name MJ had called out in addressing the devil. "Isis"? "Iris"? *Something* starting with an "I" . . . he flipped back to the start of the glossary and began running his eyes down the page, searching. Suddenly he had it.

"Iblis," he read, "the primary devil of the Moslem religion; by legend an angel who rebelled against God when Adam was created, refusing to bow down to a man of flesh who he felt to be basically inferior to him. He set out to prove his superiority over man by becoming the tempter and destroyer of mankind."

It fit, and yet didn't fit. Mike felt himself growing more confused, as if there were a lie in there which, once removed, would allow all the pieces to fall into place.

Lilith, he jotted on his scratch pad. *Adam's first wife.*

Eve. Usurper of Lilith's position. Tempted Adam to commit original sin, with resulting banishment from paradise.

Iblis. Spirit being, jealous of Adam, avowed tempter and destroyer of man . . . through Lilith? he noted, the question mark underlined twice, *or through Eve!* his pencil exclaimed in bold strokes.

He got up to check with the librarian on where he could find a King James Bible, wanting to re-read *Genesis* in hopes of finding a clue.

On the way back to his seat, Bible in hand, his attention caught on the rack of morning newspapers draped neatly over their wooden rods. The headlines were nearly identical: "Medical Miracle Rocks Vatican: San Francisco

206

Archbishop to be Acting Pope."

He grabbed the nearest paper from the rack, carelessly dislodging the support rod which fell to the floor with a loud clatter. The dyspeptic-looking librarian eyed him with disapproval.

Oblivious to her, Mike stood there immobilized, reading the article. His shock and sense of dismay grew with every line.

There was, beneath the sensationalism, something naggingly familiar in the story; something that teased at his memory. It had to do with the Pope's particular infirmity and his strange, spontaneous recovery from a state of virtual brain death. And then his subsequent selection of Archbishop Quillans, of all people, to exercise the powers of the Papacy in his stead, including the enforcement of any mandates the stricken Pontiff might by some later miracle originate. Where was it he had heard this tale before, and why did it give him such a feeling of impending doom?

Suddenly Muldoon had an inkling of what it might be and he felt his skin grow icy, his scalp crawl, at the first hint of an idea so heinous. He dropped the newspaper and began to flip through the Bible.

The thin, bird-faced librarian was on him like a harpie.

"Sir!" she exclaimed in a shrill, outraged stage whisper, "You must be more careful of library material or I shall have to ask you to leave!"

Mike looked up from the book, his eyes far away, while she made an exaggerated struggle to put the paper back in order and re-insert it in the rack. "Sorry," he mumbled. He sat back down at the table where he'd left his other reference works and continued through the New Testament pages to the Book of Revelations, chapter thirteen.

I stood upon the sand of the sea and saw a beast rise up out of the sea, having seven heads and ten horns, he read silently, *and upon his horns, ten crowns, and upon his heads the name of blasphemy.*

And I saw one of his heads as it were wounded unto death; and his deadly wound was healed: and all the world wondered after the beast.

He hadn't known he'd begun reading aloud until the librarian hissed at him, a finger against her thin lips. He read on in silence for a while.

And I beheld another beast coming up out of the earth, and he had two horns like a lamb, and he spake as a dragon.

The hissing sound erupted again, the librarian shaking her head violently. Several people looked up from nearby tables, some annoyed, a few amused. Mike looked her directly in the eye and continued to quote aloud.

"And he *exerciseth all the power* of the first beast before him, and causeth the earth and them which dwell therein to worship the first beast, whose *deadly wound was healed.*"

"Sir, *please!*" the outraged woman shrieked, hurling herself around the desk in breathless agitation, sliding to a stop before him. "I'm afraid I'll have to ask you to leave. *Now!*"

Mike shook his head as if awakening from a trance. His eyes slowly cleared and he looked up at her in bewilderment. "What was that?" he asked. "What did you just say, ma'am?"

"You h-heard me," she sputtered in self-righteous anger. "Now will you go quietly, or do I have to call a guard and have you *thrown* out?"

Acutely embarrassed and only vaguely aware of what he'd done to offend the woman, the priest hastily gathered the books into his arms and began walking toward the door.

"Not so fast! Are those *my* books?" she accused pointing a bony finger at the three volumes Mike clutched tightly to his chest.

"This one *is* yours," Mike apologized, handing her the Bible. "The others I brought with me."

Not satisfied, she painstakingly checked all three book jackets with irritating thoroughness before she would finally let him go. "And don't come back," she ordered smartly to the door once it had closed behind him.

He walked the long, steep trek back to Joe's apartment on Telegraph Hill, his mind embroiled in half-formed realizations, his heart pounding from an excitement that bordered on terror. It was the thought of his own old leather bound Bible still packed away somewhere with the rest of his personal belongings that pulled his tired legs relentlessly up the hill against the pain. He couldn't waste a minute getting back to this research.

He also found himself wanting very badly to talk to Joe and Marija about all this, but when he got back to the little flat it was empty. He felt strangely let down, wandering bleakly through the empty rooms. Finally he noticed that the note he'd been left that morning, held by a magnet to the refrigerator door, had been replaced by a new message in Marija's neat backhand.

"Dear Mike," she'd written, "We've gone to my mother's in Walnut Creek. She called me this morning — pretty hysterical over the newspaper accounts of the seance. We may need to spend the weekend. Come over if you can. We could sure use your help to calm her down. Call for directions if you decide to come — 555-4015. Love, Marija and Joe."

"P.S.," she'd added below, "There's plenty of food in the fridge, so *please* take anything you like. We want you to feel this is your home for as long as you want to stay."

As he put a pot of water on for coffee, he considered calling Marija, talking to her and Joe about his speculations. The paper he'd picked up from the newsstand on the way home lay before him on the table, its headlines taunting . . . yet with one hand on the phone, he still hesitated. He would do some more research first.

Among the cardboard boxes of hastily packed books and personal papers he soon found his worn black Bible. Returning with it to the kitchen table, he quickly found the verses he'd been reading when the librarian had interrupted him. As he reached the middle of the next short chapter he paused, his finger jabbing at one line emphatically: *Babylon is fallen.* That struck a familiar chord, something he'd read about Babylon — "the great whore that sitteth on many waters." But where? Quickly he skimmed the next few chapters until he found the reference he was seeking.

And I saw a woman sitting upon a scarlet-colored beast, full of names of blasphemy, having seven heads and ten horns, he was reading aloud, his voice a rough whisper, skipping over lines as he went. *And upon her forehead was a name written, MYSTERY BABYLON THE GREAT . . . and here is the mind which hath wisdom: the seven heads are seven mountains on which the woman sitteth.* He scanned silently for a minute, then once again spoke aloud, his finger following the lines of the text as he read: *"And the ten horns which thou sawest are ten kings, which have received no kingdom as yet, but receive power as kings one hour with the beast.*

"These have one mind and shall give their power and strength unto the beast."

Ten! Wasn't that the number who had participated in the secret consistory? He picked up the newspaper. Yes. The seven cardinal-bishops of Rome, the Eastern Patriarch, and Quillans, and the Pope. These ten now formed the top echelon of power and authority in the Catholic world!

Mike mumbled his way through another verse of the recondite predictions before reading aloud the next, almost dropping the Bible in his excitement.

"The waters which thou sawest, where the whore sitteth, are peoples, and multitudes, and nations, and tongues . . . and the woman which thou sawest is that great city which reigneth over the kings of the earth."

"My God," he shuddered, sitting heavily back down in his chair, a sinking excitement washing over him from forehead to bowels. "It all *fits!* It *all* fits! The city on seven mountains, that's got to be the seven hills of Rome—and the Whore of Babylon," he shook his slowly, "is the Vatican itself."

Swiftly he flipped back through the flimsy pages to a vaguely remembered passage in *Ephesians: Put on the whole armor of God, that ye may be able to stand against the wiles of the Devil,* Saint Paul had written. *For we wrestle not against flesh and blood but against principalities, against powers, against the rulers of darkness of the world, against spiritual wickedness in high places.*

His fierce joy at the sudden realization of what this all meant was tempered by a clammy dread. What did it mean to him personally, what was the responsibility of having such knowledge . . . and how could he ever hope to convince anyone with the authority to stop this atrocity that he was telling the truth?

For he knew now, with a knowingness that went beyond all thought or reason, that the ailing Pope who'd recovered from his "deadly wound" and the Auxiliary Pope Sixtus the Sixth were the two evil beasts prophesied in *Revelations.* Archbishop Quillans—Sixtus—was the one about whom it was written, "And the dragon gave him his power, and his seat, and great authority."

He'd never fully believed the prophecies of *Revelations* before. Not that he doubted the concept of a day of judgement . . . but the rest had always seemed so abstruse, so buried in symbolism, subject to too many different interpretations to have much value as a guide to

211

predicting God's plan for mankind. What truth it contained had become so tarnished over the ages, made ridiculous by an endless succession of street-corner doomsayers who saw "signs of the end of the world" in every natural and unnatural calamity, that by now conventional religions scorned such views altogether, lifting their robes and tiptoeing away from the subject of apocalyptic signs in embarrassment—himself included.

Yet here it was, crystal clear, coming to fruitation *exactly* as St. John had envisioned, and yet apparently no one else in the entire world had recognized it for what it was!

The last vestiges of twilight gave way to the violet velvet of night. The first stars began to twinkle from across the great black void of space, their light penetrating the thin glass window and wasting their final energy on the receptors of the unfocused eyes of Mike Muldoon. Still he sat, bearded chin on clenched fists, looking only inward. His mind raced with possibilities, complexities, doubts, and truths—and cold gnawing fear—as he contemplated what must be done. And why, it seemed, he must be the one to do it.

"I *must* have been chosen for this task by God," he said aloud, "else why should Truth have been revealed to me like this? Yet," he sighed, getting up at last to turn on the kitchen light, "there's some detail I'm missing, some insight. I don't know how to proceed, don't feel *ready* to proceed. And I don't know why."

His eyes fell on the note still tacked to the refrigerator door.

"Marija," he whispered tentatively. "It *has* to have something to do with her! That's what got me involved in this in the first place."

He grabbed the Bible, his hands shaking so badly he had difficulty turning to Chapter Twelve, the chapter the book had fallen open to that night of her first visit to the rectory . . . the chapter directly preceding all the prophecies he'd just discovered!

And there appeared a great wonder in heaven; a woman clothed with the sun . . . he scanned quickly, . . . *and the dragon stood before the woman* . . . *And there was war in heaven: Michael and his angels fought against the dragon; and the dragon fought and his angels!*

He closed the book with a bang, then with trembling fingers dialed the number MJ'd left. The repetitive buzz of the busy signal answered.

"Damn!" he exploded; "Why didn't she leave the address?"

Running back to the closet where his gear was stored, he gathered together the Catholic fetishes: a vial of holy water, the tiny silver box of consecrated host, the cake of incense, and his own large wooden crucifix with the ivory Jesus, secured at hands and feet by golden nails. These he stuffed into the oversized pocket of his navy pea jacket, along with the manual of *Rituale Romanum* and the book on white magic.

Rifling through his canvas duffle he found and donned a badly wrinkled clerical shirt, slipping the heavy wool jacket on over it. He tried Marija's number again, but it was still busy, so he tucked her message into his pocket and left for Walnut Creek.

A rising surge of anxiety quickened his pulse. He had a premonition that whatever climax all these events had been leading to it, was going to happen very very soon. He could only hope he'd get there in time.

Fighting his way through the heavy Friday night traffic on the clogged Oakland Bay Bridge, he finally reached the relative peace of Highway 24 on the quiet country stretch leading to Walnut Creek sometime shortly after 10 PM.

Mike's car wound through the mountainous landscape

213

dotted here and there with small weak, lights, cabins and mansions peeking out from behind the dense foliage.

The big, plain, pie-faced clock on the wall of the brightly lit ARCO station in Lafayette read 10:35 when he pulled in for gas and directions. From there it was only about three more miles northeast on 680 to Walnut Creek. He asked the attendant for change for the phone.

His call was answered on the fifth ring; the voice was old, female and decidedly grumpy.

"Marija?" Muldoon faltered.

"No, this is her mother," the woman replied. "Who is *this*?"

"Mike Muldoon, Ma'am . . . *Father* Muldoon? We met at the hospital last week?"

"Oh, yes, Father Muldoon," the woman's voice softened considerably. "How are you?"

"I'm fine, thank you uh. . . . Mrs. Draekins."

"Do call me Dolores, won't you, Father?"

"Yes, certainly. Pardon my abruptness, but may I please speak to Marija now? It's quite urgent." He found himself clenching the receiver, winding and unwinding the cord around his fingers as he strove to keep his voice calm and polite.

"Oh, I'm *so* sorry, but she's not *here*, Father."

"Is Joe there, then? I really *must* talk to him." Mike found he was losing patience.

"*Neither* is here, Father," the woman signed with a touch of petulance. "They went for a little drive about an hour ago, needed some 'fresh air', she said. Frankly it was a bit of a scene here today, I can tell you that. I don't know what's the matter with Marija anymore. I mean, she *is* my daughter, and of course I love her no matter *what* she's done; but frankly she's never been what you'd call completely *normal*, you know? These crazy ideas she has — even when she was a *child*. And now this horrid scandal!

214

Well, frankly, Father Muldoon, I think she's just gone *clear* off the deep end this time, I really do. Just like her father. Now *there* was a dreamer. No sense of reality whatsoever. . . ."

"Please!" Mike shouted through the barrage of words. "Please! I'd be glad to discuss this with you any other time, but right now *it is absolutely imperative* that I find her and Joe immediately! Did they mention *where* they might be going?"

Marija had known it was going to be difficult handling her mother, but she hadn't realized just how difficult. On the drive over she'd decided that the best tack would be one of unblushing honesty: she'd simply sit her mother down and explain as clearly and unemotionally as she could exactly what had been going on for the past three weeks.

Two days ago the mere thought of confiding such experiences to her mother would have immobilized her. But now there was only an inner calm— the lingering cathartic effect of the seance, she supposed—as she mentally rehearsed what she would say.

She had, however, vastly underestimated the rigidity of her mother's stance on the occult. As soon as Marija broached the subject, her mother, with set lips and narrowed eyes, had firmly closed her mind.

Her mind had snapped shut, but unfortunately her mouth had not.

She was narrow-minded, true, but she was also glibly clever, and she'd done her homework well. Her first line of defense was an attempt to discredit everything Marija said by quoting excerpts she'd dug out of *Psychology Today* for the occasion: "Drug flashback," "executive burnout," "paranoic schizophrenia," and other such phrases.

After she ran out of prepared quotes to confuse and undermine her daughter's story, she resorted to self-righteous denouncements on the subject of spiritualism in general—and on Marija's interest and participation in such goings-on.

When MJ started to laugh, the older woman's face flushed red and she quickly moved to her final coup.

"Well, *you* may think this is all very funny," she cried in contemptuous outrage, "but I hope you realize that you've completely *ruined* your lives, Marija—Joe's as well as your own. Not to mention that nice young priest! I mean, have you even considered what you're going to do for money—provided you don't end up in prison—now that you've lost your job . . . and probably cost poor Joe his job, too!?"

She bestowed a look of sympathy on the man, expecting his tacit agreement, but the cold anger in his eyes reviled her.

Marija, who'd given up trying to contradict her mother during this final tirade, was blinking back tears of frustration and rage when she finally stood up in defeat. "I need some fresh air," she announced to the room. "The bullshit in here is beginning to stink."

They left without another word, slamming the door behind them.

Twenty minutes later, sitting in the parking lot of a nearby McDonald's, watching the steam rise from their coffee, each waited for the other to speak.

"Where to, lady?" Joe finally broke the silence.

"I don't know. I'm not ready to give up yet . . . after all, she *is* my mother."

Marija paused, swallowing back the pain that had risen in her throat. "I'm just so damned tired of arguing about it, defending myself. Sometimes I get to believing her opinion of me, doubting my own." She sighed heavily. "Why don't we go for a drive somewhere, out in the

216

country of something. I need to get my head together before we go back."

The roads carried them along for a while, an unplanned route of sudden turns which led out of the suburban affluence of Walnut Creek and onto a lightly traveled thoroughfare heading south. It was a poorly lit rural road which, after a few miles, dipped into a long expanse of pleasantly rolling farmlands before beginning to wind gradually upward through hilly twists overhung by the shadowy forms of live oak, spruce, and Monterey pine. Ten minutes into the mountainous wilds a large sign loomed up unexpectedly in the glare of their headlights, just before a white metal gate, chained and locked, which blocked the road ahead.

Mount Diablo State Park, the sign read, *North Gate — Day Use Only. Overnight Visitors Please Use South Gate Entrance.*

There was a small parking area to the left of the turnaround in front of the barrier and a rustic, unlit park restroom beside it a short ways off the road.

"Let's stop here for a bit, okay, Joe?" MJ said, breaking the silence that had enshrouded them ever since they'd left the fast-food restaurant. Her voice was strangely distant and thoughtful. Then she added lightly, "I need to use the john, anyway."

After he'd seen Marija safely to the women's room, Joe went over to the other side of the old wooden building to take care of his own needs. When he emerged she still wasn't out, so he lit a cigarette and watched the stars for a while. It wasn't until he'd finished his smoke that he realized she'd been in the restroom an inordinately long time. He walked over by the entrance, the first vague edge of unease gnawing at him.

"Marija! You about done in there?"

Silence. His uneasiness escalated into alarm.

"Marija, are you in there? Answer me, please!"

When there was still no reply he hesitated a minute, then pushed open the door and walked inside. A quick search by the flickering flame of his disposable lighter revealed no sign of his wife.

"Marija!" he yelled, running back outside. "Where the hell are you?"

The moment she'd heard the rust springs on the wooden door of the men's room squeak closed behind Joe, Marija had quietly exited the building, a distracted look on her face. Without seeming to hurry, she'd walked quickly into the surrounding woods and disappeared.

She was not fleeing anything, yet her feet moved forward purposefully, as if under the direction of some other mind, toward a particular destination of which she knew nothing.

Joe's voice was calling her name as she topped a narrow ridge a hundred yards above the parking lot, but Marija couldn't hear him now. She couldn't even hear the wind whispering warnings through the pines, the concerned question of an owl. Her head was filled with other voices: a low buzzing hymn, a fused gregorian chant, white noise that filled her ears, blocking out all external sounds, dizzying her senses in a high vertigo.

As she started down the steep incline on the other side of the hill, her foot slipped on a loose stone, pitching her head first into the blackness below. Her cry was swallowed back in her throat as she tumbled into the unseen depths.

There was a momentary blinding flash of pain, followed by a slowly closing blackness. As she lapsed into unconsciousness, she felt herself separate from her body, watched it grow smaller beneath her while she floated lazily higher and higher, no longer knowing or caring about the pain.

Suddenly her speed accelerated, doubling and redoubling and redoubling again. She was hurtling beyond space now, into the blackness of dimensionless existence. A wave of bodiless, deranged laughter reached out to grasp and tear at the fabric of her soul as she flew by, but she was moving too fast, too far, for it to engulf her in its realm.

After an eternity, or a moment, she abruptly entered an arena of blinding white light where all sensation of time ans space ended—and began.

"Hello, my dear," said a familiar voice, slick and oily and full of perfumed hate. "I knew you'd come to me eventually. How could you not? You've always been mine . . . Lilith."

Joe held onto the thought that MJ had returned to his car while he was still inside the building. That *must* be it . . . she was probably sitting there right now with the windows up against the chill, playing the stereo, wondering where *he* was. He raced toward the parking area, hope trying valiantly to combat the burning pit of fear in his stomach.

But the car was empty, the radio silent. He shook his head back and forth like a panicked animal, reached in through the open window, and began honking the horn over and over while his fear bloomed into anger. Where the hell had she gone? "She'd better have a damned good reason for doing this to me," he raged aloud; but inside he hoped . . . God, how he hoped.

Mike had managed to extract from Marija's mother a random list of places her daughter might possibly have gone. Automatically eliminating any across the bay as too far to search, and unlikely in any case, he found that even the pared-down list encompassed a range of over six hundred square miles, from Berkeley to Clayton. Within that area must be thousands of miles of back roads and major highways crisscrossing the countryside.

Nearly overwhelmed by the task before him, the priest went back into the service station to purchase a local map. Returning to his old VW, he turned on the dim interior light, carefully unfolding the road map, and with it the realization of just how tiny he and the two people he had to find were against the scale of the area he had to explore.

He contemplated the maze of colored lines, names, and markings, trying to envision the land it represented, imagining himself high in the air, a giant looking down on the countryside. He found his own approximate location—a small, insignificant dot on the roadside between Lafayette and the intersection of Highways 24 and 680—too tiny even to be seen.

Then, as he continued to stare at the map, a strange subtle transformation occurred. The red and blue lines faded, becoming instead gray concrete ribbons. The printing disappeared, changed into sparkling dots of light amidst an undulating sea of brown earth and deep forest green.

He *was* above the land now, *actually* above it, and with a peculiar twist of vision he could see himself, a miniscule man bent over a map beneath the blue and white ARCO sign, his ancient beat-up Volkswagon a blue metal insect squatting on an island of light amidst the darkened countryside.

After a moment he saw something else far off in the distance: it was Joe! He was alone, standing outside his red Alfa, angrily leaning on the horn while he seemed to be scanning the surroundings. The look on his face told the story. He was in some sort of hilly, wild-looking area to the southeast of where Mike's own tiny body sat, still fixated on the map. Between the two men tiny glow-worms of light sped along a dark macadam artery — obviously a major highway leading south. But Joe was some distance east of that highway, in a remote stretch of land that looked empty and forbidding.

Mike wondered at the strange tricks of perception he was experiencing, the way he was able to see Joe with absolute clarity — first from a great distance, then close enough to see the lines of worry etched in his face. Space had lost its usual meaning, dropped its physical barriers to him. It was as though his ability to perceive a particular thing had become directly related to his desire to do so.

In the next instant he discovered the missing woman as well. She was lying beside a great jagged boulder that glowed dully in the moonlight, just over a thickly wooded hillock from the clearing where Joe waited, her body crumpled and unmoving. So still — dear God, she was lying so still! He knew he had little time left; he had to find that wild area where the couple had gone and lead Joe to Marija before it was too late.

Instantly he was back in his car, just a weary black man staring blankly at a map. But his index finger was now pointing at a green shaded zone on the paper. "Mount Diablo State Park." he breathed.

Gunning his tired engine, he lurched out of the bright neon oasis and onto the dark gray expanse of highway, heading south as fast as the old car would go.

"No . . . that's not true," Marija was crying, pleading; "I can't be yours. You're evil. *The* evil. I've always *tried* to be good."

Her desperate pleas dissolved into a shuddering silence as the beast began to physically materialize out of the darkness.

First came the eyes: red, almond-shaped orbs glowing like those of a wild thing caught in a spotlight's glare; then the feral gleam of teeth in a wicked lipless slash of mouth. Next appeared the facial mask of scaly greenish skin tattooed in scenes of horror — wars, murder, genocidal hate, and sexual depravity — graphic evidence of the degree to which man continuously blasphemed God's most treasured creation, himself.

The odor of the beast was like the stench from a million rotting corpses, a ton of reeking feces — those things which profaned and mocked the sacred gift of life with the crude reminders of its ultimate, inevitable product and end: death, stink, and decay.

"Lilith," the empty hollow of his voice reasoned smoothly, "you're being silly. What is 'good' and what is 'evil,' anyway? Two meaningless words levied on acts committed to enhance one's survival in a timeless void where one can do nothing but survive. Look at it this way: we all continue to exist for infinity regardless, so what's the difference how we go about it? How can any one act be judged good or evil when the only true sin is to do nothing at all?"

"But there are basic moral laws, precepts of right and wrong!" she protested weakly.

The devil snarled in disgust. "Have you forgotten how you pledged yourself to my cause when God betrayed you by creating Eve? Perhaps you need to have your memory refreshed, my dear. Look!" the voice hissed; "Look and remember who broke the promises first!"

In the center of the white space where Marija cowered, a figure began to present itself. It was a man: young, with thick, curly black hair, long muscular limbs, glowing eb-

222

ony skin. She gasped at his beauty, his unadorned elegance . . . and at the first stirrings of an old, old memory, like every sad love song ever written.

"Oh, yes, he *is* gorgeous," the wide lipless mouth snickered, "a beauty to take your breath away, is he not? But beware, there is venom hidden in the spines of the exquisite lion fish, a thorn beneath the blossom of every fragrant rose. Beauty can be a trap to draw one close, lower one's defenses for the deadly strike. You of all people, Lilith, should know that!" Mocking laughter filled the blackness around their little region of light.

Within the arena now appeared another form so like the first it might have been its clone, but this one was female. Equal in height, long-limbed and lithe, with blue-black hair and skin, she came and took his hand. As their eyes met, it was as if one person were looking into himself — all the best in himself that he would never have been able to see without this mirror image opposite.

"It's you, Lilith — yes," the dragon chuckled. "God's perfect little creations, weren't you? Pieces of Himself that he could play with as a spoiled child dallies with his toys." His voice was softly threatening, a thin razor of sarcasm beginning to expose its edge.

"Paradise, Lilith . . . you see there, you even had little ones. God was replicating Himself through you, filling his chess board with tiny, insignificant pieces of His spirit and energy."

As he spoke, two more human forms had manifested themselves nearby: a small boy and a smaller girl. Both were elfish miniatures of the adults, playing quietly at their parents feet, now and then giggling mischievously behind cupped hands at a shared secret of childhood.

"Ah, but you know how God is, Lilith . . . He *does* get bored so quickly." The dragon's teeth gleamed wickedly out of the blackness.

Suddenly the globe was filled in one sector with a gray eddying cloud. The four figures looked over at it — curious, but not alarmed. They had no knowledge of fear, no reason for distrust. Not then.

The cloud slowly congealed, and in its midst a figure began to take shape. Gradually it solidified as the mist around it cleared until it was discernible as another human form, another female. She was somewhat shorter than Adam and Lilith, fuller of breast and thigh. Her skin was lighter, with an exotic olive cast to it, her hair a deep auburn cascade, her eyes green and catlike, her lips full and inviting.

No wiles or pretensions were put up to mask her intent: she simply walked over to Adam, put one hand on his chest and one hand on his groin, and locked her lips onto his. And that was that: Adam was enchanted, beguiled, entrapped, "in love." Lilith had ceased to exist.

He and the new woman — Eve — faded out of the arena, leaving Lilith and the two children alone and bewildered in the dimming light. And now Lilith knew pain and despair, and the impotent fury of loss.

"Yes," breathed Marija. "I remember now."

"You were betrayed, Lilith; betrayed by God Himself," the dragon spat, whipping his tail around viciously. Sparks of light flashed behind the movement, scarring the dark void as the three lonely figures faded away. He leaned conspiratorily toward her, his foul breath choking her senses as he spoke.

"He wanted to experience pain, so He gave *you* pain. He wanted to know despair, so He gave *you* despair. He wanted loss and grief and anger, so He *used* you, manipulated your feelings in order to experience these emotions Himself *through you*. And," the demon leered wickedly, "He wanted to feel *lust*, so He gave Adam Eve."

"But it was *I*, Lilith, who gave you the sweet comfort of

revenge, *I* who taught you how to hate . . . and how to get even," the voice purred slickly. "You haven't forgotten *that*, have you, my dear?"

"I haven't forgotten."

"And in return for my gifts, my friendship, you promised to be mine, mine forever. To do my bidding. To aid my own plans for vengence."

"Yours forever," she intoned numbly.

"Come then, Lilith. Come to me now. I have one last little task for you to perform. . . ."

Joe had harnessed the frenetic energy of his terror after minutes, setting it to the more directed course of trying to determine which way Marija might have taken in her flight.

As he wandered about the rest area, he discovered a small, worn path winding through the soft amber grasses on the other side of the rest room, trailing listlessly through the spicy sumac and sage before rising sharply through manzanita and scrub oak to disappear in the dense vegetation above.

With no better possibility in sight, he began to follow it, working upward around columns of maple and pine, skirting yard-wide boulders, scrabbling on hands and feet over steep rockfalls of loose earth and shale.

As he neared the top of the ridge, panting heavily from the exertion, he heard a voice call out his name.

"*Joe.*" It was soft, almost part of the wind. He turned his head, trying to tell which direction it had come from.

"*Joe, help me.*" It was Marija! But he still couldn't tell where the voice originated; it seemed to be all around him.

"Marija!" he yelled to the trees and sky. "Where are you?"

"Here, I'm here," the night answered back. "Please, darling, I need you. Come to me now."

"I'm coming, Marija," Joe called, standing atop the ridge. But before he could take another step, he felt its solidness waver beneath his feet, saw the surrounding trees soften, weaving drunkenly against the moonlit sky like so many columns of smoke. His heart began to lurch.

"Just keep talking," he begged the wind. "Show me the way to you."

The stars moved in, no larger, just closer, the firmament taking on the appearance and texture of Madame Le Beuc's ceiling—low, flat, non-dimensional, speckled with counterfeit planets, constellations, galaxies.

"Please hurry," the woman's voice entreated, *"Hurry, Joe."*

The man looked up in confusion; the voice seemed to be directly overhead, but how could that be? He felt the heavy ceiling of sky and stars press down on him. Then, as he watched, it began thinning out, becoming semi-transparent—like a one-way window losing its refraction. He thought for just a moment that he could see a shadowy form beyond its dark glass, a huge black phantom moving behind the night sky.

Joe shook his head to clear it: just clouds passing over, his mind explained reasonably, but the shadow went *behind* the stars! Just a trick of vision, then; tired eyes, he insisted, rubbing them with his fists.

The beast chuckled, a slender black ribbon of tongue flickering out, running across the horny plates which formed his upper lip, anticipating the joy of victory so near at hand. He had waited, plotted, manipulated so long and so carefully for this moment. With this antagonist defeated and the other soon to fall, there would be no witnesses to warn the few who might listen, no one to pull his servants down from the ultimate throne of power they were, at this very moment, on the eve of assuming.

A silent roar of malevolent triumph exploded upward from the dragon's belly at the thought, bulging his throat and pouring from the ugly slash of mouth with a pungent odor. Marija cringed, hiding her face from the fiery blast.

Convinced of her own evil, knowing she was lost, she'd called Joe into the trap as the demon had ordered. There'd been a perverse sort of comfort in the act. Resolving the issue of which side she was on once and for all was a relief, no matter which side she'd chosen.

But as Joe drew under the devil's control, and he switched his attention fully to the task of overcoming the man's last vestiges of resistance, his hypnotic influence over Marija lessened, and suddenly she found some of the old doubts and uncertainties returning.

How *could* she have been on Satan's side all this time and not known it? Must she continue this betrayal just because she'd once been betrayed herself?

"No!" she yelled in sudden defiance. "I *won't* do it; it has to stop somewhere. Joe, get out of here; it's a trap, a *trap!*"

Joe recoiled as if struck, the force of Marija's warning shoving him back into the physical world. The ground rose up to meet his rump— hard, hurting, reassuringly solid once more. He looked around in bewilderment.

The moon darkened angrily to a bloody hue, then faded away altogether; the sky seemed to shiver. Massive black clouds boiled up over the far horizon like a distant tidal wave, hurtling toward him in cold fury. A tremor rolled ominously through the earth under his feet.

All at once a brightly glowing object shot across the sky. To Joe's amazement it traced a slow, curving arc that ended not in a fiery meteoric burn-up, but an abrupt, calculated stop, hovering in the air some fifty yards away.

It was so close he could feel its heat, so bright it cast a long, milky shadow across the ridge.

As Joe struggled to rise, the shadow behind the sky screamed and roared, writhing his monstrous head in frustration and rage. From out of his black domain exploded a great shower of burning meteorites, hurtling through the heavens to explode against the invisible walls of air in fiery red puffs, the smoke of their destruction turning into distorted, tormented images before slowly fading in an agonized wail.

"It appears the legions of Satan have arrived." a voice above him stated calmly. *"Make yourself ready for battle."*

Michael Muldoon had reached the southern entrance to Mount Diablo State Park at about the same time Joe was nearing the top of the ridge above the north gate a few miles away.

Not wishing to arouse undue suspicion in the bored-looking ranger at his late-night arrival, the priest leaned casually out his window and asked, in as off-handed a voice as he could muster, if the man remembered seeing a young couple in a red Alfa Romeo come through about an hour ago. "Maybe they left a message?" he added hopefully. "We were supposed to meet earlier, but I was tied up."

"Nope," was the taciturn reply. "That'll be six dollars for overnight use, if you're gonna stay."

"Sure," Mike replied, extracting a five and a one from his worn leather wallet and handing them to the ranger. "You couldn't have missed them . . . the couple, that is . . . could you?"

"Been here all night; the only thing through since sundown has been a couple of vans full of hippies . . . Mexican hippies," he grinned.

The priest managed a polite smile. "Is there any other entrance to the park they might have used?" he inquired lightly.

"North end, but that'un closes at dusk. Day use only, that side of the park." The ranger had come out of his booth and was leaning against Mike's window now, making Mike decidedly uncomfortable with his closeness.

"Is there any way to get over there from this side?" the priest asked, letting up on the clutch slightly so he could begin to ease away from the man.

The ranger backed up, his voice cooler now. "Just follow the main road. 'Bout halfway up the mountain it branches off. Take the left fork."

"Thanks," said the priest, starting to pull away.

"Only you can't drive all the way to the gate; road into the day section's chained off at night. You'll have to hoof it the last half mile or so."

"Okay, sure. Thanks again," Muldoon said over his shoulder.

"If you find yer friends, tell 'em to get the hell outta there. Day section's closed."

Well, it was better than nothing, Mike thought as he drove away.

"Deadbeats," the man muttered under his breath as he went back in to the warmth of his little green booth and his whiskey bottle.

Mike restrained his urge to hurry, keeping his speed exactly to the prescribed 15 mph until he had rounded the first curve of the park and was safely out of the ranger's sight. Then he pressed the pedal to the floorboard, pushing for all the power he could get out of the tired engine.

The sense of grave urgency that had begun to impress itself on him earlier that evening in San Francisco had grown with every mile since. He gunned the engine to little effect: the car stubbornly plugged along at a reluc-

229

tant 25 mph.

"Running would be faster than this!" he fumed, banging his hand in frustration against the steering wheel.

It was almost a relief when he came to the chain across the road and was forced to abandon the exhausted vehicle and put his body to the test.

The religious artifacts in his jacket pockets clanked and bobbed as he ran, threatening to spill out, yet bringing a measure of comfort with their presence.

As he topped a small rise he saw the north gate station, still several hundred feet away at the base of a long gentle slope; and in the asphalt parking lot just outside the gate was Joe's red Alfa. His heart leapt as he began to sprint toward the familiar car, then hope failed when he realized its owner was nowhere in sight.

Where had he gone? Had he found Marija? Mike stopped, his eyes groping the darkness, tracking slowly up from the car, trying to spot the ridge he'd seen in his vision, below which he knew the woman lay.

Suddenly a bright glowing object shot across the sky, circling in a slow, curving arc to hover like a street lamp just above the rim of the hill that hulked behind the parking area.

The monsignor broke into a dead run, his mouth working in a breathless prayer that he wasn't too late.

The dragon had screamed and bellowed in a convulsion of fury at Marija's betrayal, his voice filling the void around the spot where she cowered with a blinding spectacle of colors. Liquid fire erupted from his mouth and flaring nostrils like a flood of molten blood — swirling, eddying, hungrily licking at the boundaries of her luminescent white mole. But it couldn't seem to touch her now.

"I'll be back for you, bitch, he had roared. "and when I

230

do, I'll teach you what it means to defy my will!"

With that, he had disappeared in an implosion of black-ness, leaving a deafening quiet behind.

Mike drove through the brush like an angry bull, scrambling up the steep slope as fast as his muscular legs would take him.

Halfway up the hill he began to notice an odd sensation, as if time were slowing down, making his limbs less effectual. As he neared the top he felt as if he were moving through heavy molasses, every muscle pulling against the unbearable load of its own mass. A huge, invisible hand seemed to flatten against his chest, holding him in place, making him strain for every inch of forward progress.

The very air had grown thick and viscous, charged with an electrical energy that stood his body hairs on end, while he continued to struggle through an invisible sea, running on useless limbs that twitched beneath the bed-covers, bathed in sweat. He cried out, his voice a gut-tural, drawn-out wail: *"J-o-o-o-o-e . . . h-e-l-p m-e-e-e-e!"*

A blinding flash of lightning shredded the air around him, and a pine tree exploded into flame and flying cin-ders. The acrid scent of ozone swirled in pungent clouds beneath his nose. Reflexively he dived to one side, float-ing heavily to the ground. As he landed he hit his hip with bruising force against a round gray rock, the glass vial in his pocket shattering—a crystalline sound, each minute concussion of the breaking shards hitting his ear-drums with perfect clarity. The spilt holy water filled the pocket of his navy pea jacket and began to seep coldly into his trouser leg.

Struggling to his hands and knees, he began to climb laboriously upward once more. It was impossible to tell

how much time was passing; it was measured in his movement, his infinitesimal progress forward—inch by difficult
inch—toward the crest of the rise just above.

All at once he felt a pair of hands attach themselves
firmly beneath his armpits, felt himself being drawn to his
feet. He looked up into the face of Joe Marten.

"Thank God," the priest wheezed, his voice, his time
sense suddenly back to normal. "Have you found her yet?
Have you found Marija?"

But before he could answer, the rolling tempest Joe had
seen approaching across the valley was upon them.

All around the two men the heavens were bent into
awesome displays of energy and power. Ball lightning
dropped and exploded in mid-air above their heads while
hundreds of jagged bolts zigzagged viciously into the earth
in every direction, setting off a myriad of small fires in
the tinder-dry forest.

This close-up display of might was set against an almost
continuous backdrop of sheet lightning, brilliant curtains
of electricity short-circuiting across the sky one after the
other. The din was enormous, shaking the ground beneath their feet with the intensity of a major earthquake.

The glowing sphere that had hovered above the ridge,
guiding the priest to Joe—trying to guide Joe to himself—
was no longer in sight, apparently having abandoned the
pair of friends to face the wrath of Satan alone.

A sudden cessation of the enveloping din startled both
men back to a studied alertness. Now a deathlike, menac-
ing stillness filled the air; a hushed anticipatory quiet like
that preceding an earthquake or hurricane. They watched
the sky, standing back to back, not daring to breathe, to
speak, even to think.

The temperature seemed to be dropping rapidly; the
sky, all at once totally devoid of light, closed in around
them like an icy fist.

Then a violet-hued shaft of light began to descend from a rent in the heavens. As it came lower, they could make out a form enclosed in its beam, a vision fabricated out of the stuff of nightmares.

It had a reptilian shape, with heavy muscular hindquarters covered in glistening green scales, the upper arms and torso of a man. Its broad back was bent under a ridge of ten spikes, proceeding up the spine from a thick tail and ending at the top of the strong bullish neck where its huge, dragonlike face began.

Mike felt a sickening dread gnarl his stomach at the sight of a monstrous instrument of copulation, swollen with sexual excitement, protruding stiffly from beneath the belly of the beast. As the creature descended past the men, dropping below the rim of the hill where they stood transfixed in horror, he turned to fasten a pair of mocking crimson-colored eyes on them.

Joe broke first, followed closely by Mike, running to look over the ledge, first to see Marija's unconscious form lying in the narrow ravine below, a small puddle of blood beneath her tousled hair turning the dusty soil dark and wet.

The beast was already clambering atop her, his scaly, clawlike hands lifting her limp hips, tearing away the fabric of her jeans as if it were paper.

"*Nooo!*" Mike hollered, teetering on the rim of the crumbly shale cliff while his hands shuffled frantically through his pockets. He withdrew the large wooden cross and hurled it down upon the broad horned back sixty feet below.

The monster let forth a piercing shriek, half-pain, half-rage. Dropping the woman, he clawed at the smoking crucifix that had embedded itself in his flesh, finally dislodging it. Where it had lain a blackened brand now smoldered amidst the glistening scales.

233

Satan's big ugly head revolved by slow degrees on the coarse neck, circumrotating a full half-circle until it was looking backward, up at the men, with a hatred so profound it was palpable. The beast seemed to hesitate, as if debating whether to come after his antagonists, then a look of malicious glee supplanted the hate in his eyes and he turned back to the insensate woman, raising her bared buttocks with his claws to meet the thrust of his organ.

Joe and Mike hurtled over the crag—half-leaping, half-falling as the shale crumbled beneath each plummeting step. It was only sixty feet to the base of the little arroyo, but before the men could attain it, they saw a change occur in the luminescent tunnel of light through which the demon had entered their world. It began to separate from the ceiling of sky, whirling like a tornado as it darkened to an ugly red; it and the wildly pumping dragon were rapidly disappearing in a spinning vortex into the body of the woman he rode.

By the time they reached her side it was too late: the beast had vanished altogether, the light was gone, and the remaining darkness was pregnant with their dread.

As Joe reached out a tentative hand, lightly touching her cheek, Marija's eyes flew open—pupilless crimson eyes that glowed wickedly in the stygian gloom—and her lovely soft lips parted to release a black slender ribbon of tongue to taste the night.

Instinctively he recoiled in horror, leaping away; but as he did the priest moved forward, dangling a rosary protectively before him as he squatted down near the side of the possessed woman.

"The cross, Joe—get the cross," Mike whispered urgently, holding the little crucifix on its string of polished prayer beads closer to Marija's face while she snarled and cringed away from the holy object.

The smaller man obediently salvaged the still-smoldering cross from its landing place in the dirt nearby, tossing it gingerly from one hand to the other. "Hot," he explained.

"Wrap it in a handkerchief, then, and hold it above her. Quickly," the priest warned, seeing the woman's body begin struggling to rise against the weak talisman he held in front of her.

Joe stood above that which had been his bride, swallowing hard. He held out the cross with both hands against the red-eyed demon she had become. Immediately the woman fell back against the ground, writhing and screaming, the foulness of her language exceeded only by the foulness of her breath. Her hands were thrown protectively over her face, her black tongue snaking at the air.

"Keep her there," Mike wanted to say, but hesitated to voice it, afraid now to speak in the presence of the beast for fear of giving him an advantage.

But Joe heard the other man as clearly as if the words had been uttered aloud.

Mike slipped the silver pyx of consecrated host from his jacket, carefully removing one of the paper-thin wafers of wheat which symbolized the body of Christ, before replacing the little box in its hiding place.

"Distract her," he whispered, at the same time beginning to edge closer to Marija's thrashing body. Joe immediately responded, leaping across to her right side and jamming the crucifix threateningly toward her face.

As she howled and turned her head away, Mike thrust himself on top of the woman, using his thumb and forefinger to jam the host into her mouth and down the back of her throat, too deep to be spit out.

Instantly a look of fury utterly transformed the delicate features of the woman: the jaw clenched shut, grazing the priest's fingers as he hurriedly leapt away. Her lips pulled back in an ugly snarl, the crimson eyes bulging in their

235

sockets at the outrage. Her entire jaw was lengthening, thickening; her even white teeth grew sharp and elongated, protruding grotesquely from bluish-black gums.

"Satan!" Mike enjoined forcefully. "By heaven be ye exorcized; by earth be ye exorcised. In the name of God and Christ Jesus I command you. *Come out of that woman!*"

The bulging throat erupted, the clenched jaw releasing a torrent of evil-smelling vomit on which rode the hated little wafer. It spewed out like magma expurgated from the bowels of the earth, covering Mike, Joe and the woman herself with its vile, blackish green liquor.

"Fuck you, asshole!" the body bellowed, the voice a deep, unearthly bass that sounded as if it were echoing from a bottomless well.

Joe pushed the crucifix at her again, but the beast appeared to be gaining strength, becoming more resistant to the sacred power of the cross. She snarled, withdrawing only slightly this time.

While the other man kept the demon occupied, Mike pulled out the incense he had stashed in the deep pocket of his woolen jacket, his hands shaking. Using parts of the black cake that had crumbled during his struggle up the hill, the priest made a circle in the dirt around the supine woman, lighting each piece of the fragrant resin in turn, hoping to trap the monster that possessed her within its pungent ring of smoke.

During the past few minutes, the far-off wailing of sirens had begun to intrude into their consciousness, gradually growing louder, closer. Joe, suddenly remembering the multitude of small lightning fires that had been set off during the freak storm earlier, now became aware that there was a strong smell of wood smoke combining with the odor of the burning incense.

"Shit," he swore under his breath. This new external threat meant their time was even more limited: the exorcism must be complete before the fires had them completely surrounded.

"We've got to discover the name of the deity this demon most fears," Muldoon broke into Joe's thoughts. "That plus his own name are all we really need to bind and exorcise him. The rest of this stuff," he indicated the burning incense, the crucifix in the other man's hands, "are simply artifacts which buy us time, help us keep him under control until we can get rid of him once and for all."

"Well, time is one thing we don't have a lot of," Joe informed him, looking at the sky. A reddish glow encompassed them on three sides, replacing the blackness with its ominous doomsday hue. Brighter spots and flares could be seen here and there where the fires raged out of control: the smoke was becoming thicker, and they noticed a fine mist of ash beginning to dust their heads and shoulders.

A subdued, distant crackle could be heard through the thin night air, and though the temperature immediately within their narrow ravine remained abnormally frigid, they could see where the heat from the approaching conflagration was distorting the surrounding atmosphere into wavering streams, sucking the available oxygen into the cooler strata above.

Mike blew on his stiff, aching fingers to warm them, casting one more worried glance at the burning forest before returning his attention to the task before them.

The dragon was leering out at him through Marija's blood-colored eyes, a sarcastic grimace distorting her misshapen, twisted face.

"Fuck you, priest," the hollow voice rumbled. "You'll never get rid of me. I *like* it in here."

With a gleeful snort, the monster began contorting the woman's body, heaving the hips and red-stained pubic area up and down in a grotesque parody of fornication. The slender, delicate hands were flung convulsively to her chest, ripping open the cotton blouse, tearing apart the flimsy brassiere beneath. She began to knead and tease the soft, full breasts until the nipples stood erect and rigid with excitement, all the while rolling her hips suggestively.

"Getting turned on, cocksucker?" the heavy voice sneered. Then, whipping the girl's head around to face Joe on her other side, it tormented, "How about you, hubby? Don't you want to fuck your little bride?"

The distorted mouth that had once smothered his in gentle kisses opened wide in ugliness, emitting a high keening squeal of derision, that of a pig at slaughter, the stench of putrescent death riding the foul breath. Her black ribbon of tongue flicked out an amazing length, lapping playfully at his genital area.

It was too much.

A cold, shaking rage overtook the man, replacing the pain and fear with a killing fury. But as Joe raised the crucifix above his head like a club, he felt a muscular arm reach out to stay his hand.

"No, Joe," Mike warned, his thoughts piercing the other man's anger. "Don't you see? That's what he *wants* us to do. If we kill her body with him inside it, Marija is lost forever . . . and so are we. If we kill *her*, we can never be free of *him*: he will own her soul *and* us by the act!"

As Joe slowly lowered the cross, tears pooling in his downcast eyes, Mike extracted the book on white magic from his coat, flipping to the glossary of deities. He was prepared to recite every name on the list — provided the fire didn't envelope them first — from the gods of ancient Egypt and Babylonia through the entire litany of saints in the *Rituale Romanum*, if necessary, until he found the one holy being that this horrible incubus would bend to.

In actual fact, it took only a few seconds, for when he

reached the seventh entry under "monotheistic deities," calling out *"Jehovah."* the demon shrank within the body of the woman, momentarily restoring her normal features as he threw her arms protectively across his eyes.

"Jehovah, from Hebrew JHVH, 'he that is'." Mike pronounced the name again carefully, testing the initial reaction for verity: the body writhed and began to flip-flop about on the ground like a beached fish, gasping in apparent distress.

"That's it!" he exclaimed triumphantly, starting immediately to thumb through the last few pages, looking now for the roster of demons. But before he reached it he paused, struck by the hope that perhaps—from the beast's reaction to *"Jehovah"*—invoking that name alone might be enough to exorcise him. Maybe he wouldn't need to evoke the demon's own title as well.

He was all too aware of the sky reddening around them, growing brighter with each passing moment; of the sibilant thunder exploding through the forest, growing ever closer as it devoured the trees with a hungry ferocity. Time was running out; he decided to try it.

"Hear me, Satan! In Jehovah's name, I order you out of this woman!" he commanded loudly, drawing a worried glance from Joe, still holding the crucifix above his prostrate wife.

In response, Marija's body again started to flail wildly, then went totally limp. An odd, soundless hush fell over the little ravine, and in the midst of it the woman began to rise slowly from the ground.

"By Jehovah be ye exorcised!" Mike chanted more forcefully. But the body continued to rise.

With a growing sense of desperation, the priest shouted, "In the name of Jehovah I bind thee!" The woman's supine form paused now, floating nearly five feet off the ground.

"In the name of Jehovah I exorcise thee!" the black man screamed.

Marija's face turned toward the men, staring at them with cold, dead eyes. The lips bent into the faintest hint of a smile, the body revolving slowly in their direction, two pale, flaccid arms reaching out to them. Then she was flung, unresisting as a rag doll, headfirst into a twenty-foot-high boulder on their right.

The two men stared in stunned horror as blood poured down the woman's shattered nose, staining her exposed breasts and belly and spraying off in dark wet droplets onto the ground below. Still floating, she was suddenly jerked up into a vertical position and hurled back across the narrow gorge toward them, bouncing off the shoulder of the startled priest with such force that he was knocked to the ground. Abruptly she switched directions, once more flying loose-limbed and helpless toward a second self-immolation against the granite face of the large rock that filled the center of the hollow.

Dropping the cross, Joe leapt as if released from a spring, grabbing the woman about the knees in a flying tackle before she could hit the boulder's jagged surface. He tumbled with her to the earth. The strength of the beast within was enormous. Even as he fought to hold on, Joe could feel her slipping from his grasp, wrenching away.

"The cross!" he cried out feverishly. "Muldoon, get the cross!"

But the priest was one step ahead of him; he'd already snatched the wooden symbol from the ground where Joe'd dropped it, was beginning to press it down against Marija's naked chest even as Joe spoke.

They smelled the sickly sweet odor of her searing flesh, felt their guts being torn by the screams of pain that seemed to go on forever before the woman finally sagged

240

into unconsciousness beneath their touch.

"Oh, God, what have we done to her?" Joe cried, lifting himself off the body of his wife and snatching the cross from her smoking chest with his free hand.

A blackened outline of the crucifix was emblazoned between her soft, pale breasts, the charred areas fissured with raw, seeping scars where the pinkish meat of her flesh showed through the darkly crinkled skin.

Her eyes were closed, her breath struggled weakly through the once-delicate nose, now hideously bent to one side. It released a steady stream of bright red blood which ran down through the lines on either side of her mouth, dribbling over her jaw line and down her neck to congeal in a thick, sticky mass among the strands of her fine dark hair.

"Marija!" he cried, weeping.

"It's *not* Marija, not anymore," cautioned Mike harshly. "Now hold the cross over her, close to her face: we've got to keep the monster in check or he'll kill her before I can find out his name and complete the exorcism."

As soon as Joe'd complied, Mike began to read from the book of white magic again intoning the names of known demons from its glossary while watching attentively for the slightest reaction from the possessed woman:

" 'Tiamat,' 'Set,' 'Pazuzu,' 'Satan,' 'Beelezebub,' 'Lucifer,' 'Mephistopheles,' 'Mara,' 'Ahriman,' 'Nemeroth,' 'Iblis,' 'Abaddon' . . . "

A tree exploded and fell nearby, near enough that they could feel the heat, the sudden brightening of the sky as its sparks and embers flew in all directions. *"Hurry,"* Joe implored him.

Mike finished the list without result, then doggedly went through it again, reading each successive name with increasing urgency: still nothing, not a blink, not a sigh. *Nothing.*

241

"Do you think he's still in there?" Joe asked. "Maybe you got rid of him the first time after all."

As if in answer, the woman's eyes opened and the red orbs of the beast glittered out wickedly. But aside from that, it made no overt move. It seemed to be waiting now — perhaps for the fire to finish off the work it had begun.

"Damn, what do we do now?" Mike despaired, slamming the book closed. "I was so sure I'd find it! I was half expecting it to be 'Iblis' — that's the name it responded to at the seance."

"Maybe this isn't the same demon," Joe suggested. "Or maybe Satan has many faces, many names, all part of the whole entity? However that may be, I've got a gut feeling that the one we're dealing with here is the big gun, the original, if there is such a thing."

"Of course!" the priest cried, slapping the book against his palm, his voice all but lost in the roar of the approaching conflagration. "The final battle."

Joe looked at him quizzically.

"I'll explain later," Mike promised, "but you *are* right about who it is we're up against here."

"Mike," Joe volunteered, shifting back to a low whisper in an attempt to avoid being overheard by the red-eyed beast peering up at them from the woman's battered face. "When I started checking into the occult, after Marija's first supernatural episode, I found out that one could supposedly summon up Satan by reciting the Lord's Prayer backward. I even tried it," he admitted sheepishly, "but nothing happened, so I figured it was a crock. I think now I may know *why* it didn't work: I think you have to *pronounce* each word backwards as well, as if you were reading them in a mirror."

"In a mirror?" Mike mused. "You mean as if . . . as if Satan is the *mirror image* of God?"

"Yes," he said after a minute, his voice hoarse. "That which twists the truth into a lie so deceptively close, yet so exactly opposite, that one cannot tell which is which. *That's* how he deceives mankind so well and so completely!"

"Then if Satan *is* the perfect mirror image of our concept of God," Joe continued the thought excitedly; "and if the name of this God is Jehovah, then the demon's name must be . . . " he paused, both men struggling with the transposition, "Havohej! He who is *not!*" they cried aloud in unison.

The woman's eyes opened wider, but where before there had been a cooly mocking hatred, there now was fear. Her back began rapidly to arch in a convulsed tetany, bending at the waist like a hunter's bow, threatening to snap in two. Joe pressed the cross closer to her face, but that kept only her head down; the back continued to bend alarmingly while her mouth screamed blasphemies unto the heavens. Out of the corner of his eye Joe noticed the priest incongruously tearing off his jacket.

"Here, help me put this over her." the man ordered.

"What for?" Joe yelled back, straining to press her back down, keep her from breaking her spine.

"It's soaked with holy water; it might help," Mike explained, flinging the garment over her nude torso. Immediately the rigid form relaxed, collapsing to the ground in a crumpled heap.

"Havohej! He who is not!" Mike shouted over the crackling thunder of the fire, now exploding trees a mere one hundred yards beyond the barren ridge above them. "In the name of Jehovah, He who *is*, I bind thee! Havohej. He who is NOT! In Jehovah's name I exorcise thee!"

A tremendous wailing shriek split the air; the female

243

body jerked violently, throwing Joe to one side. From the place between her splayed legs an eerie light appeared, rapidly becoming a whirling reverse vortex of the light that had gone into her earlier. As it eddied outward and up, they could see within its cloudy glow the trapped fury of the vanquished dragon raging impotently at them as he rose higher and higher, until he and the beam of light had disappeared back into the black void beyond the sky.

Behind lay his discarded pawn, the woman called Marija, battered and broken on the bloodstained earth.

Chapter 17

The heavy jowled homicide inspector retrieved the folded newspaper from his desk where Detective Muñoz had tossed it with a terse "Read it and weep" a moment before.

"Go ahead, read it," the sergeant urged, "It's gonna give a cosmic enema to your favorite case."

The older man sighed and opened the afternoon edition of the San Francisco tabloid. "Which?" he growled at Muñoz, who was hovering behind his left shoulder.

The sergeant reached over and poked a stubby finger at the top of the page. "Headline, man; page one."

"Freak Electrical Storm Sets off Fire in Mt. Diablo Park; Three Campers Missing."

"So?" he snarled.

"Read it!" Munoz repeated in exasperation.

Lieutenant Grogan read:

245

"A freak electrical storm hit central Contra Costa County late last night, downing power lines between Alamo and San Ramon and start a number of flash fires throughout the heavily wooded area immediately surrounding Mt. Diablo State Park. Hardest hit was the park itself, where three San Francisco residents, apparently trapped in a remote area, are missing and presumed dead as a result of the firestorms which ravaged the northern perimeter of the popular camping area.

"Nah," breathed the aging detective, shaking his head at the first inkling of what was to come. "*Can't* be." Almost reluctantly he read on:

According to park ranger Alec Harding, the electrical storm which struck without warning from a previously cloudless sky shortly after 11:30 PM Friday night, was the worst he'd seen in twenty years of park service.

"Luckily most of our campers were in the lower campgrounds, like they were supposed to be," Harding reported, "so we were able to get them all out okay. But just before the firestorm started an unidentified male came through the south gate looking for some friends. Against park rules he went on up to the day area to see if he could locate them. I don't know what happened after that; the fire blocked off all access to the area almost instantly. There was nothing we could do!"

A later report from Contra Costa Fire Department officials revealed that two burned-out vehicles were discovered shortly after dawn in the vicinity of the north gate day campground, one matching the description of that driven by the missing camper. An immediate search of the area was launched, and a little after 8 AM search-and-rescue teams found a badly charred jacket and a pair of women's shoes in a narrow ravine nearby, but no traces of the missing persons.

Detective Paul Grogan felt a queasy shock pass through his bowels. He mopped the heavy film of perspiration from his brow with a stained handkerchief. "Fuck me," he said, taking a swallow of cold coffee from the paper cup at his elbow. Grimacing, he picked up the paper again and continued.

In a bizarre twist to this story, the cars destroyed by the fire were identified through DMV records as belonging to two prime suspects in the 'Seance Double Murder' case that rocked this city only two days ago: Reverend Michael Muldoon, former pastor of St. Jude's Parish here in the city, and Joseph R. Marten. It is speculated that the unidentified third camper was probably Marija Draekins Marten, the other suspect in the case.

Though no trace of the missing trio has yet been found in the rugged terrain, fire department and state park officials concur that the probability of them having escaped on foot is minimal, due to the extreme speed and intensity with which the fire converged on that area."

"Ah shit!" the overweight lieutenant blew up, throwing the paper down on his desk in disgust. "Why the fuck wasn't I notified about this earlier?"

"I checked," the sergeant shrugged, unruffled. "So far

247

the case is still being handled by the local sheriff's department . . . *So what* that the broad and her missing lover-boys are prime suspects in one of our biggest murder cases? You think those yokels give a shit about San Francisco police biz?"

"Well *I*, for one, don't believe it!" the older man stormed, his beefy face red with fury. "I don't believe this disappearance was any fuckin' accident; and I don't *believe* the three of 'em are lying about out there somewhere like a bucket of Colonel Sanders' extra crispies . . . and I *don't* believe that my whole fucking case has gone up in smoke just like that!"

"Believe it," the other man advised, suppressing a smile at the totally unintentional pun of the humorless inspector. He popped a sunflower seed nonchalantly into his mouth, proffering the cellophane bag to Grogan, who slapped it away in disgust.

"When I see it, my young friend, when these tired cynical, overworked eyes gaze down upon the french-fried carcasses of those three killers — flat and cold as the stainless steel dissecting tables they're laid on — *then* maybe I'll believe they're all dead; then I'll let go. In the meantime, the case remains open."

Chapter 18

Sunday, June 17th
Rome

The pair of American travelers trudged wearily down the ramp of the Italian airliner, their shoulders drooping with the weight of their flight bags.

They paused momentarily as they reached the tarmac, squinting up at the early morning sun, then continued their slow procession toward customs.

Both were clean shaven, but there was a lightness around the jaw line of the taller man which contrasted sharply with his dark brown cheeks and forehead. A similar white patch, less noticeable, lay across the upper lip and down the sides of the mouth of the sandy haired male, giving him a wistful appearance. Had anyone bothered to sniff closely, they'd have caught the unmistakable scent of wood smoke on their skin and something akin to burnt chicken feathers clinging stubbornly to their hair, despite hasty shampoos in the Oakland Air Terminal restroom prior to their noon departure the previous day.

Their clothes were new and clean, if somewhat rumpled from the overnight flight, and purposely nondescript: cheap, short-sleeved pastel polo shirts, tan polyester slacks, sport jackets slung casually over their arms.

Though physically quite different, there was yet something strikingly similar about the pair: a quality in their carriage, an intense, almost haunted look about the eyes, as if the men had been hollowed out, scraped clean of their humanness by some incomprehensible horror, then refilled with an all-consuming purpose that went beyond any normal passion: beyond hate, beyond love, beyond fear or vengeance. As they moved deliberately to the terminal, that hollow fire caused more than one fellow passenger to take a second look.

The customs officer searched their canvas travel bags with extra care, made suspicious by their itchy energy, which he mistook for nervousness, their lack of the usual tourist accoutrements. But there was nothing to justify his mistrust; just underwear, socks, toiletries, a change of clothes. A Bible.

"Traveling light, signori," he commented obliquely, frisking the lining of their bags with sensitive fingers.

"A rather impromptu trip of faith, I'm afraid," Mike replied lightly, clenching his fists in his pockets to keep his voice from shaking. "We decided at the last moment to attend the coronation of the new Pope. It *is* today, is it not?"

"Ah yes, signore," the official assented, his attitude suddenly more cordial, relieved, as he tucked their belongings back into the canvas satchels. He checked the big chrome Timex on his wrist: "You will have to hurry; it begins in less than three hours. There are rental cars available outside," he suggested helpfully, zippering their bags back up and waving them through. "Welcome to Italy," he called after their rapidly retreating backs.

250

"Three hours," sighed Joe once they were out of ear-shot. "If you are right in what you told me, if this is the only way to be sure Marija is forever free of that beast . . ."

"It is," Mike assured him.

"Then somehow we must in the three hours remaining to us, change the opinion of the world about the sacredness of the Pope . . ."

"No, just the College of Cardinals," interjected the priest, thinking perhaps there was little difference at that.

". . . and stop the papal coronation, because if we fail . . ." He looked at his companion.

Mike shrugged, swallowed against rising tears. All they could do was try.

In a quiet room of a large Oakland hospital a woman lay sleeping. Her face and chest were swathed in bandages. Her identity was swathed in mystery.

No one had seen her come in the night before, but that was not unusual with the chaos typical of an urban ghetto hospital on a Friday night.

Someone, the admissions clerk who worried over such matters speculated, *must* know her: someone must have brought her in.

She was too badly injured to have come in under her own power, the doctors concurred: she had a serious concussion, a badly broken nose and arm, and numerous bruises . . . not to mention a pair of strange-shaped third-degree burns, ones that looked as if they might have been inflicted with a branding iron.

"Wife abuse," the interns whispered, nodding sagely.

Their consensus was confirmed a few hours later when a male voice called to inquire about the mystery woman's condition, but hung up when pushed to give her identity or his own.

Well, they'd all done *their* duty, the hospital personnel agreed. They could only hope that when the woman regained consciousness she'd finger the creep that did this to her so they could bring the police in on the matter and have the shitheel arrested . . . if the woman would press charges.

Most of the time they never did . . . .

Two
The Coronation

and all the world wondered after the beast.
Revelations 13:4

Chapter 19

There was an aching lump in the man's throat and chest, and he bent over almost protectively, holding the pain to him. It was all he had of the woman right now. The pain, a few memories which hurt too much to look at, and the uncertain hope that this quest he was now irrevocably committed to might bring the bittersweet release of revenge . . . and bring Marija, the *old* Marija, back.

He forced his tired legs to quicken their pace. The taller man, who had shaped the design of their dubious mission, had begun to outdistance him, pushing through the misty sunlight with a coldly burning passion, a determination to stop the abomination scheduled to take place within the hour.

Joe wished he could share the fervor that glittered from the priest's dark eyes, the conviction which spurred his worn, ash-blackened boots forward against the weariness that must be wobbling his limbs as much as Joe's by now.

255

All Joe wanted at this point was to get it over with, to get even — and to get some sleep.

The taxi they'd taken in from the airport had let them off more than a kilometer from St. Peter's Square, across the Tiber from Castle San Angelo.

They'd crossed the Tiber, the sluggish, slate-blue river which dissected and immortalized the eternal city to which it had given birth, over an ancient, arched stone bridge. There were no cars on the bridge, just a slow, steady stream of pedestrians, all heading west, just as they were. Roadblocks had been set up the night before across all arteries and thoroughfares that led to the Vatican. Only official Vatican limousines and those of card-carrying dignitaries were allowed to proceed inside the city gates . . . plus, of course, the official cars and sound trucks of the media, who could always go anywhere, it seemed.

Anyone else who wished to witness the historic coronation of the world's first auxiliary Pope would just have to hoof it: there was no special parking for the handicapped today, Joe mused sardonically.

Early-morning sun radiated off pastel stucco buildings on either side of the broad avenue with a golden apricot glow. Muldoon took in the beauty of his surroundings with an ironic expression on his tightly set lips. It's come full circle, he thought, this holy city where the first Christians provided endless entertainment for the elite of ancient Rome before the snapping jaws of half-starved lions. He shook his head.

The Vatican itself had been erected over the site of Roman Emperor Nero's public gardens and circus, where many early Christians suffered martyrdom, and where, according to Catholic tradition, Saint Peter himself was crucified and buried. Over his very tomb, it was said, the main altar of St. Peter's Basilica now stood.

Mystery Babylon the Great, the priest thought, shuddering despite the warmth of the sun. "Drunken with the blood of saints and with the blood of the martyrs of Jesus. . . ."

He hadn't realized he was speaking aloud until Joe stopped him with a gentle hand on his arm, a questioning look.

"Nothing." He shook his head, smiling ruefully.

As the two men neared the eye of the keyhole-shaped plaza that widened into St. Peter's Square, the sudden surge of the crowd became stultifying. The combined heat of thousands of hurrying, sweaty bodies turned the air around them into an oven. Joe felt giddy, nauseated. The buildings on either side loomed up huge and overpowering, then they too wavered and danced in his vision.

He swiped a perspiring palm across his eyes, his hand slipping down to give a nervous, habitual tug at the thick mustache that was no longer there. He scratched the side of his mouth instead, as if that was what he'd meant to do all along.

More than forty hours without sleep was taking its toll on him, erasing the steadying effect of physical reality, substituting dreamlike qualities to the structure of the world around him.

The crowd thinned slightly as it poured from the narrow bottleneck of the entrance into the broad plaza, giving the two companions a momentary sense of expansiveness, relief. But less than fifty yards ahead they could see that the mass of humanity again grew tightly packed as everyone pressed relentlessly towards the Basilica at the far end of the immense square. It was there that the momentous event they had all come to witness would shortly occur, unless the two Americans could find a way to stop it.

"Mike," Joe called above the murmuring river of people that carried them along. "We'll never get through this crowd in time. How can we hope to prevent"—he caught himself, looked around for eavesdroppers—"things now?"

He immediately hated the way his voice sounded, the despairing, self-pitying whine of it. He sounded like a tired and petulant child. There had just been so much lately, so damn much . . . he swallowed hard.

Muldoon stopped to consider his friend carefully. The light faded from his eyes momentarily, revealing the compassion and understanding that comprised the essential core of the man.

"I know, Joe," he said, his voice a sighing whisper that somehow carried above the crowds, his words encompassing not just their present dilemma, but the whole of the other man's misery, their shared misery and loss.

He broke eye contact then, the pain too personal, and began to scan his surroundings, taking in the tall, red granite obelisk that towered over the central piazza like a finger pointing accusingly toward heaven, the majestic double colonnades that encircled the huge arena drawing the worshipers forward like embracing arms to the awesome basilica at its head. Along the roof of the colonnade were set a series of great marble statues—some badly decayed, but still awe-inspiring—the embodiments of saints and apostles in seemingly endless procession. Stately, serene, their frozen expression of divine piety acted as uncomfortable reminders of the sacred traditions they guarded. Their sightless marble eyes seeming to glare in silent accusation, as if they knew his purpose and were already condemning him.

But for his *intention*—or for his probable failure?

258

"Let's go around to the side," he muttered, turning from the accusing eyes of the statues. "Maybe we can find a way through to the Vatican offices." He consulted the pocket-sized Baedeker he'd picked up at the airport which had a map of the Vatican inside. "If we try to stop this travesty out here in the square, in the middle of the ceremony," he explained, taking Joe by the elbow and beginning to edge the two of them toward the perimeter, "we'll get ourselves arrested and deported, if not stoned. I think our best bet is to find someone in authority, high up enough to do some good . . . maybe even the secretary of state himself. Then we convince *him* to stop this thing, or at the very least, postpone it until there can be a full investigation of our charges."

"If there's anyone in authority left who'll listen," Joe responded grimly. "Maybe it's too late, everything's too late. . . ."

He was remembering Marija.

It wasn't until they were somewhere over the polar ice cap on their hurried flight to Rome that Mike had at last filled him in on the full scope of what was happening, of where the possession of Marija and their involvement in the battle to save her from it fit into a much greater war.

"Look, Joe," the priest had said, bringing out his worn, slightly singed Bible from his overnight bag. "This is what I was coming to tell you about last night, you and Marija . . ." His voice had caught on the sound of her name.

When Mike had finished explaining the whole thing for him, Joe had shrugged doubtfully, not entirely convinced, his mind whirring with input overload, his heart still too full of pain and worry over his wife to care much whether or not two "beasts" were taking over the Catholic Church.

259

"Okay," Muldoon had acknowledged, almost as if Joe had expressed his reservations aloud, "then check this out. Maybe this next section will bring it all together for you."

He'd flipped through several more pages until he came to the allegory about the whore of Babylon, then handed the small black book back to Joe, explaining the text as Joe read. -

"The seven mountains upon which the woman sits," he said patiently, "are the seven hills of Rome. It *has* to be Rome, don't you see?"

Joe nodded contemplatively.

"And here it speaks of a scarlet colored beast with ten horns that the whore — the Vatican, if you will — sitteth upon. That's the same beast that it talked about earlier, in Chapter Thirteen. And here," he pointed to another verse on the page, "where it says that the great whore sitteth on many waters, and these waters represent peoples and multitudes and nations and tongues — this indicates a state or organization which has influence over a great portion of the world. So *you* tell *me*, what other religious, political, or financial institution has reached its fingers into as many areas of the world today as the Roman Catholic Church?

"Joe? Think about it, who else *could* be the whore of Babylon? It's got to be Vatican City, Joe. It's what the seat of the Roman Catholic Church will become if Havohej's plan to put his beasts on the throne of power is carried through."

Joe had nodded with reluctant belief. If this was what it was all about, okay. Then he'd come to the right place to avenge Marija. That's all he really cared about.

And now, here in the very shadow of Saint Peter's, as they pushed and wriggled their way through the endless tides of the faithful, the not-so-faithful, and the merely curious, on their way to find someone with the authority and willingness to stop the coronation of the second beast, to stop the final transfer of the vast spiritual, political, and financial power of the Catholic Church into the teeth of the Dragon, Joe still thought of revenge.

Chapter 20

Sunday, June 17th
San Francisco

Lieutenant Paul Grogan was not a particularly genial man. At his best — usually after the Forty-Niners won a football game, provided he'd had the afternoon off to watch it — he was gruffly cheerful. At his worst he was a blazing asshole, as his former wife had pointed out fifteen years earlier when she made her final exit from his life.

Today his mood ranged somewhere between Ivan the Terrible and Godzilla. Even Sergeant Muñoz, who'd learned to roll with the verbal punches over the years, had gladly parted company with a twenty dollar bill to get the day officer to fake an assignment that would get him out of going with Grogan to the fire scene.

Before he left, Grogan put in a call to the Contra Costa County sheriff in charge of the investigation. In a moment the tired, patient, softly-accented voice of Sheriff Cardenza came on.

"Yes, Lieutenant Grogan, what may I do for you?" he

inquired.

"You found 'em yet, Sheriff?"

"You mean the three missing campers?"

"Campers, my ass! Give me a break, Cardenza—those people are cold-blooded murderers!"

"Oh? There has been a trial already, then?"

"All right, murder *suspects*, then . . . *alleged* murder suspects. According to you, alleged accident victims, I suppose. But damn good murder suspects, let me tell you, and I'm not about to let them off the hook on the supposition that they might have been victims of some damned brush fire. Tell me, Sheriff, any positive evidence of their *allegedly* incinerated carcasses yet?"

"No, Lieutenant, nothing so far."

"I'm coming out there, Cardenza. I want to have a look at the scene myself, if you don't mind."

"Suit yourself . . . *Grogan*. Do you want me to meet you there?"

After the call to Cardenza, Grogan immediately punched the button to connect with the PBX operator in the station exchange.

"This is Grogan. Page Muñoz and tell him to get his ass up here on the double." He hung up without waiting for acknowledgement. Muñoz appeared almost at once.

"What's up, sir?"

"Put out an APB on Muldoon and Martens, statewide; then start checking all points of egress from the bay area: buses, taxis, airlines, the works. You can reach me through the CC Sheriff's department if you come up with anything."

He jammed on a dirty, misshapen brown felt hat and

263

squirmed his way into a nondescript cloth overcoat which had grown noticeably smaller over the years. Then he scooped the contents of his desk top indiscriminately into the jacket's oversized pockets.

He took a moment to light the disheveled looking Roi-Tan he'd been grinding between his yellowed teeth half the morning, peering over the flame at his unmoving assistant.

"Well, what're you waiting for, Muñoz, a gilt-edged manifesto? Get your ass moving!" he belched in a cloud of pungent smoke.

Chapter 21

The Vatican

The two Americans pressed forward through the crowds beneath the sheltered colonnade, Mike leading Joe by the arm, edging toward the inner wall of the huge covered walkway. Next to its granite columns squatted a group of full-breasted mothers blithely nursing their chubby infants while withered old men leaned against the cool pillars as if for support, leering sidewise at the happy show of breasts. Out from the wall lumpy old women in flowered dresses shifted their weight, fanning themselves distractedly against the heat.

A hundred feet farther on beneath the open-faced passageway the men came upon the Portone di Bronzo, a huge bronze door flanked by a small ticket office and two young Swiss Guards, which served as the main entrance to the Vatican Palace. Beyond the door was a vast, ornate chamber which, though far from deserted, was much less congested than the Piazza. As they moved inside, the priest found himself suddenly diminished by the incredible grandeur of religious art that seemed to

assault him from all sides. As they walked the long Cor-
ridoro del Bernini toward the broad staircase at its far
end, the gilt and gold and glory stared down at him
from every square inch of the vaulted ceiling, every
carved, lighted niche along the frescoed walls.

It was like walking inside a work of art. Magnificent
murals depicted biblical scenes—mostly saints being mar-
tyred, he observed wryly, who stared down at his effrontery: he entered their hallowed presence with dirty boots,
fire-singed hair, a blemished soul and secret purpose.
"What are you *doing*, Muldoon?" they seemed to scream
in their perpetual agony, their ecstatic bliss.

He shook his head, rubbed his eyes, steeled his resolve.
It was *for* their faith, their ultimate sacrifice, that he
must do this, not *against* it. I'm here to join you, a part
of his soul cried back. It is to preserve that for which
you lived and died. One day my likeness may be painted
there among you, immortalized—but whether as saint or
demon . . . .

He approached one of the quaintly costumed Swiss
Guards who stood immobile against a marble column in
his bright blue, gold, and crimson striped pantaloons and
blouse.

"Scusi, signore, but could you direct me to the office
of the secretary of state, please?" Muldoon requested,
hoping his voice conveyed none of his inner turmoil.

"That would be across the Cortile di San Damaso, the
inner courtyard," the guard answered politely, indicating
the direction. "Up the elevator to the third story. *But*," he
added hastily as the wild-eyed visitor turned to leave,
"one cannot meet with His Eminence unless one has a
prior appointment, and is as well . . ." he paused, looking obliquely over Mike's cheap polyester slacks and shirt,

his worn boots and canvas bag . . . "a personage of, shall we say, some importance."

"I assure you, the business I have with His Eminence is of such urgency that the cardinal secretary will have no objection to this slight breach of protocol . . . not once he hears what I have to say."

"I am sure you are telling the truth, signore," the guard nodded somberly. "But I am afraid that any audience today, no matter how 'vital', is completely out of the question. The cardinal secretary is in the midst of preparations for this morning's coronation of our new Pontiff. . . ."

"But that is precisely what we came to see the secretary about!" Joe found himself blurting out. "He must be convinced to stop this coronation. "It *cannot* be allowed to take place!"

A short, rotund figure approaching the trio paused in his slow, rolling gait upon hearing this proclamation, then slipped back into the shadows. His heart had begun to accelerate at the words. Archbishop Luigi Magliano thought he was the only person in the Vatican, perhaps in the entire world, who entertained any serious doubts about the impending coronation, the purported "miracles" that had shaken the papal throne over the past ten days.

But what was this now, these two strangers with their colorless clothing and burning eyes, demanding that the coronation be stopped? Hot tears of hope sprang to the emotional Italian's eyes. "God, what have you sent us here?" he prayed.

The arguments down the hall were getting louder, more heated. The guard sounded testy. Perhaps he should break in before these two—Americans by their accents—found themselves being escorted into the custody

267

of the Italian police.

"Signori," the guard was saying in a tight, angry voice. "You are being foolish in your demands, dangerously foolish. This is a holy place, a place of God, and you are coming very close to blasphemy in what you say. I must ask you to depart at once, before I am compelled to have you forcibly removed."

"Please, if I may intercede," Luigi broke in as he hurried forward, mopping at his brow with a stained handkerchief. "Allow me to introduce myself. I am Archbishop Magliano, public relations representative for the Vatican. The papal secretary is, I am afraid, not in his suite at this hour, not even in the building, I fear." This was said in a most apologetic manner as he laid a pudgy hand on the small of the larger man's back, another on the arm of his slender companion. He began to apply a gentle pressure against the two men, steering them gently away from further confrontation with the guard, talking rapidly to distract them.

"Perhaps I can be of some service to you, if you would tell me what this is about."

If he was hoping for an instant exchange of confidences, a flurry of revelations, he was quickly disappointed. The imposing black man who seemed to be the stronger of the pair apparently had his mind set on finding the cardinal secretary and making his disclosures, his appeal, to that figurehead alone. For his part, Magliano was not about to risk exposing his own antagonism toward the Pope-elect to virtual strangers, not until he was sure what these two had in mind, what their actual feelings and motives were.

"You may indeed, if you will just tell me where I can find the cardinal secretary," Mike answered his escort once they were out of earshot of the guard. "It is he I must tell my story to, only he who has sufficient power to stop this fiasco now."

"He's on the other side of the Piazza di San Pietro, in the Pope's own offices, getting ready for the ceremonial procession, I'm afraid," Luigi answered in a low voice.

"*Are* you afraid? You *should* be," Mike accused, turning to direct a disconcertingly penetrating look on the nervous little Italian. "Perhaps," he amended, his eyes thoughtfully probing the other man's, "perhaps you really *are?*"

"You will never get through these throngs of well-wishers in time to see him in any case," the archbishop sighed, shaking his head, avoiding the strangers' perceptive gaze, the uncomfortable question he had posed. "Even if he *would* listen, which I doubt."

"We've got to try anyway, *got* to!" Mike avowed grimly, taking Joe by the elbow as they bounded down the marble steps beyond. He stopped halfway down the brief flight to turn his brown eyes back onto the worried face of the Italian archbishop. "Thank you, Your Excellency," he said with a nod, then hurried away.

Luigi Magliano watched the pair as they ran loudly down the quiet, nearly deserted corridor toward the bronze door which opened onto the Piazza.

Your Excellency, Luigi thought. He must be familiar with church protocol to know to call an archbishop by that title. Who is he, where did he come from, what does he know?

Then, making the sign of the cross, he began slowly and reluctantly to follow.

Chapter 22

Mt. Diablo State Park,
California

Cardenza turned out to be tall and slender, with an aristocratic hook to his long, straight nose, full salon-cut hair, and a heady intelligence behind his mutable hazel eyes. In his sharply pressed khaki uniform he looked like the poster boy for a recruitment campaign. Certainly too damned young and good looking to take the job of fighting crime seriously, Grogan sniffed, unconsciously sucking in his own flabby girth, which only imperceptibly receded from its comfortable overhang above his rumpled trousers.

He locked up his decrepit Ford and climbed into the sheriff's unit for the ride in from the park entrance.

The line where the fire began—or ended—was as clearly marked as if it had been laid out by a surveyor's transit: on one side the scrub oak, manzanita, and Monterey pine scrambled for footing in the sun, as green and vigorous as anywhere else in the park. On the other was a barren wasteland of blackened ruin. Infrequent pines stood here and there like dark sentinels over the charred remains of smaller trees and bushes; even the rocks were covered in a pall of gray ash. In some places along the demarcation line of the fire an oak, pine, or manzanita stood half-ruined, one side a blistered, black, denuded skeleton, the other untouched, green, and alive.

"Whew," remarked Grogan as they turned onto a side road into the heart of the fire path. "Some inferno this must have been!"

"Now maybe you can see why we thought it impossible for anyone to have escaped it on foot."

"Yeah, well . . . " Grogan begrudged even the smallest admission of a possible misjudgment on his part. This terse comment was all the sheriff was going to get.

The two burned-out vehicles belonging to the priest and to Joe Marten had already been towed over to the sheriff's substation in Danville, but Cardenza pointed out where they'd been: Muldoon's here, where the chain had been blocking the road into the day camping area; Marten's over there in the outer parking zone, near the restrooms.

The sheriff pulled into a space near the north park entrance where the second car had been found. Two other vehicles were already there, a cream-colored sedan with the insignia of the Contra Costa Sheriff's Department, and a red four-wheel-drive truck belonging to the fire department's search-and-rescue unit.

"Still lookin', huh?" Grogan grunted with a nod toward the latter.

"Still lookin'," Cardenza acknowledged.

The trek up the steep hillside behind the restroom made the out-of-shape detective more winded than he cared to let on in front of this powerhouse who'd been leading the way at a killer pace. He stopped halfway up the hill, leaning against the charcoal stump of what had once been a stately pine, making an elaborate show of lighting a bedraggled cigar. Cardenza noted, grinning, that the old guy didn't bother to trouble his lungs with smoke from the damn thing once he'd taken an interminable time to get it going.

From the other side of the ridge, the youthful sheriff pointed out the spot where a jacket and other evidence had been found at the bottom of a fifty-foot ravine. About thirty feet from the base of the cliff was an enormous white boulder, some twenty feet in diameter and nearly forty feet tall, it's top rounded by wind and weather to a smooth lumpiness.

Blue circles had been drawn in two places about five feet up its southern surface, marking the areas where embedded pieces of flesh, hair and blood had been discovered.

Today's blood typing and medical records had verified that these had come from the missing woman, Cardenza told him. "We think she must have been fleeing the fire and fallen over the cliff in the dark."

"You trying to tell me the lady fell off the cliff over here?" Grogan squinted at the scene, shifting the squint briefly to Cardenza, then back to the ravine. "That she somehow managed to bash her head against that big rock over there in mid flight? And then got up and walked away? What was she, Superwoman?"

"Well, it *is* quite a distance," Cardenza admitted, squatting down at the edge of the cliff and idly tossing a pebble over the edge. "But the forensics boys surmised that had she been running toward the cliff when she fell . . ."

272

"At mach five," Grogan threw in sarcastically.

"Well, it *is* possible," the sheriff persisted petulantly.

"Yeah, right . . . anyway, how the fuck do we get down there?"

Cardenza wordlessly rose to lead the way along the edge of the ravine edge until they came to a more-or-less negotiable path that traversed the face of the cliff at a reasonable angle, ending at the bottom some fifty feet from the base of the boulder.

"*Hullo!*" a man's voice rang out as they approached the scene, his footsteps crunching through the underbrush at the far side of the gully. A young blond officer in the uniform of the county sheriff's department appeared from behind the rock, fastening his belt. "I was putting out a residual hot spot," he observed cheerily. "You bring me a replacement?"

"Not quite, Briant," the senior officer replied. "This is the chief homicide inspector from SFPD, Lieutenant Grogan: He thinks what happened here may be related to a case he's been working on. I brought him for a look-see."

"Help yourself, Inspector," he said. "I've already seen it, thanks. If you've got any questions, just holler."

As he stumped off, Grogan could hear the sheriff from Martinez quizzing the local deputy about the area's likely night spots.

"Life goes on," he grunted, staring at a vague outline in the dirt before him.

He glanced over at the blue circles five feet up the face of the boulder, then speculatively up at the top of the cliff again, shaking his head. Back his eyes went to the blue circles and then to the disturbed dirt, as if tracing the flight of the woman in her supposed plunge.

273

"Shit," he concluded.

He squatted, the strain of his bulk threatening to split the seam in the shiny rear of his worn brown trousers, and carefully inspected the ground where the jacket had been found.

Strange . . . there was a huge amount of ash and cinders rained randomly about this entire area, but unless his eyes played tricks on him, there appeared to be a little pattern as well, a thin, circular marking of blackest ash that encompassed the exact spot where the jacket had been found. He reached down and pinched a small sample of the questionable cinder, holding it close to his nose, sniffing thoughtfully. The smell brought back an instant recollection of the dimly lit altar where he'd knelt with his mother every Sunday as a little boy, the white-cassocked priest shaking clouds of choking white smoke at him from a tall silver censer.

Chapter 23

The Vatican

The surge of the crowd beneath the hot glare of the midday sun was rough and unruly, more befitting the heathen gatherings that had crushed their way into a similar plaza two thousand years earlier, hoping for a good view of a bloodbath, than a group of pious worshipers gathered to witness the coronation of a twentieth-century pope.

But a circus is a circus.

Many had been here since the predawn hours, some since the night before, hoping to edge close enough to the coronal procession route to receive a papal blessing from His Holiness.

His Holiness! Michael Muldoon felt a desperate sort of laughter edge its way up his throat at the thought.

From his personal experience, the man who had been head of the San Francisco archdiocese in which Mike had served had never been what one would call a holy man, never what the clergy liked to term "a priest's priest."

He had achieved the position of archbishop by being a

politician, not a pastor, and once in that prestigious office had shown himself to be a pushy, snobbish, self-important dictator.

Muldoon hadn't liked or agreed with the archbishop's policies back then, but now he understood a far more shocking truth about this claimant to the throne of Peter: he was not merely a misguided liberal, an egotistical over-achiever — he was the devil's own handmaiden. And this was the man who was to be given total and absolute authority over the worldwide Catholic Church unless they could somehow stop him.

But too late . . . the clarion call of a score of long, silver trumpets suddenly resounded through the noisy square, cutting through the hum of conversation like cold steel: the procession had begun.

Mike grabbed for Joe's arm again, but this time the smaller man was already taking the lead, pushing through the seemingly solid wall of bodies ahead like an icebreaker, ignoring the muted curses and protests of the people they shoved aside — protests that, had it been anywhere else, any other occasion than this most holy of holy events, might have taken a more physical form of expression. Italians were not renowned for their passivity.

All at once the two Americans found themselves at the boundary of a thirty-foot-wide aisle formed by two shoulder-to-shoulder columns of brightly costumed papal guards who held back the pressing sea of bodies on either side like a human dike.

There, eighty feet away and moving toward them, was the papal throne, its golden canopy jerking twenty feet above the heads of the worshipers as six brawny Swiss guards marched in slow cadence, bearing their precious burden toward the entrance of Saint Peter's Basilica.

"What do we do now?" Joe shouted into the priest's ear, seeking to be heard above the din of the wildly cheering crowd as the fringed canopy swayed slowly closer.

"I don't know, I—don't—know!" Mike cried back, desperation in his voice.

Just then the portable throne swung slightly in its snaking path through the assemblage, coming into full view of the pair. Mike Muldoon looked up into the iced steel of Pope Sixtus's eyes and a white-hot shock tore up his spine, exploding in his brain.

His mouth opened and words not altogether his own poured forth above the noisome cacophony around him.

"And I stood upon the sand of the sea, and saw a beast rise up out of the sea, having seven heads and ten horns, and upon his horns ten crowns, and upon his heads the name of blasphemy"!

"Hey what is this?" a portly, well-dressed man beside them growled in astonishment.

"What'd he say? What's he talking about?" a pretty blonde questioned her companion.

But the austere figure on the canopied throne heard. He knew. And his eyes began to blaze as they focused on the source of the disturbance.

"And I saw one of his heads as it were wounded unto death," Mike shouted defiantly, *"and his deadly wound was healed: and all the world wondered after the beast: and they worshiped the dragon which gave power unto the beast: and they worshiped the beast, saying, 'who is like unto the beast'?"*

Pope Sixtus's eyes met those of Muldoon. The hate emanating from their flat gray irises was a palpable force, a burning cold. Joe felt a wave of nausea pass through his bowels—something akin to fear, but danger-

277

ously close to awe. The crowd nearby was growing surly, threatening — but Mike seemed totally unaware of their presence.

"And all that dwell upon the earth shall worship him, whose names are not written in the book of life . . ."

Someone from behind them made a grab at the speaker: a burly, deeply-tanned Italian who looked like a longshoreman . . . probably *was* a longshoreman. Joe reached out and pushed the aggressor away.

The procession had stopped directly in front of them now. The Swiss guards and gendarmerie, holding back people trying to push their way through for a closer look, could do nothing to thwart the disturbance behind them.

A crimson-robed church official, probably one of the Vatican's cardinal-deacons, was setting afire a small bundle of flax fibers tied atop a long thin reed at the side of the portable throne, speaking the traditional words of homage in Latin: "Holy Father, thus passes the glory of the world." *sic transit gloria mundi.*

Mike's voice rang forth above the deacon's, even stronger and more commanding:

"And I beheld another beast coming up out of the earth; and he had two horns like a lamb, and he spake as a dragon. And he exerciseth all the power of the first beast before him, and causeth the earth and them which dwell therein to worship the first beast whose deadly wound was healed!"

His finger was pointing directly at Sixtus in accusation.

"If any man have an ear, let him hear . . . for we wrestle not against flesh and blood, but against principalities, against powers, against the rulers of the darkness of this world, against spiritual wickedness in high places!"

For a moment everything stopped. Time froze and

they stepped away from it, these three: the new Pope, resplendent in his white silk robes, his tall pointed miter embroidered in golden thread, his ornately jeweled papal clasp; and the two Americans in their dusty slacks, their polo shirts.

Then the scene wavered, changed. The Pope's tall, peaked cap became a crown of horns extending down the back of his thickened muscular neck; the white silken robes of office vanished, exposing a thick, taut skin of glistening green scales beneath. The coldly handsome face became a reptilian fantasy from some grotesque horror film: wide, flaring nostrils replaced the thin, aquiline nose; black-ridged face plates covered the high cheekbones. Two enormous almond-shaped eyes glowed with wicked red humor from the distorted dragon face, while the wide lipless mouth pulled back to expose a series of long, daggerlike teeth.

"Don't you *see* it?" Joe screamed at the sea of frozen faces around him. "Can't you see what he's become?" But the faces remained rapt, caught in a stop-action frame in which the image of the serenely magnificent Pope-elect was caught with them, *all* they saw . . . all they could *ever* see.

Suddenly the demon threw back his huge, clumsy head and laughed, a terrible evil crowing call of triumph and derision, as his long narrow black tongue snaked wickedly at the sky.

Time abruptly restored her grip on reality; sound and movement returned to the world like a motion picture film that has finally started rolling again. Pope Sixtus had resumed his papal identity; no one else had seen. The procession began its slow trek forward once more, leaving Mike and Joe standing in shock, their mouths

279

agape.

But the nearby crowd had not forgotten *them*. It was as if Mike's last entreaty, quoted from *Ephesians*, had just now left his lips. Several men were jostling the pair, grabbing at them angrily, shouting curses in Italian that needed no translation. A matron in a red print dress spat in Mike's face.

Joe began pulling at his friend's arm, urging him away from confrontation with the hostile group, leading him back toward the left colonnade where people were as yet unaware of the furor that had been created by their pronouncements against the demon to whom these fools had come to pay blind homage.

The worshipers seemed willing to let them go, turning their attention back to the pomp of the coronation procession. But one man followed at a discreet distance, one man who had heard the words, seen the biting hatred in the look the new Pontiff had given the offenders, a man who had been vaguely aware of the momentary blurring of time, a wavery sensation that had passed through him and was gone. He hadn't been near enough to see the transformation of Sixtus into the beast of the pit, but he'd felt it in his gut. And the things the tall, dark American had said had exploded in his gut as well.

So Magliano followed them as he had ever since their encounter in the Vatican palace a half-hour earlier, followed them like a man who's been searching for answers without knowing the question, and at last hears the question posed. Whether they had any answers he did not know; yet at the very least he knew he must follow, must find out.

Chapter 24

Mt. Diablo State Park, California

Detective Grogan held the pinch of incense to his nose, still smelling it.

"Cardenza!" he bellowed, waiting in the same squatting position for the sheriff to come running. "You got any evidence bags on you?"

"Briant?" The sheriff asked hopefully, chagrined that the inspector had managed to find something they'd missed after all.

"Got a couple of little ones left," Deputy Briant said, fumbling through his jacket pockets until he fished out a pair of sandwich bags.

Grogan waddled around the circle of ash, gathering up samples of the burnt incense.

"Note it down, Cardenza," he puffed in satisfaction. "There is a perfect circle of burnt incense here—fragrant resins, if you prefer—indicating some sort of religious rite performed either before or after the alleged accident."

He got up, grimacing at the arthritic pain that shot through his lower legs as circulation was restored. Handing the bags to the sheriff, who promptly turned them over to the deputy and followed worriedly behind the inspector, Grogan began a systematic inspection of the narrow canyon. Two hundred feet south of the boulder the gorge abruptly ended in a sheer wall of rock down which groundwater seeped in green and orange stains. The side opposite the cliff from which the woman had fallen was covered in heavy brush, much of which had somehow been spared the ravages of fire, but a closer look showed that the cliff towering behind the skirts of sage and manzanita were as steep and unclimbable as the other canyon walls. This left only the northern end, where the ravine gradually narrowed to a point some three hundred feet distant. It, too, appeared to close off altogether.

"What's down that way?" Grogan asked, pointing with the smoldering end of his cigar.

"It dead-ends, if I remember right. Briant?" The sheriff passed the buck to the local boy again.

"Yeah, squeezes right down to a little gap, barely big enough for one full-grown man to push hisself into. After five or six feet it seems to stop altogether . . . The way we've got it figured, the campers could *only* have gotten out on that narrow path you two just came down . . . assuming, of course, they got out at all."

Grogan gave the upstart a hard look, held it until he could almost see the deputy's balls shrivel. "Let's go have a peek, shall we?"

The gap mentioned by the deputy was small, all right, and seemed to end about six feet into the rocky cliff. But Grogan was never one to take something for granted. He squeezed his large bulk into the crack, inching his way forward. As he approached what had first appeared to be the end of the tiny chasm, he discovered that rather than ending, it made an abrupt left turn, gradually widening as it proceeded.

"Cardenza, squeeze your ass in here!" he yelled back. "I think we've found our so-called fire victims' escape route."

He and the sheriff followed the narrow gorge through its tortuous path, finally emerging into open country more than a mile from where they began. Fifty feet behind them the land was in blackened ruin; ahead it was lush and green. They were out of the fire zone. Two miles further on, down the left hand side of the gently rolling foothills, they could see a gray ribbon of road winding through the broad valley. Highway 24! The three murder suspects could be anywhere by now.

"Mexy, you cost me a day and a half," Grogan muttered.

Chapter 25

St. Peter's Square, Vatican City

By the time the Italian archbishop pushed his squat, sweating body through the throngs in the square, the Americans had already disappeared from sight, as had the Pope-elect, who'd since been carried on his canopied chaise with only a minor degree of tipping and tilting, up the broad stone steps and into the central chamber of the huge cathedral.

Now Magliano moved slowly along the shadowy causeway toward the entrance to Saint Peter's, his worried brown eyes scanning the crowds in the square for a glimpse of the pair he'd been tagging.

Within the church, he surmised, the ceremony of homage would be taking place: all the scarlet-robed cardinals coming forward in turn to bow before the new Pope and kiss his foot, this in front of a small, select audience of some forty thousand or so important church officials, lay people, and media representatives. Significantly Magliano had been omitted from the guest list — a slight which was unheard of for an archbishop of Rome and former member of the Vatican's diplomatic corps.

"Ah, just as well," he sighed, giving a disparaging tweak to the tip of his mustache. "I want no part of what is going on in there today."

Still, a part of him felt let down, left out—the kid peering longingly through the hedge at a neighborhood playmate's birthday party, wondering if his invitation got lost in the mail.

Soon the formal display of homage would be complete, the high mass begun, with Pope Sixtus officiating at the enormous altar in the central cathedral, his tall, soldierly figure diminished by the elaborate bronze baldacchino that the great artist Bernini had constructed in the seventeenth century. Above him would rise the magnificent central dome designed by Michelangelo himself, vaulting like a spirit more than four hundred feet from the floor of the nave. Its size and grandeur were enough to make any mortal feel his own insignificance, but somehow Magliano doubted it was having that effect on Sixtus. Nothing was large enough to challenge an ego of such proportions.

Pope Sixtus VI looked over the rows of cardinals kneeling before him, heads bowed and eyes closed, waiting for him to deliver the holy sacrament of communion, and he smiled benignly. All members of the sacred college were present, with the exception of the four highest ranking, who officiated with him at the mass.

"This is my body," he murmured, holding aloft the symbolic wafer of unleavened bread. "This is my blood," he intoned over the silver chalice of unconsecrated wine. "This do in remembrance of me."

285

As he reached to dip the first small wafer into the wine, he looked into the black, ruby depths of the chalice and saw, staring up from the inky liquid, a pair of almond-shaped crimson eyes with vertical slits for pupils.

("This is *my* blood," one of the eyes winked — and the pool of blood became filled with gruesome, slithery, crawling things that splattered about wetly in the thick, demonic liquor — "and by it" — Sixtus placed the wetted wafer on the first cardinal's outstretched tongue — "I am become the master of you all . . . bloodmaster over this unholy city and all its unholy servants, who shall carry *my* sacrament back to the peoples of the world.")

Beyond the walls of the basilica, Magliano's private worries about the ceremony were cut short by a minor disturbance near the base of the steps that led to the broad portico framing the entrance to Saint Peter's. He hurried his pace.

Yes, it was the pair. He could just see them now, in some sort of confrontation again with one of the navy-blue-and-white uniformed gendarmes posted about the front entrance to keep out the uninvited. Two more guards were approaching the trio curiously. Magliano pushed through the remaining crowd, all but omitting entirely his perfunctory nods and indecipherable, mumbled apologies to those unfortunate enough to be in his path. He was on the verge of hailing the guards, interceding again on the strangers' behalf, when a slender arm reached out to accost him.

"Excellency?"

He turned to the source: it was the pretty, intelligent, and impertinent young reporter from *Il Messaggero*, Signorina DiGuccione. He groaned inwardly, even while pasting on a polite smile at the totally awful timing of the chance encounter. The woman showed remarkable consistency in her ability to meddle in his life.

The big brown eyes within the small oval face regarded him seriously. "It *is* you, then, but why are you not at the coronation, archbishop?" It was phrased as a question, but he sensed she knew the answer, knew and regretted it, perhaps . . . as well she should.

"Why aren't *you?*" he retorted, but immediately felt shame for his petty attack when he saw the chagrin wash over her face.

"I, um . . . I'm really sorry about that article. I hope it didn't make too much trouble for you."

"Too much?" He enjoyed watching her squirm for a moment, just as she'd made him squirm. Then he relented, shrugged eloquently, easing the tension between them. "It is of no import, signorina. You only printed what was true, in here," he thumped his chest, "I could not have disguised my feelings much longer in any case. So perhaps I do not belong in there after all." He gestured toward the huge building that overshadowed and overwhelmed the mortals at its gates, noting as he turned that the two Americans were no longer in view and all the guards seemed to be back in position.

"As God wills," he prayed silently, turning his attention back to the small, pretty woman.

"Well, if it's any consolation, *that* article's why I'm outside too." She attempted a wan smile, but it never reached her teary eyes. "Someone called my editor, someone from the Vatican—highly placed, I gathered—who didn't like the allusions I'd made to His Holiness's rather liberal record. I'm now on probation!" She made a wry

287

face, tossing back her thick, short mane of hair. "Restricted to society stuff: charity teas, debutante balls, weddings. Not much opportunity there to ply my skills as an investigative reporter . . . nor to make waves, I guess. Today I'm here only as one of the curious multitude."

"I'm sorry to hear that, truly," he told her, laying a gentle hand on her shoulder. He spoke with her another minute or two, not wishing to seem hurried, partly because he didn't wish to appear unfeeling, more because he didn't wish to arouse her suspicion. With her intuitive nosiness, she just might follow him to the two Americans, seeking out a story with which she could redeem herself . . . possibly at the expense of whatever purpose these two were sent to fulfill.

He was just leading their conversation into a polite excuse to part company when suddenly the crowds in the square broke into a wild display of jubilation. Out of a glass door opening onto a small balcony 75 feet up the enormous facade of St. Peter's, a miniaturized figure in white vestments had appeared, followed by a short, red-robed ecclesiastic who Magliano recognized as the senior cardinal deacon of Vatican City.

A strategically placed microphone carried their voices clearly through a hundred amplifiers spaced along the upper edge of the double colonnade surrounding the huge piazza, making it seem as if the words came from everywhere at once. As the new Pope knelt before him, the red-gowned cardinal ceremoniously placed the three-tiered gold crown of papal office on Sixtus VI's close-cropped head, solemnly pronouncing this man "Father of princes and kings, ruler of the world on earth, and vicar of our savior Jesus Christ."

For we wrestle . . . against principalities, against powers, against the rulers of darkness of this world. . . . The American's words thundered back into Luigi's mind, sending chills across his back. He almost cried with the realization, but it would have gone unnoticed anyway: many in the crowd were crying openly by now.

Pope Sixtus now stepped forward, raising his arms high above the golden crown that rested uneasily on his head to accept the cheering acclamation of the several hundred thousand faithful packing the square. The minutes passed, the crowd roaring itself hoarse, but the new Pope held the posture of triumph on and on, wanting more.

Magliano could see the cardinal deacon at last lean forward to whisper something in the Pontiff's ear. Sixtus shook his head imperceptibly, and raised his arms still higher in a gesture reminiscent of Nixon or Juan Peron, milking the crowd for every last drop of adulation, grinning until the cheers finally began to die of their own exhaustion.

Only then did he give the traditional blessing, "Urbi et orbi"—*to the city and to the world*—to the crowds of worshipers and TV cameras focused in on his finely hewn face.

As if on cue, the cardinal deacon disappeared beyond the door to the inner recesses of the church. Soon he reappeared, pushing before him a wheelchair. In it was a tiny shrunken, whey-faced creature hunched over to one side. Saliva drooled from his slack gray lips, his withered hands formed into permanently twisted claws against the silken vestments of his holy office. But the oversized black eyes set deep within the cadaverous face were bright, alive, sparking with a dark, knowing humor.

"My children," Pope Sixtus's rich baritone boomed out

289

through the hidden amplifiers, immediately stilling the wondering murmur of the crowd, "Most of you by now have heard of the great miracles that have been manifested within this holy city over the past week, of how our revered Pope Marcus, after suffering a massive cerebral hemorrhage, given up as dead by his physicians, came back to us with wondrous proclamations, declaring himself our direct link with the Supreme Being, his voice now God's own messenger to the wanting world.

"But we understand, even as Christ Jesus himself once understood, that in the frailty of human faith it is sometimes necessary to provide even the most devout with some sort of visible proof, some act that defies the laws of nature as we mortals understand them, in order that all last, lingering doubts may be stilled, that you will all truly believe in his Divine immanence."

"No, no . . ." some voices from below carried up. "We believe, we believe!"

His imperious hand stilled their protestations. "You wish to believe," he corrected, "and you will believe. For I give you now Pope Marcus, I give you now the proof you seek. I give you . . . " with a dramatic flourish he stood aside, waving his arm toward the withered body in the wheelchair . . . "a miracle!"

He stepped quickly behind the wheelchair—a maneuver orchestrated like all the rest. Then slowly, amazingly, the crippled, ruined frame of Pope Marcus began to rise, the withered arms—scarred with fresh red needle marks from the placement of intravenous tubes—still clutched spastically to his sunken chest. He rose gracefully, as if pulled on invisible wires, to an upright position and then—no, it couldn't be!—he was rising further, floating up from the wheelchair, up above the balcony itself!

Gasps of wonder escaped from the multitude. No one dared speak, lest he or she be responsible for breaking the spell, sending their beloved Pontiff crashing to the pavement twenty-five meters below.

He'd transcended gravity. Sailing softly and slowly over the crowd, his pallid feet dangling bare and limp below his upright form, he moved on his invisible path until he achieved the very center of the enormous plaza, hovering directly above the apex of the eighty-five-foot-high Egyptian obelisk, his dangling feet just grazing the pointed tip of the red stone structure, looking like a twisted ivory angel atop a granite tree.

Then he spoke. His voice was a hollow, horrible thing echoing up from some unfathomable depth, a hole in space or a bottomless well, rasping and growling like a record played at too slow a speed. It resonated and rumbled as if magnified by a faulty PA system, yet it was obvious there could be no electronic equipment at that inaccessible spot.

Men and women were crying openly now. Many— most—had fallen to their knees, hands clasped in an attitude of prayer, lips moving soundlessly, eyes glued to the tiny, frail figure far above their heads.

"Children," the hollow voice reverberated, "Hear me well. I am the voice of the Lord, thy God speaking through this empty vessel of our servant Pope Marcus the Third. Blessed are those of you present here today, blessed are those to whom you will take today's glad message. Your salvation is at hand.

"As you trust in me, trust also in your new servant—to be henceforth known in title as 'Secondary Pope Sixtus the Sixth'—for he has been chosen to act on my behalf, to carry out my directives and achieve my great plan for

291

the world."

All of a sudden, in the midst of the awestruck silence, a voice screamed up from the crowd below, slashing the reverence like a bloody sword: "Blasphemer! Blasphemer! You are *not* God's chosen one, but *Satan's*. You are *not* the source of light to this weary, half-blind world, but the Prince of Darkness and its ultimate enslaver!"

It was Muldoon, shaking in fear and fury, standing just outside the colonnade across from the obelisk above which the transported Pontiff hovered. Joe stood close at his side, silently mouthing the words.

People looked about in an absolute horror of confusion, as if caught in a waking nightmare. They were too stupefied to dredge up any emotion for or against the man shouting in their midst. But already a wedge of uniformed guards angrily pushed their way through the crowds towards the reviler of their holy sovereign, the man they were sworn to protect. Their duty at least, was clear.

"He deceiveth them that dwell on earth by means of these miracles, which he has power to do in the sight of the *beast!*" the monsignor quoted loudly, his voice carrying over the growing rumble of the worshipers, up with exquisite clarity into the ears of Pope Marcus. Deep within the Pope's black, black eyes, a purple light began to emanate, focusing downward into a pair of needlelike beams.

"Behold, the jackals already bay at the Holy See, trying to dissuade and confound you with their nihilistic interpretation of The Word!" the Pope's unearthly voice thundered.

The eyebeams flashed suddenly brighter, more intense, elongating down at increasing velocity toward the accusers like two fiery fingers of death. They hit the space above the Americans' heads just as the Vatican gendarmerie were reaching for the two men; but rather than destroying the pair, the rays began to bend and diffuse, as if striking an invisible barrier. Their white-hot heat surrounded the intended victims, forming a wall of electrical force between them and their would-be attackers, who fell back in pain and disarray, shielding their faces from the burning radiation.

Women were screaming, men shouting. The floating shell of Pope Marcus, high overhead, hesitated, as if taken by surprise at this turn of events.

In that moment a short, heavy arm reached through the shimmering aura that encompassed the two strangers: to the squat mustachioed man attached to the other end of the appendage there was no heat, no pain; it was merely light and illusion.

"Come with me, come quickly," he whispered urgently to the tall, dark preacher and his smaller, sad-eyed companion. They moved at his word without hesitation, as if their paths were predetermined by the script being written moment to moment in their heads.

A minute later the Pope withdrew his fire into himself: his targets had disappeared. The police looked around in bewilderment, asking questions of the nearby witnesses, burling about like ants in a termite nest, while the power in control of Marcus—the ultimate strategist, father of politicians and used-car salesmen—was already turning the incident to his favor.

"Behold! The hand of God has vanquished the deceivers!" He proclaimed in his terrible bass rumble. "Can there be any doubt remaining in your hearts that the true God is before you? You have witnessed the wondrous proof that it is He—for who else can create and uncreate anything of this universe, who else can bend, change or circumvent the very laws of nature but *He*, because they are *His* laws!"

And from deep in a dark, musty tunnel beneath the colonnade, following behind the dim, wavering beam of a tiny penlight held resolutely in the fingers of their new benefactor, Mike and Joe heard the crowd's roar of approval, the swelling tidal wave of voices cheering on and on in near-hysteria. The two men stopped and looked at one another in hopelessness.

Magliano halted as well, turning to these strange, driven men who were now crying bitterly at their failure. He shook his head at them.

"No, it is not over *amici usque ad aras:* You are the Olive Trees . . . ." Surprisingly, embarrassingly, he dropped to his knees, bent forward into the darkness and kissed both their feet—a gesture of ultimate homage and servitude, of shining humility. "I will do all I can to help you," he whispered hoarsely. "My honor and my privilege."

Chapter 26

Contra Costa County,
California

By the time Lieutenant Paul Grogan finished his inspection of the fire scene and returned to the park entrance to pick up his car, it was nearly six PM. He was
tired, pissed off, and ravenous.

It wasn't until he'd driven all the way back up Highway 24 to Lafayette, at the intersection of 680, that he
finally found what he'd been looking for—two Big Macs,
an apple turnover, and a chocolate shake.

Now that he was fed, he decided he might as well pay
a visit to Mrs. Draekins while he was in the area, see if
she might be able to shed any light on her daughter's
whereabouts. By 7 PM he stood in the middle of her
tidy house, his misshapen hat crumbled penitently in his
big hands, peeking at the woman from beneath the overhang of bushy eyebrows while she busied herself making
coffee. For once there was no cigar hanging from his
lower lip, and without it his face look oddly empty, exposed and vulnerable.

He couldn't have said why he was acting so out of character. His submissive, respectful manner had nothing to do with being in a nice home—he'd been in much finer ones from time to time, the urge to commit murder not limited to the poor by any means. But this was no more than your average, well-kept middle-class suburban house—a rambling, wood-shingled ranch style from the mid sixties, with unlit tiki lamps around the obligatory kidney shaped pool, huge-leafed philodendrons hugging the flagstone exterior of the house, palms paired in tactfully landscaped plots here and there amidst a slightly patchy lawn.

The house was furnished in oak and maple period pieces—overstuffed sofas and chairs in muted floral prints that looked warm, comfortable, inviting . . . and unsat in, as if they were on perpetual display in a showroom window.

An ornate Black Forest cockoo clock in the entry hall—the only object in the house not rigidly American colonial—began squawking out the hour: seven questionably musical chirps. A second door in the clock face opened and out twirled a tiny painted couple, dancing woodenly to a Strauss waltz.

The woman at the kitchen counter turned to smile at him a bit too brightly, her eyes glittery with grief.

"Silly little nuisance," she commented, and he couldn't be sure whether she was referring to the clock, to him, or to the pain of her missing daughter.

She invited him graciously into the living room, setting two delicate china cups of steaming black coffee carefully down beside each other on the heavily-lacquered maple coffee table, then staring at them confusedly as if trying to remember what she was supposed to do next.

"Oh, of course," Dolores answered herself aloud. "Cream? Sugar?"

"Uh, no, ma'am, this'll be just fine for me."

It was *her*. That was what was making him as twitchy as a school boy, he realized with a sudden little start, his heart lurching in his chest. She was a good looking old broad with an indefinable aura of covert sexuality beneath her refined exterior—and Christ, what a nice ass for an old lady! He wondered if she could be had, and the thought frightened him. It had been years since he'd sought comfort in anything beside his own good right hand.

As she sat down on the opposite end of the sofa, a tiny smile softened her features momentarily, as if she sensed what he was thinking and appreciated it. She pulled and straightened the soft pink knit jersey dress to cover her knees more modestly. All the act succeeded in doing was to accentuate her nylon-smooth legs. Paul took a big swallow of the hot coffee to hide his nervousness, thinking that whoever started the trend toward putting women in slacks was either a fag or a commie.

"What would you like to know, Mr. . . . ." she searched for the name he'd given her over the phone. Damn! How could she forget it already? She prided herself on always remembering a name. Dolores shook her head apologetically.

"Grogan, ma'am," the beefy lieutenant replied. "Detective Lieutenant Paul Grogan, SFPD."

"Yes, of course. I am *so* sorry. I just can't seem to think straight since, since. . . ." There was a little catch in her voice.

"I, uh . . . I'm trying to piece together the facts concerning your daughter's unfortunate . . . accident. That and the incident she and the two gentlemen were involved in a couple of days prior, when the two people were killed? From what I've gathered so far, it appears they were in the middle of some kind of . . . religious ritual? He didn't want to risk offending her at this stage by calling it devil worship, but the middle-aged woman had no such compunction.

"Demonology!" she spat angrily. "Crazy, weird ideas! They thought my Marija was being possessed by Satan, that's what they told me that night, the night my daughter came by." She stopped, clearing her throat brusquely, swallowing hard. She wouldn't cry, *couldn't*: it would make her mascara run, her face sag. She looked so old and ugly now when she cried, not like in her youth, when a show of tears was her most effective weapon. She took a sip of her coffee, trying to wash the emotion back down into her chest.

"I tried to suggest she see a psychiatrist, but she wouldn't hear of it. She and that husband of hers took off in a huff . . . said they were going for a drive. 'Fresh air,' they said. That's the last time I saw either one of them, the last time I saw my daughter. . . ."

That did it. The last word came out in a gush of tears. Abruptly the woman jumped up, mumbling apologies, and rushed from the room. Grogan could hear water running in the bathroom down the hall, muffled sobs, the stern inhaling of breath while the woman fought to regain control. He felt a certain admiration for the old gal, trying to be so brave, so strong in the face of her obvious heartbreak.

Class, that's what she has. They don't make women like that anymore, he thought hungrily.

Within her mirrored bathroom, the woman was peering myopically into the gilded vanity. Having successfully staved off a flow of tears, she was now carefully reapplying the mascara, hoping her fifty-two-year-old eyes wouldn't puff up too noticeably.

"Damn her, anyway, how could she *do* this to me," she muttered uncharitably, pulling on a lower lid so that her powdered eye shadow would go on more smoothly.

She shook the unkind thought from her head with a vague toss of her platinum hair, pressing a pair of manicured fingertips against a throbbing little pain that had begun to develop in her right temple.

By the time Dolores Draekins finished repairing her make-up and returned to the living room, the burly detective was standing as if to leave.

"Perhaps this is too much of a strain on you right now, Mrs. Draekins," he began regretfully.

"No, no . . . do sit down, lieutenant. It's quite all right, really," she assured him. "I don't mind answering your questions. It helps a little to talk about it, actually. May I get you another cup of coffee?"

"Well, sure — if it's not too much trouble."

"It's not," she replied, picking up his empty cup and her own half-full, cold one. "Oh, lieutenant, are you still officially on duty?"

"Uh, not exactly, ma'am. I'm supposed to be off on Sundays, but I've been putting in a little of my own time on this case."

"Then could I persuade you to join me in a little cognac? I feel I could use a drop myself, but I do hate to drink alone. . . . You know what they say."

Grogan readily consented: nothing he loved better than

a shot of good brandy with his coffee. He watched her ass again as she left the room, admiring the tight little way she controlled its natural swing.

Even more, he liked the way she returned, with an entire fifth of Hennesey's Very Special and a pair of crystal brandy snifters on a silver tray.

The cognac seemed to travel almost instantly to the speech centers of the woman's brain, short-circuiting the locks and lubricating the gears on her jaw. Soon she was rambling on about her daughter in far greater detail than the detective asked for, needed, or particularly wanted to hear. Nevertheless he listened with intense politeness, especially as his talkative hostess kept generously refilling his glass while giving him an abbreviated life history of Marija's odd behavior, filled with backhanded compliments and damning praise. "Trusting to a fault" seemed to be her personal favorite.

The picture that began to evolve was that of an emotionally susceptible young woman who'd begun falling apart shortly after entering a relationship with this character Joe and the quasi-priest Muldoon.

Obviously the two were engineering and orchestrating the mental takeover of her daughter—though to what purpose, Dolores said, she couldn't imagine. Neither, Grogan agreed, could he.

But the final conclusion was inevitable: Marija had been the innocent dupe of these two fanatical cultists and may well have been beaten and kidnaped by them when she refused to go along with their Satanic practices any longer.

"I *know* my daughter, Paul," Dolores said, nodding her perfectly coiffed head and grabbing his arm for emphasis, leaning closer until he could see the slightly unfocused

300

blue of her eyes, until her musky perfume was competing with the aromatic cognac that permeated his palate.

"She's a good girl. Maybe a bit, how did you say . . . 'flaky'? But basically she's decent, Paul. She *must* have been brainwashed into believing all that crazy stuff about Satan trying to possess her. . . . Yes, I'm *sure* that's it! Those two *brainwashed* her, and then I must have broken through that brainwashing . . ." The woman was getting quite excited now, the alcoholic clarity of her thoughts coming through like inspired perceptions. ". . . That night when I pointed out that what had been happening was all in her mind. I must have—what is it they call it? *Deprogrammed* her. That's it—I deprogrammed her!" She was clutching his arm so hard that her bright red finger-nails could be felt beneath the heavy material of his jacket, biting into his flesh.

"*That's* why she turned on them, threatened to go to the authorities. I just realized that in a way, in a strange terrible way, it's *my* fault she's missing, hurt . . . maybe even killed!"

Dolores threw herself dramatically into Paul Grogan's arms, sobbing loudly in seeming despair.

The detective's drink slopped out over his hand and was dripping onto the brown shag carpet. He gingerly set the glass on the coffee table, dragging his fingers across the carpet on the return trip to remove the last traces of cognac before awkwardly beginning to pat the woman's heaving back, muttering words of comfort, squeezing the too-soft arms, imagining they were breasts.

Jesus, was she soft! A picture flashed unbidden across his mind: that softness all naked and unfettered, lying vulnerable and passive beneath him while he plunged his hardness into it, over and over and over. He shuddered.

You puke, you asshole, he chastised himself, gritting his teeth against the incipient erection. Here's this poor lady, her heart breaking, and all you can offer is to rape her in your mind.

But the fifty-two-year-old matron in his arms took her time letting go of his comfortable bulk, even after the last of her sobs had subsided, and when she did at last pull away, her mascara was remarkably intact.

Later that night, much later, as it turned out Dolores Draekins and Paul Grogan ended up falling asleep in each others' naked arms . . . both happily surprised.

Chapter 27

Sunday, June 17th
Vatican City

Joe Marten answered the coded rap on their door, opening it to admit in the twilight, a portly mustachioed man who carried a greasy paper bag in each hand.

"Archbishop," he nodded, taking a bag and shaking the soft, damp palm that had clutched it. He shut the door quietly behind them.

"I brought you a little supper, signori," the Italian said inclining his head politely.

Mike came across the bare cement floor of the tiny kitchen where he'd been tinkering with the ancient plumbing, wiping the grease from his long fingers with a soiled rag.

"Welcome, Your Excellency," he said with a warm smile that hid the dark fatigue and hopelessness in his bloodshot eyes. "Please come in, be seated." He had an arm around the shorter man's shoulders, steering him toward a shabby sofa. "We will talk."

"Yes, certainly, thank you," Magliano said. "But first,

eat," he insisted, shoving the second bag of food into the black American's hands. "I am sure you must be . . . how do they say in America . . . 'starved'? Eat, the talking will wait that long."

"Smells great," Joe commented, coming around the other side of the couch to plop himself into a threadbare upholstered chair, his nose already deep into the brown recesses of the paper bag.

Mike sat too, proffering the bag in a gesture of invitation to the Italian, who shook his head. "No, no please, go ahead. I have already eaten my fill, thank you."

Magliano, to avoid watching them eat, began looking more carefully at their surroundings: the filthy kitchen alcove, the tiny bath with its cracked and stained porcelain fixtures, the seepage and mildew-stained wall beneath the dirt-streaked transom.

"But it is so, so . . . shabby!" he blurted aloud, wringing his hands.

He knew the abandoned apartment, located in the basement of one of the older complexes that flanked the rear of the Vatican gardens, was a perfect hiding place for the two uninvited visitors. Its brush-enshrouded outside at the bottom of a leaf-strewn cement stairwell was almost invisible to the infrequent passerby. With a little caution one could come and go at almost any hour without being spotted.

Magliano, who'd been aware of several such abandoned apartments in the Vatican, had led the fugitives to this one after their narrow escape from the gendarmerie earlier, never imagining anything in the ornate, well-kept city could be in such sad shape. He sighed loudly, looking around again.

"If we'd wanted thick carpets and color TV, we could

304

have stayed home." Joe smiled kindly at the distraught man as he licked the last crumbs of sweet Italian pastry off his fingertips.

"Yes, please don't give it another thought," Mike added; "you've already done more than we could have hoped for."

Luigi Magliano blushed again, shaking his head.

"So," Mike turned to the topic that was on all their minds. "Have you had time to consider all we told you of Pope Marcus and Sixtus?"

"Yes," the archbishop answered very quietly, studying the worn asphalt tile.

"And will you help us pull the plugs?" Joe blurted, lacking the priest's finesse.

Startled by such abruptness, Magliano looked up, held the man's eyes a moment, then muttered "Yes."

"You will?" Joe sounded genuinely surprised.

"Thank God," breathed Muldoon.

"I, I still pray it is the right thing. To take a life, any life . . ."

"But we aren't, not really," Mike argued gently. "We're just turning off the manmade mechanical devices that have prevented God from taking the man at his rightful time. It was Satan, not God, who ordered he be kept alive on machines."

"I know. That is what I thought about all afternoon; that is why I decided to help you end it . . ."

"So!" said Joe.

"So . . ." Mike echoed.

"So, what do you want me to do?" asked the archbishop, his palms upraised and his expression so quaintly comical that this time the smile did reach Mike's eyes.

305

Chapter 28

The sun had set, the twilight snaking purple and gold fingers through the sky above the Vatican palace when Archbishop Magliano turned at last from his third-story window with a sigh.

Locking the door of the small, tidy bedroom behind him, he put on a look of indifference as he forced his gait to a casual stroll down the long, carpeted hall of the east wing apartments, heading toward the business offices of the palace.

Nodding, smiling, passing the time of day when necessary with the few ecclesiastics and other palace personnel he happened to encounter, the archbishop made his way slowly down two flights and through a short maze of hallways to the suite of rooms that constituted the Vatican infirmary.

Guards were posted outside the wide double door that led to the hospital waiting room, a hospital now devoid of all patients save one. Magliano recognized them, and clutched at his memory for their names as he paused as if to exchange pleasantries with the bored and foot-weary pair.

"Ah, Pietro," he smiled broadly, reaching out to take the first man's hand firmly, "how is it with you? And *you*," he turned to include the other costumed sentinel with a friendly clasp to the shoulder, "Lorenzo, isn't it?"

"Why yes, Your Excellency," the younger guard smiled, flushed with pleasure at recognition from the well-known nuncio.

"And how is your young bride, Lorenzo? Anxious to have you home to supper, I would guess."

"I, suppose so, sir . . . that is, Your Excellency . . . but I'll be off at nine, that's not too long now."

"You too, Pietro? Will you finally get to rest your tired feet?" he smiled kindly.

Such social niceties were so natural to the archbishop's demeanor that neither guard had the slightest inkling they were being questioned for a purpose. Even Luigi's own guilt and nervousness did not surface sufficiently to compromise his habitual friendliness.

"Yes, Your Excellency," Pietro grinned, shifting to the other foot, "and glad of it, too!"

"It must be a tiresome duty," Luigi commiserated, looking from one to the other. "What with no public allowed back in this area now to keep you busy. Do they even have guards all night?"

"No, we're the last on until morning. We're only here to catch the occasional stray tourist . . ."

"Or reporter," Pietro interjected.

". . . who slips by the watchmen at the entrance to this wing. Actually *he's* here for *that*," the younger man grinned. "I'm just here to keep him company."

307

"But now that the public entrances are locked for the night, and all visitors have been ejected, there's no need for us," Lorenzo concluded helpfully.

"And how is everything within?" Luigi nodded toward the closed door with a concerned expression. "Are the doctors still running in and out at all hours, or has it settled down to the usual routine?"

"Ah, now, Excellency," the first guard ventured, "Of course they tell us nothing of Il Papa's condition, but we do have eyes and ears. It appears the machines within whirr on without trouble, doing their jobs as it were, and nothing much changes for the better — or the worse. He shook his head sadly; the young blond guard shook his in silent mimicry. "The doctor visits four or five times a day, checking the machines and charts — as a matter of fact, he's in there for his last visit now — and of course there are two nursing nuns on duty round the clock, but that is all. No, nothing changes, except if, like this morning, God wills it, then just for a little while, it seems."

"Hmm," said Archbishop, "a sad state of affairs, yes? A sad, sad state. Well, all we can do is pray, my little soldiers."

Just then he heard noises in the inner waiting room - a man's voice giving curt directions, a soft woman's murmur of compliance. Magliano checked his watch.

"Well now, how the time files! Here it is ten to nine already; soon you will be flying home as well."

Luigi wanted to get out of there, to leave before the doctor saw him and later when the deed was done, made the connection. But the pull of the priesthood was too strong in him.

"Kneel, then, if you will, my brothers, and I will

308

pronounce a blessing on you to see you safely home."

"Thank you, Excellency," the pair muttered, kneeling and bowing their necks while the gentle holy man made the sign of the cross on their foreheads.

The doctor exited upon the scene, but averted his eyes and hurried quietly away so as not to interrupt the sanctity of the moment.

Only one pair of eyes, hidden in the recesses of a dark side hall some fifty feet away, continued to watch Magliano . . . as he had for the past fifteen minutes with great interest.

The owner of those eyes skulked farther back into the shadows now as the archbishop waddled past and on down the dimly lit hall, exiting out a side door that wheezed shut and locked behind him with a small click. Then the figure emerged from his cover and began to follow.

Outside the night was dark, a thin ground mist rising to blot out the meager twinklings of the first handful of stars to be thrown against the palette of sky. The stranger could barely make out the rounded form of the archbishop as he slipped quietly down the broad alleyway between buildings and headed toward the unlit secretive expanses of the Vatican gardens.

He hurried his pace, afraid to lose the man among the twisting hedges and shrubbery. Finally he saw his quarry far ahead, turning into a disused path alongside one of the older apartment buildings near the rear of the walled city. Slinking carefully behind the overgrown bushes that nearly covered the path, he saw the archbishop suddenly turn toward the building and disappear. The crisp night air carried the sound of quiet tapping, then a door squeaked open on ancient hinges and a voice said,

"Come in, my friend."

A distinctly American voice!

Magliano was harboring the Americans who'd made such a scene at this morning's coronation! Half the Vatican gendarmerie were looking for them throughout Rome, and here they were right under everyone's nose!

Cardinal Bishop Paolo Bertini shook his head in stunned disbelief, then carefully, quietly slipped away and hurried back to the palace.

The thin intense man lay open-eyed on his bed in the austere little suite. He couldn't have slept that night if he'd been drugged with morphine.

The Americans! Damn them, all his old doubts and fears had returned because of them, because of what he'd heard them accuse Pope Marcus of this morning after the coronation.

It was *their* fault he'd found himself restlessly wandering the halls this evening, his feet drawing him subconsciously toward the infirmary where the source of his confusion lay, *their* fault he'd inadvertently stumbled upon Magliano questioning the guards.

And questioning it was.

He knew the archbishop was up to something, even though the guards did not. He knew, because he knew that Magliano had openly opposed the election of Sixtus and gotten himself brought down because of it. He knew because . . . he was up to something himself, wasn't he?

Because he couldn't shake the feeling that something was wrong—deeply, terribly wrong.

Because though he'd prayed long and fervently, prayed until his bony knees had ached and swelled from the hours spent pressed into the hard floor of the little apartment he'd been assigned in the palace, still the edgy disease would not leave him, the nervousness that had gnawed at his insides ever since his first summons to the dying Pope's bed side.

The gray, wizened remains of Marcus had looked out at Bertini and his colleagues with those too-bright eyes and unapologetically declared himself the voice of God. Only . . . only Bertini hadn't felt the touch of God in that awful voice, nor did he feel it in that of the successor, Pope Sixtus VI.

So. What was he to do about Magliano and the Americans?

He didn't even know what to do about himself.

Chapter 29

Archbishop Magliano slipped behind the hedges and down the crumbling cement steps at precisely 8 PM.

The door opened even before he knocked, admitting him to the squalid little apartment.

In one hand he carried a large plastic bag which bulged softly, in the other a pair of grease-stained paper bags similar to those he'd delivered the night before.

He was perspiring heavily, even though it was not a particularly warm evening, and his sweat had an acrid smell which embarrassed him.

Not much was said. It had all been discussed in detail the night before, when the archbishop had returned with the infirmary schedule. There was nothing left but to do it, and the three preferred to face this idea alone.

While the Americans ate, the Archbishop withdrew the garments he'd brought from the larger bag, laying them carefully over the back of the decrepit sofa and gently, busily smoothing out their few wrinkles with his hands.

They were long, cream-colored hooded robes made of heavy wool which, he knew, were liable to be oppressive in the mild Rome weather—but that couldn't be helped. Brown braided waist cords and black-beaded rosaries completed the effect.

When the men finished eating, he helped them into their disguises, then stood back to appraise each carefully.

"Well?" Joe said, attempting a model's turn and pose. "Do I make it as a monk?"

The little Italian smiled despite his tension. "You'll pass," he said, "but *you* . . ." He tweaked his large mustache insultingly at the other man.

"I know, it's hard to make a religious man out of a ghetto ganglord," Muldoon grinned.

"Well, it's true that few of your color have chosen the monastic life . . ."

"Probably second thoughts about the vows of chastity," Joe gibed, then fell quickly silent at his own poor taste.

". . . but it's actually the tennis shoes I was referring to," Luigi finished.

Mike looked down at his feet. The robe had obviously been intended for a man several inches shorter. His size-twelve Reeboks hung out all the way to the tops of his red-striped socks.

"Shit," he mumbled, shaking his head.

"Ah, well, too late now. Let's just hope no one notices," the archbishop shrugged, checking his watch. "So, if you are ready?"

The trio proceeded in silence across the gardens and through the twilit alleys of the huge complex, the "monks" with heads bowed, their faces lost in deep shadow beneath the overhang of each broad, peaked cowl.

At the rear of the palace's eastern apartment wing the

313

Americans waited nervously for Magliano to fumble his personal key into a locked door, then followed him quickly inside.

"What now?" Joe whispered, the first words he'd uttered since leaving the safety of their refuge.

"It is only five to nine," Luigi whispered back. "We don't want to arrive at the infirmary before five or ten after, to be certain the guards have gone. I suggest we take a slow stroll the long way around."

"And remember," Mike admonished his friend, "there is no need to speak, even when spoken to. Many monks take a vow of silence, so such behavior is not considered unusual. Let Luigi do all the talking, if any explanations become necessary."

On the second floor of the Vatican palace, in an enormous and magnificently decorated apartment, a small party of diners had just completed their sumptuous main course at the same moment the trio of would-be-assassins entered the opposite side of the building.

At the head of this enormous oval table presided the newly elected pontiff in a thronelike chair. To his right sat Cardinal Secretary Mendice, his tiny hands folded together where his plate had been. To the left of Sixtus was Patriarch Synarus, carefully brushing crumbs from his beard with a clean linen napkin. On either side of these men across from each other sat Dean Falliano and Camerlingo Bertini, the first, thought Sixtus, a proud and decisive lion, the second a shrewd but nervous little weasel, someone to be watched.

The rest of the company hardly counted, a quartet of palsied and liver-spotted old fools who were as incapable

314

of contributing anything to his plan as they were of opposing it.

"So, this is it," he thought, "my home guard, my mighty phalanx with which I shall conquer the world." His smile became rueful. "Oh well, these oldest cringing dogs are nearly useless, but at least they will cause me no problems — no doubts raised, no trumpets sounded. They'll go along with the program, any program, just so long as it doesn't threaten their security. They're too old and entrenched in church dogma even to consider questioning the mandates of their Pope: *that* would be tantamount to questioning everything they've ever believed in."

The other four, at least, were still powerful, vital men, capable of wielding tremendous influence in the world he sought to control . . . capable, he knew, of being dangerous, had not the Master delivered them into his hands. It was too bad they would aid his cause simply out of blind stupidity, rather than any true commitment to the *real* ruler of this earth.

Anyway, that was their problem: in the end they would realize their mistake too late and end up with no side at all. Neither good nor evil would have them. Barred from the presence of God for their betrayal, they would also be denied the pleasures of Mammon by their own confused consciences . . . which only served them right.

None of this showed on the Pope's tanned, impassive face; there was nothing but the little smile, which could have been interpreted as warmth and friendliness, so long as one didn't look too closely into the cold gray flint of his eyes.

He signaled his personal steward to bring the dessert, and later, some champagne.

315

As hoped, an eminent member of the Vatican staff escorting a pair of cloaked and mute religious brethren attracted no undue attention during their trek through the labyrinthine passages. The trio arrived at the entrance to the hospital infirmary without incident.

The time was now 9:10. The last guards had gone home to supper and the door lay unattended; no sound could be heard within. Magliano tried the latch, but it was locked. Not surprised, he rapped loudly on the door.

After a minute there was the sound of hushed footsteps. A moment later the door cracked open just enough for a white-robed nun to peer through.

"Sister Mary Margarita?" the archbishop inquired gently. "It is I, Archbishop Magliano. May I speak with you a moment?"

The nun's face went through a subtle series of colorations. She had orders to admit no one, he was sure, but at the same time she had vows to respect the authority of such as himself . . . . Besides, they were friends. After a moment she wordlessly opened the door, yet when she spotted the hooded figures behind him she hesitated again, her look now one of outright dismay.

"Please," he said gently, "these are friends and brothers, Benedictine monks from Wales who have traveled a long pilgrimage to pay homage to our Pope. Mayn't we have just a moment of your time?"

A younger nun had appeared, peeking curiously out the swinging doors which led from the waiting room into a large examination area and nurses' station.

"Good evening, Sister Teresa," smiled the Italian archbishop, stepping forward with a gallant little bow. The monks moved in behind him, twin shadows.

The homely nun returned the smile warmly, her face aglow. "What's the harm?" she said to the other sister, who shrugged and let them by.

As the door closed and latched behind them, the two hooded men simultaneously let out their breath. They were in; it was as good as done.

While the archbishop continued explaining the purpose of their visit, the Americans, wanting to look about but not daring to, forced their eyes to inspect the patterns on the marble floor at their feet.

"But they have come all the way from Scotland. . . ."

"I thought you said Wales?"

"Yes, yes — Wales . . . I meant Wales. Dear Me. Anyway, they have come all this way to offer a special prayer and benediction for the Holy Father's recovery . . . surely you can make an exception in this case?"

"Well, Excellency," the elder nurse responded, "I myself can see no harm in it, but Doctor Frederico left strict orders that no visitors were to be admitted without the express written consent of the Pope himself."

"But surely that is silliness . . . a misunderstanding," he corrected. "Il Papa cannot even speak, let alone write!"

"Not Pope *Marcus*," the nun exclaimed.

"Ah yes, of course . . . Sixtus."

"Perhaps I could call his suite, see if his personal steward could convey your request?" the woman suggested helpfully.

"I suppose . . . yes, all right . . . if there is nothing else we can do.

It was their prearranged signal.

Mike began to edge quietly toward the younger nun while Luigi, hands thrust deeply in his pockets, followed closely behind the other, approaching the swinging doors

317

that led to the switchboard at the nurses' station inside.

Suddenly both men acted. Each clasped a gauze-filled hand over the nose and mouth of his respective captive, his other arm clamped tightly around the sister's waist and arms. Each pulled a struggling woman into the other room and held her down until the flailings ceased. Then the men rose, looking shaken.

"You keep an eye on them," hissed Mike to Joe. "Give them a little more ether if they start to come to."

He turned abruptly and followed the archbishop, who was weeping quietly, down the broad hallway that led to the hospital room where the comatose pontiff lay helpless to stop them.

The champagne glasses had been filled, the dessert plates cleared, and at his signal a large cardboard portfolio had been placed on the table beside Pope Sixtus.

"I have here," he told his audience, his large hands fiddling with the soft edge of the folio, "preliminary sketches by the renowned Italian artist and sculptor Artelio Rowena, depicting the miraculous flight of Pope Marcus at my coronation. I have commissioned him to make a great statue in front of the basilica to commemorate the event."

A spontaneous murmur went up from the group, eight senior statesmen all shuffling at once in their chairs, exclaiming to themselves at the unexpected news.

Pope Sixtus chuckled. "I see you are taken by surprise—but surprise, I hope, of the agreeable variety. Or was not the occasion sufficiently miraculous to warrant some form of lasting memorial?"

The cool challenge was understood beneath the gentle

phrasing, the congenial tone.

"I have already selected one," he went on, smiling, "so I will not take up your time with the rejects. This," he said as he pulled a large sheet of art bond out of the folder with a tiny flourish, "will soon become a new symbol of hope and faith for our churches across the globe."

"Aaahhh." The sound, a sigh of admiration and wonder, escaped the old, dry lips as one long exhalation, a whisper of fall wind slithering through a pile of withered brown leaves. Every one of them leaned forward to peer more closely at the design. It was a watercolor of the red granite obelisk that stood in the center of the piazza. Atop it was the artist's impression of Pope Marcus, his pale, unshod feet pressed against the pyramid like a diver just leaving a springboard. The long white cassock and loose-fitting surplice flowed out behind like unfolding wings; a golden aura surrounded the Pope's head like a multi-layered halo. Rowena had kindly omitted the slack-lipped drool, filled in the gray, cadaverous cheeks with a glowing radiance, unbent the spastic tetany of the Pope's arms and sent them reaching for heaven.

Engraved in a gold banner spiraling the base of the obelisk were the words, "Il Papa sera Il Niño."

As he read this inscription, Cardinal Paolo Bertini felt an icy chill begin its slow climb up his spine.

Pope Sixtus VI was sitting before them with his newfound infallibility, proposing a "new symbol of faith" for their religion which would, in essence, declare Marcus the Son of God. . . . this was the Second Coming of Christ!

"Il Papa sera Il Niño," "The Father becomes The Son". Or worse, "The *Pope* becomes the Son!"

The icy chill suddenly penetrated his heart.

The tall black man in the too-short monk's robe and the squat Italian in his perspiration-stained suit burst as one through the glass-paned door into the hospital room . . . and stopped short.

Across the sterile white cube from them, on a metal hospital bed, lay a gaunt, wizened figure that looked more mummy than man.

His shrunken flesh was taut and gray and what little hair still clung to his mottled scalp was pure white, fading to invisibility against the bed linens. The eye sockets were deep pits of purplish blue.

For a moment they thought he was already dead, that this whole thing was an enormous hoax.

Then they saw the tubes and wires that crept from beneath the sheets to a bank of machines near the bed. They heard the rhythmic whir of a pump, the quieter hum of other monitoring devices. They saw the series of slow blips that popped and dipped with electronic regularity across a flowing green screen, proof that life of a sort was proceeding.

The six tiny wires taped to Marcus's skull were connected to a machine which had recorded, for the most part, an unwavering series of straight lines since the day after his massive cerebral hemorrhage.

"Okay," whispered Mike after another minute. "Let's get this over with."

Neither man noticed the sudden ominous jiggle of the needle on the EEG printout.

As they moved a little closer to the foot of the bed, the eyes of Pope Marcus popped open—deep, dark obsidian eyes with a fire still in them.

"Stop!" an unearthly voice rumbled from beneath the

320

cracked white lips.

It jolted them like a command. Sweat sprang to their suddenly icy foreheads.

"You cannot do this," the voice charged in an eerie, echoing growl. "You *must* not interfere with God's will. Are you not so sworn?"

Mike found his voice first, but it proved unconvincingly weak. "You are not God, you're Satan! You . . . deceiver!"

Pope Marcus, or whoever spoke through him, laughed—a terrible sound, full of pain and hate and malignancy.

"You *are* Satan," Magliano cried, his voice a smear of anguish.

"Of course," Marcus smiled, his slack lips parting hideously to allow a string of drool to escape. "But that doesn't make it any *less* God's will."

"Wha . . ." Mike began, but a cold horror was beginning to dawn on him.

"Oh, come now, Muldoon," the voice spat. "You who are forever throwing lines of prophecy at me like so much dogshit . . . who do you claim *wrote* that book you're quoting from?"

"But . . ."

"*Who*, Muldoon?" Marcus shrieked, his cadaverous head rising a few inches off the pillow. "Do you refer to that black leather Bible you're always carrying as 'The Word of Satan'?"

"No."

"What, then? The word of *what*, Muldoon?"

"*God.*" It was a forlorn whisper.

Magliano's face was buried in his hands, his body shaken with racking sobs.

"What was that, priest?" the voice asked with a slithering sweetness. "I didn't hear you."

"God. It's the Word of God!" Michael cried.

"You get an 'A' choirboy," Marcus laughed, his head collapsing on the pillows, his eyes dark and sparking inside the pits of dying flesh. "And if the Word of God says that this is what is *supposed* to happen, as part of *His* grand design, then who in hell—and I emphasize *in HELL,*" he snickered—"are *you* to try to stop it?"

Muldoon bowed his head, knowing the demon was right. In the final test of faith, it appeared, there was no clear line between good and evil; they were merely opposite faces of the same coin that spun endlessly on its edge until in a blur, the two faces merged into one.

He put his hand on the weeping little Italian archbishop's shoulder. "Let's go, my friend," he said.

Within a minute or two of playing guard over the unconscious nuns, Joe Martens gnawing impatience had grown to anger. He'd flown over 7000 miles to avenge Marija's rape, to free her once and for all from the beast that had repeatedly tormented and terrified her; so what the hell was he doing watching a pair of oversized penguins snore?

He'd given them a couple more whiffs of the ether-soaked cloth, then hurried down the broad corridor in search of his co-conspirators, arriving outside the hospital room just in time to hear the demon's last argument, to see his friends—overwhelmed by their own faith—give in to the deceit and start to withdraw.

And the anger in him exploded into a wild, burning thing.

He had no tenets of organized religion to confuse him. All he had was a huge ache of love for a certain woman and a too-clear memory of what this monster inside the lifeless shrunken zombie of Marcus had done to her.

Joe still knew right from wrong, in all its grand simplicity.

He leapt across the room with an animal roar of rage, pushing the two priests out of his way.

Marcus's eyes, suddenly wide with alarm, caught his in their insane power for an endless moment. Then Joe turned his gaze slowly to the machines, the life-giving machines.

"No!!!" the voice screamed as the small, lithe man launched himself at the carefully stacked electronic devices.

The components flew, landing with explosions on the white tile floor, Joe falling among them painfully. One sharp corner caught his rib with a solid cracking sound; an exploding monitor screen sent slivers of glass into his face. He reached behind him with a groan and, grabbing a handful of rubber-sheathed wires, yanked the multitude of terminals from the wall.

The tall, sleekly tanned pontiff had risen from his seat, champagne glass raised ceremoniously in the air.

The other eight men in the room rose slowly as well, holding their own glasses lower, like candles in a processional.

"I would like to propose a toast," Sixtus began. "To the new symbol of faith for the entire world: to Pope Marcus, 'Il Papa sera. . . .'"

He dropped the glass, its shattered crystal exploding in a dreamy, musical scream as it hit the table, and grabbed the sides of his head in sudden agony.

The pitifully shrunken waste of Pope Marcus heaved itself up from the bed in a final frantic effort to survive. Writhing half suspended in the air, he seemed to go through a series of convulsions, gasping and clawing at his throat with skeletal yellow fingers, a string of indecipherable blasphemies erupting from his mouth in a guttural noise that shook with each new spasm.

The trio of assassins looked on with a strange passivity.

As the seizures subsided, the deeply sunken eyes began to bulge outward, expanding and expanding, looking surprised, amazed, astounded. Changing color as they grew, from deepest black to brown to swollen dark red, they became large, froglike orbs, crimson balloons . . . then all at once they burst, spraying twin gushers of blood across the pristine whiteness of the sheets, the walls, the tile floors, spattering the faces of the men who watched.

Yet not one of them blinked.

The pope's blue slash of mouth opened wide in the final agony of death, but instead of a scream or a rale there came a furious wind, a huge black rushing wind that stole all warmth and light from the room, plunging it into the depths of outer space, a vile-smelling evil wind that raged in lunatic laughter around the three stonelike assassins until at last, whirling and shrieking, it hurled itself down the hallway and was gone.

Sixtus had released his temples and clutched the table edge, his entire body rigid. His neck and head arched backward, his eyes rolling up in his head until only the

324

whites were seen. Then a piercing howl erupted from his parted lips.

The eight cardinal bishops stood just as they'd been, their hands still gripping the wineglasses raised in toast. No one appeared to be able to move.

One of the eldest dropped his glass after a moment, but he seemed not to notice it shatter.

As Sixtus roared, a wavery film passed across the eight men's eyes . . . or was it across the room? The wavery film again—and suddenly it was not Pope Sixtus before them, but a creature from a nightmare, a huge, hideous lizardlike creature with blackish-green scales, great clawed hands, slit-pupiled crimson eyes. A long, reptilian tongue flung itself ceilingward as the screams continued to boil from his bulging throat.

Bertini looked at Falliano, Mendice at Synarus; the four identical looks of knowing horror instantly confirmed the shared reality.

Two of the eldest cardinal bishops had fainted dead away and would never remember what they'd seen. The other two later chose to explain it away as drunken hysteria, closing their minds almost instantly. But the four nearest the man had seen . . . and knew.

All at once the seizure passed and Sixtus came back to himself, his normal features instantly restored. He showed no hint of awareness that he had undergone a transmutation in their presence, but what he did say was almost as shocking.

"Pope Marcus has just been murdered!" he announced coldly, and then immediately strode toward the door, the cardinals who were still able following watchfully behind.

Chapter 30

The knock on the door broke the silence and interrupted the tense net of fear within the room like an explosion. All conversation stopped instantly.

Joe saw a sudden end to his plans for reunion and a happily-ever-after with Marija.

Mike saw a quiet life of solitary prayer and reflection . . . in prison.

Magliano saw a million faces turning away from him, a life in exile from the human race.

No one moved to answer the door.

The death knell sounded again, longer and harder. This time an urgent whisper accompanied its hollow sound. "Archbishop!" the voice cried. "Luigi, please, let us in!"

The Italian sighed wearily, pushing himself up from the sagging armchair. He might as well be the one to answer.

As he opened the door, four figures in long robes

swept swiftly past.

"Well," Cardinal Falliano said after a moment, agitatedly pushing his fingers through a thick mane of silver white hair, "Don't just stand there dumbfounded, archbishop—introduce us to your Americans."

Magliano continued to stare open-mouthed at the visitors. Joe and Mike had risen when the four entered, but remained where they were, silent.

At last the archbishop found his voice.

"Father Michael Muldoon, Mister Joseph Marten, may I present you to Cardinal Bishop Mendice, Secretary of State of Vatican City," he said formally, automatically starting with the highest ranking official.

Joe heard Mike inhale audibly, then genuflect to kiss the sapphire ring of the tiny man whose apple-cheeked face was ringed in a fringe of soft white hair. "Your Eminence," he uttered humbly.

Joe carefully followed his example.

The same ritual was repeated through the next three introductions: Cardinal Falliano, Patriarch Synarus, and Cardinal Bertini.

Once the formalities had been completed, however, an awkward silence followed.

"Won't you please be seated," Mike finally offered, indicating the worn sofa and chair.

"Watch out for the springs," Joe warned with a quick grin as the cardinals began to sweep their robes up.

That helped break the tension. The cardinals smiled back, Mendice even emitting a little chuckle.

"So," said Falliano, again taking charge, "Tell us why you murdered Pope Marcus this evening. Tell us *everything*; everything you know, everything you . . . suspect."

"Yes, *everything*," breathed Bertini.

327

The three assassins paled visibly, as if each had been struck a blow.

Joe and the archbishop turned as one toward Mike, who raised an eyebrow, shrugged, and accepted the task.

It was nearly 3 AM before he finished the telling.

Only then did the four top men in the Roman Catholic hierarchy reveal the transformation of Sixtus they had witnessed that night.

"We apologize for putting you through this," the diminutive secretary of state said, nodding to the three fugitives as he rose.

"But we needed confirmation," affirmed the tall, sad-eyed patriarch, rising with the others.

"We needed to know everything," repeated Bertini for the third time that evening.

"But, but wait . . . what are we to *do* about it?" Joe blurted.

"Don't worry, my friends," Falliano assured them gravely. "It will be taken care of."

"In the meantime, pack your things as quickly as possible," Mendice advised. "A limousine will meet you outside the northwest gate at," he checked his watch, "four AM. That gives you forty minutes."

"And I, Your Eminence?" Magliano faltered.

"You too. You're going with them."

Chapter 31

Joe was sitting on the edge of Marija's bed holding her hand when Mike burst into the room carrying a folded newspaper. He could see the red "Special Edition" banner even before Mike handed it to him, pointing excitedly at the headline. "THE POPE IS DEAD," it read.

"Yeah, I know," Joe grimaced, handing it back.

"No!" Mike yelped, pushing it at him again "Not *Marcus, Sixtus!*"

"What?" Joe let go of Marija's hand and opened the paper, reading quickly.

Pope Sixtus VI died suddenly this morning in his Vatican City apartment, only two days after his coronation as Acting Pontiff of the Roman Catholic Church, making his the shortest pontifical reign in history.

According to Vatican spokesperson Cardinal Secretary of State Mauricio Mendice, who was breakfasting with the Pope when he was stricken, Sixtus VI suddenly clutched at his chest and collapsed on the table without a word. He was pronounced dead at the scene a short time later by his personal physician, Dr. Gilberto Federico. The cause of death, after a preliminary medical examination, was determined to be a coronary occlusion leading to massive heart failure. No autopsy is planned.

"I'll bet," mumbled Joe. He continued to read.

Sixtus's predecessor, Pope Marcus IV, whose alleged miraculous feat of levitation at the coronation Sunday is now being described by Vatican officials as mass hallucination on the part of a hysterical crowd, was discovered dead in his hospital bed at the Vatican infirmary only hours earlier. A temporary power failure apparently shut off the life support systems that had kept the comatose pontiff alive since he was stricken by a cerebral hemorrhage ten days ago. . . .

"A power failure!" exclaimed Joe. "Now, why didn't *we* think of that . . . it would've been a lot easier!"

He shot a look at the other man in the room. The portly Italian tweaked his mustache in response and shrugged eloquently, as if to say, "You can't think of everything."

Marija just laughed, so he kissed her.

Afterword

Marija recuperated quickly that summer. With the aid of cosmetic surgery, her finely shaped nose was restored to its former beauty—with the exception of a small scar. Joe claimed it made her look slightly dangerous . . . after which she stopped covering it with makeup altogether.

With the aid of Joe's love, Muldoon's counselling, and the absence of any more supernatural events, Marija healed emotionally as well, though more slowly.

On August 6 of that year, the Seance Double Murder Case was formally shelved by the San Francisco Police Department for lack of evidence that a homicide had been committed. To the department's astonishment, Detective Grogan didn't raise so much as an eyebrow over the decision, let alone a formal protest.

He'd also begun whistling lately.

Fall began on a Saturday that year, at 12:01 AM. Twelve hours later, Marija Draekins Marten and Joseph Richard Marten were remarried in a formal ceremony at St. Jude's Chapel, with Monsignor Michael Muldoon officiating.

The prenuptial High Mass was said by the acting head of the San Francisco archdiocese, Cardinal Luigi Magliano.

It was a beautiful ceremony. The bride was radiant. Marija's mother cried until her mascara ran. Grogan handed her his handkerchief, and agreed, grudgingly, that they did indeed make a lovely couple.

The Dragon didn't mind, not really. He was, after all, now bloodmaster over the more than one hundred fifty top officials of the worldwide Catholic hierarchy. Each time one of these performed the Holy Eucharist, consecrating the wine into *his* blood, they would unknowingly bring more souls into the ranks of his unholy army.

All except the four.

The four who'd missed taking his first communion at the coronation mass of Pope Sixtus, and later who had betrayed him.

Ah well, no matter. Perhaps it would take a while longer than he'd intended for his plan to come to fruition — he'd have to wait a few years before making any overt moves that might alert that highest cadre of cardinal bishops to his insinuating presence in the Church.

But to one who stands outside of time, the delay would be less than the blink of an eye; whereas men grow old, grow forgetful, and die. . . .

PINNACLE'S FINEST IN SUSPENSE
AND ESPIONAGE

WARBOTS by G. Harry Stine

#5 OPERATION HIGH DRAGON   (17-159, $3.95)

Civilization is under attack! A "virus program" has been injected into America's polar-orbit military satellites by an unknown enemy. The only motive can be the preparation for attack against the free world. The source of "infection" is traced to a barren, storm-swept rock-pile in the southern Indian Ocean. Now, it is up to the forces of freedom to search out and destroy the enemy. With the aid of their robot infantry—the Warbots—the Washington Greys mount Operation High Dragon in a climactic battle for the future of the free world.

#6 THE LOST BATTALION   (17-205, $3.95)

Major Curt Carson has his orders to lead his Warbot-equipped Washington Greys in a search-and-destroy mission in the mountain jungles of Borneo. The enemy: a strongly entrenched army of Shiite Muslim guerrillas who have captured the Second Tactical Battalion, threatening them with slaughter. As allies, the Washington Greys have enlisted the Grey Lotus Battalion, a mixed-breed horde of Japanese jungle fighters. Together with their newfound allies, the small band must face swarming hordes of fanatical Shiite guerrillas in a battle that will decide the fate of Southeast Asia and the security of the free world.

#7 OPERATION IRON FIST   (17-253, $3.95)

Russia's centuries-old ambition to conquer lands along its southern border erupts in a savage show of force that pits a horde of Soviet-backed Turkish guerrillas against the freedom-loving Kurds in their homeland high in the Caucasus Mountains. At stake: the rich oil fields of the Middle East. Facing certain annihilation, the valiant Kurds turn to the robot infantry of Major Curt Carson's "Ghost Forces" for help. But the brutal Turks far outnumber Carson's desperately embattled Washington Greys, and on the blood-stained slopes of historic Mount Ararat, the high-tech warriors of tomorrow must face their most awesome challenge yet!

DOCTOR WHO AND THE TALONS
OF WENG-CHIANG   (17-209, $3.50)
by Terrance Dicks
Doctor Who learns a Chinese magician, the crafty Chang,
and his weird midget manikin, Mr. Sin, are mere puppets
in the hands of the hideously deformed Greel, posing as
the Chinese god, Weng-Chiang. It is Greel who steals the
young women; it is Greel who grooms sewer rats to do his
bidding—but there is even more, much more. . . . Will
Doctor Who solve the Chinese puzzle in time to escape the
terrifying talons of Weng-Chiang?

DOCTOR WHO AND THE MASQUE
OF MANDRAGORA   (17-224, $3.50)
by Phillip Hinchcliffe
It is the Italian Renaissance during the corrupt reign of the
powerful Medicis. Doctor Who, angry because he was
forced to land on Earth by the incredible Mandragora Helix, walks right into a Machiavellian plot. The unscrupu-
lous Count Frederico plans to usurp the rightful rule of his
naive nephew. This, with the help of Hieronymous, influential court astrologer and secret cult member. Using
Hieronymous and his cult members as a bridgehead, the
Mandragora Helix intends to conquer Earth and dominate
its people! The question is, will Doctor Who prove a true
Renaissance man? Will he be able to drain the Mandragora
of its power and foil the Count as well?